I0760954

USA TODAY BESTSELLING AUTHOR
SARAH M. CRADIT

ISBN: 978-1-958744-40-6

Cover and Interior Design by The Illustrated Author Design Services
Map by The Illustrated Author Design Services
Hardcover Art ("The Well") by Nora Adamszki of Adamszki Art
"Until the Sky Falls" Art by Alexandra Curte
Fen and Pesha Portraits by Stephanie Brown of Offbeat Worlds
Editing by Novel Nurse Editing

Publisher Contact:
sarah@sarahmcradit.com
www.sarahmcradit.com

For the selfless.
Your happy ending is waiting.

PRAISE FOR THE HAND AND THE HEART

"Lush and heartwarming! Cradit's ability to weave both a heartfelt romance and epic world is to be commended."

~Elle Beaumont, author of the Immortal Realms Trilogy

"Sarah has done it again! From the first page, The Hand and The Heart will entrap you in another beautiful tale of love and family. Through brilliant storytelling, every moment felt natural between the characters and their interconnected narratives. Don't miss the magic!"

~Kay Marie, @booksinparadise

"This is one of my favorite fantasy romances from Cradit yet!"

~Candace Robinson, Author of Spindle of Sin

"Delightful escapism, full of complex characters that sizzle on page. Hits the spot for fans of romantasy, found family, and friends to lovers."

~Megan, @bookish_megeen

"THATH is easily one of my favorites in The Book of All Things series. With a rollercoaster of emotions and the magnificent look into the Medvedev world, Sarah brings to life this romantic fantasy like the Weaver of Worlds that she is."

~Rachel, @rachelsbooktea

"The story, the setting, and the magic system are so incredibly unique and intricate, I absolutely loved it. And oh WOW, this sweeping story of two men on a journey to find themselves while they find each other is just beautiful. Absolutely a must-read for fantasy romance lovers!"

~Jordan Fischer, @julietfoxreads

"Sarah Cradit has done it again! The Hand and the Heart is the perfect edition to the Darkwood Cycle of The Book of All Things series. Perfect for Epic Romantasy readers that enjoy medium-to-high spice, intricate world building, and a tale about redeeming love."

~Kate, Instagram Blogger @DarkenedLibrary

INTRODUCTION

There exists a kingdom set upon an isle, surrounded by a sea no one has ever traveled beyond. The Kingdom of the White Sea it is called, or simply the kingdom, for they have no other name for it.

But long before men came to the White Kingdom, there were another people who lived quietly and freely: the Medvedev. They were and are a powerful druidic race, sharing most of their physical characteristics with men, aside from two significant differences.

Every full-blooded Medvedev is born with an animal familiar. If their familiar is aquatic, the Medvedev has naturally blue locks. If terrestrial, green. And if airborne, violet. Often these are the only ways to spot a Medvedev with the naked eye.

Little is known of these elusive peoples beyond their borders, but much is whispered.

King Carrow, the first man to claim a throne in the kingdom in many generations, saw the prudence of coming to an accord with the Medvedev, avoiding a war that would decimate both sides with no true winner. The Termonglen Accord maintained that the Medvedev would keep all of the Hinterlands, their home and the largest Reach in the kingdom, and men would respect their borders without question. The only safe passage from north to south became one of the Compass Roads. As long as men stay to the agreed upon path, all is well.

For centuries, the accord has been honored.

While the Hinterlands has always been safe for Medvedev, the same cannot be said for the rest of the realm. Any who dare leave the haven of their forestland must take great precautions to avoid being captured, sold, or studied. They use magic to cover their remarkable hair and are careful never to address their familiars in public. Although they have committed no crime, it is the life of a fugitive they must lead if they choose to live in the kingdom proper.

The only way for Medvedev to live in peace is to never leave their home at all.

Nearly thirty years before the start of this story, a group of Medvedev *did* leave their home. Speculation abounds on the real nature of their rift with Chieftainess Aoife of Asgill, but only the Forsaken—as these banished refugees came to be known—know the true story.

Stiofen Thornheart and Pesha Trevanion are both sons of Forsaken. Their lives have been very different—Stiofen, having spent most of his years on the run with his twin sister, bouncing from home to home, and Pesha, hidden away in a glorious manor with his half brother, never experiencing the world beyond—but they have both, in their own ways, suffered as Medvedev living in the kingdom. Disconnected from their culture, never able to fully *live,* they have borne the stigma of their late parents all their lives.

The sins of the fathers have become the sins of the sons.

It is said the Forsaken can never go home, but that's precisely where Fen and Pesha are headed. They travel with Pesha's half sister, Farren, a Medvedev whose familiar was murdered eight years ago, a tragedy that resulted in her becoming feral. The Trevanions' efforts to help her ever since have lost their efficacy, and they are out of both time and options.

Though Farren was born on Asgill lands, neither Pesha nor Fen have been there. Everything they know about their culture and people was passed down from embittered, disenchanted parents. They cannot know whether they will be welcomed with open arms, turned away with prejudice, or swiftly punished with malice.

What they do know is that if the Asgill Medvedev cannot help Farren, no one can.

If she cannot find relief soon, she'll die.

Pesha and Fen have shouldered the grief, pain, and fear for the people they love for as long as they can remember. Fen as his sister's protector and handler, and Pesha as his brother's trusted right hand. Neither has given much thought to their own happiness, because a life of crisis only allows for chaos.

Even now, as they risk everything to save Farren, they are acting in service to others.

But the truth and absolution they seek cannot be found in their siblings, nor in the lush homeland they've never been to.

Forgiveness. Understanding. Love.

Those gifts can only be found within.

And, perhaps, with the only other person who understands the internal battle that has waged unabated for far too long.

To help Farren, they will need to learn to do the impossible: accept they need as much help as they have always offered others.

Fen and Pesha will either break this chain…

Or die trying.

TERRITORY OF ASGILL

Reach
Hinterlands

Chieftainess
Aoife

Chieftainess's Family
Mairead, 23, daughter (familiar: Adir)
Niallan, 20, adopted son (familiar: Lian)

Other Asgill Medvedev
Ruairi, 6 (no familiar)
Datu
Theta
Kaia
Cassair
Fiachra
Gellais
Esta
Fanne
Elodie

SHADOWFEN HALL

Village
Darkwood Run

Baron and Baroness
Desemir Trevanion II, 27
Siofra Trevanion, 19 (familiar: Aio)

Baron's Family
Stiofen Thornheart, 19 (familiar: Eshe)
Pesha Trevanion, 18 (familiar: Atio)
Farren Wintersin, 28 (familiar: Nera, deceased)

Others at Shadowfen Hall
Euric (Desemir's Guard)
Wulfhelm (Desemir's Guard)
Cassius (Desemir's Guard)
Gisela (Attendant)
Lieken (Attendant)
Lotte (Head Mistress)

HOWLING SEA
N
W
E
S
MIDNIGHT CREST
ICEBOLT MOUNTAIN
MIDWINTER REST
WITCHWOOD CROSS
WHITECAP
NORTHERLAND RANGE
FOREST OF LYCANA
9
WULFSHEAD HAVEN
TORRIN'S PASS
6
WESTPORT
EASTPORT
DUNWOODE
1
DARKWOOD RUN
SALTHILL
WULF'S NECK
7
MAYKE
SALEEN
ASGILL
2
DRUMAIN
BYTHESEA
TERMONGLEN
RUSHWOOD
WHISPERING WOODS
12
VALLEYBROOKE
STREAMSTOWNE
EVERLEIGH PIKE
EVERHART THICKET
WILDWOOD FALLS
PARTH
RESPLENDENT RELIQUARY
THE SEPULCHRE IN THE SKIES
10
5
GAP OF EVER
THE SEVEN SISTERS
BRIARHAVEN
RIVER RUSH
WINDWATCH GROVE
GREENFEN
PINE BLUFF
WHITEWOOD
OLDCASTLE
FIONN'S PASS
3
OAK HILL
WHITE SEA
EAST DERRY
IRON HILL
BLACKPOOL
STONE MAWR
NEWCARROW
4
SANDYMOUNT
GREENCASTLE
GOLDTHORPE
SANDYCOVE
LEECASTER BAY
11
HORNSEA
PORT WORTHING
CAMP ATONEMENT
GREYSTONE ABBEY
WHITECLIFFE
8
CAMP RESTITUTION
1.) NORTHERLANDS
2.) HINTERLANDS
3.) WESTERLANDS
4.) SOUTHERLANDS
5.) EASTERLANDS
6.) ISLE OF BELCARROW
7.) DUNCARROW
8.) WASTELANDS
9.) WULFSGATE
10.) LONGWOOD RUSH
11.) WARWICKTOWN
12.) WHITECHURCH
KINGDOM OF THE WHITE SEA

THE ONES WHO SERVE

ONE
CHAOS IS ALL YOU KNOW

Fen was absolutely convinced they were seconds away from the wheels flying off the carriage.

Pesha bellowed for the horses to go faster, *faster,* the same harried command he'd been shouting for miles. His knuckles had lost their color as he gripped and snapped the reins, his entire face painted with wild fear. The horses weren't faring much better, already foaming at the mouth, which neither he nor Pesha could do a thing about because their aggressors showed no signs of slowing.

The end was near, one way or another.

Looking behind was a fool's errand, an invitation for more unneeded terror, but Fen, with his heart stuffed in his throat like a bag of bricks, couldn't stop himself. Instinct and experience prevented him from ignoring the frightful problem at their backs. One look was enough to validate his concerns. The rabid lawmen had gained considerable ground since they'd all whipped out of the forest and onto a sturdier path. He could practically feel their zealous spittle spraying his neck.

"We have to go back into the forest!" he cried, dividing his fevered attention between Pesha and the men looking after a fruitful bounty. Once caught, they'd lock Fen and Pesha inside a spellbound prison and write to the Sepulchre, demanding a reward in exchange for the location of the "illicit" magic users. "In there, I can slow them, but there's nothing to slow them on the road."

"We'll *crash* in there. This coach isn't made for it," Pesha said, threading the words through a tightly clenched jaw. "They'll eventually give up. Come on, faster!"

"I don't think they will," Fen said distantly. Pesha hadn't been chased before, had never been kidnapped, abused, or exploited for his magic. His secluded upbringing in Darkwood Run had sheltered him from the harsh certainties of an exposed life in the realm. The Sepulchre, to many, was a necessary institution, designed to oversee and regulate the use of divine gifts. To Medvedev, their agents were death incarnate. But it wasn't just the Sepulchre and their agents. It was all men who feared what they didn't understand and couldn't conquer.

Pesha didn't understand the savage determination of men like that.

Fen gripped the back of the jostled bench and turned again. One of the lawmen mimed reaching for his sword and pointed the phantom weapon Fen's way. Eshe's tank sloshed against the straining leather bindings, overflowing and spilling over the sides. He couldn't discern from his angle how much she'd lost, how much would be too much. "Pesha, we *have* to get off the road. Now!"

"They'll fall off, Fen. We just have to—"

"Now, Pesha!"

Pesha's face squinted in raw determination. His dark hair fell over his eyes, but he didn't seem to notice or care. "No."

Fen hopped on the bench to face him. "Listen to me—"

"I said *no,* Stiofen." Pesha's mouth drew into a tight circle.

Stiofen. Pesha had taken to calling him by his full name more and more, the frequency commensurate with the tension blooming between them that Fen could diagnose but not cure. "This carriage is going to break *down*, Pesh, you push it any harder. When it does, what will we do with Eshe? With Farren?"

Pesha grimaced, his brows fusing into a hard line. Fen knew mentioning Pesha's sister would either motivate or infuriate him. She was deep asleep inside the carriage, oblivious to the horrors of the chase—as long as the magic held anyway. They both knew how bad things could go—and how fast, if it slipped even for a moment.

Overhead, Atio kept a conservative distance. She occasionally swooped in to monitor the escalating situation, but never long enough for Fen to fear the men would see the falcon and know her for what she was: his familiar. The other half of his soul.

Atio would be fine, but Eshe, Pesha's familiar, was another matter. So was the feral Medvedev, magic-bound inside the carriage.

Fen turned and, gripping the back of the bench with both hands, carefully climbed onto his knees. The jostling threw him into Pesha, who pushed him off with an angered huff, another knife to the gut in what had been an entire voyage of them.

Fen strained down to tighten the straps on poor Eshe's water tank. Things were about to get worse, and she was already losing so much water.

"What the fuck are you doing?" Pesha hissed, spurring the exhausted horses.

"If you won't…get off…the road…" Fen's teeth clacked from the force of the bumps. He met the eyes of one of the two lawmen who had seen too much and would never, no matter what Pesha tried to tell himself, let it go. "Then…I have…no choice…"

Flourishment had gotten them into the mess, and he hoped it would be enough to get them out of it. The lawmen had been hiding in the forest, watching, when Fen had flourished his and Pesha's meager meal into a feast. They'd seen him continuously refill their mugs with ale, and add needed thickness to their blankets on the chilly night.

"Get down!"

It was Fen's turn to refuse. "They won't stop," was all he said before pushing Pesha's radiant anxiety into the background of his thoughts. The panting horses, the spilled water, the beady eyes of determined men all fell away, and all he could see or hear were the sounds of the forest on both sides of the path.

Flourishment built upon what already existed. It would have been easier to use in the forest, full of potential obstacles, but the road was, though rutted, clear of useful debris.

Fen chanced bending over the bench to root around in the cargo area. There wasn't room for much else after they'd strapped Eshe's tank in, which was the reason he'd had to flourish most of their meals, their bedrolls, and other provisions they'd needed on the road.

"You're going to fly off. Sit *down*," Pesha commanded.

Fen heard the words, but they stoked nothing in him aside from bland acknowledgment. His hand connected with one of the rocks they'd used to tether their satchels in place. He swatted at it until it rolled into his palm.

He didn't want to hurt the men, no matter what their intentions were, but he was running out of options. Pesha wasn't wrong about the forest, but that didn't make him right about the road. There wasn't a safe way to lose their assailants.

That was what Fen told himself as he hurled the rock, turning it into a boulder that crashed onto the path between the men. The horses squealed, and the men shouted in stunned indignation, but the diversion did little to slow their advance.

Fen picked up another rock, then another. One by one, he launched rocks and morphed them into boulders from the back of the wagon. Sweat streamed down his face as he dug deep, dredging his well of strength. Every flourishment drained him, but he had no time to replenish.

"What in the world is going on back there?" Pesha shouted. "Fen!"

Fen grabbed a handful of dust and chipped rocks from the bed of the wagon. He closed his eyes, cocked his arm, and launched a barraged assault into the road. This time, one of the horses reared hard enough to throw its rider into the woods. The other one veered off the path but kept on, holding its pace. The remaining lawman only briefly glanced toward his fallen comrade before gritting and bearing down, slipping back onto the road.

Their accosters had agility and nimbleness on their side, but they'd held back *just enough* for the entire pursuit. They must have known they didn't need to overtake the carriage, just exhaust it.

And they were, objectively, exhausted.

Fen was out of rocks, at least the ones he could reach. There wasn't much else in the back of the wagon, just a thin, worn blanket they'd been using to cover Eshe's tank—

Fen brightened with an idea. He lifted the blanket, turning it into a chute that caught the force of their ride. It bowed toward the remaining rider, who seemed to know what was coming but did nothing to avoid it, hunkering lower to go faster.

With a hard clench in his belly, Fen released the blanket. When it grabbed the air, the thin cover turned into a canopy, as broad as a celebration tent. It landed perfectly, horse and rider disappearing behind a gray cloud of moth-eaten wool. The man howled in fury, spewing curses and threats Fen couldn't make out under the crash of hooves and wheels. The horse came to a sliding stop, its whinny desperate and shrill, ignoring the wheezing commands of its defeated rider.

Fen, breathless, dropped back onto the bench. He tucked his head between his knees and tried to recover himself.

"You going to tell me what happened back there?" Pesha demanded without turning. His eyes flicked sideways.

"We've lost them. Finally," Fen answered as he sat back up. "But they'll find us again if you don't get us off this road *right now,* Pesha."

"Fine!" Pesha cried. "Fine."

He snapped the reins and gave the command for the horses to shift left. The carriage left the ground altogether when they jumped from road to trail. A thump sounded inside the cabin, and Fen looked through the curtain to see Farren had been jolted to the floor. He was still too dazed to do anything but stare and hope her sleep kept her from suffering.

Fine was the last word Pesha said for hours, even when they briefly stopped to give the horses time to recuperate from running so hard.

Fen, who had been matching his silence, pulled out the map and shoved it under Pesha's nose.

"What is this?"

"We're close to the cabin," Fen said quietly. The hours had done nothing to restore his own energy. He'd never felt so depleted. He was surprised he could even gauge direction at all, when the forest looked the same on all sides and his senses had dulled to nothing. "Another hundred yards or so to the east."

"Great." Pesha stared quietly forward. His hands had relented somewhat on the reins, but the rest of him hadn't relaxed at all.

Fen had spent weeks trying to understand Pesha's increasing reserve…his hot-and-cold handling of both Fen and the situation. His mercurial moods came and went in an instant. Fen had followed his friend on the voyage because he'd thought he'd been needed. That he'd been…wanted. More and more, he wondered whether he'd imagined it.

Tonight, though, Fen was done. Pesha could have his moodiness and secrets.

The only cure for the day's chaos was sleep.

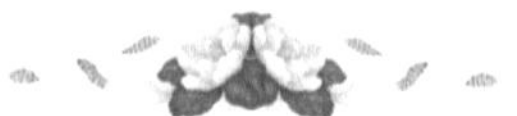

They reached their stopping point, somewhere in the Wulf's Neck, just after dusk. The accommodation was a disused hunting lodge, yards off a furrowed path and tucked into the forest like a dark secret. Moss disappeared the roof, and vines climbed the walls. A stream trickled nearby.

It seemed more like a place a man might take a mistress than hunt a bear.

Fen wondered how Desemir had found the damned place, and to whom it actually belonged. He'd wondered that every night they were leveraged one of the baron's many connections, but tonight the thought made him *angry.*

He was wound tighter than one of Desemir's newfangled timekeepers by the time Pesha had parked the carriage under the bowing pine branches, behind what the owner had no doubt called a stable but was more accurately a rickety barn with sparse utility.

"Just get the fire started. I'll handle the rest," Fen muttered, brushing past without making eye contact.

Pesha shifted his weight to one hip with a grunt. The garish moonlight revealed the trail of lines around his eyes had deepened, reminding Fen of the potholes on their harrowing trip. "Don't let pride make things harder for you. I'll help."

"Pride is the last thing on my mind right now," Fen retorted. He squeezed the sleep from his eyes and squinted into the dark, melodic forest. The acrid tang of sweat on his tongue made him suddenly aware of his empty belly. "Just go. If I need your help, I'll come get you." The last words were a lie, and Pesha clearly knew it too.

"If you say so, Stiofen." Pesha threw up his hands and marched toward the back of the carriage.

"I do," Fen said, too tired to mute his exasperation.

With a pointed look, Pesha scooped their satchels into his arms, blinked hard at Fen, and trudged down the snow-covered path toward the door.

Fen waited until Pesha had disappeared inside before starting their evening routine. He peered through the tank at Eshe for signs of distress, not sure what he was even looking for. She'd been jostled quite a bit on their traumatic chase, but her water level was still in a healthy range, and the little seal was still coiled in the same position as always, slumbering away. They could add more in the morning, to be safe, but for now she was fine.

Atio landed on a railing with a distressing squawk.

Fen cast a quick glance toward his falcon and went back to work. "I know what you're thinking. But not tonight." He rooted around the sides of the tank until he heard the familiar tinkling of the bell net. With a tug, he freed it and gave it a shimmery shake into the night air before climbing up onto the wagon step and draping it over Eshe's tank. The seal swirled once in her water world, as she always did when the net was settled. He liked to think it was her way of saying thanks.

It wasn't a ward, but if anyone tried to mess with Eshe's tank, the bells would warn them. Eshe would too, Pesha insisted, but Fen chalked that up to wishful thinking. She would remain in stasis until she could safely swim in warmer water.

Fen palmed the net. "Sleep well, girl. Sorry we lost your blanket, but we'll find another. I'm sure there's something inside the cabin." He glanced at Atio. "Keep an eye on her...Yeah, yeah, I know you always do, but I just have a bad feeling after today. And stay warm. Looks like there'll be more snow tonight...*again.*"

Atio squawked in confirmation.

With a heavy sigh, Fen moved to the carriage and opened the door.

Farren still stole his breath every time he saw her, thin and delicate from eight years of magic-induced slumber but otherwise unchanged by time. She was near thirty years of age but physically looked not much older than him, forever arrested in time to the day her poor familiar, Nera, had been brutally ripped from the world by Ludwik Trevanion. Desemir and Pesha had spent the years since doing everything they could for her, but every effort was ephemeral and, eventually, useless.

If the Medvedev of the Hinterlands couldn't help her, no one could.

Pesha had shifted her back to the bench when they'd stopped to water the horses and catch their breaths. Her legs were curled up into an opening created by her arms, and she slept through Fen's slow unfurling of her limbs as he tried to guide her off the seat without hurting her. Pesha was right. It had been easier with two of them.

"It's all right, Farren," he said, draping her arm over his shoulder for the third time. As with the prior attempt, it flopped back to her side. With a grunt of exasperation, Fen nudged himself against her instead and hoisted her over his shoulder. She was so light, he wondered why he'd tried to get her to her feet at all.

Fen kicked at the lodge door to open it and stumbled inside. The place looked like all the others they'd found succor in: modest, with one room on the main floor and stairs leading to a small loft. The kitchen was only a stove in the corner, which would take an hour or more to heat, and from the looks of it, Pesha hadn't even lit it yet.

He set Farren in a chair before returning to the door to shut it. As he shrugged off his layers and hung them on the rack, he caught sight of Pesha, pacing back and forth in front of the hearth. That, at least, had been started, and the fire had picked up enough life to generate meager warmth.

Pesha's face twitched as though reacting to a conversation only he could hear.

Rolling his eyes, Fen spun and returned to the door.

"Where are you going?" Pesha barked. Not a question, a demand.

"To relieve myself?" Fen scoffed. He flicked his hands out. "That all right with you, or would you prefer I piss on the rug?"

"Glad one of us can find some relief tonight." Pesha crossed his arms and stared at the fire.

"If you want a fight, pick one with the trees," Fen said and reached for the door.

"You've gotten so *reckless* with your flourishment, Fen." Pesha turned his head upward with a laughing scoff. "And you don't even know it."

The words landed right between Fen's shoulders. He squared up, growing hot. "My flourishment? You mean the skill that keeps us fed and warm?"

"In *private*. When no one is looking!"

Fen released the door and shoved back, sensing the interaction was going nowhere fast but unable to stop himself. "*You* were supposed to be on lookout, Pesha. So I could do it safely. So we could avoid *exactly* the situation that happened to us today."

"Well, Farren was coming around, and I can't tend to her *and* be your fucking minder at the same time, can I?"

"So you should have said something!" Fen cried. He started forward several paces. "Flourishment requires my entire focus. You know that."

"And then you *kept* doing it when they chased us, when if you'd have just been patient, they'd have dropped off and convinced themselves they were only seeing things."

"Is that a delusion you're actually entertaining?" Fen palmed the back of Farren's chair, briefly wondering how much of their bickering she'd absorbed over the past weeks. "Really? Because they were on our heels for over an hour, and *I'm* the only reason they stopped at all."

"Chaos is all you know." Pesha rolled his head toward the ceiling. "You don't understand subtlety."

"I understand I came to help you, but all you've done is criticize everything I do," Fen replied, pinching his shoulders. Every muscle in his body screamed for some kind of release. Sleep. Pain. "This entire trip has been nothing but you reminding me of all the reasons I disappoint you."

Pesha went silent. The fire crackled and popped. Farren stirred but didn't wake. "I never asked you to come, Stiofen."

Hot, uninvited tears flooded across Fen's eyes. He scowled to counteract the raw grief finding its way in, squeezing past the barriers he was too tired to reconstruct. "No, Pesha, you didn't. But I cared enough about you to not want you to face this alone. I would do anything for my own sister, and if it were me on the road…I wouldn't want to be alone either. But that's all *you* know, isn't it? You wear your solitude like a badge of pride and honor, like your sacrifices are your greatest strengths." Fen wiped his eyes with a furious grunt. "Well, fine, Pesha. Stand proud and tall and *alone.* But I'm fucking tired, bone tired, and I've given all I have to the day."

Fen didn't linger for Pesha's reaction. He was already so close to the edge, waiting to fall, and even a whisper of derision or pity would send him hurtling into the void.

He sluggishly climbed the ladder into the loft. He barely had his boots unlaced and off before he collapsed onto the hard mattress and sobbed into the crook of his elbow.

Nothing...*Nothing* had gone to plan.

Pesha was cold, distant. *Angry.*

Farren needed more magic every day.

And Fen...Fen had never, in all his life, been more alone.

He wiped his eyes on his sleeve and tucked his hand under his head, where a pillow should have been. Beyond the frosted glass of the tiny window under the eaves, snow spilled. Atio would be fine. She always was. Eshe had lived most of her life hibernating at the bottom of a frozen lake. Her needs were simple...simple, as he'd believed his own to be.

He missed Siofra. Aio. Wulf and Lottie and Euric. Even Desemir. He craved the warmth and love of Shadowfen Hall, which had been the most unexpected but most wonderful gift of his life.

He missed the way things had been with Pesha.

Hunger pangs tore through his belly. He'd forgotten to eat, and now it was too late. No power in the world could make him climb back down that ladder before morning.

Fen closed his eyes and pulled the thin blanket tight around his shoulders with a shiver. He didn't have the heart or reserves to flourish it into a thick quilt.

He'd just drifted off when the ladder rungs creaked.

Find your own place to sleep, he thought, but his heart raced with every hollow thump of Pesha's boots on the loft boards... with every pass of fabric across flesh as Pesha removed his layers.

The mattress shifted with his weight. Fen clenched and increased his grip on the blanket. Moments later, Pesha's hand slid along the edge of Fen's shoulders. He peeled the blanket away and nestled his face where it had lain, then trailed his hand down, tucking it over Fen's belly with a firm but gentle tug, his fingers splayed in penitent invitation. Fen tentatively brought his hand over Pesha's and let Pesha lace and lock them together.

Pesha sighed, warming the back of Fen's neck with his apology. Fen closed his eyes and fell asleep.

TWO
BLIND TRUST

Pesha moved through the forest with blind trust. Eyes closed, he tilted his face skyward and stepped indiscriminately through broken trees and scattered detritus. Frogs scampered below; birds cried above. Somewhere in the distance, Atio blurted her shrill morning song into the air, creating a sense of disorder in the calm.

Blind trust. Those two words sent a coil of fear straight into his empty belly. All his life, he'd stood by his brother, Desemir, with both eyes wide open. His mind he'd trained to listen for threats unspoken. There wasn't time or prudence for his thoughts to wander when Desemir had a list of adversaries a mile long.

And trust…He'd never *truly* trusted anyone, he realized. Desemir, yes, but how many times had his brother promised to do one thing to appease Pesha and then done as he pleased anyway?

Fen though…Fen was…

Pesha inhaled the fresh pines, breathing them in through his nose and letting them settle in his chest. The trees in the

Wulf's Neck smelled like light and promise, unlike the rich musk of the Great Darkwood that had provided the background of his life.

He didn't know where they *were*, exactly, but Fen did. Fen had tried to show him, but he'd swatted him away like a nuisance. Even as he'd watched, his chest aching, as Fen deflated with rejection, Pesha couldn't stop himself. His rash cruelty was an out-of-control carriage careening into a gulch, the crash inevitable.

Pesha wanted to feel *something*, but it wasn't kindness.

It wasn't love.

He groped around the area, his eyes still stubbornly closed, until he found a tree. He moved toward it until he could touch it with both hands, palms spread along the rough, jagged bark.

Breathed in. Held it.

Eshe.

Pesha heard her splash in his mind. He hadn't wandered too far then.

As he exhaled, a flutter passed through him. His eyes welled with hot, stinging tears that evoked rage, not grief. He liked the rage. Maybe a little too much.

Do you remember what Lottie used to say about my father, Esh? About how terrible men never knew they were terrible until they were dropped into someone else's world? No one ever sees themselves as the villain unless they're forced to confront their darkest truth.

Eshe couldn't respond to him the way Atio responded to Fen. All Medvedev were different, their relationships with their familiars wholly unique to each individual bond. But he felt her indelible sorrow like a soft blanket.

I don't believe in fate. I don't believe in the Guardians or any godlike creatures exacting divine judgment. But this trip... This trip has been nothing but one failure after another. Pesha dipped down to wipe his eyes on his sleeve. *I would be a fool to expect the rest to go any smoother.*

Eshe's sadness deepened his. He'd failed *her*, day after day, year after year. The little seal had spent her life at the bottom of a lake that was frozen more than not, and he'd uprooted her and stuck her in a tank so small, she could hardly swim around. He'd carelessly dragged her along on his foolhardy quest because he couldn't bear to be parted from her for so long.

They're not going to help Farren, are they? They'll expel us the moment we step foot on their lands, if we even make it that far. They'll take one look at the three of us, children of the Forsaken, and we'll be lucky to make it out with our lives.

Eshe's response filled him with confusion. She disagreed, but it was unclear why.

Farren was suffering before, but what if I've only made it worse? And Fen, I've dragged him from his sister, from everything he knows, and have done nothing but inflict a hundred tiny cuts from a dagger I never intended to wield.

His familiar went silent, but her glow radiated, wrapping him in a gentle embrace his first instinct was to reject. He didn't deserve comfort, or absolution.

I should send him home. I could buy him a horse at the next trading post. He's good with maps. He'll find his way. You don't agree, Eshe? Then you haven't seen the way he looks at me. As though…as though I'm someone else, some man he's built up in his mind and convinced himself is real.

"There you are." The sound of boots crunching followed Fen's declaration. He tromped through the branches and leaves and sidled up next to Pesha. "Everything good?"

"Fine," Pesha lied, blinking hard to shift from one moment into another. He glanced at Fen's hands, each holding a steaming mug.

"It's not your favorite," Fen said, holding one out. "I couldn't find the tea you like. The bergamot. It may have been lost when we packed in a hurry…"

Pesha accepted the tea with a sheepish half smile. He braced for the dressing down he deserved, but it didn't come.

"One more night, and we'll be in the Hinterlands." Fen breathed in and closed his eyes. "From there, we're on our own. No more hidden cabins."

"So soon?" Guilt clogged Pesha's throat. Fen had every right to confront him, but he seemed to let it go instead. *Another reason to send him home, where he'll be surrounded by people who won't hurt him day in, day out.*

"So soon?" Fen's laugh had a hard edge, the first sign his wounds had yet to heal. "Pesh, we've been on the road for weeks. We've been in the Wulf's Neck alone for days. We're right on the border of Asgill lands, according to the map. Might even get there today, if we snag ourselves another wild chase." His mouth twitched, almost grinning, as he drew a sip from his mug.

Scream at me, Fen! Give me your worst. I don't deserve your jests, your efforts to make me *feel better. Stop acting like I haven't been a total fucking monster.*

Pesha buried his gaze in the conciliatory tea.

"Are you ready for this?"

"I'm not sure," Pesha said quietly. "I don't even know where we're going once we cross the border. What to say."

"My mother told us there are no maps of the Hinterlands. She said a Medvedev knows when they're home."

"That doesn't make any sense."

"Not to us anyway," Fen agreed with a short laugh. He squinted against the sunrise peeking through the canopy of trees. "My mother hated 'home,' enough to betray their chieftainess. Perhaps her advice shouldn't be taken as wisdom."

"At least your mother had advice for you. I barely knew mine," Pesha said. He drew out a sigh. "My memories are corrupted. I always thought she was the one who had taught me what little I know about our Medvedev roots, but it was Farren. My sister was the only one who bothered to give me any insight into who or what I was. My mother was too enraptured with her venomous lover to have anything but scorn for me."

Fen didn't respond right away. "Siofra and I had a complicated relationship with our parents too. I don't know that the Forsaken considered much how their actions would affect their descendants. Until the day they died, both my mother and father stood firm that they'd made the right decision."

"Maybe they did," Pesha said. He swallowed a deep sip of tea and then overturned the rest of the contents into the gloaming.

"Maybe." Fen shuddered his shoulders. "Oh. Our messenger raven returned this morning. Atio found her circling and guided her in."

Pesha turned with a frown. "Is there trouble at Shadowfen?"

"No," Fen said quickly. "No, Desemir wrote to tell us Siofra is doing fine, still pregnant, but...but they've confirmed our suspicion she's having twins." He sucked his teeth.

Pesha crossed his arms and turned away. It was even more reason to send Fen back to Shadowfen Hall, where he could comfort his sister in the last weeks of her convalescence.

"Should I send a response back?"

Pesha drew in a lungful of pine air, desperately trying to re-center himself, to quell the rising tide of rage that had been blooming and building for months.

"Nothing at all?" Fen asked.

The urge to snap at Fen was so powerful, Pesha had to bite down on his tongue. Copper filled his mouth, steadying his incomprehensible fury. "Desemir said she's fine, but I know my brother, and he'll be scared to death. His focus belongs with his wife and the twins."

"We'll send one when we arrive then." Fen dumped his mug. "I'll secure the wagon if you want to clean up inside."

"Sure."

Fen lingered. He looked around, obviously waiting for Pesha to say something else. Pesha *owed* him something else—a mountain of apologies, an explanation, anything but the silence he gave instead.

Fen at last nodded, collected Pesha's mug, and retreated.

When the sound of his regret disappeared into the distance, Pesha lowered to a crouch, buried his head between his parted knees, and sobbed.

"Hope it wasn't too cold for you last night, Eshe," Fen said. He balled the bell net up and shoved it into a canvas bag. "I guess you don't feel cold like we do though, with all that time you spend at the bottom of a frozen lake."

Atio squawked, her wings fluttering.

"I know *you* don't get cold," he said, smirking. He went to adjust the tank straps for the day's ride when a thought occurred to him, one he was shocked he'd not wondered about before. "You've always talked to Aio. Can you…Do you…communicate with *other* familiars? Like Eshe?"

Atio responded in the affirmative.

"Does she understand *me*?"

Another yes.

Fen pulled his shoulders back in astonishment. All this time, he'd spoken to Eshe the way he might a tomcat. But though she wasn't *his* familiar, she was one nonetheless, and it heartened him to know his comforting whispers hadn't gone unheard.

Farren was inside the carriage already. He checked on her to ensure she had a comfortable position and that her blanket hadn't slipped away, as it sometimes did.

Everything was fine. She was curled up on the bench like a lynx, her quilt tucked around her like a swaddled baby.

Fen closed the door and locked it, but he couldn't shake a sense something *was* wrong with her. But she looked the same as always. Nothing was out of place. Her gentle snores went on, uninterrupted.

Pesha jogged down the path, holding up the satchels. "Everything good?"

"Yeah," Fen said, shaking off the foreboding creeping through his thoughts like weeds. "Ready?"

Pesha threw the satchels into the back and climbed up onto the bench. "Have to be," he said, staring ahead as Fen joined him. "You know, Fen—"

"I'm a little tired," Fen said, cutting in. He'd been anxiously waiting for Pesha to say the words, but it didn't mean he was ready for them. "May just close my eyes for a few, if you don't mind."

"Right." Pesha spurred the horses, and the carriage jerked into motion. "Of course."

THREE
PALE-BLUE PONIES

Pesha kept both eyes fixed on the road. At the early hour, there were mostly traders traversing the Compass Road. He noted the way they kept to the center, as though fearing an accidental slip into the Hinterlands without realizing. The Unfortunate Denouement, some called it, because most men who veered off the roads and into the forbidden forests were never heard from again. Many travelers along that stretch, it was said, wouldn't even speak a single word until they were clear of the badlands and safely within the borders of the Westerlands, Southerlands, or Easterlands.

Although the foreboding warning signs were yet miles ahead, Pesha didn't need them to know they were still in the Northerlands. The only time he'd ever traveled beyond Darkwood Run was when he'd gone south to Newcarrow to rescue Fen and Siofra. But he'd never, *ever* forgotten the way he'd felt the moment his wagon had skipped from the familiarity of the Northern Reach to a place that should have been home but never had been.

Fen moaned and stirred against Pesha's shoulder. Pesha's gut twisted in an endless quagmire of convoluted wants and needs. How easy it would be to loop an arm around Fen and pull him closer. To lean down and brush a kiss across his soft mouth. He could mend what had broken between them. Fen, with his achingly large heart, would forgive everything, all of it.

Pesha opted to let him sleep.

He's only so exhausted because I've been an incomprehensible asshole.

Eshe stirred to life in her tank. She seemed to agree.

"You always take his side," Pesha muttered. He nodded at a family passing on their way north. The man driving their carriage returned the nod. *He might not have, if he could see my true hair color. Or Fen's.*

Or the spelled Medvedev inside the carriage.

He wondered what Desemir was doing. He no longer worried *how* his brother was, not since he'd settled into his marriage with Siofra. Pesha had been managing Des's capriciousness, his whims, for so long, it felt unnatural to stop now, but the habit lingered, just like the last conversation he'd had with his brother before he and Fen had left Shadowfen Hall.

Why not look at this as an opportunity for fresh beginnings for yourself as well?

What do you mean?

From the time our father died, you've been determined to save me from my mistakes. And I am eternally grateful for your sacrifice, Pesh. I couldn't have asked for a truer brother than you. Whether I deserved it is a matter beyond my deciding.

But?

But can you honestly say you *have lived? Mistakes are a part of living, brother. They guide us toward the paths we inevitably take. Is it not time for you to turn your attentions to your own needs?*

Pesha didn't even know what that meant. *His* needs. What needs? Everything he'd ever required was easily found within the boundaries of Shadowfen Hall and the surrounding forests.

Several more travelers—traders, from the looks of the goods piled in their wagons—passed. Pesha offered more perfunctory nods, but the growing number of people on the road tickled his anxious nerves. With a glance at the sky, darkening from a coming storm, he decided it was time for their first break.

Fen jolted awake when the carriage left the road. He wiped his mouth, muttering something unintelligible.

"Taking a necessities break," Pesha said, pulling back on the reins to guide the horses toward a surer path.

"How long was I sleeping?" Fen returned to his side of the bench. "Where are we?"

"Not long," Pesha lied. "We're about a half-day's ride from our last stop. I thought we could take a bite, let the horses rest."

"I'm famished," Fen said with a breathless sigh. "I should've eaten this morning."

"I agree, you should have," Pesha said with a pointed peripheral look.

Fen rolled his eyes. "Yes, Father."

Pesha made a *pfft* sound. His heart skipped at the soft chuff Fen made in return. It felt good to be playful with him again, but so much had gone wrong in the past weeks, and there was no place for mirth in all the failure. It wouldn't last. It couldn't.

The uneven path stretched on, guiding them deeper into the forest. Pesha searched for anything resembling a decent place to set up a quick reprieve. A clearing. A stream. But the farther they went, the less likely it seemed.

"Pesha…the trees."

"What about them?"

"*Look.*" Fen didn't point so much as gesture all around.

Pesha glanced up, his breath catching. He'd been so focused on the path, he hadn't noticed the leaves had gotten lighter. *Bluer.* Which was…impossible. He may not be a worldly man, but Pesha had devoured books at the same rate as Des, and there'd been nothing to suggest there were blue-leafed trees anywhere in the kingdom.

"It has to be an illusion of sorts." Fen grabbed the upper rail on the footboard and turned away from Pesha to get a better view of the forest. "Even the bark...What is this?"

Yes, even the bark, Pesha realized. His senses tried to catch up. The bark was dark, like ebony wood but with a hint of midnight. Perhaps it was an illusion, like the way some said the skies above were so blue because of the sea's reflection. That had been disproven by the Reliquary scholars but was still a strong-held belief by many who didn't know better.

Light ahead promised a change of scenery. Pesha eased the horses in that direction, his heartbeat uneven as he wondered if it wasn't an illusion but a trick. A trap.

The forest opened up into the strangest thing Pesha had ever seen.

An entire pasture of blue grass lay before them. It shimmered in the breeze, carrying the first whispers of rain. But the grass was the least of the oddities staring back at Pesha and Fen.

It was the horses.

Ponies might have been a more apt description, for they were small, like mules, but broader and with considerably more hair. And they were all, every one of them, a very pale blue.

He stopped the carriage at the edge of the clearing. Perhaps foolishly, his fear faded, supplanted by wonder. Fen leaped off the bench and bounded into the grass.

Wait! Pesha wanted to yell after him. Instead he watched, bewildered, his breath trapped in his chest as Fen intrepidly approached one pony, hand fearlessly outstretched. The beast looked up, its mouth full of blue grass, and sounded a gentle, inviting nicker.

Pesha choked out a stunned laugh, watching Fen light up in awe as he ran his hands down the pony's unusually long, silvery mane. The pony nudged him for more, causing Fen to giggle in delight. He looked back with a smile so boyish and authentic, it liquefied Pesha's angst.

Two more ponies moseyed toward Fen, and soon he was struggling to divide his gleeful attention between them all. He laughed, picking handfuls of grass, feeding it to them, and trailing his hands down their manes and snouts.

A memory took hold of Pesha. The first time he'd laid eyes on Fen, in that jail cell in Newcarrow. The dark distrust brimming behind the caged boy's narrowed eyes. The fear he tried so hard to hide but was as bold and obvious as his anger. Week by week, Pesha had fought to break those barriers down to dust, to show Fen he was safe. Safe at Shadowfen Hall. Safe with *him*.

Pesha shook off his daze and jumped out of the carriage. His legs wouldn't obey the command to move until Fen shot him another excited look, beckoning him over with a wild nod. An unexpected smile spread across Pesha's face as he jogged into the clearing. He slowed when he drew near.

"Aren't they incredible?" Fen whispered, as though anything more substantial would disrupt the strange forest paradise they'd stumbled upon. His face was a picture of pure joy as he traced his fingers down the shimmery mane of the pony nearest him. "This *is* real, isn't it? I'm not dreaming?"

"You're not dreaming," Pesha replied, though he couldn't be certain of it. He heard his own voice through a fog of delirium. He'd never hallucinated, not when drunk on spirits nor when he'd eaten the intoxicating mushrooms Wulfhelm had insisted were "utterly safe."

Fen, his face split with a broad grin, reached for one of Pesha's hands and brought it to the mane. He watched, waiting for Pesha's reaction.

Emotion choked Pesha's throat, blooming across his chest. How could something so wondrous exist in the same world as him and Fen? No one would ever believe them. He wasn't even sure he wanted to tell anyone. It seemed like a moment created just for the two of them, when they desperately needed amnesty.

He laughed. At first, the sounds were fragmented, but by the time the tears came, his unrestrained bliss was the only thing he could hear at all. Fen laughed with him, his hands wound through the pony's hair as he nuzzled his face back and forth against the gentle beast's snout.

Pesha dropped to a crouch and feverishly grabbed at the blue grass—no, it was silver when the sunlight hit it, ah, but then it was blue once more when a cloud passed overhead—and moved from one pony to another, offering them each a generous handful, whispering sweet words as they accepted his gift.

"Apples," Pesha said, an idea coming to him. "Horses love apples. Maybe the ponies will too."

Fen brightened and bounded back to the wagon. He returned with one apple, which he quickly flourished into dozens. He dropped them onto the grass, flashing a sideways smile at Pesha as they watched the ponies form a sort of haphazard line.

"They're taking turns," Fen said, his voice filled with wonder. "Like a society would."

Pesha and Fen alternated feeding the ponies, one by one, until the apples were nearly gone.

"Should I make more?" Fen's question had another lying just beneath the surface. Pesha recognized the childish hope, and it reminded him he was the one who would have to make the call to stay or go. If they left, they would make it to their next cabin by suppertime. If they stayed…

Pesha twisted his mouth to the side and nodded. He swayed into Fen. "One more round."

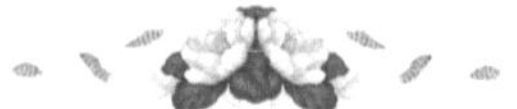

One more round had turned into three, then four. It was nearly dusk before they looked up and realized they'd squandered an entire day in the meadow with the pale-blue ponies.

They'd have to push hard. No more stops. But no matter how Fen examined the consequences of their idyllic detour, he found no cause for regret. He couldn't remember the last time he'd felt so light. So free. If he ever had.

And Pesha, no matter what he might say later, when the yoke of responsibility returned, had been just as free. As light. As happy.

They said nothing about the ponies once they were back on the Compass Road, headed south. Pesha stared forward, his lips curving into occasional half smiles. Fen's heart swelled with something he couldn't define. It wasn't quite happiness but the absence of angst—the acceptance that faith wasn't linear but a series of broken lines, testing his ability to follow. His mother used to say, *Your worst days are behind you,* and he'd roll his eyes, because it both made perfect sense and none at all.

But their worst days *were* behind them. He had to believe it. He *chose* to believe it, because the Guardians, or whoever was responsible for them, wouldn't have diverted them to a place filled with such hope and wonder if there weren't better days ahead.

Pesha leaned back on the bench and sighed. He shifted the reins to one hand, and the other fell beside him, landing inches from Fen's leg.

Fen placed his hand next to Pesha's and waited to find out if it was an accident or an invitation.

Pesha's pinky tickled Fen's. Fen wiggled his back until Pesha climbed his fingers over the top of Fen's hand.

With his attention still pointed ahead, Pesha smiled.

Fen blinked away tears and smiled too.

Better days indeed.

FOUR

THE FORESTS ARE MAGIC, AREN'T THEY?

The final overnight on the road included the smallest cabin yet. There was one large central room and a loft, similar to the ones before, but there was no stove for food making, and the only privy was a hundred yards into the woods.

Fen flourished Farren's blanket into an entire stack of them, and they settled her near the fire, close enough to keep warm yet far enough that she wouldn't accidentally roll into it and launch another chain of unfortunate events.

After the lovely—and deeply needed—afternoon in the forest clearing, Fen wasn't leaving anything to chance.

Pesha leaned against the hearth, his eyes glazed from the spirits he'd started on several hours back. He swayed as though responding to music, and Fen, for a moment, wished there *were* music. Emboldened by the healing the day had offered, he wouldn't have hesitated to cozy up to Pesha, slide one arm around his waist, and whisk him over the threadbare rug into an awkward but fulfilling waltz.

Exhausted though he was, the thought put a broad smile on his face.

Pesha chuckled softly from across the room. "How I wish I could draw. Sketch. Anything. No one will ever believe us."

"Never," Fen agreed with a peaceful laugh. "Even if we *could* draw those magnificent beasts, they'd think we were drunk on spirits."

Pesha's teeth flashed through a boyish grin. "We *are* drunk on spirits, Fen."

"*You* are," Fen said, teasing. A bottle sailed toward him. He barely caught it before it went crashing into the wall. His eyes flew wide in astonishment. "You could've killed me."

"Why would I want to do that?" Pesha gaped at him in affected offense. "Drink up."

Fen sighed at the dusty bottle in his hands. He'd taken the reins from Pesha an hour ago, when he'd nearly run the carriage into a copse of trees. One of them had to be responsible.

But it was night, and they were drunk off more than liquor. Pesha wasn't inviting him to imbibe; he was inviting him to join him in letting go.

For once.

Fen's eyes fluttered back in surrender as he uncorked the bottle and tilted it back. Pesha made an approving sound, which quickly heightened to excited whoops as Fen drained the remnants and gave the bottle one last theatrical shake as he finished. He aahed and chucked it back at Pesha, who caught it with a shit-eating smile.

"What would Siofra think?" Pesha cajoled with a smirk. He dropped the glass bottle into the fire without turning, then winked with mischief.

"What would Desemir think?" Fen replied, blinking hard enough to make his eyes ache. The spirits had hit him fast. He stumbled to the wall but recovered quick enough to hopefully make it seem like he'd meant to do it. "What would…would *Euric* think?" Fen clomped down on his lower lip. He didn't know what had compelled him to bring up Pesha's once-lover.

"That crusty old demon?" Pesha snorted. He closed his eyes and smiled. "Took more spirits than this to get me into his bed."

Fen lowered a hard gaze Pesha's way. "He coerced you?"

"Nooooo." Pesha cackled. "No, no, no. I'm the one who came onto him, but fuck if it didn't take some drunken courage to make it happen. I think he regretted it more than I did."

"Oh." Fen's mood crashed in an instant. He tried to cover his disappointment by turning his attention toward Farren, sleeping quietly in her mound of blankets.

Pesha squinted one eye. "You're not jealous, are you?"

Fen's face flooded with heat. "Jealous? No, why...Why would I be? If you're into Euric..." He cleared his throat and grinned. "Into *older*, eh, *grumpier* men..."

"The grumpier the better," Pesha replied with a dreamy look upward. "If they're not growling, I'm not finishing."

"Pesha!" Fen felt himself grow hotter. If the floor were to open up, he'd happily swan dive through it. "Forget I...Forget I said... How did we even get on this topic again?"

"You're blushing, Stiofen."

"Of course I am. Will you listen to yourself?"

Pesha crossed his arms. His mouth pursed. "You're the one who brought up Euric."

"Yes I did, because...because I can't—" Fen hiccupped, making Pesha cackle. "He shouldn't have said what he said that night. About seeing your ass."

Pesha's face crumpled in boozy amusement. "He was thoroughly pissed. Hammered. Loaded. Ta—"

"I get it." Fen lifted his hands in wobbly surrender. "No need to run through a hundred other words that mean the same damn thing."

"Which is?" Pesha watched him with a deliriously patronizing stare.

"That you—" Fen halted, flummoxed. The spirits jumbled his thoughts, diverting them off the path. "Have been with all these men, and I…"

Pesha's cheeky grin dissolved. "Only a few. A few that were *safe.*" He turned toward the fire, gripping the hearth with both hands as he bowed close enough to the flames to kiss them. "I know you think I'm being obstinate, that I don't have the experience you do in…in running from trouble. And you're right. You're *right.* My world is small. Always has been."

"Pesh, I didn't mean…" Fen tried to move, but he was rooted in place. He could almost feel himself go to Pesha, wrap himself around from behind, and rest his face in that divot between his strong shoulders. But he was too much of a coward to move. "Siofra and I spent most of our lives cowering in fear, belonging to others. All that running…" He bowed his head, swallowing a lump. "It doesn't come without cost."

For a while, the only sounds in the small room were the crackle of fire and the occasional breath from Farren in the corner. Fen's heart pounded, escalating through the silence and drowning it with the uncertainty of expectation.

"Stiofen," Pesha said. Low, husky. "Come here."

"No." Fen surprised himself. "You come here."

Pesha's shoulders tensed under his shirt. His back lifted, pinched, as he curved in and then shoved off, turning. A dark blush lit the tops of his cheeks, his eyes wide and glistening.

He took one bold step, then another. Fen staggered back, unsure why, until he hit the wall.

Pesha drew nearer, enough for Fen to feel and smell the ripe liquor on his breath. Enough to feel the air change, the warmth increase, and his belly clench. Pesha's hands landed on either side of Fen's head, pinning him to the wall.

"I shouldn't have brought up Euric," Fen said weakly. His voice squeaked, high and shrill. "That's your business."

"Mhm." Pesha scorched him with the intensity of his stare. "But it's not the first time you've asked, is it?"

Fen, his jaw clenched, shook his head. The room spun.

One of Pesha's hands left the wall and landed on Fen's shoulder. He squeezed and moved it south, running a flat palm down Fen's chest. Fen's eyes rolled upward, his breath hitching as he inhaled and held it.

Pesha's hand moved farther down. Fen went as still as stone. Pesha's eyes never left his as he fingered the waistband of his trousers. "Why did you come with me on this trip?"

Fen battled the cotton in his mouth as he searched for a response. "I didn't want you to be alone."

Pesha flattened his hand and dipped his fingertips under Fen's trousers, tickling his flesh, eliciting a pathetically desperate whimper. "Is that the whole truth?"

Fen tore his gaze away, searching for his sense of control. He looked down, but seeing Pesha's hand in his pants left him more vulnerable. "Des has Siofra. They have each other, but you… me…."

Pesha's hand moved deeper. He brushed the base of Fen's cock, and Fen's knees buckled. Pesha caught him before he went down, using his body to fix him to the wall. "We're the ones who serve," he whispered, running his words along the side of Fen's face.

Fen didn't recognize himself, didn't know himself at all, as he shoved one of his own hands inside his waistband and twined it around Pesha's. Pesha grinned, tracing his tongue along the inside of his lip, and together their fists formed a knot around Fen's cock.

"Ahh!" Fen cried, stretching to the tops of his toes. His head rolled to the side as he and Pesha moved their joined hands, stroking his hard length. No one had ever touched him like that. Even he rarely touched himself, leaving no room for frivolity when there was always something more important, more necessary.

Pesha slid his thumb over the head of Fen's cock and swirled the pre-cum beading there. Fen's toes curled and he pitched forward, biting down on Pesha's shoulder as he came, spurting against Pesha's thumb, which was still moving in concentric passes. It happened so fast, he wasn't even sure it *had* happened, until Pesha removed his hand and rubbed his cum-soaked fingers together. He pressed one to his parted mouth. His tongue lashed out for a taste. Fen slammed one hand against the wall to keep from coming again.

"These forests *are* magic, aren't they?" Pesha mused to himself, turning away with a small shake of his head, as though the interlude had been a dream to shrug off. Fen's cock throbbed in agony, ready for more. He was afraid to ask. He didn't know how to ask. He didn't know what the fuck he was doing at all.

Pesha staggered into a chair on his way to the ladder. Fen watched, frozen, as Pesha climbed. Fen stayed to the wall, clamoring to breathe, to will himself into motion. If he could only find his courage, Pesha was waiting for him in the loft, and he didn't have to be experienced to know that whatever had just happened was only a tease of what could happen.

But he didn't move at all, until he heard Pesha's snoring waft down.

He sighed, sagging in near relief. Wanting something was one thing. Getting it was another.

Fen didn't know what he wanted anymore. The night had shown him that.

But when he climbed up and flopped onto the bed next to Pesha, one hand draped over the other man's waist, he knew the answer wasn't far off.

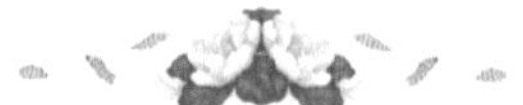

Pesha woke so suddenly, he knew it had been no mere chance. He squinted against the luminous moonlight spilling through the tiny window and across the meager bed. Fen was faced away, his breathing slow and easy. For once, he hadn't been the cause of Fen's nightmares, but the source of his dreams.

It was almost enough to distract him from the sense something was very, very wrong.

He blinked hard and rubbed his eyes, sucking in a gulp of air. A sickening wave of nausea hit him, and he had to clap a hand over his mouth to keep it at bay. He'd drunk too much. Said some things. *Done* some things.

It was still night. He couldn't have been out for long. Sleeping through the nights on the road had been an unsurprising side effect of running hard from dawn to dusk. Exhaustion hit him as hard as the nausea.

He closed his eyes and settled onto the hard pillow with a sigh. If he fell back asleep, he could still garner a few more hours, and—

Pesha bolted upright in the bed.

"Fuck. Fuck. Fuck. Fuck. No. No. No. *Fuck.*" His mouth fell open as he ran through as much of the night before that he could remember. Not a lot. Not much at all, except the most important part, when he'd forgotten to renew his magic on Farren before retiring for the night.

Fen rolled over with a groan. "It's not morning yet."

"Fen." Pesha couldn't hear himself over the hard throb of his heart. "Fen, we have…We have a massive problem."

"Hmm?" Fen nestled the pillow and tucked the blanket tight under his chin.

"Far…Farren. I forgot…I can't look."

Fen's eyes flew open. "Pesha. No."

"I can't. I can't look. I can't."

Fen scrambled out of bed and crawled to the edge of the loft. He fell back on his heels with a sigh and half turned. He paused for a moment and then spoke. "She's not there."

Howls sounded in the night.

Pesha threw back the blanket and leaped up. He raced to the window and gasped. "She's outside! Fen, she's—"

But Fen was already gone.

FIVE
WULVES

Fen leaped from the loft to the floor below and landed with a devastating thud before rolling across the moth-eaten carpet. He was up before he could register the pain, yanking on his shirt at the same time he was hopping into pants. He didn't waste time lacing his boots, instead tucking the leather straps inside to prevent a hard fall from slowing him.

Pesha's shouting declined, the desperate sound growing farther away. He wasn't following. It didn't matter. Fen had heard the wulves, and if there was more than one, there was a pack.

He ripped the door open, pausing only long enough to close it again. Somewhere in his mind, he registered that Farren would need warmth when he got her back inside, same as he'd thought ahead about the laces. It was the kind of forward thinking that had saved his and Siofra's asses time and time again.

When everyone else panicked, Fen acted.

The moon was the only illumination in the otherwise dark forest. He heard Eshe shift in her tank, restless, as he passed the lean-to where they'd stuck the carriage for the night. He launched into a sprint that left no room for error. Instinct compelled him over hidden logs and bade him duck when rogue branches sprung out to waylay him. He had only one thought as he raced for Farren's life: *if you waste time thinking, she'll die.*

He came to an abrupt, sliding stop when the forest opened into a clearing. Probably the same clearing Pesha had spotted Farren in from the window. Despite the dim shroud of night obscuring the field, Fen saw her right away.

She stood, half crouched, in the center of a pack of wulves. Six, maybe seven. It was hard to tell, when there were so many shadows. They circled her, their haunches flared, bouncing low growls between them. Fen briefly calculated his odds, which were not good at all, and moved toward the circle.

"Fen, no! Stiofen!" Pesha screamed from somewhere behind him. He knew without wasting precious time to look that Pesha was still in the loft, frozen in place. Fen remembered that kind of fear, enough to know he had no use for it anymore.

Pesha's petrified proclamations followed Fen as he stepped sideways toward the pack, careful to not draw the wulves from Farren. Not yet anyway. Not until it was time to act.

Atio cawed overhead, circling in the sky. *Let me handle this, girl. You get too close, they'll tear you apart.*

She held back but hovered overhead.

Farren's red braids flew as she arced her head back and howled. This only incited the wulves, and they closed in tighter, narrowing the circle into a chokehold. Farren grinned and bayed again, pursing her mouth to resemble a wulf's snout.

She's playing, he realized, but the wulves weren't. They were toying with their kill, which was giving Fen time to assess whether there was anything nearby he could use to distract them.

He drew close enough for his shadow to climb over them, so he slowly lowered until his hands touched the cold ground. Breath low and uneven, he blindly dug around in the dirt, his eyes on Farren and the wulves as he searched for something, *anything* to flourish.

Pebbles, grass, and dirt. Nothing more. Only small things that would need to become very big things to make a difference. The more extreme the flourishment, the quicker it spent his energy. He'd be able to turn a handful of pebbles into boulders before he ran out of steam, then he and Farren would both be dead.

But as his fist closed over a handful of earth, another idea occurred to him.

Fen had never tried it before, but it didn't mean it wasn't possible. He really had no idea what his limitations were. He'd spent his life resenting a gift others exploited for their gain. When he wasn't exhausting his vitality in indentured servitude, he had no desire to practice or expand the magic that had caused him so much grief.

Farren reached for one of the wulves, and it gnashed its teeth, lunging toward her. She hopped back with a delighted giggle that sent chills radiating down Fen's spine and into the soles of his feet. Atio's horrified caw screeched through the night.

Fen tilted his head toward the sky, filled his lungs with air, and howled.

The wulves all snapped their attention his way. Farren waved at them, trying to get them back, but they didn't stop their advance. Their shoulders rippled as they shifted direction, one pace at a time, their yellow eyes glowing with malice.

Atio's heavy wings battered the air. Fen couldn't see her, but he felt her descending.

No, go back!

"Farren," Fen cried. "I don't know if you can understand me, but you need to run back to the cabin now! Right now!"

Farren launched another braying howl into the moonlit sky. Atio's squawks heightened as she flapped just above Farren's head, talons curled and ready to grab hold.

She doesn't understand friend from foe, Atio. Up, up!

He filled his other fist with dirt and uncoiled to full height. His pulse pounded hard enough to make his chest hurt, and he feared his heart was legitimately readying to burst and kill him on the spot.

Atio hadn't listened and was battering the air, chasing wulves back and forth. Low enough that if one thought to leap up and grab hold of her, she'd be done.

Fen acknowledged his fear and buried it, lifting both hands to his sides as the wulves closed in.

Pesha screamed for him to stop. He screamed for Farren to run. For Atio to fly. He screamed and screamed and screamed, and it became the background notes of Fen's courage as he lifted his hands, mouthed a silent prayer, and launched the handfuls of dirt into the air.

The contents metamorphosed into a storm of dust and serrated, dense soil. It churned through the air, clipping the wulves, lifting one and carrying it off into the forest. Fen ducked low for more handfuls, hurled, and flourished, screaming as he watched the wulves, one by one, peel away from the force of the tempest.

Atio swooped low and landed close enough for Fen to rethink his strategy. But then he saw what she was doing: closing as much dirt and rock in her talons as she could carry. She took to the skies and met his gaze. Fen choked out a breath and nodded to show he understood, and then Atio rained earth over the melee while Fen transmuted it into violence.

For every two wulves he sent flying, one would come back dazed but furious. He wiped the sweat from his brow as he swayed on his feet, digging deep for vigor he no longer had. All the while, Farren howled, Atio screeched, and Pesha cried out for all of them.

But Fen heard only one thing.

If you give up now, all three of you die.

Siofra had once told him she heard their mother's voice from time to time, doling out wisdom she'd never bothered to give when she was still living. For Fen, it was their father, Rohan, who showed up for him in death in a way he never had in life.

Rest comes later, Stiofen. End this now.

The final two wulves descended on him, circling with their teeth bared, fat drops of saliva dripping from their mouths and disappearing into the grass and dirt. Wheezing, Fen forced himself to a squat once more, never taking his eyes off the predators ready to make a meal of him.

Fen closed his fists around the biggest clods of dirt he could carry and sent them hurtling through the air before he even made it back to his feet. Atio scooped and dropped more dirt, but there was too much going on for Fen to divert his focus to flourishing everything. The two wulves went spiraling into the funnel cloud, yelping as they were carried up, up, so high there was no danger left when they finally came down and slammed to the earth with catastrophic thuds.

He fell to his knees and bowled over. A shadow crashed over him. Panting, he forced himself to look up, to face death like a man, but it was only Farren. Thank the Guardians, the gods, whoever, but it was only Farren.

"We have to..." He couldn't finish. Wheezing, he flapped a hand toward the cabin. But Farren didn't move. Like the wulves, she bared her teeth, spittle dripping from her mouth, down her chin. Her emerald eyes practically glowed. "Farren. Farren, you need to—"

Farren landed on him with a triumphant screech. She threw her head back with one final howl, twisting her neck in thrall to her song and drawing the other wulves to her side. Fen watched in abject horror as she then turned her gnashing on him. The other two surviving wulves flanked her right and left.

Atio screamed a blood-curdling cry into the night.

As Farren's teeth burrowed into his clavicle, Fen lost the last of his fight, surrendering to darkness and pain.

The success of Pesha's entire life hinged upon his unwillingness to overreact, even in the most dire circumstances. He'd watched enemies dance in and around his older brother's legacy for years,

Pesha acting as the soft-spoken voice of reason to a man who, in just the right mood, would have blown up all of Darkwood Run to keep Shadowfen Hall safe.

These men will destroy our entire world, Pesh, unless we get ahead of it.

Des, these men wouldn't know courage or boldness if it was inked on their foreheads. Let it rest. Show them you're the man with infinite patience, and they'll fear that far more than any aggression.

But as Pesha watched Fen blindly race into danger to save *his* sister, he realized it hadn't been patience that had kept Desemir and the Hall safe, but the illusion of protection offered by an isolated keep in the middle of a forest so valuable, no one dared risk harming it.

There was a moment. Always. Everyone said so. It was never the moment it should have been, the high-adrenaline worst of the worst, nor the one that could have prevented the terrible thing from happening at all.

For Pesha, it was watching Atio hook her beak into Farren's shirt and try to lift her off Fen. It was the way the bird never gave up, even though her eyes clearly betrayed her acceptance that death was coming for them both.

Pesha pulled a tunic over his head, not bothering with his pants or boots before rushing outside into the night. His feet crashed into sharp branches and dead leaves as he pounded through the forest, slicing his soles, but he kept on until he reached the clearing.

What he saw there sent the world to a crashing halt.

The wulves were being baited away by Atio, but they weren't a danger to Fen, not anymore.

Farren was tearing away at his neck like a member of the pack, blood and gore pouring down her chin like a triumph.

Pesha raced toward them, his chest heaving and his hands out. He closed his eyes and ran the rest of the way blind, focusing on the magic that had kept Farren safe—had kept them all safe—for so many years.

When he was close enough to smell them both, he opened his eyes again and whispered.

Farren's head whipped upward. Her mouth, dripping with Fen's blood, gaped unnaturally in a soundless scream, and her eyes were blown so wide, he thought for a moment something had attacked her from behind.

She snapped back, her spine arcing like an invisible hand was bending her away from Fen. Pesha stomped closer, still whispering, still focusing all his effort on subduing the beast his sister had become without the needed calm of magic.

"It's all right, Far. Everything's fine," Pesha said, unsuccessfully masking the tremor in his voice. *Don't look at Fen. Not yet.* He couldn't hear or see Atio anymore either. "Listen to my voice and know you're safe."

Farren shuddered. She sniffed at the air and dropped to her knees with a whimper. He stared in horror as she stretched her hand to her mouth and licked, mingling her own blood with Fen's.

She rocked in place. Her eyes fluttered back. And then she toppled onto her side, spent.

Pesha opened his mouth wide and gasped for air. Nothing was enough, no gulp satisfying or steadying. He stumbled to the side and lowered down beside Fen and Farren both. Farren was…It was hard to tell if she was injured, but it didn't seem so. Fen, on the other hand…

His neck was ripped open, blood spurting with his rapid pulse. Part of the flesh covering his jaw had been torn off, and one of his hands, presumably in trying to protect his face, was missing a finger.

"Not like this," Pesha whispered and folded himself over Fen. He transferred his vitality to the boy who had saved his life when he'd come to Shadowfen Hall angry and lost. Pesha had been angry and lost too; he just hadn't realized it until he'd observed his own truths reflected in the eyes of Stiofen Thornheart.

He heard Atio chasing the last of the wulves away. Felt Eshe crying out for him, sharing his pain in a way only she could. But the sound that brought Pesha back to life was Fen's heart rate gradually slowing to normal. The sensation of his flesh reforming, his finger regrowing, and his beautiful jaw, the one Pesha had imagined trailing kisses along a hundred times but had never been brave enough to try, restoring.

Fen finally lost consciousness. Pesha curled Fen into his arms and held him there, taking a moment to reflect on everything he'd almost lost because he'd been irresponsible and indecisive.

No, a coward. A fucking coward.

Fen was right about him. Pesha didn't understand how to thrive in chaos. He should never have taken the journey at all, but bringing Fen along had been nothing more than selfishness. He'd *wanted* Fen at his side. He couldn't bear to leave him behind, so he'd convinced himself it was better this way. That together, they'd have a stronger chance of success.

Pesha carried Fen back to the cabin and settled him onto Farren's bundle of blankets. He returned to the field and gathered Farren in his arms, but exhaustion caused him to lose his bearings, and the path was darker on the return. Atio appeared overhead and cawed once to indicate Pesha should follow, guiding Pesha the way back to the cabin, Farren bouncing like dead weight. Pesha raised his head to thank the falcon, but Atio was already gone.

He set Farren beside Fen. There was no way he was carrying either of them up the rickety loft ladder. After the horrors of the past hour, he didn't have the heart to go up either.

Pesha tugged at the blankets to make them stretch wider and settled in beside Fen. He draped his arm over both of them, needing to feel they were still breathing, still calm.

Only then did he allow himself a few moments to think. To really accept what had almost happened.

When he was certain Farren would not spring back to life, and Fen's heart was still beating steady, Pesha closed his eyes, buried his face into the edge of Fen's hard pillow, and wept.

SIX
THE WORLD AS WE KNOW IT

Fen had noticed the vegetation changes around midday. Salthill was the only treeless town in the Northerlands, and the Wulf's Neck had been a barren landscape of the same views, over and over.

But now there were more trees, richly hued with a painted-on look, similar to the towering giants of the Great Darkwood but different enough to leave him unsettled, like he was bearing witness to something not meant for him.

Beside him, Pesha held the reins in one hand. His good hand. The other bore a Farren-sized bite mark he'd stubbornly refused to heal. Fen had had to resist a hearty eyeroll when Pesha had grunted about being fine. Even a few days ago, he'd have argued with Pesha about it, tried to make him see reason. But that was another time, and he had been another person then.

A valley of trees dotted with white-tufted blooms, like cotton, filled the left and right of the road. The clusters were so dense, it felt like the carriage was getting packed in, being funneled through the Compass Road to another dimension.

Pesha hadn't said a word. Nor had Fen. Even Eshe and Atio were quieter than usual.

Farren, of course, slept—as she should have been doing when she'd traipsed into a pack of wulves and nearly gotten herself, Fen, and Atio killed.

It wasn't even anger he felt. He tried to turn the churning tension into rage, because *that* was manageable. It had purpose, boundaries. Meaning. Whatever dark thoughts were spinning through Fen's troubled mind at present, they were worse than looking up into Farren's glowing eyes and knowing he was in terrible trouble.

Back and forth he'd waffled, for weeks, on whether he should have come. Whether he was needed, wanted. But it wasn't even about that anymore. He didn't *want* to be there, to be needed, to be wanted. He didn't want to feel like an expendable force in Pesha's life. Like…a pleasurable distraction, sometimes required but mostly not.

Pesha grunted in pain.

Fen braced in annoyance.

What a fool I've been, thinking I was falling in love with you.

He'd already decided what to do. The only thing left was to tell Pesha.

Fen uncapped his waterskin and took a hearty swallow. He sheepishly passed it to Pesha, who didn't even acknowledge the offer. The snub was the last bit of courage he needed to say the words. "Look. I'll help you find the way to Asgill lands. I'll help you get Farren settled. I'll—"

"I never should have brought you." Pesha's mouth parted in a sigh. He let it hang that way, commanding the agonizing silence, stealing the moment from Fen. "It was selfish to accept your offer. I just didn't want to be alone, but I could've brought anyone else. One of the guards. Anyone really. It never should have been you. It's not your battle to fight."

Fen flinched from the force of Pesha's confession. "I wanted to fight this battle with you, or I wouldn't have offered."

Pesha ran his broken hand through his dark, wavy hair. "Maybe I don't need you to, Stiofen."

Fen balked, scoffing. "No? Well, good, because that's what I was trying to say before you rudely interrupted me and made it about you. Once we get there, I'll find my way home with the carriage, and I'll have Des arrange for someone more suitable to bring it back to you. Good?"

Pesha's nose curled up. "Perfect," he gritted out.

"Great. Then it's settled."

"I'd say so."

Twisting away, Fen gathered his cloak tighter and gazed into the strange forest, still shifting and changing every hundred yards. Conifers with needles so dark they seemed purple sparkled in the breeze, while strange-looking critters danced around the forest floor in peculiar choreography. He didn't remember any of it from the long carriage ride from Newcarrow, when Pesha had whisked him and Siofra out of a musty jail and offered them a different life. To be fair, Fen remembered very little from that time at all, except how much he'd wanted to distrust Pesha, despite how at ease he'd felt in his calming presence. Learning to trust anyone except Siofra had taken weeks—months—and he had to wonder if it had all been for nothing. A long con. A fantasy of happiness that was as fleeting as a storm.

The carriage slowed. Fen turned his attention back to the road, where a large wooden sign greeted them on the right side. The words were carved deep and rutted by weather and time but were still clear.

"Notice to travelers," Pesha muttered. "A hundred paces south, the Compass Road will take you through the Hinterlands. If you wish to continue onto the Westerlands, Easterlands, or Southerlands, your journey henceforth must keep to this road. If you stray, you are subject to the capricious mercy of the clahnns of the Hinterlands. May the Guardians be with you." His face scrunched together. "I forgot about this sign."

"Well, how are we going to stick to the Compass Road when it's Asgill lands we're looking for?"

"We aren't." Pesha spurred the horses, and the carriage shot back to life. "We'll have to veer into the forest soon."

"Asgill lands are vast."

"I know."

"How will we know where to go?"

"You ask like I've been there, Fen. I don't *know*. We'll…feel it, like your mother used to say." Pesha rolled his shoulders and shifted in discomfort. His mouth puckered.

Fen felt it too. They didn't need words. It was more of a sense anyway. The border warning hadn't been necessary, because it was obvious they weren't in the safety of the Northerlands anymore.

But it was the dread…the sinking, damning dread. He didn't remember the sign from his fateful trip north, or the feeling, but he'd been so wounded and distracted to think of anything except how to keep Siofra safe.

His jaw throbbed from phantom pain, and his neck quickly followed suit. His hand traveled up to remind himself he was still whole, that Pesha had seen to his needs quickly enough to leave him with only mild scarring. When it mattered, Pesha had acted.

But if he'd acted faster, none of it would have happened at all.

Except, it was partly Fen's fault too, because he'd enabled Pesha to get drunk and distracted…had fully taken part in what had happened after, however brief and confusing.

Pesha drew a deep sigh and guided the horses toward a rutted path leading off the road. He mouthed something to himself as they left the safety of the Compass Road and entered the forest.

Fen held his breath. The woodland seemed like all the others, similar but not the same. The deeper they went, the more vibrant the trees, the flora. Even the forest animals were *more,* with longer quills and richer coats.

Eshe sloshed in her tank, spilling water over the sides. Fen turned around to check on her, but Pesha kept his eyes trained on the path, which was less defined the farther they traveled. Soon there was no path at all, just a quagmire of obstacles to creatively dodge.

Atio dipped below the canopy of trees and hovered near the carriage.

Pesha bolted straight on the bench. He whipped an arm out to his left and pinned Fen in place like an overprotective mother.

What, Fen started to say, but it quickly proved unnecessary.

Rustling sounded from all sides. The carriage came to an abrupt halt, and they watched, in dumbstruck awe, as several dozen Medvedev swept in from the perimeter and surrounded them.

"Hello!" Pesha cried. His voice was cracked and weak. "My friend and I are Medvedev, and we've come a long way—"

A large net came down from the trees and encased the wagon. Fen swatted at the thick rope, crying out to Pesha, who clawed and kicked.

"You don't understand!" Fen yelled, but no one listened. Strong arms lifted him from the carriage bench, still wrapped in netting, and he was hurled over someone's shoulder. He swung around, trying to spot Pesha, Atio, anyone, but then the netting was removed, and a burlap sack was shoved roughly over his head.

"Say nothing, Fen! Say nothing to them! It's a trap! We were wrong! We were—"

Pesha had heard the expression "it was all a blur" enough times to wonder how so many people could relate to such a peculiar claim, but until he'd watched Fen and then Farren ripped away from him, amid a flurry of damning accusations, he'd never had his world distorted while he was standing in it.

Atio's screeching cry as they roped her talons took his breath away.

But Farren, howling in agony, was worse. So much worse. He hadn't been sure at first what he was hearing, which could have easily been *hoot, hoot, hoot,* but even in his disarray, he knew what his sister was screaming and that, for the first time in over eight years, she was making words from her sounds.

"Wulf, wulf, wulf!"

That was the moment. The one that broke him.

"No, Farren, it wasn't your fault! It wasn't your fault. This isn't your fault!" Pesha thrashed, opening his mouth wider to scream the words louder. He couldn't let her get taken thinking she'd caused their capture. If she could make words, she could understand them, or so he prayed. "Farren, please listen to me. *Hear me.* We'll figure this out, but you did not cause this to happen. This is not your fault!"

Her howls turned to desperate screeches. "Wuuuuuulf!"

Everything was spinning so wildly out of his control. He'd had no time to react. "This isn't your fault! Farren!"

Wulf, wulf, wulf soon faded to distant echoes, muffled by the rustle of trees.

And then it was gone. She was gone.

How many times had he screamed the truth? That Farren was his sister, and Fen his friend, and they were both desperate to help her. That they meant no harm to anyone. That the murder of Farren's poor familiar had been enacted by someone long dead, and that they'd come to right the man's terrible wrongs.

Soon, though, his words sounded like the other sounds, of rustling and grunts and a hundred unanswered questions.

Pesha thrashed against his bindings, but there were at least four men, maybe more, surrounding him, and nowhere to go even if he could fight back.

He felt Eshe somewhere nearby, but he almost wished he hadn't, because all he picked up was unfiltered panic. Wherever she was, she was no less a prisoner than he.

It was all—all of it—a blur.

A blur of fear and confusion.

Of terror.

He was no longer sure what was real and what was fantasy.

The air shifted. If his mind hadn't been so muddled, he might have had the clarity to describe the shimmer—no the *bend*—when they clearly passed from one place to another. Place was the only word he could find for it, because there was no way he would even consider a word like *dimension* or *world* without losing his sanity altogether.

Time turned fluid.

The Medvedev occasionally passed brief conversation between them, and though it was in another language, he understood it perfectly. Their cadence was more clipped than his, wasting no time with filler words. Perhaps they knew he could decipher it, because they were saying nothing about his crime nor his fate. Nothing at all about Fen or Farren or the poor familiars.

I'm sorry, he thought, but he didn't know who the words were for. Fen, for putting his life in danger, repeatedly, for him? Farren, for not knowing how to fix her? Des, for leaving him, after all these years? Siofra, for taking her brother and confidant away?

Himself, for failing all of them?

A rush of bright light flooded his vision. He squinted against the intrusion, wishing his hands were…Ah, but they *were* free. The bindings had been removed with the blindfold. His shoulders screamed when he moved them from their locked position, but he was *free,* and there was nothing around him except spectacularly vibrant forestland, unlike any he'd seen before, and when he took a step forward, he—

Pesha rocked back in pain. He shook his head to clear it and tried again, more slowly. There was nothing in front of him that he could see, but there *was* something there. An invisible wall.

He carefully traced the rest of it with his hands, patting solid air until he had a sense of the full size of his unseen prison cell.

It was then he noticed the ground was several feet beneath him.

His cell was floating.

Invisible.

Impossible.

Motion in the distance caught his notice, and when he looked over, he saw Fen, suspended in air like him and waving his arms in delirious circles. Pesha shook his head and slapped the air wall to show him he was in the same predicament. Fen reared back and slammed himself into the magical wall. Once, twice. Pesha shook his head in wide passes, begging him to stop, but Fen continued on and on and on, until at last the force knocked him unconscious, and he fell to a heap on the floating ground.

Atio screamed and tried to take flight, tugging at the rope binding her to a nearby tree.

Pesha's chest caved inward. He had no choice but to sit, or he'd have gone down as hard as Fen. Legs crossed, he rocked, thinking and pleading with whoever was listening to intercede on their behalf.

But there was no one. Because…

Say it. Fen would. He wouldn't shy away from the truth. He'd confront it. Say it.

"Because we're no longer in the world as we know it."

SONS OF THE FORSAKEN

SEVEN

RAISED BY MEDVEDEV, EXPLOITED BY MEN

The fellow called himself Cassair. Fen's instincts flared with immediate caution, for there was no reason for the guard to give him a real name, yet nothing in the man's solemn expression indicated cleverness or trickery. Indeed, he seemed to have little guile about him at all. After two decades of navigating the bumpy, unpredictable nature of men's motives, Fen would be refreshingly surprised, if the circumstances weren't so unfortunate.

Cassair was built solid, his muscles so pronounced under his clothing that Fen might have believed he was made of stone. Of course, his light-green hair and fox familiar meant he was just as Medvedev as Fen, so they had at least that in common. Except Cassair was sitting on the right side of the interaction, and Fen was balancing on the edge of a crevasse of unknown depth.

"You. Here. Reason." Cassair had been parroting some version of the stilted question over the past hour, rewording it slightly each time in a hurl of solid words marked by solid stops—*Reason. Come. Tell. Reveal. Secret. Intention*—each time as though he thought little of Fen's intelligence. But Fen had already adjusted to the Medvedev's speech, how any but the most essential words were dropped altogether, and his mind filled in the blanks whenever the guard—no, *sentry*, Cassair had emphasized when correcting Fen—spoke. It was a swift, natural transition in understanding that he assumed was abetted by some form of useful magic.

"I've already told you why we're here. My answer won't change, no matter how many ways you ask it," Fen said. He eyed the wooden bowl and mug that had been set out for him, untouched. His belly rumbled as he watched the porridge congeal, weighing the odds it was poisoned. It seemed far more likely the Medvedev would deal with their supposed transgressions in a more ceremonial manner, but he couldn't rule out a quiet, tidy dispatch either.

The hut was a generous single room, sized for two or three people. There was a bed, which had a rough, hand-carved look to it, and two tables, including the one at which he engaged the stoic sentry, playing an unwinnable game. There was even a touch of decor, a handful of stitched stars and moons dangling from the supports that swayed whenever one of them shifted.

The floor was rough beyond the pelt rug, a fact Fen had discovered because his boots had been confiscated along with his other clothes, replaced with a simple tunic and loose pants, but nothing for his feet. He noted Cassair had boots on but didn't know what it meant, if anything.

All things considered, Fen's present arrangement was still better than the invisible prison he'd slept in.

"That is not the whole truth," Cassair said, his harried blinks the only visible sign of his growing impatience. The man was otherwise placid. Fen studied him, overcome with the sense that though he and the sentry were both Medvedev, the guard belonged there and Fen didn't, a disparity that went well beyond the obvious power imbalance.

His mother's words, *that is no home*, came back to him.

"History, when told through by those who came later, isn't history; it's just a story," Fen answered, balancing truth and abstraction. He knew the words by heart, having said them at least ten times in half as many hours. "I wasn't there for most of it. But everyone who was has been consistent in their accounting. Ludwik Trevanion was a sick man who had a torrid affair with Arenn Wintersin, Farren and Pesha's mother. He turned his eyes on young Farren until she finally stood up to him and then he *murdered* Farren's familiar. Arenn killed Ludwik, then herself, leaving his sons to manage the mess he left, which included Farren's complete and total break from reality. They did the best they could, with no one to help. Pesha and Desemir love Farren. Everyone at Shadowfen Hall does, including me, and I don't know her as she was." A shiver tore through him as memories of the wulves came rushing back. He shook them off. "She's family. We want to help her, and we've run out of options. There's nothing more to it than that."

"The man is dead," Cassair said, "so he cannot defend himself."

"Ludwik?" Fen snorted. "No, not unless you've got an 'in' with the spirit realm."

Cassair didn't crack a smile. "And you were not present when the familiar was executed."

"As I said, I didn't even *know* the Trevanions back then. I was too busy running from other evil men. Because, you know, Ludwik isn't exactly a rarity in the realm."

"Your travel partner was not there either."

Fen's toes curled in annoyance. "He *was* there, but he was just a little boy. I don't know how much he remembers, to be perfectly honest with you." *And he won't talk about it, so good luck to whatever sentry got stuck interrogating Pesha.*

"The aggrieved, Farren, cannot speak to confirm or refute anything you've said."

Except, that wasn't what Cassair had said. It was more like, *Aggrieved. Farren. Cannot refute.* Fen's mind no longer had to slow down to catch up, but sometimes it still caught him off guard.

"*No*, but that's why we're here," Fen said testily. He heard others milling about outside, more people who belonged there. Probably curious about the rogue Medvedev caught sniffing around their forests uninvited. *More accurately, three Medvedev.* "As you can see, she's…broken. Pesha and his brother have done all they can, but all it's done is prolonged—" He slammed his mouth shut with a deep groan, shaking his head. "*Why* am I telling you all this again? You're not the one in charge. You're not the chieftainess. I want to speak with *her.*"

Cassair regarded him with profoundly concentrated scrutiny, across one of the most uncomfortable silences of Fen's life. "You. Here. Reason."

"*Fuck y*—no. Nope. Not saying another word." Fen crossed his arms and flopped back, only to recall there was no back to the chair he was sitting on, which was no chair at all but a stump that had been smoothed and converted into a broad stool. He inelegantly flailed about, while Cassair watched unwearyingly for him to finish. Fen regained his balance, but the frustration of it all snapped what was left of his calm. "I've told you everything. I'm done. Torture me. Beat me. Starve me. I don't care anymore."

"Torture is your way."

Fen's face scrunched in incredulous amusement. "I've never tortured anyone in my life, sentry."

"You. Men." Cassair waved a hand.

"I'm full-blooded Medvedev," Fen said with a humorless chuckle. Outside, more Medvedev milled about. They were gathering. For him? Had to be. But were they curious or hostile? Cassair wouldn't explain any of it, so there'd only be one way to find out, and Fen wasn't looking forward to it. "Why do I even bother telling you anything when you won't listen?"

"Raised as man."

"Raised by Medvedev, *exploited* by men. Not the same. But you wouldn't know about that, would you? In your little sylvan paradise here, where apparently everyone does as they're told or they're expelled?"

"Forsaken." Cassair's nose briefly wrinkled in disgust.

Fen rolled his head back. The flesh on his neck stretched taut, almost stinging. When he pitched forward, he slapped his palms onto the table's edge. "Cassair, neither of my parents ever bothered to explain what that means. What they did. What happened here. All I know is they weren't happy, they made it known, and they left. So that slight does nothing but confuse me."

"You. Here. Reason."

Fen laughed when he realized the difference between hearing Cassair's language as it was meant to be heard and the way Fen's mind processed it was directly proportionate to his level of annoyance with the sentry.

Cassair cocked his head with a bemused look, as if to say, *What's funny?*

"I'm done answering the same questions over and over," Fen said, bobbing his head in swift nods. "*Done.* Your turn. Tell me where Pesha is."

Cassair locked his hands.

"No? Tell me where our familiars are."

Cassair blinked.

"How about Farren? The one we came here to save but will more than likely hurt herself and others unless she's magicked?"

Voices joined the melee outside, shifting Cassair's attention to the door for the first time.

"If you don't want to talk about me and mine, maybe we could talk about why the trees and flowers look *nothing* like the ones in the rest of the Hinterlands. Even though we traveled, what, a half tick of the sun at most?"

The sentry's brows knit. He was still watching the tent flaps.

"Ah, didn't like that one?" Fen wanted to burrow more questions into the sentry until he split, like a dowel under a nail, but it seemed far more likely Fen would just waste his energy, and there was no telling how much he'd need. "I suppose we'll just sit here in the silence then." He held out several minutes before flopping forward with an exasperated groan. "*Tell me* where my companions are."

Cassair's eyes fluttered briefly upward. He inhaled through his pinched nose. "Safe."

"Safe? Can you perhaps define *safe* for me? In your own words."

The sentry not only did not define the word, but he offered no more of his own either. Another grueling hour passed, Fen alternately sighing, pacing, or picking at the food that, more and more, he was thinking *wasn't* poisoned.

The tent darkened. Dusk had settled, which meant Fen had been in the hut far longer than he'd calculated. He didn't relish the idea of walking into throngs of curious Medvedev in the dark.

Cassair tilted his head upward, whispered something Fen couldn't make out, and stood. "That will be all for today," he said. It had been more like *all today*, but Fen was positive it was magic instilling intent upon words.

"You mean that absolutely pointless waste of time, breath, and energy?"

Cassair waited at the door to the hut, his gaze fixed just beyond Fen.

"You're not taking me back to that floating—"

Fen yelped, arcing forward from the thrust of an unseen hand between his shoulders. Cassair's mouth twitched, a hint of a grin, as Fen was dragged on the tips of his bare toes.

Abruptly released by whatever foul magic had propelled him, Fen staggered out of the tent and into the cool night. He swallowed a greedy gulp of air and looked up at a sky of endless stars. On the hard nights that had followed hard days, he would count them, and the highest number he'd ever reached was three hundred and seven. But there were a dozen times more than that tonight. A hundred times. There were so damned many stars that just as Fen started to count, his vision blurred.

Cassair waited with presumably endless forbearance.

The lovely scent of cedar ripened in the forest, and Fen took that in too. He heard the trill of nocturnal insects, which sounded similar to the ones in Darkwood Run but different enough to give him pause in identifying them. There was a song rustling along the forest floor, a mournful hymn that made him feel at peace.

Cassair finally nudged him into motion. Fen muttered an insult his heart wasn't into anymore and then he noticed there were at least a hundred sets of eyes staring directly at *him.*

The trepidation he'd felt hearing them amass outside the tent was momentarily paused by the sheer awe coursing through him at the sight of so many Medvedev—and familiars.... in the air... on land... they were everywhere—in one place. Until he saw them all together, curious faced and staring, he'd not realized there were nuances to the emerald, sapphire, and violet hair he thought of as one-dimensional. Some took creative flair to their styles, piling and braiding, while others had a more simplistic approach, cropped close and neat. But there was as much variety in the Medvedev ogling him as there were in the men of the world.

Cassair said nothing, and the stern look he passed around the crowd seemed to be what kept them silent as well. But no words were needed to read the distrust, the accusation. He wanted to jump onto a log and preach his innocence, but he didn't even understand the crime, and he could already see it was a tough audience.

So Fen averted his eyes and followed his sentry until the curious Medvedev were behind them.

They marched through a sea of various-sized huts, each as individually unique as their occupants. They were arrayed in patterns, and when Fen paid closer attention to where the bonfires were placed, in the center of each arrangement, he realized the patterns formed familial territory. Or perhaps micro-societies.

So many questions. Not one answer.

More Medvedev were gathering around these fires, cooking their meals and talking and laughing. They passed their wineskins and encouraged each other to fill their plates to full. Fen was almost relieved at how normal it felt. Despite the sense he'd gone beyond the borders of the known world, enough of what he saw felt close enough to home to soften the disorientation.

One gathering stopped their merriment when Cassair and Fen walked by. A Medvedev, with violet braids woven behind his head, spat and hissed, "Forsaken." The others followed, one by one, and Fen continued to feel their eyes boring holes in him from behind after they passed.

"They really don't like me," he said when they were clear of the encampment.

"They remember the great betrayal. They suffered for it."

Fen whipped his head toward the sentry at the unexpected answer. "You know I wasn't even alive when it happened, right? I've never even been here before. My mother and father refused to tell us anything. Until we got here, I couldn't even be sure it was real."

"Reason does not close the wounds of the injured."

Fen made a sputtering sound. "At least you're acknowledging my reasonability."

"It's not for me to decide," Cassair said. He outstretched his arm. "In."

Laughing, Fen flapped his arms. "In *what*?"

Another ephemeral force surged up to punt him forward. Just as he regained his footing, he saw the sentry tapping a strange pattern into the air with his fingers. Fen started to ask him what he was doing, but he felt the air shift as the invisible prison formed around him, and the answer was clear.

The ground separated away from him and he floated upward, courtesy of the magical orchestration of the sentry, until Fen was about two feet off the forest floor.

He glanced at the spot where Pesha had been locked up, but it was empty. Not that he could discern distance or borders—or anything.

"Fiachra," Cassair stated and sashayed away.

"What in the blazes is a feeawkruh?" Fen rushed forward, beating his fists against air that had no business being solid, knowing before he even raised a hand how it would go. In some ways, it was like he was establishing a routine, defining his own role in the seemingly defenseless situation he had no clue how they were getting out of.

When he was sure he was alone, or as alone as he could be in a foreign land with his rights stripped away, he curled into a ball and faced the empty spot where Pesha should be. All that remained to him was anger as he stared into the dark, glittering forest. He repeated in his mind all the slights and offenses perpetuated against him by someone he trusted as much as his own sister, inviting the building fury that followed and encouraging the tingle in his limbs to roar to life and weaponize into something useful for once.

Where are you, Pesha?

He was probably trying to reason his way out of imprisonment. Smooth diplomacy was Pesha's hallmark, and it had served him well at Shadowfen Hall. But if he were there, Fen would remind him diplomacy was useless when they had no advantage to speak of. Clever words landed soft.

But when Pesha finally returned, Fen wouldn't say any of that. He'd turn and face the other direction. Though he imagined himself with an intense, glowering stare that would chill the heart of any man, he was more afraid of wearing his own heart in his teary eyes, and he'd already given too much of it away to someone who didn't want it anymore. Maybe never had.

Whatever the truth, it didn't matter in the lawless Hinterlands, the land of a million stars and a forest no one would ever believe, if they ever made it home.

Across the hours, he'd been soothed by the nearness of Atio, but he had not earned even a glimpse of her. Atio was trying to reassure *him,* though she was silent, so Fen could only guess at why his familiar had run out of fear.

I'm sorry, Si. I really wish we'd sent that raven now.

With nothing left to do but sleep, he did.

Pesha was determined to win the standoff.

It hadn't started as one. The sentry perched across from him in the surprisingly cozy hut had made what he assumed to be the Medvedev version of small talk on their walk through the encampment—itself harrowing, judging from the inexplicable glares he'd earned like an array of medals—and then, once he'd been properly settled and served a meal he wasn't sure would be wise to touch, the softness in Fiachra had disappeared in a flash, so fast it had startled him.

Like a flame she could turn off and on at will.

She asked him why he was there. He answered the first time and the second, but by the third, he recognized the tactic she was using, because it was one Desemir had perfected with the cocksure barons of Darkwood Run.

Arms crossed, he closed his mouth and waited.

Fiachra crossed her arms too. It was only when he caught her touching her mouth when he did, and then again when he scratched the back of his scalp, that he understood she was mimicking him.

Mocking him?

He had no idea.

He knew fuck all about his so-called people, and she wasn't making things clearer.

Day turned to dusk. His belly ached for relief, but he'd already held out so long that even if he believed they weren't trying to make him sick, his pride would have him starving before he touched his food.

Fiachra flipped her blue braid over her shoulder. She closed her eyes, opened them, sighed, and smiled. "Time."

"Time for *what*?" Pesha retorted, feeling a small burst of arrogant pride at not having lost the war of silence.

Fiachra gestured upward, but all Pesha saw was more brown tenting. He shrugged and grumbled his annoyance.

She tapped a finger against her chin and squinted. Stood. Though she didn't speak, she did glance at him over her shoulder, an invitation to follow. It was more a command, he thought, for what would happen if he stubbornly planted himself on the stump and refused to leave?

Nothing good.

Then again, maybe that was a language they'd understand.

Across the hours of bloated quiet, he'd listened for signs of Fen. Of course, there hadn't been a single one, which seemed as intentional as shoving them in separate cells and interrogating them individually. Imagining Fen spitting mad, cursing and glowering at whatever sentry had been unfortunate enough to get assigned to him, was *almost* enough to put a smile on Pesha's face.

He followed Fiachra out of the tent, but they didn't return through the encampment. Instead, she led him deeper into the strange forest, weaving a path he'd never retrace on his own—which was probably the point. As they neared the sound of a babbling stream, Pesha's heart nearly exploded, and he broke into an ungainly sprint.

Eshe!

In the chaos of confusion, he'd blocked all thoughts of her. He rarely let himself appreciate how truly tragic it had been for them to live their entire lives so separate. It was unnatural not to need her in the way others did, and he hadn't fully embraced that until he'd felt the joy radiating from her as she swam freely.

Fiachra approached the riverbank—not a stream after all, but a deep, broad body of water that would require a vessel to cross—and knelt.

A bright-pink salmon splashed out of the water, cresting and diving back in. It did this again and then again, until Fiachra, laughing in delight, clucked her tongue. To Pesha it sounded like she was implying, *Show-off.*

"Eshe," Fiachra said, standing. "You see?"

Pesha started to say he could feel her but there was nothing *to* see, until there was. Eshe breached the river's current with a giddy little flip that sent his heart spinning. He could have sworn he heard her laughing too.

"Only death can separate Medvedev from familiar."

"Then why can't I be with her?" Pesha asked as he watched Eshe move with a grace and ease she'd not been afforded in her frozen lake at Shadowfen Hall.

Fiachra frowned at him from the side. "Do you not feel her everywhere you go?"

"I suppose I do. But the farther we are from each other, the harder it is. It feels like I've left a physical part of myself behind."

"Distance means nothing here." Fiachra's hands lifted at the sides as she breathed in. He'd already grown accustomed to her strange way of speaking, so he no longer needed to fill in the missing words. "You have not been in pain."

It wasn't a question, but he answered anyway. "Not that kind of pain."

"Sacred," Fiachra said, nodding as though it was all the explanation required. "It was not my charge to bring you here, but now that you have seen, perhaps you will see fit to speak, Pesha."

It was the first time she'd said his name, and it seemed significant. "I told you why we're here, Fiachra."

"There are facts, and there is truth."

"I don't know what that means."

"Aoife will want truth. Not facts."

"Aoife?"

"The chieftainess."

So he *would* be speaking to her. The question was when. "Fiachra, tell me where my sister is."

"Safe." Fiachra swished her mouth from side to side.

"All right. I want to see her. With my own eyes."

"You cannot go."

"Excuse me?" Pesha shifted, his anger swelling back to the surface. "Why not?"

"Nor can I," was Fiachra's only answer, a continuation of her prior statement. "In due time. Tomorrow, you must speak clear and true. It is not for me to decide the next."

"The next? The next what?"

But Fiachra only smiled that strange, languid grin she'd been giving him all day and walked away from the river.

"You brought me out to the river for a reason, right?"

The sentry kept on.

She didn't stop or speak until they'd returned to a part of the forest he recognized. They marched right past Fen, who was sleeping in his cell. Fiachra made a little encouraging sound for Pesha to step into a patch of clover.

He obeyed. What else could he do? He had no authority. Reading whispers was only a useful skill when he was the sole magic dealer in the room. But in Asgill lands, surrounded by those who had been cultivating their abilities their entire lives, who could detect and deflect any attempt at infiltration?

Fiachra tickled the air with her fingers, and his surroundings shifted. The walls had been built.

She tapped the invisible front wall, offering a gentle smile he trusted no more than he did her little detour to the river. It was a tactic, and if he understood anything, it was the strategy of politics. If Desemir were there, he'd remind Pesha there was nothing that spoke more clearly for an adversary than what they didn't say.

Pesha waited for her to leave before searching for signs Fen was awake. They couldn't hear each other so far away, so caged, but he wasn't sure he needed words. One look in Fen's eyes would slow his pulse, cool his blood. It always did. Always had.

But Fen was faced away, his body lifting and falling with the slow breaths of rest.

Pesha sank to the invisible floor. He pulled his knees tight to his chest and laid his head across the top.

He couldn't remember ever being so tired, but if Fen was sleeping, Pesha would stay up and keep watch.

For what, he didn't know.

But he had a hunch they would soon find out.

EIGHT
NIGHTMARES AND RELAYS

Siofra hadn't been plagued by such a terrible dream in months. The horribleness of it sent her hurtling awake, thrust into an immediate awareness of everything around her. The quiet bedchamber was bathed in inky darkness, beset by the dimmest glow from a fire long since burned to embers. Balcony curtains billowed in on the storm's wind. A swash of light shocked the room, followed by a clap of thunder.

Beside her, Desemir slept with his mouth flung wide. A tiny gathering of drool on his pillow was a solid judge of her own performance that night, several incredible hours when it had just been she and he, exhaustion their only hindrance. In these final—or what she could only assume were final, with what little she and the others at Shadowfen Hall knew of Medvedev births—weeks of her pregnancy, sex had become more a game of inventiveness and adventures in flexibility, but her husband relished the challenge. Relished *her*.

Siofra had everything she had ever dreamed of, so why were the nightmares back?

She turned under the silk sheet and faced the other direction; the heavy oaken doors loomed in the distance. Beyond, the night guards would be standing watch—Wulf, Euric, and Cassius having retired when Siofra and Desemir had turned in. The evening crew was just as competent, but then why did she feel like they were so exposed?

It's your fear talking. Go back to sleep, before you wake Des.

"Si."

Too late.

"I'm fine, love, go back to bed," she said, softly to avoid rousing the concern of the guards. Slithering under the covers, she rotated back, to face him. His eyes were wide open. "Really, Des. Was just a dream."

"Are you sure it wasn't a nightmare?" His hand shot out to her forehead. He blotted the sweat away and brushed her hair back off her face. Another bolt of lightning flashed. "Your face is completely flushed. Let me light a lantern."

Siofra sighed. "I wish you wouldn't."

"Want me to apologize for fussing over my wife?" Desemir growled. "You'll be waiting a long time for that, Si." He twisted his nude, toned body, stretching it toward the nightstand. Even in the darkness, with the terrible dream fresh on her mind, the clean lines of his back and shoulders stirred something illicit within her. She could just make out the swollen red trails left by her fingernails.

Desemir carried the lantern toward what remained of the fire. His ass tightened with each step, making her mouth water. Maybe this was all she needed to clear her head, a visceral reminder of the way Desemir made her feel, day and night.

When the lantern was lit, he swung it her way with a sleepy smile. She forced herself to avert her gaze upward. Feigned her own smile.

"Not fooling anyone, especially not me," he said. On his way back to the bed, he reached for a robe but dropped it, grinning with sleepy mischief when she made a pitiful groan. "Maybe you're just pretending to have a nightmare so I'll fuck you again?"

"Is it working?" she asked. Joy wavered on her face, unable to land. The vision of Fen's wild eyes and grime-colored face was enough to extinguish the desire stirring between her legs. Dreaming of her brother wasn't unusual, and she was even used to it, her mind's way of keeping him close when he was so far away. He'd never, ever been so far away before. All their lives, throughout the turmoil of change and trauma and exploitation, their one constant had been each other. Fen, her twin, her best friend. Her protector through so much. Her best friend in all the world.

For the first time in months, Siofra had the deep, innate call to sing. To serenade the world with her deadly melody until there was nothing in the wake of her terrible gift but devastation and calamity.

"The only thing stopping me from fucking you into next season is that look on your face," Desemir said as he returned to the bed. He leaned down and kissed her. "Talk to me, Si."

"It was about Fen." She pulled her knees as close to her belly as her pregnancy would allow and burrowed her face into the pillow. "He was hurt. Filthy. It seemed like he was...a prisoner, but I saw no cell, no guards, no...I don't know. Maybe I'm not supposed to understand. It was just a dream."

"If it was just a dream, it wouldn't have you like this." Desemir lay down beside her, watching her from his pillow. "But your dreams aren't prophecy, are they?"

Siofra shook her head.

"I'm afraid for our brothers too," Desemir said. He threaded a sharp inhale through his teeth. "I think about them all the time. Every day, I regret letting Pesha go, letting Fen go with him. It wasn't my choice to make though, and it wasn't yours. Our want to protect them only extends as far as they allow it."

"I know that. I know that, Des. It's just that...My dreams have never been prophecy before, but...How would I know if that was still true? What if I'm only just coming into other abilities? My mother said she'd only discovered half of her own magic before she'd had Fen and me."

Desemir went quiet. He chewed the inside of his mouth, his eyes turned down in thought.

"You're thinking the same, aren't you?"

"I don't have the experience to know the answer," Desemir said. "We have ravens from every stop except their last one, which should have been two days ago. That means nothing. Delays happen all the time on the road. Only thing you can be sure of on a long journey is timetables are just estimates."

"Why does it sound like you're trying to convince yourself?"

Desemir smiled at her. His eyes hung heavy with the call of sleep. "I was trying to ease *your* mind."

"When yours is not at ease?"

He sighed. "It hasn't been at ease since I watched the wagon roll away with our brothers and Farren." His hands found hers, and he gave them a tug, nudging her closer. "You know we have a relay raven. If you want me to, I'll use it."

Relay ravens were a rarity in the kingdom, possessed of impeccable precision in scent and direction, reserved for the wealthiest only. Unlike most messenger ravens, who had memorized a set of paths, relay ravens could go anywhere and could find anyone, so long as the person they were searching for was someone whose scent was available for them to learn. The Shadowfen relay raven knew all of their scents, even the staff's, a precaution taken by Desemir, who was always prepared for the worst of anything.

"I don't know," Siofra said after careful consideration. "It's tempting, but they'll think we don't trust them."

Desemir's mouth drew tight. "It's not about trust."

"Isn't it? They said they'd send us a raven if they ran into trouble."

"They also said they'd send us a raven when they reached the Hinterlands," Desemir countered. "If they had run into trouble, the absence of a raven should be explanation enough."

"I thought you were trying to calm me down," Siofra said with a pained laugh. "Now my mind is spinning even faster!"

Desemir shook his head and breathed in. "Yeah, I was, wasn't I?"

"Excuse me. Si? Des?"

They turned toward the door, where a disheveled Wulfhelm stood, unarmed and in his nightclothes.

Desemir sat all the way up. "What is it, Wulf?"

"I don't know...I feel like a right fool at present...but I had this terrible dream, and I had to make sure you were both all right. I see you are, and so I'll, eh..." His face knit together in a mortified wince. "Good night. Sorry."

"No." Siofra gathered her shawl from the floor and wrapped it around her on her way toward him. "Was it about Fen? Pesha?"

He raked a hand down his stubbled neck as he swallowed. "No. Farren."

Siofra turned back to look at Des, who seemed just as surprised. "Farren? You dreamed about Farren?"

"It was just a dream, and now I feel foolish. I should not have woken the two of you for something so trivial."

"We were already awake." Desemir grunted. "Why were you dreaming about Farren?"

"I...cannot say. I really am sorry for disturbing you both."

"Stay," Desemir commanded.

Siofra clutched her shawl tighter, working through her thoughts. Wulf might feel like a fool, but there was nothing foolish or silly about his timing. She didn't believe in coincidences. "Des, I...Send the relay. Please."

Desemir leaped from the bed in the nude. He stretched and reached for his robe. Siofra noted Wulf's apathy toward Desemir's nudity, realizing he must have seen it a thousand times.

"Relay? Why the need for a relay raven?" Wulf asked. He squinted and rubbed his eyes. "Wait, *did* something happen?"

"Fucking hope not," Desemir said, tightening the belt on his robe. "But we're gonna rule it out just the same."

NINE
WOUNDED BIRD

Fen may have fallen asleep in an invisible floating cage, but that wasn't where he woke.

His surroundings came into focus in slow, surreal revelations, prompting a mystifying blend of relief and fear when he recognized where he was. It was the same hut he'd been interrogated in the day before.

Fen wasn't surprised to have company, but when he squinted and strained to adjust, it wasn't Cassair he spotted standing along the far side staring at the wall but a young woman, with deep-violet hair woven in byzantine rivulets down her back. A bow was propped nearby, the dark wood of the curved weapon matching her flowy cream tunic and green fitted trousers.

The woman turned, her smile broadening as she came into view. Her flushed apple cheeks had a youthful effect that seemed unlike the air of poise about her, and he wondered her age.

"Stiofen Thornheart. I am Mairead, or Mair, but since you've been raised by men, it may suit your preferences to think of me as Mairead de Medvedev, despite that we do not track or recognize such familial designations here. Whether you prefer Mairead Mair or a full and proper accounting of my name, we are well met."

If the first thing Fen had clocked about Mairead de Medvedev had been her soft, cool confidence, the second was the way she spoke just as he would. His mind—or the magic, he hadn't decided—didn't need to fill in missing words because there weren't any. "You don't talk like the others."

Mairead's entire face lit up with a grin. "Was I very convincing?"

"I'm sorry?"

She laughed and tossed her hair behind her shoulder. "I've been practicing."

"Practicing talking like men?" Stiofen asked, hitching his upper lip. "Why would you want to do that?"

"Well, this very scenario."

Fen sat up on the cot. "Did you know we were coming? Did you…" He tapped his head. "See it?"

"I didn't know *you* were coming, but you aren't the first Forsaken to return home, looking for succor." Mairead gestured toward the table before making her own way there.

Fen tried not to stare at her lithe, graceful movements or the dimples that didn't require a smile, but he was too tired to be subtle.

"Nor, I expect, the last."

Fen rocked forward on the cot and pushed himself up to go join her. He took the stump across from her, averting his eyes from the dazzling grin sending his heart into uninvited palpitations. "Pesha and I aren't Forsaken though. Our parents were. We've never even been here, or any of the Medvedev lands."

"The appellation is attached to blood."

"I thought you didn't recognize familial designations."

"They are not the same." She was still smiling, still drilling holes in him with her lilac eyes. Her mouth parted, and a delightful little trill escaped, one he couldn't quite believe had come from her mouth. With a laugh, she closed it again and rolled her eyes.

All Fen could do was stare, dumbfounded.

"Adir," she said with a playful but chastising scowl. "You've already announced yourself with your song, so may as well come out and reveal yourself."

A purring flutter filled the air as a tiny little songbird descended from a rafter and daintily landed on Mairead's shoulder. She tsk-tsked her familiar with a loving stroke, and in answer, he tilted his chin and ruffled his tail-feathers with a prideful flutter.

"He's a songbird," she explained. "And he can never resist living up to his name, can you, Adir?"

Adir responded with a cheerful little melody Fen almost wished he could understand.

But no matter how charming the beautiful Mairead and her little songbird were, the fact remained that Fen was their prisoner.

"You said Pesha and I are Forsaken, regardless of us having nothing to do with it," Fen said. "What about Farren?"

"Your companion's sister is a unique, if rather heartrending, case, and her guilt will be decided in the matter of the fallen Nera if and when she is competent to stand for it."

"Her *guilt*? Am I understanding this right that you've already decided Farren is responsible, when I've told you, and Pesha no doubt has told you, that Nera was *murdered* by the man who was assaulting Farren?"

"I have decided nothing," Mairead said. She flicked her hand to dismiss her familiar. "Because it is not for me to decide." A strange expression passed across her face as she leaned in. "Though I think it was rather bold and brave for the two of you to venture here, knowing you'd be unwelcome."

Fen swallowed hard. Unwelcome. As if he needed confirmation. "We would never have come if Pesha and his brother hadn't already tried everything else."

Mairead nodded slowly with a scrutinizing look. "I would have done the same, I think."

"But you have no qualms about locking us up?"

"You are not a prisoner, Stiofen. Would you like to leave?"

Fen nearly leaped from his chair. "Yes!"

Mairead wrinkled her nose. "Is it the food?"

"You're not really serious."

"Yes, Aoife said you can leave," she said with a thoughtful look. "But Farren stays."

Fen deflated, groaning. Of course, she wasn't dangling simple freedom in front of him; if she were, they'd already be back with their wagon. "We aren't leaving without her."

"We assumed as much." Her nod was curt, authoritative. "In accordance with our laws, any Medvedev who has been severed from their familiar is sent for rehabilitation. At the end of her stay, Farren will either bond with a displaced familiar, who has been grieving their own loss, or she will surrender her soul to the Light to fuel our cycle of rebirth and renewal."

Fen had to replay her words to understand them. No matter how friendly sounding they were, the meaning was clear. "Farren has to bond with another familiar in your little familiar farm? And if she doesn't, you're going to execute her?"

A dark cloud passed over Mairead's gentle disposition. "There is only one crime for which a Medvedev can be executed. The murder, or attempted murder, of a Medvedev or their familiar. Farren is like a wounded bird who will either fly again or not. And there is no magic to tell us what she needs or how she'll fare. Unlike a physical wound that can be healed through medicine or magic, the severing of a familiar starts and ends at the soul. Fortunately, or perhaps unfortunately, she cannot endure the trials if she is not possessed of her full wits."

"So you plan to kill her, whether or not she heals? Either because you think she killed her own familiar or because she failed to bond with a new one."

"No one wants to hurt Farren. Still, there are laws and ways we must follow."

"Never been much for laws, since most of them cause me harm."

Mairead had nothing to say to that.

Was Pesha receiving this same terrible speech? "We didn't bring her here to *die*. We brought her here to heal, Mairead. And I should think that Farren would have a say in this."

"And a beautiful thing that would be, should her soul heal and find a new mate. But a severed Medvedev cannot make any choices for themselves." Mairead smiled. "All hope is not lost, Stiofen. You were right to bring her here, for if there *is* hope for Farren, it lives within our borders, not without." Her softness again faded. "But you must understand and prepare yourself. Understand... that what happened to our chieftainess was unthinkable. The banishment enacted upon your parents and the other Forsaken was cross-generational. Your being here is a conundrum of sorts, for while you are not directly responsible for the crimes of your forebears, your presence here violates Aoife's decree."

"Why am I here? What are these interrogations?"

"You brought yourself here," Mairead stated. "As for why you are *here*, in this hut, with me... Well, I have been selected as your mentor for the duration of your time in the Territory of Asgill. This hut where we sit will be your home, and the *questions* have been for us to discern whether it is prudent for you to meet with Aoife or not."

"Why wouldn't it be prudent?" Fen asked. He stored her comment about the hut being his home for later.

"She's determined that it *is* prudent, and so we await the word of Cassair, who will arrive when the chieftainess is ready to receive you."

That was something, at least. A part of him had feared they'd toil for months, or even years, wondering when the heck they were going to get some answers. "And..." Was asking a sign of weakness? Another test? "Atio?"

Mairead frowned. "Do you not feel her nearby?"

"I do feel her, or I'd be..." Fen coughed. "Is she still *chained*?"

"Yes. For now."

"Why?"

"You aren't the first outsider to come to Asgill."

"How does that answer my question?"

"We've learned much from those unfortunate visits." Mairead shook her head with a woeful glint in her eyes. "Atio is not tethered out of cruelty. She is tethered for her safety."

Fen's throat went dry. "Her safety? Why would she be unsafe here?"

Mairead tilted her head. "You have a twin sister, I understand. Siofra."

Fen groaned. Nodded. There was no point in denying it or any statements disguised as questions. It didn't matter how they'd come across the information. What mattered was they had it. "Why is Atio unsafe here?"

"Why did your sister not join you?"

He started to hedge, but it was an opportunity to inspire trust. It was what Pesha would have done, and where Fen may have excelled on the road with danger on their heels, Pesha was strongest in a room he could influence. "She's with child." No point in adding there was zero chance he'd have let her come, a decision he'd never had to make but knew he'd have been fully justified if he had.

"Is she now?" Mairead's mouth parted. "Will the child be a halfling? Like Pesha?"

With a long sigh, Fen nodded again. "Children. Twins. Pesha's brother is the father."

"Pesha and this man share a father?"

"You must already know, the way you're asking me."

"No," Mairead said slowly, a touch of melancholy in her tone, "but the other halflings who have come to us…Their mothers all had one thing in common."

Fen understood the implication, but it wasn't accurate. "Pesha and Farren's mother was not taken advantage of. She was a more-than-willing participant in an affair that…" His mind wandered to the imagery he'd constructed for history that predated his time at Shadowfen Hall. "Ended up wounding the whole family. Farren worst of all." He cleared his throat. "I want to see Atio. I've been more than patient."

"You will." She nodded with a slight smile. "When we venture outside, you will see her. I'll make sure of it."

Fen's heart fluttered uncomfortably. "And Pesha?"

"That is not up to me." When Mairead stood, it reminded him of the graceful moves of a cat unfolding after a long nap. "Cassair has arrived."

"What?" Fen whipped his head around. "Where? How do you know?"

Cassair peeked his head into the tent with a nod and then retreated.

Mairead raised both brows as if to say, *See*? "Are you ready to meet Chieftainess Aoife, Stiofen?"

"Right now?"

"Right now."

"Will she…" But there wasn't a question burning there, only doubt. The questions would form later. "Am I dressed appropriately?"

"You are dressed as we are dressed, which is as she will be dressed."

"Will Pesha be there too?"

"That I do not know." Mairead reached for her bow with one hand, and the other she stretched across the air. "Come with me, Stiofen, and you will see we are not who you fear us to be." With a clouded glance at the tent flap, she added, "not unless we must be."

Pesha greatly disliked Niallan, and they'd only just met.

Was it the beady, knowing look he offered in place of words? The sly cat, Lian, who had been circling Pesha's legs for the past hour? Maybe it was more simple than that; Niallan, like Fiachra yesterday, stood between Pesha and answers.

"I want to see Fen and Farren, and I want to see them *now*."

Niallan tucked his dusky-green hair behind his ears before leaning down to coo at his familiar. Pesha crossed his arms and rolled his eyes.

"Fiachra has arrived. It's time," Niallan said, his first and only words since *this will be your home, Pesha. I will be your mentor, and the one who will see to it your needs are met with adequacy.* He rose and went to the tent flap. "Come."

"Go where?" Pesha retorted, but he followed anyway, loathing every step that inched him closer to blind obedience. "Niallan—"

"Niall, if you please." The Medvedev held the tent flap open.

"I have done everything you and your friends have asked of me. Now I want something from you."

"I am not the one to grant it." Niall wore a perturbed scowl. "But I'm taking you to the one who can. Will you join me, or shall I inform Chieftainess Aoife you are declining her goodwill?"

Niall almost made Pesha miss the haughty barons back home who loved taking verbal swings at his brother. Even when they won, they lost, because Shadowfen Hall only had one master. But the reverse was happening now, and Pesha was one of the barons, in search of compromise with his tail tucked between his legs.

Instead of answering, Pesha brushed past him and out into the sunny morning. He took in a breath of fresh air and forced his tension to clear. *Breathe. Neither Niall nor Fiachra have the authority to answer my questions. But the chieftainess does.*

A female Medvedev with violet braids walked past, glaring, but not at him. Pesha followed her gaze to find it was pointed at Niall.

Well, well, well, we have something in common, stranger.

But Pesha's self-satisfied grin died the moment he saw who was with her.

"Fen." He choked the word from the back of his throat.

Fen glanced over and, with a hard swallow, averted his eyes and kept walking.

"Fen!"

"He'll come around," Niall said, following the two as they walked away. He added a sigh on the end, and Pesha began to understand Niall might have landed himself in a similar situation, with the woman.

"You've misread things," Pesha grumbled, stuttering into step beside the mentor he hadn't asked for. "Are they..."

"Yes," Niall said, staring wistfully after Fen and the violet-haired Medvedev. "It seems they're coming with us."

TEN
THERE'S TRUTH AND THERE ARE FACTS

The dining hut was similar in design to the one Mairead had said would be Fen's home, but it was rectangular and long, built to hold the banquet-style table that was the only furnishing inside.

No one needed to point out Chieftainess Aoife. Though she was slight of physique, there was an energy rolling off her that could have been described as either malevolent or benevolent, neither descriptor wholly right or wholly wrong.

Her violet hair was cropped short, dusting the edges of her jaw. Her simple tunic and trousers matched the way Mairead and Pesha's mentor, Niallan, were dressed, except hers were a vibrant green, stitched at the edges with silver thread. Fen was so occupied wondering how they made silver thread in the forest that he missed the introduction altogether.

Fen watched the chieftainess as he was escorted to his seat. He couldn't help but stare at the enigmatic sovereign who had to be older than his parents but looked younger than him.

He flinched when Pesha's warmth materialized beside him. Pesha started to speak but cut himself off, just as Mairead and Niallan each took a seat on either side of the chieftainess. Adir fluttered above Mairead's head before landing on one of her shoulders. Hissing floated up from under the table. Fen was in no hurry to see the creature who had made such a feral sound.

He glanced around at the emptiness of the table to the left and right of him.

Pesha made a contemplative sound and then said, "Huh."

"Thank you, loves." Aoife's treble voice was nearly as pitched as the songbird's.

"Of course, Mother," said Mairead.

Niallan nodded in respect.

"Mother?" Fen whispered under his breath. Then, louder, "You're her children?"

"Never mentioned *that,*" Pesha muttered.

"Mairead is the daughter of my womb. The only one," Aoife said, speaking in the parlance of man. "Niall is the son of my choice."

"Your 'choice'?" Pesha asked in a petulant tone. It would no doubt go over really well with the present crowd.

Niall leaned behind his "mother" and exchanged a glance with Mairead, who swiftly averted her gaze.

"Did you and your brother not choose your family when you brought Stiofen and his sister into your lives?" Aoife asked, in her disconcertingly soprano tenor.

Pesha kept trying to catch his attention, but Fen kept his focus pointed stubbornly at the chieftainess. The past couple of days had stretched into a series of little eternities, and he should miss Pesha—he *did* miss Pesha. But absence had only deepened frustrations that now seemed bigger than anything else competing for placement in his mind.

A bowl appeared in front of Fen. It was a thick stew of sorts, the scent welcoming and delicious. The entire experience was so disorienting, it didn't even occur to him they might have been taken to a dining hall to *eat.*

"My children tell me you've eaten nothing put in front of you." Aoife lifted her bowl to her mouth and drew a deep, slurping sip. She dabbed her sleeve to clear the excess from her mouth. "I shall sip from every bowl if you like. We do not debase ourselves with such underhanded assaults. In the rare event of crime within our borders, we have our own justice, but those on the other end are never surprised by what comes."

"Wouldn't be the first to train yourself to be immune. There are whole communities of women in the Westerlands who have been eating poison for breakfast their entire lives," Pesha said. With one hand in the air like a fussing mother, he added, "Fen, don't eat it."

Fen defiantly lifted the bowl and slurped loudly. He clenched in anticipation of Pesha's annoyance. He no longer thought the Medvedev were going to poison him, but if they were, it would at least put a swift end to the misery.

His gleeful disobedience was cut short by a hard squeeze to his upper thigh. A warning. Fen ground his jaw and took another slurp, ignoring the pinch, the painful dig of Pesha's thumb and forefinger into his tense muscles. Fen bore down, flexing, and swallowed more of the bland but serviceable stew, his cock growing insolently hard as Pesha's hold on his thigh became an immovable vise.

Their captors watched with rapt interest.

"Ahh. We do not eat poison for breakfast or otherwise," Aoife said. "We can pause until we've discerned whether Stiofen will live or die, or we could continue on."

Pesha's hand snapped free, but he didn't retrieve it from its resting place on Fen's leg.

"It's fine," Fen said. His thigh throbbed from the sudden release. "It's not Lotte's cooking, but it's not going to kill us either."

"Death isn't the only punishment they could devise, I'm sure." Pesha's mouth wrinkled into a scowl, which Fen normally found sexy but at present was only annoyed by.

"Continue on. Please," Fen said. He glimpsed Mairead's approving smile, and his cock grew *even* harder, confounding him. Pesha's hand twitched on his leg. Fen wanted it gone, but removing it would require acknowledging the very real hold Pesha had on him, literally and figuratively.

"You have come a long way on Farren's behalf," Aoife said. "Now that I have had the opportunity to look in on her myself, we know you are not responsible for her present condition, beyond the matter of her continued existence. Magic alone has kept her in stasis?"

"Thank the Guardians." Fen huffed with a relieved whistle. "I'm glad you see it now."

Pesha held fast to his silence.

"The magic?"

"Oh." Fen nodded. "Yes. It was the same magic that protected Eshe from harsh winters in a frozen lake. Pesha and his brother did the best—"

"Fen!" Pesha's fingers pinched.

Fen twisted sideways, wrenching free with an affronted grunt. "Did the best they could, but all they could do was calm her, not fix her."

"Will you *stop talking*?" Pesha hissed from the corner of his mouth.

"It was your idea to come here, Pesha! Guardians' sake!" Fen took a swallow of the dark liquid in his mug. It was surprisingly sweet. "*You* believed they could help her. Remember?"

"That was before they took us captive, Stiofen."

"You are not captive," Aoife said in her childish voice, tilting her head. Her violet hair brushed the hollows of her cheeks when she leaned forward. "Though our law decrees the blood of the Forsaken forfeit all rights coming back here, we recognize you do not understand our laws, and are content to let you leave, with the promise you'll not return unless invited. But even more sacred to us is our charge to those who have been severed from their souls. By bringing Farren here, you have surrendered her to our care."

"I've done no such thing," Pesha retorted. He shoved his bowl across the table, where it went spinning and tipped to its side. The thick stew spread and congealed on the wood. "I brought her here for help, not kidnapping. Farren can't consent to this."

"Farren cannot consent to anything in her present state. On that we agree," Aoife said. "And until she can, we have an obligation to her."

"I don't think you understand. My brother has the means to raise an army if it comes to it."

Here we go, thought Fen with an inward sigh.

Aoife trained her hawkish gaze on Pesha. Mairead buried a grin, and Niall smirked.

Pesha's nose flared. "You don't believe me?"

"I believe you say what you mean," Aoife said. "But your armies would never find our borders. Even if they found them, they could not breach them. Have you not noticed the trees, the air...None of it looks here like it did when you were in the Hinterlands?"

"Of course we've fucking noticed," Pesha muttered.

Fen bit the inside of his mouth. "Mairead said Farren's guilt would be decided. I want to clarify how that has changed now that you've seen Farren yourself, obtain some reassurances there'll be no more talk of guilt or punishment where she's concerned. Because, Chieftainess, you just said—"

Pesha slammed his hands onto the table, startling the rest of the words out of Fen, and leaned forward. "Guilt? *Guilt*?" He sputtered. "She was taken advantage of by a powerful man and then destroyed by him!"

Aoife blinked. "Your father, yes?"

It was Fen's turn to clamp a hand over Pesha's leg. Pesha angled his flushed face toward Fen in sour acknowledgment but didn't look at him. "His father, yes. A man who was terrible to everyone, but especially his children. Desemir was more a father to Pesha than Ludwik ever was."

"They don't *care*, Fen. Don't you—"

"We know of Ludwik Trevanion," Niallan stated, raising his voice above Pesha's. "You not only have the blood of the Forsaken, Pesha, but also the blood of a monster. How peculiar you carry not one but two bloodlines of destroyers. And you wonder why we struggle to trust you?"

"Niall." Aoife's supple mouth turned to a pout. "There is yet time for the past. Here we approach the future. Stiofen, Pesha, you are welcome to stay until Farren is either healed or has rejected her healing. You are not prisoners but guests. *My* guests. And yet I fear that will not be enough for our people. Even the word, Forsaken, is anathema to many of them. I cannot protect you from their gazes, their damning words…only their hands. Harming another Medvedev or their familiar is punishable by an interruption in existence. Stiofen, we will unbind Atio, and you can be assured her time here will be free of violence."

Pesha snorted and whipped his gaze around the table, a sardonic smile splitting his features. "You can't even say murder, can you? Execution? You'll kill them?"

"Use whatever words helps you to understand," Aoife said, "that they will not harm you, and you will not harm them. But words are weapons too. And you do not perhaps have all the defenses you require to resist the ones that will be laid upon you here. Others will heap the sins of your parents upon your shoulders, and there will be no pity, no understanding to be found in their eyes."

Fen was suddenly aware of an absence he should have noted right away. "Chieftainess…Where is your familiar?"

Niall's eyes fluttered closed as though in pain. Mairead bowed her head.

"Like Farren, I no longer have one," Aoife said, measuring each word. "But that is a tale for another day, if at all." She turned her glossy eyes on Pesha. "You wish to see your sister. I cannot grant you the level of access you desire. Not for cruelty or punishment, but for the sake of her healing, which requires a complete estrangement from the past. She may know, in some deep and inaccessible part of her, that you are not answerable for what your father did. But she is beyond reason. If she does not embrace the safety of the Menagerie, opening her heart, mind, and soul to the possibility of rehabilitation, then her fate will have but one destination."

Fen sat back, wordless. Even Pesha closed his mouth. Aoife might not want to explain how she came to be without her familiar, but Fen could guess where it had started. It seemed Pesha was making the connection too.

"Why the interrogation then?" Pesha cleared the hoarseness from his voice. "Why put us through the past two days of thinking we were prisoners?"

"There is truth and there are facts," Aoife answered. She swayed slightly. "You have both communicated the facts as they are, but neither of you has addressed your truth. Perhaps you will find it here, but only if you're searching." She glanced at Mairead and then at Niallan. "While you are here, you will be expected to work, as we all do. Stiofen, you will assist Mairead with the foundlings in the Hatchery."

"Foundlings?" Fen asked.

"You would call them orphans. We do not have so many in our world as you do in yours, but we do for them what we can. Mairead does for them what she can."

Our world, Fen thought. Not just *our land.*

"And you, Pesha, will assist Niallan in the Menagerie."

Pesha straightened. "Where Farren is?"

"Yes," Aoife said, "and no. She is there, but you will not interact with her. You will work with others like her. Indeed, you may understand her better through this work."

"And our familiars?" Fen asked, his heart suddenly racing. "You promised to unchain them."

"Eshe is more free now than she's ever been. Would you not agree, Pesha?" Aoife laughed softly. "Atio has already been unchained. She soars our skies unfettered right now, as we speak of her." The chieftainess's mirth faded. "You are free to wander as well, just be mindful of the steps you take and the words you use with others. Do not say Forsaken. Do not ask them about that time. If you find some to palaver with, we have already spelled you both with the magic needed to understand every word we leave unsaid. You will find even more clarity as time passes." She reached a hand toward each of her children. "Mair and Niall have shown you to your huts. If you have needs we have not foreseen, tell them, and they will do their best to accommodate them. But I..." Aoife frowned. "I find myself confused, as I observe the two of you together. Should we have only prepared one hut?"

"Yes, *please*, Fen and I would like—"

"No," Fen blurted. He inched his chair farther to the right, away from Pesha. "Separate is better. Thank you."

Pesha pivoted in his chair. "*Fen.* Come *on*."

"Nothing I said before has changed," Fen said, shoving back from the table. He avoided Pesha's searching gaze, his stumbling disbelief. "Is there anything else? I need...some air."

Aoife nodded at Mairead. "Mair will escort you back. You'll learn your way soon."

"Fen!"

Fen squinted, nudging his seat under the table with his heel. He felt every emotional beat of Pesha's hurt and anger, and with a touch of disgust, Fen realized he was enjoying being the one on the other end of the pain.

He couldn't say why it felt right or even why he did it, but Aoife seemed to approve of the gentle bow he afforded her before slipping out into the warmth of midday.

Mairead exited just after him, Pesha right behind her.

"Talk to me. Now." Pesha snatched his hand and dragged him away. Fen yanked back, but Pesha was stronger, pulling him to a nearby tree. Fen ripped his hand away and tucked both under his arms.

"I already said everything I have to say." Fen glanced at Mairead, who seemed to be waiting for a signal to intervene. And what would she do if he gave one? Nock an arrow onto her impressive bow and pin Pesha to the tree?

"We *need* to stick together." Pesha tore at his hair. He craned his neck back and growled. "You're angry at me. I deserve it. But, Fen, *listen—*"

"I'm done listening to you!" Fen bowed his head, thinking of all the moments of his life when he'd had to decide fast—how those moments had saved him and Siofra time and time again. How could he ignore that same instinct now, when it was crying out for him to find his own way?

Unexpected warmth on his face made Fen jump. Pesha cupped his cheek. His head shook slowly. "Stay with me, Fen. We don't have to talk. We don't have to do anything. I just need to know you're near."

"How could I be anything but near here?" Fen demanded. A rogue tear spilled and trailed over Pesha's hand. Fen's shame deepened. "There's nowhere to go. If you need me, I'll be around. But you won't, will you? Because you never have."

Pesha's other hand came up and slid along the side of Fen's neck, tightening. He sucked in a deep breath, pursed his mouth in thought, and pulled Fen's face in for a forceful kiss.

Fen froze under the hot command of Pesha's lips…the authority of his tongue prying the edges of his mouth. More tears spilled as he melted in compliance. A gathering swarm of sobs locked his throat, the force of them sending his own arms up and around Pesha's neck. There they stood, wrapped in desperation, fear forcing them together and tearing them apart.

It was Pesha who retreated. Another slight, another weakness of Fen's laid bare before not only Pesha but their mentors. Mairead would look upon him with unwanted sympathy. *Knowing* sympathy.

"Please," Pesha whispered. His thumb swept the sharp edges of Fen's cheekbone. "Stay with me. We'll figure this out. Together."

"I can't," Fen answered, closing his eyes as he broke away. The charged air between them dissipated. "Good luck in the Menagerie."

He returned to Mairead without looking back. He could hardly meet her eyes as she waited for him to make his way over.

"Some things do not change world to world, do they?" Mairead asked. She sounded elsewhere, drawn into her own statement.

Fen's face wrinkled in confusion. "Yesterday I thought you and Niall were together…but he's your brother?"

"He is not my brother," Mairead said with a disdainful look toward where Pesha and Niall had gone. "I cannot say what he is, and I'm weary of trying." She grinned and feigned a long shiver. "I could return you to your hut, but the hours are yet long ahead, so I'd like to introduce you to the foundlings. Would you like that?"

"Please. The distraction will be most welcome," Fen said, sparing one last glance at Pesha before following her.

ELEVEN
THE DISPLACED

"This is it?" Pesha asked, standing next to Niall on the top of a hill overlooking a broad valley full of low-growing shrubs and stunted trees with orange and violet leaves. A handful of birds flew in formation from edge to edge of the valley bowl. Roaming the thick grass were terrestrial animals of all sorts, from elk-kind to rodents to a tiny white lynx that stalked the perimeter alone. At the far end was a lake surrounded by more trees, and to the east and west of it, two different encampments.

"The Menagerie," Niall answered with a wistful sigh, bobbing his head in a sweeping assessment that mirrored Pesha's. "The displaced familiars roam free, unaware there are borders keeping them from truly wandering."

"Same magic you used on me."

"Yes. But these must be maintained at all hours, or there are… Well, you're well aware of the consequences, aren't you?"

Pesha searched for Farren, but the encampments were too far away to make out anything but the tents. "They're all like that?"

"They're all *different*." Niall pointed. "The displaced live in the huts, same as they do all over Asgill, but there are a dozen watcher Medvedev who live here as well, charged with keeping all displaced safe through their rehabilitation. I'm one of them."

Pesha sucked in. "Displaced. You use that word a lot. Is that what you call what happened to Farren?"

"Our ancestors were clear about what has happened to every creature you see in this valley." Niall crossed his arms and breathed in. "Victims. All of them. Most back there—" He nodded in the direction they'd traveled from. "They believe there is no hope for the displaced, that we are merely proffering mercy in their final hours. But to be displaced infers a return to where one belongs is possible."

Pesha swallowed. He'd been teaching his brother to confront hard truths for years. All that counsel meant nothing if he couldn't do the same for himself when it mattered. "How often…"

"One in ten find a new mate. Sometimes less, sometimes more." Niall sighed again. "Even *one in a hundred* would make all of this worth the effort." He pointed again. "Farren is in the East Watch. We'll be in the West Watch. The encampments may seem close from back here, but they are separated by the lake and a hearty walk. If you are discovered in the East Watch, for any reason, Aoife will see that as insubordination and order your re-imprisonment." He turned toward Pesha. "But we don't have to worry about that, do we? Because you brought her here to heal, not to interfere and cause further harm."

Pesha shook his head. A daze had stolen over him the moment he'd watched Fen walk away outside the dining tent, and Pesha hadn't shaken it. He'd never expected their sojourn to the Hinterlands to be a simple matter, but it had never occurred to him he might be separated from Farren altogether…be ostracized by Fen. The first he had no choice but to accept, but the second, he couldn't. *Wouldn't.* Fen's broken heart was entirely his fault, which meant it was entirely in his power to mend it.

Pesha hadn't missed the searching looks Mairead aimed at Fen throughout the brief meal—the rising flush in Fen's cheeks when he'd noticed it himself. They'd never discussed Fen's preferences, but Pesha had always assumed Fen liked men and women both, unlike Pesha.

"Good." Niall checked the sky. "We've just missed the Hour of Blessing, where we carefully pair up the displaced for a heavily observed meeting. We judge their compatibility. Most get ruled out within the first few moments of their greeting. Anger. Violence. Nothing that would surprise you. Some tolerate one another long enough to complete their session, but have no spark. But we can usually tell from the very first meeting whether the Light has deemed them a match. We move through the tests because we must, but we know. As soon as we detect a connection, they are moved to another part of the valley, where their true rehabilitation begins." Niall glanced at the ground. "Farren has met with two displaced so far, and both have been failures. Unless she fared any better today, she'll continue to join the Hour of Blessing until she has run out of pairings."

Pesha closed his eyes to ground himself, but the unknowns were chipping away at his fractured resolve. "And then what?"

Niall clamped a hand onto his forearm. "A worry for another day."

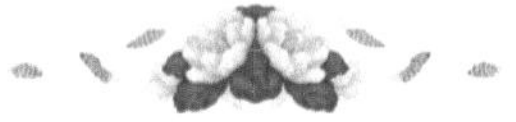

There were three foundlings, two girls and a boy. One of the girls was young, only a couple of years old, but the other was closer to an adult. Mairead explained to Fen that while she usually managed their care on her own, there was a rotation of recently delivered mothers cycling in to act as wet nurses. The little boy was a bit older, perhaps seven or eight.

"Esta, Fanne, and Ruairi," Mairead said, nodding at each child as they stood in the row in the center of the foundling hut, locked in respectful formation. The girls both smiled, but the boy, Ruairi, seemed more curious than happy.

"Go play," Mairead said, ruffling their hair as she gave them each playful nudges. Ruairi was the last to fall in line, following the girls with his head down.

Fen watched them disappear from the tent. "What happened to their mothers and fathers?"

"Esta and Fanne's mother passed on, I'm afraid," Mairead said. She moved around a nearby table, collecting bowls from a recent meal. "Ruairi's mother was..." She stood straight with a sigh. "Banished."

"Banished?" Fen held the dish basket out for her. "But wait, where are the fathers? Should the children not be with them?"

"Their fathers are not Medvedev," Mairead said quietly. She grabbed the basket from Fen with a grateful smile and cast a thoughtful glance away. "There are men in this kingdom who look upon us and see..." She breathed out slowly. "Well, you would know, wouldn't you? You and Pesha have both seen what the world is like for us out there. But not all are so vigilant. Not all understand men will say and do anything to get what they want."

Fen nodded to himself as he pushed the stools in. He hadn't expected to find evidence of the outside world within Asgill lands, and it made him angrier, somehow, than anything he'd experienced so far. "Unfortunately, yes."

"The poor mothers..." Mairead wedged the basket against her hip and leaned against the table. "We are not meant to join with man. We may look similar, but we are not the same."

Fen froze. "You're saying these mothers died because their child's father wasn't Medvedev?"

"We've seen it time and time again..." Mairead pursed her mouth. "And the mothers, they are too afraid to tell us who they've lain with, and so we're never prepared to aid them through the worst of it. Ruairi's mother knew it would save her life to tell us, but the cost was banishment. Others prefer death."

Fen's breath left him before he could say *Siofra.* Her name choked him at the back of his tongue.

"Oh! Fen, forgive me. Please. I should not have worried you so, with your own sister carrying a foundling." Mairead rushed to his side. "Not all struggle. There are signs we know to look for, and once known, we can address them, before they become all-consuming."

"I don't even know..." Fen bowled over, gripping his knees. Had he not foreseen there might be a problem with the delivery? Had he not convinced himself she wouldn't need him when it did? "I don't even know when the child is coming. What if I'm *here* when it happens?"

"Hm. That is hard to say. It is different for all mothers of foundlings. Women gestate for nine months, but for Medvedev, it's closer to eleven. Those traits are foremost in both races and so impossible to predict with any precision. We have seen mothers deliver anywhere along that spectrum, and even outside of it."

"She's..." Fen didn't know how far along she was. The timeline between their dramatic rescue from the Newcarrow jail to their strange but beautiful life at Shadowfen Hall was foggy enough, but everything since was a downright blur. "She could be anywhere on that spectrum."

Mairead reached for his hand and covered it with hers. When she leaned in, one of her braids swept his knee, causing him to look up. "I predict you will not be here very long. There are only so many displaced familiars for Farren to attempt bonding with. You'll be home before you've had time to miss it."

Too late, Fen thought, wondering how a place he'd claimed could never be home was calling to him so loudly. It wasn't just Siofra. He missed Lieken and Lotte and Wulf and Euric. Even Desemir. He missed the strange, dark halls of Shadowfen and the inky, towering trunks of the Great Darkwood. The way standing on the veranda made him feel utterly exposed and yet also protected, another world within a world.

Pesha was part of this too, and maybe...maybe when they returned, it would be easier to go back to how things were, before he'd fallen so hard and so deep for a man who had no stomach for commitment.

Mairead pivoted completely toward him. "I am a midwife, Fen. I learned the trade from my father, and he from his mother before him. I've been training Air—that is, Ruairi—to be my adept, and I could train you at the same time. I could show you what to look for in a foundling birth, so that you can help your sister through her final confinement."

Fen chuckled at the thought of ever developing such a skill. "I have no experience in childbringing, Mair."

"Nor does anyone. Until they do." Mairead butted her forehead into his with a spirited grin. "You are adaptable in a crisis. You can bring a calm upon yourself that allows space for thought. I saw that same potential in Air, and I see it in you. Maybe *that's* why you're here with us, Stiofen. Not for Farren or Pesha, but for yourself. For your sister. You can do more than save her. You can make it safe for other Forsaken to have families beyond our borders."

Fen looked around in a panic. "That sounds an awful lot like blasphemy around here."

"No one wants the Forsaken to perish," Mairead said, standing. "But how can they not, when the knowledge they need to thrive exists only here?"

"Are there a lot of Forsaken out there?"

"Too many. But less every day." She clapped her hands together. "Supper will arrive before we know it. Help me prepare the afternoon lesson and then we'll return to the encampment to draw for our evening chore."

Everything Mairead had said stirred within him a call for more questions, but he nodded, smiled, and said, "Show me how to be useful, and I will."

TWELVE
DUSKTIDE GATHERING

Following Mairead around like a lost puppy reminded Fen of his early days at Shadowfen Hall. Except Shadowfen Hall was a manse, and the Asgill lands seemed to stretch on forever, their borders unknown even to his mentor, who'd explained there were no maps or guides. *We recognize our boundaries on instinct,* she'd said, and that was both the most ludicrous pile of nonsense he'd ever heard and yet somehow completely consistent with how strange and different it had felt crossing into the Territory of Asgill.

They passed many other Medvedev on their way to the Dusktide Gathering. He was assailed with more accusing looks, but he hardly noticed them anymore, because he was too enthralled by the Medvedev's easy, carefree existence. It was evident in their casual gait, how they seemed to almost be unaware of their familiars, which ran and flew and swam freely. He'd stopped magicking his violet hair to make it brown, but he realized he must still have an "otherness" about him because he was drawing even more scrutiny, as though he was missing some critical element of being Medvedev.

Every few steps, Mairead glanced over with a smile that made the ice around his heart melt just a little. She'd shift it into a glare for anyone looking their way with anything but pleasant greetings.

"Dusktide Gathering. As I was saying…" Mairead burst into speech after a long stretch of silence, smiles, and scowls. "Every evening, we join together to divvy up responsibilities for the next fortnight. Some cook, some mind the children, and some fetch water from the well stream. It's a new choice every time. While we all have different roles to play in the clahnn, different trades if you will, at Dusktide we are all equal."

Fen scrunched his brows. "What if you can't cook?"

"Like me?" Mairead laughed and winced. "Not every meal is splendid."

Fen grinned in spite of himself. "My father used to say, there are some battles you expect to lose but must fight anyway." He froze as soon as he'd said it. No one had mandated he couldn't speak of his parents, but he doubted anyone wanted to reminisce about the Forsaken.

"Your father must have been thinking of Dusktide Gathering with that little petal of wisdom," Mairead said with a sideways grin. If she was offended, she showed no signs of it.

Fen relaxed. "So when I get chosen to prepare tonight's meal, and they all start dropping one by one, will that be viewed as an unfortunate accident or calculated murder?"

"Now that you've shared your grand plan with me, I'm afraid we'll have to go with murder, Stiofen." Mairead clicked her tongue. "And there's a lesson for you. Always better to be a mystery."

"Damn."

They both laughed. It was nice. For the first time in a long time, though he had no reason to, he *felt* good.

"I'm serious. I don't know much at all about meal preparation. I know it may seem like I come from great privilege, but most of my life, I was in hiding or at the mercy of others."

"Is that how you feel about living with Pesha and his people?"

"No," Fen said. "At first, but…no. Not anymore."

"I should warn you—"

"Mair!"

They both turned and saw Niallan jogging up. Behind him was Pesha, wearing a—predictable—scowl.

Mairead rolled her eyes at Fen and clenched her jaw before she continued walking. "We're going to be late, Niall."

Niall struggled to keep up. "I daresay we're going to be early, Mair. Just as you like it."

"What would you know about what I like?"

"That is not a fair representation of my feelings for you, and you well know it."

"I know you're causing me to waste my breath, and if you *truly* knew me, you'd remember how much I despise doing so."

"What you love and what you despise change so often, how could I be expected to keep up?"

"You said it yourself, Niall. You cannot."

Fen caught sight of Pesha on the other side of Niallan. He looked as uncomfortable as Fen felt, and before, they might have shared in the absurdity of that discomfort. Pesha caught him watching and was about to say something when Mairead yanked Fen forward.

He pushed to hold her pace, nearly tripping over what appeared to be an oversized head of pink cabbage growing from the side of a stump. "What was that about?"

Mairead shot him a look from the side but didn't reply. Her face bloomed with red, and she quickened her pace.

"I fight with my sister sometimes too, but it doesn't sound… ah, quite like that." Fen panted between words.

"He's not my brother." Each word was strained. "Any more than Pesha is yours."

"Do you want to talk about it?"

"Why is it that men cannot understand the subtleties of a matter?" Mairead sighed and tried to smile. "I really am trying to be polite, Stiofen. Not all troubles can be solved with having a palaver."

"That isn't...It wasn't..." He groaned and pushed to catch up, but there was no longer any need. While he had been focused on Mairead, the whole world had opened up into a clearing. The trees along the edges were lined with a smattering of lights, lit by magic. In the center was an altar, and atop that was a massive stone bowl.

Over a hundred Medvedev were gathered in small knots of conversation. Most glanced Fen's way and then returned to what they were doing, but a few stopped, arms crossed, to stare at him as he entered the circle.

"Where's the chieftainess?" Fen whispered. No one would hear him over the din of conversation and the wind whipping across the treetops, but he already felt overexposed. Overexposure, in his experience, always came with danger.

"She does not come to Dusktide," Mairead explained. She pulled Fen to the other side of the altar. With the distance from Niallan, she seemed more at ease. "This is her time to commune with the Light."

"The Light? I've heard this more than once. What is it?"

Mairead turned all the way toward him. Her violet eyes sparkled in disbelief. "You really do not know?"

Fen shook his head, ashamed.

"The Forsaken harbor loathing for more than my mother then. I would have thought they would preserve the sacred rituals, but..." She breathed out through her mouth. "The Light is our creator, Stiofen. We come from the Light, and we return to it when our time is done."

"Is the Light the same as the Guardians?"

"It is not."

"Men believe—"

"I know what men believe. And who's to say men do not come from these Guardians they hold so dear? Who's to say a Ravenwood was not created by the gods they worship? The

Vjestik, their beloved Ancestors? There can be more than one answer, Stiofen, and it does not render any of them wrong." She straightened and nodded ahead. "Everyone is here."

"This is everyone?" Fen frowned at the gathering. A hundred had seemed like a lot when the crowd was still amassing, but not if it was all of them.

"Everyone in our chain."

"Chain?"

"There are many chains that connect the Asgill Clahnn. It's not very different from the way men live in villages, though our societies are far smaller, to preserve the accord that holds us together."

Every answer Mairead offered caused a dozen more to bloom, but the Medvedev were already lining up at the altar. She placed a hand on his back and urged him to do the same.

Fen spotted Pesha farther up the winding line with Niall. Pesha's face brightened, but Fen quickly looked away.

As he inched forward, following the chain, he felt Atio's presence nearby and looked up to see her soaring from tree to tree. And she wasn't alone. There were dozens of other birds, of all shapes and colors and sizes, flying with her. It seemed they were playing. He sensed nothing but joy in her.

"Familiars have their own little traditions," Mairead explained when she caught him staring. "You may find Atio and Eshe are the most reluctant to leave here when the time comes."

He'd never considered that Atio might be lonely. She'd always had Aio, but was that enough? And poor Eshe, all alone in a lake, living most of her life in a stasis. If it was true that familiars craved connection as much as Medvedev did, then returning to Shadowfen wouldn't be as simple as going home.

Fen took another step forward, approaching the last push to the altar. He couldn't see anything beyond the tall Medvedev in front of him in line. He wanted to ask what the altar was, how it worked, and what he was supposed to do when he reached it, but he'd already asked so many questions.

"When you reach the pool, you'll simply look into it, and it will tell you where you belong tonight," Mairead said, leaning in close from behind. She gripped his shoulders. "Whatever the answer, make peace with it, even if it means sending us all to the Light with your terrible cooking."

Fen grinned and moved with the line. "You won't be saying that when it happens, Mair." He laughed. "You won't be saying anything ever again."

She gave his shoulders a playful squeeze and released him. "You're next."

Fen swallowed, straightened, and climbed the final three steps. The bowl looked massive and foreboding from below, but when he reached the top, he found it was just a simple stone bowl, filled halfway with water. He started to look back and ask her to explain things again, but the need to gaze into the pool consumed him so suddenly and wholly, he forgot the question.

The water looked the same, but he *felt* different. He swayed on his feet and had to grip the edges of the bowl to keep from toppling into the field.

"Ack!" someone called from behind. "Too slow."

"Mind your tongue," Mairead barked. "He's learning."

Fen closed his eyes, his hands still wrapped tightly on the stone, and listened to the rush of thoughts coursing through his head.

Water.

Water.

Water.

His pulse thumped with nerves, uncomfortably aware of the line of impatient Medvedev shifting, restless, behind him. "Mair, I don't understand. I just keep hearing *water.*"

"Then that is your task, Stiofen. You're to fetch water from the well. Let me receive my own, and I'll talk you through it." Mairead gently nudged him down the stairs on the other side and took his place.

A tight smile pinched her face when she joined him. "The well is built in the middle of the east stream." Mairead laughed, but there was no humor in her tone. Something had changed, and when he saw Niall staring at them from across the field, he understood why. "I'll point you there. Dredging the well is a task for two, so there will be someone with you to show you what to do."

"What did you get?" Fen asked.

Mairead pursed her mouth in irritation. "I'll be with the children. With…Niall."

Fen whistled. "Do Medvedev believe in luck?"

"Explain?"

"We like to wish each other good luck when preparing for something difficult."

"Ah, luck. Fortune." Mairead squeezed his arm. "We make our own. So there is no need to wish me good luck, Stiofen, but you might spare a thought for my composure. I fear before the night is ended, I will have none left."

She talked him through how to reach the stream, asked him to repeat her instruction, and left to tend to her own task. Fen watched her storm past Niall, ignoring his attempt to engage, and head the opposite way Fen needed to go.

Reflex had him searching for Pesha in the crowd, but he didn't see him anywhere.

It's for the best, he told himself as he started into the forest.

Pesha stared at the well in the middle of the stream bed, pondering how he was going to reach it without getting soaked. He was mulling his options for approach when it occurred to him that getting wet might be part of the task. Niall had been as vague about the well as he had been about every other "explanation" offered.

Pesha had just hiked his trousers to his knees when a rustling announced someone's arrival.

He turned, his breath catching when he saw who it was.

Fen's eyes narrowed in distrust. He pivoted, head shaking, clearly debating whether to bolt.

Pesha's flesh crackled across the thick passage of time as he tried to gauge what Fen would do next, afraid to say anything for fear it might cause him to run. He probably thought Pesha had somehow finagled the whole "task from the altar" nonsense to get him alone.

Pesha couldn't blame him for the avoidance, but there might not be another opportunity to get him truly alone, when he could finally say what he'd been trying—and utterly failing—to say all along.

"Can you believe this bullshit?" Pesha jested, thumbing toward the stream and the well. "We supposed to just trudge in there like a couple of bears?"

Fen's mouth scrunched. "There aren't any..." He cleared his throat twice. "Stepping stones? Shallow spots?"

"Afraid not. I could put you on my shoulders and *launch* you over the fish..."

Fen stared at the well, his brows a solid line. "Mair said my partner would explain how the thing worked, but, ah, that is apparently not going to happen."

"*Mair*? You two are on such intimate—" Pesha cut himself off when Fen's expression hardened. "Well, that's more than Niall explained, which I've already come to expect from the creature."

"Maybe you'd be on more *intimate terms* with Niallan if you didn't call him a creature." Fen's tone was reproving, but his unwitting smile dulled the sting.

"Let's just say, I can see why Mairead wants nothing to do with him." Pesha rolled his trouser legs a couple more times, to secure the thick cuffs over his knee, and swiveled his head to search for Fen. "I think this is the only way."

But Fen was already in the stream, trudging across in long, bold stomps. He tugged at his pants but didn't bother rolling them or hiking them like Pesha had. When he reached the tiny platform surrounding the well, he climbed up and turned back. "It's just like any other well. Bucket. Pulley."

The way Fen said it, it was clear he'd not only used many wells over the years but was assuming Pesha had as well. But Pesha had never once pumped the well at Shadowfen Hall. That was a task for their staff, a thought that filled him with unexpected shame.

Fen was already lowering the pulley into the well when Pesha daintily stepped onto the narrow shelf, wobbling for balance.

"I'll need your help to bring it back up," Fen explained. "I can take it as far as the top, but to get it into the aqueduct here—" He tilted his head toward a wooden slide of sorts, that Pesha hadn't noticed before. It flared near the top of the well like a funnel, narrowing as it went on, stretching into the forest, where it disappeared. Pesha was still marveling at the construction when Fen elbowed him. "Are you listening?"

"Yeah. Yes. Of course," Pesha muttered. Had they conceptualized the design on their own? It was so unlike the water systems of men, but it had to be effective for it to support so many Medvedev. "You need my help tilting it into the slide."

"Slide?" Fen grunted as he peered over. "This is the most peculiar system. We're *in* a stream, but they dug twenty feet *under* it for their water." He squatted and blindly reached around the platform until he found a rock, then dropped it in. "Hear that splash? It's not shallow. Don't trip and fall in, or it might be the last thing you do."

"How can you tell?" Pesha's full attention was back to Fen.

"Something my mother taught me." Fen swung the rope around and planted his feet. "Going to try to bring it up without losing too much water."

What would Fen think if he knew his heart was thumping wildly, his breath uneven and disrupted? That watching Fen's shoulders strain with the weight, his thighs clenched and spread for purchase, was deepening his guilt and grief and shame, but also his desire?

"Fen. Put it down."

Fen, tongue between his teeth and his face deep red, shook his head. "Halfway there."

"I wasn't asking."

Fen stiffened. He shifted to transfer the weight as he turned, straining from the effort. "You can either help or leave."

Pesha leaned in. Fen's eyes widened in indignation, his scowl deepening as Pesha, his hands closed over Fen's, started to lower the pulley again.

"What is wrong with you, Pesha? What is *wrong* with you? I'm so cursed tired of asking and never getting an answer!" Fen tore his hands away, and the bucket splashed below. "You push and you pull, and you're hot and you're cold, and this whole trip is stressful enough, but *adding* your wild swings, your—" His breath caught. He looked down, at where Pesha had cupped a hand on the outside of his thigh. "No."

"Fen, look at me," Pesha pleaded, taking a step. "Please."

"I just want to finish with the water, and—"

Pesha lunged forward and kissed him. He broke away just as quickly, his face flushed with the apology he *should* have said… wanted to say. So why couldn't he? Why couldn't he give Fen the one thing he deserved? Why were the words so bloody hard?

"You're an ass." Fen's stare remained fixed on the hand still clamped to his thigh. "Go on back to your tent. Hut. Whatever it is. I can get the water myself."

"I have been an ass," Pesha said. "I know. *I know.* I should never have said I didn't want you here…" He tilted his head down, toward where Fen's gaze was locked. "I didn't mean it, Fen. I didn't mean any of it. Please look at me."

Fen's head shifted in a tight upswing. His lips knit together. "Then why would you say that to me? Why would you treat me like I was a nuisance, like I was only getting in your way? The only reason things were going wrong? I swear on the Guardians, Pesha, if you can't answer me directly, don't bother saying another word."

Pesha took a chance and laid his forehead against Fen's. Fen flinched but didn't tear away. "Come to my hut tonight. After evening meal."

"No. No, I'm not—"

"*Please.* Give me a chance to…*show* you what I can't seem to say. Fen, please, look at me."

"Pesha…"

"Please. You've come this far. *We've* come this far. One night, it's all I ask. And then you can decide whether I'm worth all this sadness I've caused you. If you decide I'm not…I'll relent. I promise."

"Fine." Fen flung his arms out. "Fine. But if this is more of the same…"

"I understand." Pesha stepped back to give him space. "Let's get this water hauled."

THIRTEEN
YOU SAVAGE

Pesha searched for Fen in the encampment as he followed Niall. There were another dozen Medvedev gathering in the area, settling onto the logs arranged around the fire, but Fen was not among them. Nor was Fen's mentor, the lovely Mairead, who had latched onto Fen with stunning quickness.

"This isn't everybody," Pesha said, but he was staring at the lights in the trees. None of it was real, just illusory magic, an astounding feat of focus and resilience from whoever was responsible.

"We only gather as a whole for festivals and ceremonies." Niall clamped his hands atop Pesha's shoulders and roughly guided him to a log. "Sit."

"Where's—"

"Stiofen? With Mairead." Niall shot him a look of warning to stay put and joined a cluster of Medvedev who were huddled around a small but broad table.

A shiver ripped through him, though the night was warm, almost balmy. As day pushed into night, the forest had come alive, its song twice as loud and animated as it had been in the light hours, as though the familiars were celebrating in their own way. Pesha had stubbornly held most of his questions with Niall after the visit to the Menagerie, but would Niall have bothered explaining anything if he *had* asked?

Niall stood and turned, carrying a woven tray back to where Pesha was sitting. He balanced the tray on the log and nodded at it. "Your sustenance."

"My sustenance?" Pesha stared at the small pile of leaves, smothered in some pink substance. The only other contents were two smooth wooden glasses, carved into broad bowls, full of an amber liquid.

He reached for the tray, to figure out what he was looking at, but Niall caught his hand and moved it back to his lap.

"Wait." Niall flipped his head in a semicircle gesture. "You see the perimeter?"

"What?"

"Of our encampment. Do you see the leaves, the petals, the shells of nuts, and the stems of berries?"

Pesha *had* noticed those things arranged around the edges of the circle. But his inquisitiveness had numbed at the edges, blurring the world so that it was almost familiar. "Yes."

"They have reached the end of their growth cycle, fallen or chosen for their ultimate purpose. They have returned to the earth, the Light. We honor them on their final passage by dedicating this meal to the life and service they leave behind."

"Leaves? And berries?"

"Do men not recognize the life all around them?"

"We don't invite them to sup at our tables, no." Pesha wrinkled his nose. "And I am only half man, Niall."

Niall flicked his gaze toward the log across from them, where two emerald-tressed Medvedev were whispering and looking their way. "They know nothing of you, except what they need to know. You are not one of us."

"Of course I'm not one of you. My mother saw to that."

"To most, the matter of your biology is more egregious than being a progeny of the Forsaken."

Pesha burst out laughing. He tried to avoid meeting the eyes of the whispering Medvedev, but his gaze kept traveling back to them. "There's a word for that in our world, Niall. And it's not a pretty one."

Niall was stone-faced. "Men corrupt. You are half man, raised by men. Corruption lies within you."

"Narrow logic comes from narrow minds."

"You are complicating what is simple. Our ways are not compatible with the ways of man. You are here because my mother decided you are not a danger to us." Niall straightened. His eyes fluttered closed, and Pesha saw the others doing the same, and he reluctantly followed their lead.

"The Light has guided this bounty to us, and we honor it and the Light in all things," said a Medvedev Pesha remembered was called Elodie. Without further ceremony, she lifted her pink-covered leaf and ate.

The others did the same, including Niall, who didn't stop to explain.

"What *is* this?" Pesha whispered? "The pink?"

"The paste is red berries and a nut varietal," Niall said, his mouth stuffed so full, half his words were cut off. "The leaf is autumn spinach." He licked his lips and lifted a cup to his mouth. "The drink is called Morning Light and is made of bee's honey, leaven, and the same berries in your meal."

It didn't sound appetizing, but it didn't sound bad either. Pesha lifted a leaf and eyed it closely. The scent was floral, delectable. But something was missing. "Is there no meat?"

Niall glanced anxiously at another Medvedev, whose brows were knitted. He was clearly listening. "We indulge in meat on every twenty-sixth day only."

"Why every twenty-six days?"

"You ask a lot of questions," said the watching Medvedev. His cerulean hair was pulled back in a messy knot.

"So would you, if you were in a land you'd never been to before," Pesha said, defending himself.

The Medvedev sneered. Niall buried his own disdain in his leaf, but Pesha caught it.

"Gellais," Niall said, a useless warning after his approving pause.

"That's your name? Gellais?" Pesha asked.

Gellais nodded, his eyes pointed at his food.

"Eat," Niall commanded. "There is nothing in this you have not enjoyed before."

How would you know? Pesha wanted to ask, but he felt in his bones that all the Medvedev staring, their mouths stuffed with berries and leaves, *wanted* him to sound ridiculous. To fit the predefined mold they'd designed for him and the other half Medvedev.

Not just half Medvedev. Half man. Raised by men. Son of a Forsaken. No wonder they hate me. I represent everything they're supposed to revile.

Pesha closed his eyes, drew a steadying breath, and shoved the leaf in his mouth. He'd decided not to chew, to swallow the damn thing whole, but a pleasant sensation spread through his mouth. The paste wasn't just tolerable. It was downright delicious. He was already reaching for another as he swallowed.

"Not so bad then," Niall said with the hint of a smile.

"Not so bad." Pesha formed the smile his mentor couldn't. He reached for the drink—a type of mead, he decided, balancing the ingredients in his mind to make a familiar connection—and that, too, was a delight. It was unlike any ale they served at Shadowfen Hall, both sweeter and also richer, like they'd let it age for years. "Why is it called Morning Light?" He gestured around at the darkening dusk.

"Just is." Niall shrugged. "It was not me who—"

"Abomination." The voice of Elodie rose above the others. "Aoife is blinded by kindness."

Niall stopped eating. Pesha tensed.

"Half-breed," another said. "We do not forget the declaration that a Forsaken will lead us to damnation. No matter what *she* says."

Murmurs of agreement spread through the encampment. Pesha stilled, his limbs turning to ice. He could neither move nor speak, locking up in a crisis, just as Fen said he did.

"We'll see," said Gellais. "We'll see."

Pesha's face bloomed with heat. "See *what*—"

Niall pinched Pesha's leg so hard, Pesha yelped. He glanced over in indignation, ripped from his spell, but the wan, terrified look on Niall's face silenced him again.

"You won't even let me defend myself?" Pesha retorted in a whisper-scream. "None of what they are saying is true! I mean no one harm here."

Niall's head shook tightly. He said nothing.

"Fine." Pesha shoved another delectable leaf in his mouth and washed it with a greedy swallow of Morning Light. He jumped to his feet, passed a glare around the circle, and marched straight to his hut.

Only when he was safely inside did he dare exhale. The weight of it had him bowing over his table as he heaved forceful breaths, summoning the stability that had been ripped from him, over and over, ever since the Medvedev had secreted them away to their world.

What had once seemed like such an inspired idea, in retrospect looked as shortsighted and careless as it must have seemed to the Medvedev, who could no longer even eat in peace because of Pesha's arrival. To them, he was a terrorist threatening their sacred ways. There wasn't enough time or convincing arguments to change their thinking before Farren's rehabilitation would be over.

Des, he thought with a lengthy sigh. *I shouldn't have left you. We'll all pay for my hubris, and only time will tell how.*

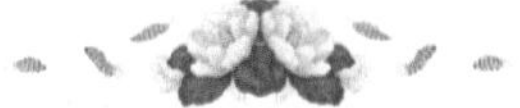

Mairead had called the ones responsible for the light, which Fen had been ogling at every step, Flamekeepers. The Keepers of

Illumination was their official name, but either title fell short of capturing the monumental hoard of light dancing along the treetops and branches and settling atop sconces and torches, bringing everything in the forest into warm but sharp relief. Even the hundreds of tiny fires scoring the clusters of family tents—all of it was magic, she explained as she walked him toward Pesha's tent. *All light and fire in Asgill is created from within. We need nothing we cannot forge or forage ourselves.*

He was still pondering the enormity of such a revelation when she squeezed his arm, said good night, and left him standing between two torches taller than he was. They were dug in on either side of the hut, the thin pelt in front of the flap an unexpectedly welcoming touch.

Listen. All I have to do is listen. If I don't like what he has to say, I'll leave, and it will be his loss.

Atio wasn't anywhere nearby, probably off frolicking with pigeons or something, but she was close enough that he felt her gentle encouragement to take the leap of faith.

Glad one of us is having fun, Attie.

There was no door on which to knock. He felt silly shouting to announce himself. But he felt even sillier standing there without a plan, full of the same childish hope that had been crushed under heel, time and time again. With these painful recollections rolling through his mind, Fen pressed on the flap and entered.

He hadn't taken two tentative steps inside Pesha's hut before he lost his footing and landed in Pesha's arms.

Fen didn't know whether to laugh or snarl at the man staring down at him with a bewildered expression.

Pesha tugged him in for a quick, tight hug. He released him and stood tall, sizing Fen up with his arms crossed over his chest. "I didn't think you'd come, even though you said you would."

"I wasn't going to." He toed the floor of the hut, which was almost identical to his own. "And then I remembered how mad Siofra was at Desemir before she gave him a chance to explain his behavior." Comparing their relationship to Siofra and Desemir's gave it more weight and shape than it rightly deserved, but if vulnerability was off the table, he wouldn't have come at all. He didn't trust the person he'd been when he'd left his hut, but he trusted who he was when he'd entered Pesha's. "I didn't come on this fool-headed journey on a whim. I came for *you.* So it would be myopic of me to refuse you the opportunity to explain yourself."

Pesha nodded, pacing away. He clamped one hand over the back of his neck and squeezed, his knuckles drawing tight. Fen watched him, waiting for him to speak, to do anything, but all that followed was a silence long enough to nearly convince him to leave. "I was scared. *Am* scared."

Fen blurted a splintered laugh. "We're both *scared*, Pesh. I thought the whole point was that it's easier to be scared together."

"Is it?" Pesha's voice climbed. He scratched his neck, and his arm went swinging at his side. "Is it better or worse to bring the people you care about into the fire with you, so you don't have to burn alone?" He sighed and rolled his head back. "Farren is safe for now."

Fen brightened. "You saw her?"

"I saw where she is. I saw others like her. I saw..." Pesha's head bowed. "I saw the effort the Medvedev of Asgill put into caring for their own. But then I learned what happens when their care fails."

Fen nodded at the ground. "Mairead said..."

"They won't even *ask* her what she wants." Pesha cackled and spun back around. "How could they? The only sounds she seems inclined or capable of making are howling...screaming."

"We won't let it happen. We'll send for Des, his army if we have to—"

Pesha cut him off with a harsh laugh. "Will we? Even if we did, would he ever find this place uninvited?"

"I...Uh, we'd figure it out. We'd..." Fen pressed his lips tight. "It doesn't matter *how,* Pesha, but we will not let them kill your sister if she doesn't bond with another familiar. That's ridiculous."

Pesha's hands drew upward in tight clenches. "And while I was supposed to be protecting her, from herself, I never even considered she might be a danger to *you.*"

Fen wrinkled his nose. His hand involuntarily traveled to the spot on his neck Farren had torn out with her bare, dull teeth. His thumb brushed along his regrown jaw flesh. A chill ripped through him as he tried to feign indifference. "It happened. You fixed it. But you've been treating me like an annoyance far longer than that, Pesh."

Pesha closed in. He skimmed his palms along Fen's chest with a sigh. What Fen needed from him seemed an ocean away, but he was ready to hear it, however hard. "I'd resigned myself to Farren's suffering years ago, horrible as that sounds, but I was the one..." Pesha grimaced and took a deep breath. "*I* was the one who rescued you from suffering in Newcarrow, Fen, and what I *should* have done when you offered to come with me on this foolish journey was force you to stay at the Hall, where I knew you were safe, where I could keep the promise I made to you and Siofra in that carriage. But I was too fucking selfish. I wanted you here with me, and I was too weak to say no."

Fen stared up at him in bafflement. "*That's* what you think, Pesha? That you interrupted our suffering and are now responsible for everything that happens to us after? Everything good? Everything bad?"

"That isn't...That's not what I meant."

"Then tell me what you meant." Fen wrung his hands behind his back. "Tell me, or I'll..." He closed his eyes. "I don't even know how to finish that thought. What the Guardians am I even doing here?"

Pesha unwound Fen's tangled hands, twining them in his. He raised them both between them, first bringing them to his own mouth, then Fen's. "Before you came to Shadowfen Hall, I had nothing I was afraid of losing. Yes, I was terrified for Desemir and his reckless baiting of all the barons, and I knew I was the only thing keeping him from total disaster, but there's a certain numbness that comes with accepting people as they are. When Siofra came around, I realized all I'd been doing was plugging the holes in the ship with bits of cork. It was exhausting, keeping him from blowing it all up day after day, year after year, but that's because *I* wasn't the one capable of calming him. I could patch him, but I couldn't fix him."

Fen closed his eyes and shook his head. "I don't know what you're trying to say."

"I don't either. I don't know a damn thing anymore, and it's eating me up inside. It's *killing* me, this…this questioning of everything I thought I knew to be true, of my own worth, my purpose in this life. If it's not to serve Des, and it's not to save Farren, then…" Pesha released their hands and buried his face in his palms. "I didn't bring you here to fish for sympathy. I'm sorry. I'm sorry. Let's start over."

Fen approached. It was his turn to peel Pesha's hands away, to bring him back to the moment. "Hey." His heart softened at the sympathy he heard in his own voice. He tilted to catch Pesha's eyes. "Pesh. I…I know what it is to serve everyone but yourself, so if anyone understands the misery that has wrapped you so tight, it's me. But don't you think the lesson we're supposed to learn is that it's time to find our real purpose? Our true purpose?"

Pesha thrust an arm out. His face glowed with red rage. "Well, we won't find it here, will we? They take my sister and deem themselves the sole decider of her fate. They put me to work in the Menagerie but won't let me see her. And when I try to be gracious, be kind, be a part of a society I don't remotely understand or recognize, they snicker and call me *half-breed* or *abomination*."

"*What*?" Fen grabbed Pesha's arm. "Who said that to you?"

"I don't know their names. Any of their names. They know mine though." He sneered, his mouth trembling. "They know every cursed little thing about me—or think they do."

Fen swelled with scorching heat. "I want you to point them out to me tomorrow, Pesha."

"I didn't tell you to get you riled up. It's fine. I can handle it."

"You're going to point them out to me tomorrow."

"Fen—"

"You're going to point them out to me, tomorrow," Fen said, the heat becoming a flame, "so I can have a fucking *talk* to the bigots about—"

Pesha gripped him by the collar and crushed him into a kiss. It was over so fast, Fen's head felt like it would whirl right off his shoulders, but he had no chance to recover before Pesha was guiding him, backing him up until they crashed into something hard. A table.

Fen's breath caught in his throat as he watched, heart pumping, Pesha lower to a crouch and tear at Fen's loosely woven belt. Fen rolled his hands along the edge of the table, his grip like iron to keep his knees from buckling.

He shook his head in lieu of words, but his hips bucked in defiance, usurping his pent-up resentment, anger, and pain. When Pesha's soft hands freed his cock, kneading it in soft, gentle pumps, Fen released a sigh so long, it unbound his mind to join his body.

Fen looked down and straight into Pesha's eyes, wide and exposed as he worked Fen's cock between his hands and cupped his testicles, sliding a finger beyond, to the area Fen used to try to reach when he had a few rare moments alone to explore his own body and what it wanted.

Pesha held his gaze when he lowered his mouth over Fen's sensitive, swollen crown. Fen's head fell back with a sharp cry, his eyes closing to memorize every drag of Pesha's supple lips, every lash of his tongue as he took his time on the first pass. He reached the base and sucked in, hard enough to turn Fen's knees to jelly. Pesha's hands shot to Fen's hips to steady him, dragging his mouth back along the thick length, and released it with a slurping *pop* sound.

Fen heaved out a breath and bowled forward, still gripping the table with enough force to make his fingers tremble. But Pesha was enveloping him once more, suckling him more gently this time. He swirled his tongue along the underside of Fen's pulsing head, so thick and ripe and growing, Fen was astounded it hadn't exploded already.

Pesha took Fen into the back of his throat and swallowed. Fen's cock bobbed along with Pesha's undulating muscles, which vibrated against Fen's shaft as he moaned, the sound so deep and savage, it seemed to come from somewhere primal, unreachable except in the act of complete surrender.

Fen's toes clenched in his boots and he stretched higher, like he might climb out of his skin. Wave after wave of damning pleasure crashed over him, drowning him…saving him. Every attempt to speak gurgled out as half-formed words, no longer important by the time they were said.

Pesha bobbed faster, tightening his mouth and increasing his suction. Fen's head fell back again, his mouth parted in a silent mewl. Pesha's fingers dug into the tender flesh of Fen's ass and thighs, and in the fleeting, blissful moment between control and release, Fen let go of the table, plunged his hands into Pesha's hair, and locked his head over his cock. Pesha's moan of approval was the last piece of the twisted puzzle, sending Fen crashing. He shook forward, held aloft only by Pesha's steely grip, as seed spilled from his cock in a violent rush. He was sighing, screaming, and whimpering with every pulse, every spurt. When he thought it was finally ended, he tried to move, but there was more built up, desperate to spill.

Pesha, his face still locked at the base of Fen's cock, slowly drew his mouth along the length, his eyes burning Fen into ash. At the end, he gave the head a little swirl with his tongue and then rocked back on his heels. His mouth was closed, but the movement of his throat as he swallowed turned Fen hard again in an instant.

All Fen could do was stare. He couldn't speak. He couldn't breathe. The closest thing he'd ever had to whatever Pesha had just done to him was that strange night in the cabin he hadn't had the courage or the heart to see through.

Pesha opened his mouth. Fen moaned at the sight of some of his cum on Pesha's tongue. He raked his teeth over his bottom lip and drew blood, entirely unsure what was happening but ready for anything.

Pesha spat the remaining seed into his hand and stood, undoing his trousers with one hand as he watched Fen with the same wild intensity. Fen reached forward to help, but Pesha stilled him with a hard look of command. *You do what I say.*

Fen gulped, his hand moving to his own appendage. *Anything.*

Pesha rolled his cum-soaked hand along his cock, spreading it over the swollen length, his eyes fluttering upward. He snaked a hand out and grabbed Fen's collar, then tugged to indicate his intent. Fen, understanding, his nerves having unfailingly returned, spun around to face the table. Pesha pressed a palm to his back to shove him forward, bending him over the smooth wood.

Fen flattened his cheek against the table, noting the sharp pine scent to ground him as he tried to remember how to breathe. He felt the head of Pesha's slick cock tracing patterns along his ass cheeks, spreading his own spend over his flesh, a message he couldn't interpret.

Pesha palmed Fen's ass and tugged, parting him. With his hands still locked there, he thrust his hips, each one teasing more force, more promise. The last one breached the entrance, enough to send Fen crawling up the table in desperation.

The future flashed through Fen's mind like a bolt of lightning—the strange, languid moments after it would be over, when they'd be forced to confront what had happened, make sense of it. Or even the days and weeks after, the critical period that would decide whether this had been real or a passing dream.

I don't know how to stop thinking about the future, the consequences. But Guardians, give me this night. Unlock the chains on my mind just this once.

"Tell me to stop." Pesha moaned. His hand slammed against the inner edge of Fen's cheeks as he stroked his cock in forceful jerks. "And I will. I never want you to—"

"Don't speak," Fen said, breathless. He flicked his tongue out to clear the spittle from his mouth. "And don't stop." His toes curled hard as Pesha's thrust went fractionally deeper. "Even if I tell you to."

Pesha leaned over the back of him and rested his face near Fen's ear. "Relax, and it won't hurt. Not for long." He rolled Fen's lobe in between his teeth and then released it, rising back to position. Fen heard him spit once, twice. Then his feet came up off the ground altogether as Pesha lined himself up and drove in.

The pain that followed was blinding, electric. Fen rolled his face downward and scraped his teeth along the table, screaming into the wood. His legs trembled, failing to land anywhere that might give him grip, but Pesha looped an arm around him from behind and locked him in place. He fingered Fen's cock with every thrust and was soon stroking it, beating it, commanding it. Fen started to relax, to find his place in the rhythm, his small but vital bit of control in the encounter.

"Fuck, I love the way your ass looks taking my cock," Pesha said, following his charged words with a frenzied plunge to the base. "How pretty would it look filled with my cum?"

"Yes. Guardians, yes. Yes, yes, yes," Fen moaned into the wood, spittle rolling off his tongue.

Every thrust was too much. Not enough. They filled him, stretched him…*changed* him. Pesha was relentless, finding the edge of Fen's tolerance and obliterating it altogether.

"From the first time I saw you…" Pesha's grunts clipped his words. His grip on Fen's hip deepened. His other hand worked Fen's cock, jerking harder and faster to match his thrusts. "You've turned me inside out."

Fen pressed his face harder against the wood to pin himself in place and reached back to spread his ass wider. The desperate, bracing sound Pesha made was the approval he needed, the *push* he needed, and he was spilling into Pesha's hand.

"Fuck. Fuck," Pesha cried. He planted a hand in the center of Fen's lower back and slowed his cadence as he shuddered into his orgasm.

Fen discovered a new pleasure, a new desire to keep him satiated on cold nights, as the warmth of Pesha's cum surged into him. *More. More, until I'm drowning* was on the tip of his lips. Pesha locked his final, trembling plunge at the base, and Fen felt every jerk, every last drop of Pesha, and silently begged for more, cursing the inevitable end to the most freeing moment of his life.

Pesha's cock slid out. He backed away, taking the moment with him.

Fen was rigid in indecision. Stand up. Stay in place. Beg for more. There was only the post-coitus haze, only the present. The future didn't exist. It wasn't real. Nothing else was.

The sound of Pesha's clothes sliding over him faded Fen's daze. Pesha returned to the table and knelt beside it, looking up at him.

"Are you all right?" Pesha brushed a band of sweat-matted hair from Fen's eyes. "Did I hurt you?"

Fen's eyes flooded with tears. He didn't know where they'd come from or what they meant.

"Fen." Pesha's expression crumpled. "Tell me what's wrong."

"You didn't hurt me. It was…" His spent cock shuddered with his pulse, slowly returning to normal. He closed his eyes. "Yes. It was yes."

Relief flooded Pesha's face as he softly laughed. "It was yes?"

Fen nodded against the wood. "You stole my ability to speak, you savage."

"That's nothing compared to what I'll do to you when you're ready." Pesha kissed him, smiling against Fen's mouth.

Fen smiled back. He rolled his lips in, tasting Pesha, tasting himself. The combination drove his cock into another frenzy, but he ignored it, suddenly aware of the exposed position he was still in.

"This was just practice, that what you're saying?" Fen asked, stretching as he unfurled himself. More than just his cock ached, but he was taken aback to discover he craved more of the pain. A quick, delicious fantasy came to him, of Pesha shoving his cock back into his ass, but this time working his fingers in beside it, stretching Fen to oblivion.

"Something like that," Pesha said. He helped Fen fasten his trousers. "Are you really all right?"

Fen nodded. "About *that*...yeah. More than all right." He smiled to reinforce his words and leaned up to kiss Pesha. "But there are still things we need to talk about."

Pesha brushed a thumb along Fen's mouth. "I know. I'm trying."

"I know." Fen kissed his thumb with a light sigh. "But I think it's best if I go back to my own hut tonight."

A flicker of disappointment came over Pesha's face, but he bowed his head, nodding. "I understand."

"You *can* talk to me, Pesh. About anything. I'll always be a safe place for you, if you let me in."

Pesha's shoulders elevated in a weighted inhale. His gaze was still fixed on the ground. "You've changed everything for me, Fen. But change takes time, and there are things...It's not you is what I'm endeavoring and failing to say."

"I never thought it was me." Fen checked his shirt and trousers. Smoothed his hair. It was pointless, for anyone within a mile radius had no doubt heard everything the soft walls couldn't absorb. "But we're in this together, Pesha, and it will be so much easier, for both of us, if you let me in."

Pesha looked up with a quick, short smile. His eyes were glossy, tired. "I'll try."

FOURTEEN
QUIVERS OF ACCUSATION

Mairead arrived at Fen's hut just after dawn with a bowl of orange berries, a filled waterskin, a flustered smile, and far less ceremony than he remembered from evening meal. Her hair was tied in a messy knot atop her head, which seemed one gust of wind away from unraveling.

"What a day for you, Stiofen! We have a child to bring," she announced, a touch of wild fear dancing in her irises.

Fen accepted the bowl and waterskin with a grateful nod. He sat, but the dull pain from the prior night's interlude had him swiftly returning to his feet. "A child to bring? You mean…"

"You shared your worry about Siofra with me. And I said…"

"That you'd teach me all I need to know," Fen said, finishing her thought and feeling himself pale. "You didn't mention there was a child coming so soon though."

"And that is why we are up with the sun." Mairead held the hut flap open. "The foundling has chosen to enter the world early, and there are things we must do to keep mother and child safe."

Fen wolfed down the berries and tucked his waterskin in his vest, following her out of the hut and into the foggy morning. "How early?"

"Incubation is typically eleven months, in the way you measure time, and she is only at nine, which may be fine if we are accounting for her Med blood, but the child is part man as well, and she's already past a reasonable time period for that, and even *then*...We've seen the pairing of man and Medvedev lead to unexpected gestations, anywhere from three to fifteen months. It's why we pay close attention to what the mother's body is telling us. And also why it is so dangerous for our women to mate with men, when we cannot easily predict their journey," Mairead said over her shoulder, picking up her pace as she dodged logs and refuse in the encampment. "I'm sure that's all very confusing, but it's important to remember Med live longer than men, Light willing. It is not unusual to find us living to one and twenty."

"One hundred and twenty years?"

"In the right environment." She swung her arms around. "When we are home, we can do anything."

They didn't know for certain when Siofra had conceived, but even accounting for small swings in accuracy, she had, at most, a month left of confinement. "And the father being a man only affects the gestation?" he asked, thinking of Des.

"That is one effect," Mairead said. She slowed at the fork at the forest's edge and switched them to another path, one he recognized. "There are other unknowns."

"Such as?"

"Complications to be aware of. Three that I've seen enough to train everyone who assists me to know the signs. Lunar interference can create energy misalignment." She shook her head. "That will not make much sense to you unless you see it yourself, but there are certain days in the moon cycle when childbirth, particularly for foundlings, is quite hazardous."

"What do you do?" Fen asked.

"We do everything we can to slow labor until a better day. There are herbs, whispers. You are unlikely to see this while you're here. What you may see, even today, is either dream dissonance or familial dissonance, which stem from the same issue but present in different ways." Mairead waited for him to catch up. "Some..." Mairead came to a halt and turned toward him. She looked around. "*Some* halfling Medvedev are not born with a familiar."

Fen gaped at her. "Some are born *without* them?"

"And it's impossible to predict, *unless* the mother presents with signs of dream or familial dissonance. These occur when her soul cannot accept what her body already knows. When this happens, she relinquishes her loving hold on her child, and the child's mind is free to wander, a quite dangerous thing when it happens before they are ready. The little one escapes into dreams where, unless we can coax them out, they will stay."

"Guardians," Fen whispered. "And the other one? Familial?"

"The same, except it happens to the mother. Most mothers know when their foundling will be familiar-less. They know and say nothing because the news is damning, but she makes adjustments in her own role in the delivery that protects the child in the absence of the familiar. But sometimes..." Mairead swallowed. "Sometimes the mother either does not know or cannot accept this fate for their child, and they enter delivery in denial. If that acceptance never comes, there is little we can do to protect the child. If we *know*, we race time to reach the mother's mind and say what she needs to hear to save her child."

It was so much to take in, and all of it he had to know if he was going to protect Siofra. He wanted to write it all down and send it in a raven, but there *were* no messenger ravens in Asgill. No means of communicating with the broader realm. He might not make it in time, and even if he did, what if he forgot something?

"I can feel your overwhelm from here. I will teach you, Stiofen. You needn't worry." She turned down another path, the last one before the Hatchery. "But now you understand that the disdain for foundlings and halflings is as much a matter of fear and concern as it is prejudice."

Fen wondered why any Medvedev who knew what Mairead had just told him would ever even chance such a thing. "What actually happens to Medvedev born without a familiar? Can they live a…*normal* life?"

Mairead shook her head but then shrugged. "They can live a life, yes. Normal in your world. Here, if there is a surplus of displaced familiars in the Menagerie, which there often is, some Med are offered the opportunity for a rehabilitation bond, but it's rare. Niall was…" She glanced around again. "Niall was a halfling born without one…"

"You say halfling. Others say half-breed."

"One is the correct term. The other is prejudice."

Fen's thoughts caught up to him. "You said Niall was born without a familiar? But I saw…" His words died on his lips at Mairead's wan look. "Oh. He was offered a rehabilitation bond?"

"Theta was my mother's counselor. When she traveled into the Easterlands, as some of our people do when they reach the age of maturity, Aoife discouraged her, same as she discouraged me years later. It's not safe for us out there, as you well know, Stiofen. Theta went anyway, and when she came back, she was with child. With Niall. Our laws decree Mother should have banished Theta straightaway, but Theta entered labor the day she returned, and Niall came along, clearly *not* full Med." She crossed her arms as she met Fen's eyes. "What could my mother do? She lost her closest confidant when she was forced to banish Theta. None of it was Niall's fault, and he didn't deserve to suffer the consequences of his mother's choices any more than any foundling does, so Aoife took Niall straight to the Menagerie when he was still a newborn mewling infant, and he found a matching mewling kitten."

"Why are you telling me this secret?"

Mairead scoffed. "It's far from a secret, Stiofen. Everyone knows. It's why…"

"Why what?"

"Nothing."

"Then why are we whispering?"

Mairead lowered her voice again. "Because…It was not a good time for the clahnn. My mother was accused of putting her personal feelings above the needs of the people. We are all still bruised from the acts of war perpetuated by the Forsaken, and there are some…some who still blame my mother. I would not stuff their quivers of accusation with more poisoned arrows."

Fen tried to knit her words into something coherent. "You're not saying…"

Adir, Mairead's songbird, fluttered down from the trees with a discordant trill.

"What's wrong?" Fen asked, watching Mairead's mirth disappear.

"The infant is cosa. We must go *now*."

"What's cosa?" Fen cried, launching into a jog beside her.

"Breech," Mairead muttered and raced ahead, bolting down the hill.

Fen pushed to catch up, but she was so much faster that he lost sight of her by the time he made it to the bottom. He remembered from his tour that infants were delivered and nursed in the large central hut Mairead had playfully called the Hatchery, so he headed there.

He entered in the middle of a flurry of activity. Medvedev rushed from one side to the other, gathering materials and passing them down the line to an elevated platform covered in furs, atop which was a cerulean-haired Medvedev on all fours, howling a silent scream.

Mairead caught his eye from the far side of the platform, nodding for him to join her. He dodged stacks of fabrics and two young men carrying a steaming tub of water on his way over.

Fen tried not to stare at the poor Medvedev's bright-red face or the perspiration streaming from places he didn't even know could sweat. Her wild hair told a story of the past hours, which, from the harried looks of everyone attending the birth, had not been peaceful.

"How can I help?" he asked, breathless, searching around him. He spotted a steaming bowl and washed his hands while he waited for Mairead's response.

Mairead tilted her head toward the end of the platform and met him there. She leaned in to whisper, "When this labor is ended, this mother will be banished. As devastating as that is, we will not add death to her misfortune today."

Fen ripped his outer coat off and hurled it into the corner. He rolled his sleeves up over his elbows. "Whatever you need."

"You want to learn what to do? For your sister? Cosa can happen to *any* mother." She pulled a log to the platform, and when she sat, she was eye level with the pregnant Medvedev's hind end. "Kaia, can you hear me?"

The woman on all fours moaned in response.

Mairead leaned in, gently parting the Medvedev's angry flesh back to inspect the area. She flicked a brief glance at Fen. "Kaia, your little one has decided he's not interested in doing things our way and wants to enter the world by his little bum. But you've been aiding me long enough to know we cannot bring him that way, can we?"

Another moan from Kaia. Her thighs rippled in a clench of pain. "Mair, is he…Does he…"

Mairead crushed her bottom lip in her teeth. She glanced down, bracing, and said, "We have but one task here, Kaia. Help me help you bring him, and then we can consider what the rest might mean." She rolled her sleeves up, and a young Medvedev pinned them in place. "I'm going to turn the child."

"How?" Fen asked.

She wiggled her fingers. "With my hands. I want you to watch, closely. You may ask questions." Mairead turned and bent backward over the platform, sliding until she was underneath Kaia. "Ah, he's just excited, isn't he, Kaia? He knows what a wonderful world awaits him. How much beauty he has yet to meet." She palmed Kaia's belly in gentle, swirling massage motions. "What's the first plant he'll take interest in, do you think?"

"I..." Kaia screamed.

"Elderberries are your favorite, aren't they?" Mairead worked Kaia's belly with her palms. Her face contorted. "Will your son love them?"

"Too...tart."

"Yes, our little boys here like things sweet, don't they?" Mairead laughed, but the humor never made it to her face. She continued her gentle twisting, her face reddening with every pass. "Remember when Kael petitioned the chieftainess to harvest fewer elderberries and more strawberries? His argument was elderberries only had medicinal use, and Aoife said..."

Kaia sputtered a snigger. "She said...She said he lacked imagination and proper taste."

"She did indeed." Mairead laughed. She buried a low, tight grunt against her arm. "And there...There he goes." Her hands flopped to her sides as she closed her eyes, panting. "There he goes. Datu, how close were her spasms?"

"Close, Mair. This child won't wait now that you've turned him!"

Mairead slid out from under Kaia. She barely made it out before Kaia screamed again.

"Who will whisper to her?" Mairead called.

"I will!" Datu cried.

"We whisper to the mother messages of peace, so that the last words a child hears before they leave their mother's womb are ones of love. It isn't very different from the way we whisper to a mother in distress to bring her across the threshold," Mairead explained. She craned her head to the side and hollered, "I need blankets. Where are the blankets? And fresh linens. Hot water?"

Everything she asked for appeared, one by one. She tapped Kaia's outer thigh. "We're going to bring this child now, Kaia. You know what to do."

Fen rocked back on his heels, settling in. He watched in awe as Mairead alternated between gentle encouragement and tough love. She coaxed the sobbing woman through what sounded to be a harrowing experience, only to result in a wriggly, soaking infant that Mairead cradled, as one of her helpers took a dagger to a long piece of flesh connecting mother and child.

Mairead made soft, cooing sounds at the infant, rocking the little one in her arms until a single sharp cry sounded. Mairead laughed through tears. "The Light has blessed you with a healthy son, Kaia. You can rest now."

The cord fell away as Mairead carefully handed the baby to a helper. Kaia slowly rotated and collapsed onto her side, sobbing as the helper placed her son next to her head.

"Datu, you can bring the rest?" Mairead asked as she pushed to her feet. She marched away, not waiting for an answer.

Fen jumped up and followed.

"Ruairi, I need you!"

"Here," the boy said, appearing seemingly from nowhere. He held a stack of blankets taller than him.

"Can you..." Mairead took the blankets from him and set them aside. "Show Stiofen how we handle the afterbirth?"

"Yes, Mair." Ruairi wiped his brow on his sleeve and gave a firm nod.

"Where are you going?" Fen asked, still reeling from the whirlwind delivery.

"To the forest..." Her eyes darted around. "To answer Kaia's question." She sighed and pressed her mouth tight. "She'll want to know whether there was another birth, in the forest."

"A familiar," Ruairi said helpfully, but there was a heavy sadness in his eyes. "Mairead is going into the forest to see if Kaia's son is like me."

Mairead glanced toward the entrance. "I have to go."

Fen's chest ached for the young boy with no familiar. Would he ever get his day in the Menagerie? What made Niall worthy and Ruairi not?

With a smile he didn't feel, Fen closed his hand over Ruairi's shoulder. "Go, Mair. Ruairi and I—"

"Call me Air," the boy said. "It's what I would have named my familiar, had I been born with one."

He trounced off, leaving Fen's heart in shambles. Mairead gave one last nod and ducked out.

Fen shrugged out his shoulders, pulling both sides into a quick stretch, and went to join the boy for his next lesson.

Pesha watched in utter disbelief as Niall first goaded the gazelle into attacking him and then let it happen.

He flinched and turned away when the gazelle barreled into Niall. Animal and Medvedev went crashing into a tree with thuds and moans. When they landed on the forest floor, they kept rolling—and rolling and rolling and rolling—until Niall was straddling the beast with a flushed, triumphant grin.

Pesha rushed over. He couldn't tear his eyes away from the subdued gazelle. Her serene eyes blinked, regarding them in peace. "Are you going to explain that?"

"Would you like to try next?"

"Do I want to…no. *No*, I don't want to tackle a poor animal into submission." Pesha stretched a hand to Niall to pull him up, but the Medvedev acted like he didn't see it.

Niall leaned forward and folded himself against the gazelle, his face against hers. He brushed his mouth against her ear, whispered something, and peeled away.

The gazelle rose to her feet, wobbled, and stared.

Niall clucked his tongue to dismiss her and she ambled away, decidedly less ornery than she'd been when the encounter had begun.

Fen stared at them both.

"You see a beaten animal, Pesha. What you do not see is the crazed, grieving creature who arrived at the Menagerie after their Medvedev was murdered in the kingdom. The many days and nights I spent with her to bring her back from the worst corners of her mind." Niall crossed his arms and watched the gazelle saunter away, gaining speed. "Today I see hope. Hope she may yet bond." He turned away, and Pesha caught him wiping a tear. "Now you will learn."

Pesha couldn't decide whether to laugh or scream, his gaze flitting between Niall and the rehabilitated gazelle grazing on the other side of the field. "I am not wrestling with animals. She could have just as easily torn out your throat, Niallan."

"Not wrestling," Niall said. "Swimming."

"Swimming?"

Niall was off without explaining, a consistent choice Pesha was realizing was a deeply embedded personal flaw. Still, he couldn't dispel the strange sight of the Medvedev inciting and then soothing the animal…couldn't help wondering what words had been whispered that had built upon weeks of rehabilitation to free the creature from her trauma.

As a little boy, Pesha had always been told that when a Medvedev died, so died their familiar. That one could not exist without the other, for they were connected by some unseen thread that once cut was severed forever. But then Ludwik had murdered Farren's familiar, and Farren had very much lived but had gone mad. He began to see what life may have been like for the gazelle when its Medvedev was murdered.

Niall stopped suddenly in the forest. When Pesha caught up, he said, "You have not been to visit Eshe."

Pesha bristled. "Is that a question or an indictment?"

"Aquatic Medvedev choose trades involving water. Build their huts near water. Eat, drink, celebrate near water." A breeze shimmered the trees above, giving life to the long pause that followed. "But not you."

"How was I supposed…" Pesha snorted. He squared his stance, welcoming the anger filling his cheeks. "Everything I have done since your people kidnapped us and brought us here has been what *you* decide I am doing."

Niall was unruffled by Pesha's edginess. "You have not asked."

"You have granted nothing else I've asked for!"

"You grow defensive."

"Oh, you are..." Pesha ripped away, folding his arms over himself. How he missed home. Des, Lotte, and even Euric and all the others. The scents he now understood were unique to Shadowfen Hall. Just the right number of candles to provide the dim but warm illumination that had colored the eighteen years of his life. He'd thought himself brave for venturing so far from home with so much uncertainty, but he'd been afraid of the wrong things. He couldn't have expected the way the Asgill lands had been pulling the walls back on his old life and letting so much more light in.

"Your bond is fractured," Niall said after a gentle reprieve. "It can be mended. But she was not made to live in a frozen lake, Pesha. She was made to be with you, and you, her."

"I had nowhere else for her to go!" Pesha slapped his palm against a nearby tree. "Maybe you don't realize this, living in your little secret paradise, but it's not *safe* for Medvedev in the realm, and every precaution and defense we built at Shadowfen Hall was to *keep* that danger from reaching us. Every single night, I prayed no one would stumble upon that lake and find her and...and..." He screamed a grunt and ground his palm against the sharp bark. Tears burned behind his eyes, too stubborn to spill. "You stand so high on your sanctimony but have never, *ever* known the fear Fen and I have known. Never had to make the kinds of choices we've had to make."

"Not all dangers come as man." Niall stepped closer. It was hard to discern whether he was smiling or scowling—or both. "I have never walked your path. But your path brought you *here*. To us. An open heart discovers joy in the lessons."

"I didn't come here for a lesson. I came here to save my sister."

Niall started toward the path again. "We're still a hundred paces from the river. Come."

Pesha couldn't though. Whether it was his mind or body failing to rise to the order, he was rooted. "I..." Heat coursed through him. He breathed in, out, sweat building. "I'm not feeling so..." The ground rushed up and then back down. He lowered into a crouch, pursing his mouth, and rocked through tingles and chills. "I don't know what's happening."

"Only what was meant to happen," Niall said. He held his place on the path. "Plenty of daylight remains. Are you coming?"

Pesha heaved breaths in and out. He couldn't expel the horrifying image of Eshe curled up at the bottom of the frozen lake, her vitals slowed to keep her alive until the few weeks in the spring when she could swim and play unfettered. How many times had he convinced himself it was fine, it was the only way—that it wasn't *ideal*, no, but nothing about life as a refugee was and they all had sacrifices to make to survive.

He needed to be at the river, with Eshe. Every inch of him called him to follow Niall, to begin the deep healing needed.

"No," Pesha finally said, hanging his head in shame. "Not today."

"You will find your own way back," Niall said and left without another word.

Fen was swaying on his feet by the time he left the Hatchery. His vision was hazed, his limbs buckling in exhaustion. Delivering Kaia's child had been the simple part. Keeping her stable after—especially after Mairead had returned with that single shake of her head, the one every single person, even Fen, understood—had taken the rest of the afternoon.

What will happen to her? Fen had asked during their brief noontide respite.

When she's well, she'll be taken to the edge of our lands, given all the food and supplies she can carry, and...

And what?

Some in the clahnn felt my mother should have barred the Forsaken from our land with magic. Mairead had bowed her head then. *In the same way we use magic to keep women like Kaia from finding us ever again.*

So the Forsaken can return any time, but a woman who has relations with a man is cast out forever?

That is the sum of it, Stiofen, yes. She'd turned her bitter tears toward the sky and went back to the tasks inside.

Dusk colored the sky between the treetops. Every few steps shifted the kaleidoscope of violet, ocher, and carnation, bathing the leaves and underbrush in a gentle canvas of light. It was almost too beautiful for words, but the effect became marred as the flesh was slowly peeled back from the truths of the clahnn. Mairead's words had been eating at him for hours. The Medvedev purported to be agents of peace, yet they'd tolerate treason but not an error in judgment? Not someone falling spell to love or lust?

Kaia had perhaps a day or two of rest ahead before she'd be exiled to a world almost completely foreign to her.

None of it felt right.

Fen drew to a sudden halt when he heard voices.

"Forsaken is a way of life. It's all you know."

Fen didn't recognize the first speaker, but he definitely recognized the second one.

"I know nothing about it." Pesha.

"You know nothing about *us.*" A third speaker.

"He never will, Cahl."

"I might know more if you didn't make it impossible to learn," Pesha stated. "If you weren't so fucking mysterious about everything."

"Abominations are what they are. You cannot change. And if you cannot change, you do not belong here, tainting our land, drinking our water, or eating our sustenance. The chieftainess is full of heart where there should be stone. But not all of us are so. Some of us would do what's right for our people."

Fen came barreling off the path toward the small clearing, where Pesha and an emerald-haired Medvedev were facing off.

"What's going on here?" Fen asked, surveying the rest of the scene. There were two others as well, hanging back and watching the one sparring with Pesha. One had their hand on their waistband.

"An education, half-breed," said one onlooker. "Care for one?"

The foul-mouthed Medvedev was quick, but Fen was quicker. His muscles remembered every twitch needed to crouch, grab, and flick. He had both daggers brandished before the other Medvedev could draw one.

Pesha's stunned eyes kept widening.

"Had enough learning for today. Thanks." Fen held his knives at his sides, lifted just enough to show the bullies he'd have no qualms using them. "And if the Asgill are so enlightened, you might better prove your point by not acting like a degenerate gang of thugs."

The Medvedev exchanged disgusted looks. "Degenerate gang of thugs?" asked the one probably named Cahl.

"Pesha is a guest of your chieftainess. You treat guests the way we treat enemies." Fen rolled the hilts in his palms, tightening his grip. "Well, that's not true. We do far worse to our enemies. Should see what Pesha's brother did to the man who'd kidnapped my sister, his wife. Suffice to say, they'll be talking about *that* night in the Northerlands for generations to come."

"Fen," Pesha said, finally speaking. His voice was choked. "It's fine."

Fen drilled his gaze into the others. "If it's fine, I'm sure they'll happily apologize."

Cahl spat. "We owe no apology."

"Oh, then it's not fine at all." Fen took another step. Cahl and the others tensed. "You must feel very brave and bold, cornering an unarmed man. But you wouldn't last a day in the kingdom. An *hour.* You talk about the Forsaken like it's a story passed down, but us? We lived it. We know exile. We know survival. We know sacrifice. We know pain. And unless you want to know all of those things in the same evening, leave Pesha the fuck alone."

"Not fit for our time," Cahl growled and stormed off. The others glanced at Pesha, then Fen and followed.

Fen knelt to refasten his daggers, breathing deep when they could no longer see. He took a moment to gather himself, then looked up and saw Pesha standing over him. "What? Did they hurt you with more than their foul mouths?" He released the buckle on his left dagger. "Say the word."

"You didn't..." Pesha set his jaw and looked away. "Get up."

Fen had only one dagger sheathed. "Give me—"

Pesha ripped him to his feet, sending the other skittering into the brush. Fen breathed in just as he was shoved hard against the tree, Pesha lifting and pinning his hands above his head with a sharp thud. The bark scored angry marks on his flesh with every shift into place.

Reeling, Fen stared into Pesha's wild eyes.

Pesha crushed his mouth to Fen's. Pesha was already hard, so cursed hard, his erection pulsing against Fen's belly brought a swift correction to a day Fen was still making sense of. From Kaia to the bullies, the stress hadn't let up for a single second, so he closed his eyes and rolled his head along the bark as Pesha breathed kisses down his neck, to the opening of his blouse.

He wilted, but the force of Pesha's open hand on his wrists was enough to hold them both in place as Pesha's kisses climbed Fen's chin and brushed his lips, until he pulled back, locking their gazes.

"Pesh—"

Pesha roughly spun him so his face was pressed to the tree, inducing flashbacks of the night before, his face sliding across the table. Fen panted, each breath catching before the next as he listened to fabric rustle...felt his trousers ripped down until they were pooled around his calves. His cheeks screamed in agony when Pesha's first powerful thrust scraped his face across the rough bark, but soon he was practically kissing it, his lower lip stuck to the trunk, drooling. His mouth filled with a raw, earthy taste that had his own cock thumping the tree.

Pesha transferred Fen's wrists to one hand and shoved the other into Fen's hair with a commanding tug. Fen's head fell back until it was upside down, his tongue dragging Pesha's chin, mouth, and nose. Pesha drove deeper, harder, each thrust a delicious discovery of pain and ecstasy, stretching him, filling him, and pulling him further and further from a day that had nearly broken him.

"I didn't ask you to stand up for me." Pesha moaned, breathless, as he released Fen's head. "But seeing you with those daggers..."

"I could use them on you. On us." Fen's face slid along the bark, tearing more scratches and sending blood beading to the surface of his tender flesh. "I could..." His eyes closed in momentary surrender. He licked his lips, tasting pine and earth. "I could take my blood...spread it over my cock..."

Pesha shrieked as he bucked upward with one hard, decisive shove. Fen tried to tilt his ass to receive more, but he collapsed against the tree.

The pressure on Fen's wrists disappeared. He went stumbling back, tripping over his trousers and straight into Pesha's arms.

Pesha craned down to kiss him. "I'm going to hold you to what you said about the daggers."

"Really?" Fen was surprised, not that the suggestion had driven Pesha wild in the moment but that he'd still want it after the thrill had passed. "You would want that?"

Pesha nipped at Fen's lower lip, dragging it between his teeth. "Bring them to my hut. Tomorrow. After supper."

Fen's throat jumped in a swallow. His head was still whirring, his body faring not much better. "Tomorrow then."

Pesha released him and walked away.

FIFTEEN
HAVING A PALAVER

What else did I say was different for halfling births?"

"Ah…" Fen grimaced, searching for the answer he *knew*, if he could just calm his mind. Mairead had been patiently asking him to recall his lessons of the day all morning, but his focus was all over the place, nowhere near the level she deserved after the time and learning she'd offered him. He was thinking about meeting Pesha at the well that night for their evening chore…of what would come after. The daggers. "The hair. The hair."

"What about the hair?" Mairead ran a finger gently down her little songbird's tail-feathers, cooing. It was good to see her smile after the way he'd left her the night before, frazzled and dejected.

Fen dangled his feet over the short cliff overlooking the river. He'd been working up the courage to jump in for hours, but his recklessness didn't extend to battling heights—one of the few genuine fears he possessed. She'd insisted it was perfectly safe, that she did it all the time with Niallan, but it was a heck of a long way down, plenty of time to regret the choice after it was too late to take it back. "Most infants aren't born with hair, so it's not an effective indicator of whether there will be a familiar when you check the forest. But if they *are* born with hair, and it is not colorful, there will be no familiar."

"Very good. Our hair is linked to our familiars. A manifestation of our connection. No familiar, no color. Well, none except the bland shades men are known for." Mairead released Adir. His high song trailed him and then disappeared altogether. Fen felt Atio's presence wane as well, which meant she'd probably gone off with the songbird. Briefly, he wondered if they spent the time squawking at each other or if there was a more meaningful connection forming.

"So there are Medvedev out there with brown or blond hair?"

"Yes. There may be more Medvedev about the kingdom than you realize. Some halflings have no trouble blending in, if they can temper their magic."

"My sister…never mind." Fen was flooded with memories of Siofra's dangerous song sending them running, forcing them from hiding spot to hiding spot. Their whole lives had been a dance of conceal and cover, until Pesha had sprung them from that moldy jail cell and introduced them to another life.

Mairead smiled from the side. "We're having a palaver, Stiofen. Go on."

"Having a palaver?"

"A palaver. Do you not know the word?"

"I know the word," Fen said, "but I'm not sure I understand the way you're using it."

"Ahh. Having a palaver is when we are free to speak openly, without reprisal or fear." Mairead pulled a rock from the dirt and sent it soaring into the river below, where it disappeared in the rush of current. "You would like to tell me about Siofra, and I would like to hear about her."

"Oh." Fen frowned. He still wasn't used to her candor. It was unlike anything he'd experienced before, and it was the opposite of the way he'd been raised. *Draw no eyes. No ears.*

"So, go on. What were you going to say about your sister?"

Fen laughed to himself, shaking his head at his lap. "I was going to say that tempering our magic isn't as simple as it sounds. Siofra, she…Her gift is song, but it's not really a gift at all, for it brings destruction." His smile died. "Death even."

"We call them melodies," Mairead said after a pause. "And they are quite rare, a good thing, for, as you say, it's a destructive magic. A terrible kind. If she were here, she would not have the freedoms you and Pesha have been given, because we must consider the safety of all Medvedev."

Fen swallowed a lump of fear. "Now that I've told you, you're not going to…go after her, are you?"

Mairead squinted toward the sun. She shook her head. "No, Stiofen, but I do not recommend sharing this information with anyone else. You understand?"

"I think so, yes."

"But you can tell me anything. Nothing you say to me will reach the ears of anyone you wouldn't want it to."

Fen felt her words were truthful—that *she* was authentic in her interactions with him. But he couldn't forget who she was and that he'd only just met her. "Not even your mother? You'd keep this from her?"

"Especially my mother," Mairead replied, but it seemed she was speaking more to herself. "Your own magic. You haven't used it here. Is there a reason?"

"Flourishment?" Fen snorted. "My whole life, everyone wanted a piece. Wanted me to make *their* lives better, bigger, *more.* If I could excise it from me like rot, I would." He bounced his heels off the cliff wall. "Is that something…something that can be done? Can I be rid of it?"

Mairead shook her head. "You are not the first to ask or to wish it were possible. Anyone who has tried…" She exhaled. "They end up not so different from Farren."

"How is she?"

"You should ask Pesha. He spends his days in the Menagerie with Niall."

He should. He knew he should. Before, he wouldn't have hesitated to sit Pesha down and make him talk. But their moments together had become a convolution of desire and anger and fear and the other things they used to talk about but no longer could. When he showed up later that night to Pesha's hut, there'd be no talking then either, for Pesha had already set the tone for what the visit would be. "Yeah. I will."

"You won't." She smiled to herself. "I hear what you're not saying. And I understand."

"Do you? Because of Niall?"

Mairead's shoulders rose in a hard inhale. She tugged her braid over her shoulder, clutching it like a rope.

"We're having a palaver, remember?"

"Clever, using my words against me," Mairead said, but her smile had returned. "We've lost the ability to speak to one another. I haven't had nearly enough time to let it accumulate in my thoughts so that I might assess the potential outcomes."

Fen chuckled. "That's your first problem, Mairead. You think logic has a place in love."

"You sound like Niall." The corner of her mouth lifted in a forced grin. "We have not had a palaver, he and I, in many months. I've tried, but he only wants one thing, and I'm not keen to provide it until we've had a proper palaver. And so on and on we go, landing nowhere except misery."

"Sounds familiar." Fen wrung his sore hands together.

"Pesha means much to you."

"He means…" Fen sighed, almost smiling. "I don't know what he means to me, and I'm tired of trying to read his mind. He refuses to…have a palaver, but I can't keep doing what we're doing without one."

"Because intimacy cannot be fully realized with physical connection alone."

"Yes!" Fen cried. He spun sideways. "*Yes*, thank you. Thank you. Why does *he* not understand that?"

"If I could answer that, Stiofen, I'd know the way to Niall's heart as well." Mairead turned to face him. "You have had relations?"

"Relations? Sex?"

She nodded.

"It's a recent development, but yes."

"You healed your face but not your hands. Why?"

Fen immediately flushed in shame. What he wanted to do was ask how the heck she'd known his wounds were related to his and Pesha's quick but scorching session in the woods last night, but he dared not. "I didn't want others to know what had happened, but I wasn't ready to forget either."

"Every memory has its own beauty. I like to consider my favorites in isolation. It means I can enjoy the ones that make me happy without dwelling on the ones that make me sad." Mairead patted his knee. "You did well yesterday at the Hatchery. You were calm under pressure, asked good questions, and you made Ruairi very happy."

"Happy? How?"

"He does not have friends. Most won't even spare him a passing glance. Some are worse." She tossed another rock into the river. "I took him on as a disciple, so that he did not end up like the others."

"How did the others end up?"

"Most are driven away," Mairead explained, sighing. "What happens to them after...Perhaps it's best not to know." She flashed him another forged smile. "We are a loving people, but we are not always so kind toward those who were not born with every advantage."

"Then you're not so very different from men."

She stared straight ahead with a heavy look. "We think we are, but perhaps you're right."

Fen hung his head and peered at her. "Are you all right, Mairead? You haven't seemed like yourself since before the birth.

I know we don't know each other very well, but since we're having a palaver, as you say, I want you to know you can tell me anything as well."

Mairead wiped her eyes with a soft smile. "You're a special one, Stiofen. I knew it when I met you. And you're kind to say so. It's only that when your trade is midwifery, you see things others will never understand. To them, banishing someone like Kaia is a means of preservation, but they can only harbor such beliefs because they were not there when Kaia did the impossible. When she was given the impossible news."

"'If I cannot see it, I need not bear it,' men say." Even the words filled him with disgust. How many men and women had turned away when Fen and Siofra had been in trouble? Screaming, huddled, terrified…nowhere to turn. It was no wonder they'd ended up with someone like Steward Stanhope in Newcarrow. Only the opportunists had had time for the terrified orphans.

"A truly terrible notion. How can we call ourselves compassionate if that compassion extends only as far as our own huts?"

"I suppose some would say self-preservation is a form of compassion, compassion for yourself when you can find it nowhere else," Fen said, his voice growing quieter with each word. By the end, he had tears pricking his eyes. "But if we all had a little more compassion for each other, there'd be no place for selfishness in this world."

"Or *yours,*" she said with a wink.

It wasn't the first time one of the Medvedev had implied they were no longer in the White Kingdom. He thought of the raven they'd never sent. Of Siofra worrying herself sick over it. Des sending an army after them wasn't out of the realm of reactions. But if Fen's instinct was right, no army would ever find them.

"You're so easy to talk to," Fen blurted. He wondered why he'd said it, but he'd been speaking his truth all morning without realizing it. *Conceal, conceal, conceal* was a constant inner refrain when talking to someone new, but not with her. Ever since she'd shown him the Hatchery, talking with her had felt like the most natural thing in the world.

"You are too." Mairead smiled at her lap. A breeze swept over them, and she closed her eyes, tilting her face toward it. "It was why…I almost didn't come home after my sojourn to the White Kingdom. We speak with candor here, but candor is only bluntness. It isn't vulnerability. It isn't Kaia, on her knees, trusting us with the most sacred moment of her life. It isn't you following your friend on a treacherous journey you could have easily begged off of."

Fen was stunned. "You almost stayed in the kingdom."

She nodded. "Almost."

"What made you decide to come home?"

"Mother." Mairead's smile faltered. "I've enjoyed having a palaver with you, Stiofen, but we must away. Noontide meal beckons and then we should look in on Kaia and her little one. Perhaps another, after supper?"

"I would love—" Fen sighed with a sheepish look. "I can't. I'm sorry. Pesha…"

Mairead nodded and squeezed his knee. "Then you must go."

"Again!" Niallan cried from the top of the platform. He leaned over the rails, his eyes darting in wild passes as he followed the movements of Farren and the deer. Two Medvedev were crouched in the field nearby, ready to intervene in case of violence, but Pesha feared it was the rain that would stop their activities for the day.

It was the third familiar they'd introduced to Farren. Each one she'd rejected. Attacked. The familiars had already been broken using the methods Pesha had observed in their last lesson. But Farren…She saw either a playmate or prey. She either frolicked too hard, injuring the animals, or she turned into the wolf who had nearly killed Fen that night on the road.

Farren lowered, squaring up. She swayed back and forth in loose, languid movements that made her seem drugged. But no drugs or magic had been used on her since they'd arrived. The feral creature they watched in the field was fully herself.

"Why do you tame the animals but not the Medvedev? She's clearly not going to bond with any of them when she's like this." Pesha jutted his arm toward the scene in the field. It was caught in the dark net that obscured their little hideaway. They could see Farren and the animals, but they could not be seen from the field.

"There is one way to tame her. Only one." Niallan leaned farther over the rail, his eyes narrowing as he studied Farren and the deer. "This way."

Pesha's heart hadn't slowed for hours. His skin was a mess of sensitive flushing. Aches in his shoulders, his hands, and his feet had taken residence. But there was nothing adequate to describe what had happened to his soul after watching Farren fail repeatedly. "It's clearly not working."

"I should not have brought you."

"Of course you should have. I'm her brother." *Fucking imbecile,* he added in his head. "I should be *down* there—"

"If she sees you, this ends."

"I'm the only one here she even knows, Niall. The only one she trusts. The only one who won't scare her near to death if she sees."

"And then she will retreat into her comforts, where she will die." Niall gripped the wood and pushed off.

In the field, Farren circled the deer, spelling the outcome of her fourth try.

"If you offer the suggestion again, I'll set you on taming the familiars."

"You're *threatening* me because I want to protect my sister?"

"Have I threatened you?" Niall was again studying the activity on the field. His frown appeared and promptly deepened. "Ester! Corral the deer!"

Pesha fluttered forward, leaning over the balcony to catch Niall's attention. "Why? She just started. You didn't even give her a chance!"

"A chance to kill the deer," Niall said. He made some gestures at the other Medvedev in the field, and one quickly roped the deer and led it away. The other stayed close to Farren, her arms out, clearly ready for anything. "The inevitable conclusion."

"How can you possibly know that when she never got close enough? She probably didn't even get a chance to *sniff* the creature. How can you know if you aren't giving her a chance?"

"She's had four chances. She will get six more, for there are six displaced familiars left."

Pesha slammed his hands onto the railing. "And she'll fail every single one if you just pull them out before she even gets to try!"

"Pesha, I have been doing this for years. I have successfully re-paired over seven displaced Medvedev and familiars. You do not know what to look for. I do. Trust me and our ways, or I will reassign you."

"Seven? Seven in how many years, Niall?"

Niall scowled and faced the field. "Ten."

"Ten years. That's not even one per year." Pesha snorted. "Would there not be a better choice for this job, someone with the talent to produce a higher rate of success?"

"You know nothing of what you speak. You could learn, if you chose to."

"From you? From the one who loses more than he saves?" Pesha spun away. "It was a mistake bringing her here. I'll talk to Fen tonight. The best thing for Farren now is to take her back home, where she's comfortable, where she feels safe—"

"You may not." Niall joined him. "It's going to rain. We'll resume after noontide meal."

"I may *not*?" Pesha gaped, incredulous. Was Fen's mentor as brazenly obnoxious as this one? Were all "native" Medvedev such pretentious bastards? "We came here in good faith, and now we're going to leave in good faith."

"You did not come in good faith." Niall sized him up with an almost imperceptible sneer. "You may leave, but not with Farren."

"Why? Why would I not be able to leave with my sister?"

"She's not your sister."

"*Excuse* me?"

"You can leave, but not with Farren."

"What do you mean, she's not my sister?"

Niallan rolled his lips into his mouth and stared.

"Tell me why!" Pesha screamed. The sound came from somewhere deep and primal, an accumulation of years and years of rage he'd suppressed for so long, he'd forgotten it was there. He waved his arms in disgusted surrender. "Actually, I don't care what reasoning you give, because this isn't up to you. You're just a henchman."

"You are right," Niall answered, maddeningly calm. "It is the chieftainess who has ruled Farren must stay."

"Why?" Pesha kicked himself for doing exactly what he'd just said he wasn't going to do.

Niallan didn't answer.

"Until when?"

Niall still didn't answer.

"Until *when*, Niallan?"

"It's going to rain," Niall said and walked away.

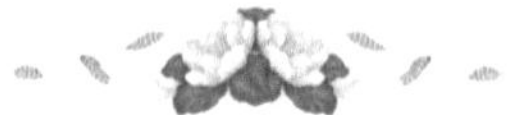

There wasn't even time for a hello before Pesha was tugging—*ripping*—at Fen's buckles, grunting, his faced flushed so red, the cause could only have predated his arrival.

Fen stumbled inside, reaching for something to stay him. He flailed for a table right as Pesha freed his cock and sent it gliding into his mouth, flesh on silk and warmth. Fen's eyes strained as they fluttered, his knees going soft, and he ignored the table, trusting Pesha's strong hands on his ass to be enough to keep him from utter disaster.

"Pesh—" His breath caught in a gurgle. Everything he'd planned to say—*Before we do this, can we talk? Can we discuss whatever this is, what it means, why it's the only way we can feel close anymore? Can we agree to try?*—disappeared in a haze of dusky desire. Every inch of him melted into the dug-in grip of Pesha's fingers in his ass, holding him aloft. Into the rhythmic devouring that had his toes curling toward the balls of his feet.

Pesha guided them slowly across the hard floor, never breaking pace. Fen gasped when the backs of his knees connected with something solid, but it was just the bed, the bed they'd never quite made it to in their interludes.

Fen crashed with a whimper and fell back on his hands, watching Pesha take his cock into his mouth in slow, delectable passes. The entirety of Fen's needs and wants pooled in the cobalt irises of the first man who had ever made his heart skip.

There'd been women here and there who'd lit something in him, though no more than passing glances and light throbs in his pants, reminding him there was more to him than what he could do for others. There *could* be more if he allowed it, but he never had.

Carefully, he stretched his hand down, reaching for his boot. He swatted the leather until he found the strap and removed the dagger. Pesha's eyes flicked to the side to watch, but his ministrations were as flawless and steady as before.

Fen hadn't realized his own intention until the tip of his dagger was marking his thumb, piercing it. A crimson trickle beaded to the surface. With his free hand, he palmed Pesha's head. Pesha slowly released his cock and sat back to watch, his shoulders lifting in hard breaths and eyes gradually widening as Fen slid his bloody thumb down the length of his wet cock. He clenched when a wave of pleasure hit him as he circled the underside of his head, swollen to smoothness.

Pesha's gaze flickered between Fen's cock and his thumb. He snaked his hand forward and clasped hold of Fen's wrist, then jerked it to his mouth, where he took Fen's bloody finger and gently suckled. Fen instinctively reached for his own cock to satiate the desire this stirred, but Pesha slapped his hand away with a scolding look.

With one last generous lick, Pesha released Fen's hand and lowered his mouth back over his cock. His primal moan vibrated down Fen's length, all the way to the base, driving a howl from Fen's throat loud enough to rouse the entire encampment. He imagined Pesha's mouth was his ass, that it was Fen taking charge, driving his cock deep and owning what he'd only before been chasing to catch up to.

Fen burrowed his fingers into the bed, his toes lifting as every muscle in his body tightened, preparing for release. And then he was spilling, erupting hard enough to briefly wonder if Pesha would choke on his spend. He bucked his hips until he'd given him every drop.

Exhaustion hit him like a solid wave of stone. He flopped back onto the bed, measuring his breaths. He could still feel the tip of Pesha's tongue scoring his length. If he could see his behind, he'd see ten angry-red indents. Later, when he was alone, he'd run his fingers along them and revisit the exchange in his fantasies.

Pesha moved to the table and uncapped his waterskin, then took a deep sip. He turned, smiling with his mouth full. His throat moved in a hard swallow that had Fen ready for another round.

"How was the Hatchery?" Pesha asked.

"Fine, but..." Fen sat up.

"I heard there was a baby born yesterday. Were you there for it?"

Fen squinted, shaking his head in befuddlement. "Are we done then? Don't you want..."

"To come?" Pesha shrugged. "That was for you."

"For me? Like...a gift?" Fen pitched forward. "Or were you doing me a favor?"

"No. No, Fen. It's not like that." Pesha spun toward the table, dropping down over it. "You said you wanted to talk. I was trying to talk. Now you want to fuck? We can do that too."

Fen's face grew hot. A tingle raced along his cheekbones. "Why are you turning my words on me like this? You *know* that's not what I meant." He suddenly felt exposed, foolish. In a rush, he leaped to his feet and buckled his trousers. His sore cock made him feel even stupider, his aching thumb a humiliation.

"I thought I was doing exactly what you wanted." Pesha's shoulders rippled as his tension mounted. They pinched together, lifting toward his ears. "But I can't win with you, can I? When I try to *show* you how I feel, you want to talk. When I want to talk, you want sex."

"What…What are you even…" Fen sputtered, surging toward the table. He leaned in and forced Pesha's gaze to find his. "There's a word for what you're doing right now, but it escapes me. It doesn't come from a good place though. It doesn't come with good intent. Whatever is happening to you…Whatever is going on in your head, in your heart…" He couldn't decide to finish.

Pesha threw up his hands and slapped them back onto the table. "Since you seem to have all the answers, go on then."

"I never said—"

"I don't know what you want from me, Stiofen!" Pesha screamed. His jaw dropped open, his throat jumping in stilted breaths. "I don't know how to *be* what you want me to be."

Fen balked, moving back several steps. The nearness of Pesha and his games, his confusion, was like standing too close to the sun. "What I *want* you to be? What the fuck, Pesha? I have only *ever* wanted…" He shook his head. "No. I'm not doing this tonight. I'm not…no. Good night."

Pesha didn't say a word. He made no attempt to stop him.

Not even a good-bye followed Fen out of the tent and into the night, more bewildered and exasperated than ever.

SIXTEEN
A COCOON OF COMFORT

Mairead was sitting on his bed when Fen returned to his tent. Her violet braid had been loosed, falling in waves. Though her head was bowed, he knew she was crying from the shake in her shoulders, and when she looked up, the tears in her eyes confirmed it.

"Mair?"

"I thought you'd be staying with Pesha tonight. Forgive my intrusion." She stood to leave, but he rushed over and nudged her back to the bed, dropping beside her. His hand hovered near her shoulder, not quite touching. He was unsure of what comfort looked like to her.

"You're not intruding. Did something happen?"

"I attempted to have a palaver with Niallan, at supper. It did not go as I'd hoped." Her chin quivered. She turned away, fixing her gaze on the wall. In her lap, her hands twisted. "I fear whatever our connection before, it has ended."

Fen took a chance, landing his hands between her shoulder blades. Her muscles tensed at his touch but then relaxed.

She smiled, but her eyes stayed on the wall. "I can be a good listener."

"You're wondering why I'm here and not in my own hut."

"I am," he said carefully. He wedged his thumb into his fist. She'd never connect the wound to the cause, but he couldn't shake the irrational fear everyone would see it and know not only what he'd done but how he'd been discarded like a toy after. "But you don't have to tell me unless you want to."

Mairead shook her head and grimaced. "There are unused huts in our encampments, but Medvedev believe our homes are embodiments of our energies. Even when we are not there, wisps of us linger. Your energy today soothed me, and I'd hoped to draw upon it. But now you're here, and I fear I've sullied your space, which was far from my intent."

"Now I'm here," Fen said. He smoothed his hand along her back. It felt right, and she didn't complain. "And I don't feel violated." *Not by you anyway,* he thought, nursing his thumb against his palm.

"You are kind," Mairead replied. She finally turned back around to face him. "Others may fling terrible words your way, trying to make you one thing and not the many things you are, Stiofen. You *are* many things. Everyone is. We are the sum of our choices, our thoughts, our beliefs, and our actions. We are not who our mothers and fathers were, not unless we want to be. We call you Forsaken, but…" She wiped the tears rolling down her cheeks. "Is it not the person wielding the word most affected by it? Is it not us who have absorbed the malignancy intended for others?"

"Mairead, what happened after I left you?"

She stared at her lap with tight shakes of her head. "Niallan is burdened with too much hate in his heart. He was born struggling and cannot forget it was Mother's charity that saved his life. He is never not wholly, painstakingly conscious of the disadvantage he carries, but he cannot grasp that is not how I or others perceive him. Yes, there are some who question my mother's affinity for him, but they've accepted it. Accepted him. Now, he turns that coldness toward Pesha, deepening the wounds that should be healing by now but are instead festering. I don't know how to reach him. Every day, he slips further and further away, traveling somewhere I cannot follow." She squeezed her eyes and straightened. "It started long before you arrived, so do not ascribe blame to either of you."

"Ah. Well, don't worry about Pesha. He's just as miserable as Niall. They're perfect for each other." Fen closed his eyes, inhaling the scent of her, of pine and blueberries and something he couldn't discern. He let it wash away the coppery reminders of the ways he never realized his heart could break. "I'm sorry, Mair. I'm sorry for the bitterness when you're already feeling terrible. I thought those days for me were…I thought things would be different. I thought they *were* different, and for a while…"

"Happiness is cyclical," Mairead said in a dreamy tone. She sniffled, laughing. "Though what they do not tell you is how unbalanced the cycles can be. Fortune favors the miserable sometimes."

Fen laughed with her. "You're sure right."

"Do you realize we're having our palaver tonight after all?"

"Not lost on me," Fen said, smiling. He had no reason to smile, but being near her left him full of the wonderful, safe sensations Pesha used to ignite in him. Her gentle but assertive kindness was both heartbreak and redemption, wrapped in one. He'd never met anyone like her, and the realization he'd soon leave and never see her again left a sharp pang in the center of his chest. "I enjoy being around you, Mairead. It may seem a strange thing to say, unprompted—"

"Not at all," she blurted. "Forgive me. Go on."

Fen flashed her a soft smile. "But you and I have both been hurt by others' unwillingness to communicate, and I like that this isn't so between us. How we can talk—palaver—and be candid, without worrying the other will respond unfavorably."

"I enjoy being around you as well, Stiofen." Mairead's smile eased, replaced by a more serious expression. "And I like the way we are with each other."

His heart thumped wildly, but his mind was a quagmire of uncertainty. All his life he'd kept his own desires locked safely away, but there'd been a cost, in the form of never having the opportunity to understand himself. To evolve each part of himself in equal measure. Eyes locked with Mairead's, he finally understood what it meant to be at peace. At ease.

So when she kissed him, her lips soft and safe, he afforded himself permission to evolve. To wind his hands through her beautiful hair and deepen the connection in the way he'd tried so hard to do with Pesha. She wasn't him—she could never be—but Pesha wasn't himself either. He hadn't been for months, and there was no telling whether the future belonged to the man he'd been or the one he'd become. Or whether Fen would still be waiting when it happened.

But there, in that moment, Fen knew who he was. Who she was. Who he wanted to be. *How* he wanted to be. So when they fell onto the bed together, wrapped in each other's weary embrace, he welcomed that too.

He pulled back and looked at her. Studied her cheekbones, high and pronounced…the bridge of her aquiline nose. Her bushy brows, as purple as her hair. "That was unexpected."

"Certainly not planned," she said, wincing playfully. "There is something Medvedev call the cocoon of comfort. It's a state of yearning that is neither sexual nor sensual but even more essential. To connect with another through touch and nearness with no expectation but kinship."

Fen chuckled. His hand found hers on the blanket. "Is that your way of saying the kiss was platonic?"

"No, for you already know that." She slid her fingers through his. "If men understood, *accepted*, the necessity of connecting on a physical level without expectation, there would be less war. Less bloodshed. Less strife."

Fen inhaled deep and released his breath slowly. "Mairead… What happened with the Forsaken? I mean, what *really* happened?"

She went quiet. He waited for her answer, only to realize her silence *was* her answer. She could neither lie to him nor tell him what he *wanted* to know, which only deepened his need to know.

"You can't tell me," he concluded aloud. "Can you?"

Mairead shook her head, but she didn't break their joined gaze. "There are clahnn secrets, and there are individual secrets. My mother is the only one with the authority to share the full story. I wish I could give you what you want, Stiofen. I'm sorry."

"What would she say if I asked her?"

"All life has wounds, and this is her deepest one. Would you re-open yours?"

Fen closed his eyes and sighed. "I don't think mine ever truly closed, Mair."

"The biggest ones never do." She brushed a kiss on his cheek. "Would you like me to stay?"

"Cocoon of comfort and all that?"

She nodded.

"I would like that. Very much." Fen closed his eyes and was asleep in minutes.

Fen woke abruptly. He rolled sideways and found Mairead gone, but he wasn't alone. When he opened his eyes, it was Pesha he saw, huddled at the end of his bed with his face in his hands.

"I sent her away." Pesha looked up, facing the door. "I don't blame you, Fen. She's beautiful. Kind. Not completely fucked in the head." He buried his face back in his hands, tugging at his hair.

Fen groaned and shifted, squirming to shrug off the heavy pall of sleep. "What are you doing here?" He closed his eyes again, swaying in exhaustion. His nose caught the scent of pungent liquor. "Have you been drinking?"

"We've made better spirits in our soaking tubs at Shadowfen," Pesha mumbled, his words split in half by a hiccup. "I can't remember which one…his name…but how could I say no? They have all the power here." Hiccup. "We have none."

Fen rolled his face against his pillow to stifle a scream. It still smelled like Mairead, like peace. "You're drunk. Go back to your own hut and sleep it off."

"You know…" Pesha's eyes fluttered, his mouth flapping wide, then closing. "I liked life better when it was simple. When I knew what to expect with every day. Wake, check on Des, eat, check on Des, business, check on Des. Watch Des fuck every midnight woman in Darkwood Run and hope they didn't kill him. Sleep."

Fen took a breath and held it. "Pesha. Go. To. Bed."

"But you…*you*…" Pesha clucked his tongue and snorted. He swiped at his nose, missing. "You and your fucking…" He screamed into his hands. "Seeing you in that cell in Newcarrow was…Ah, fuck. It was…It woke something in me, and I've been trying to put it back to bed ever since."

The acrid spirits burned Fen's nose. A queasy sensation rolled forward, from either the stench, the words, or both. "You can put your feelings, and yourself, back to bed." He clapped his mouth shut to keep the bile down.

"I came for your bed." Pesha's flushed face grew solemn. "I just didn't expect to find *her* in it."

Fen could've eased Pesha's mind about Mairead, but what would be the point? "Save your drunken confessions for the moon and stars. For the Guardians. For…anyone but me, Pesh. *Anyone* but me. I've reached the utter limit of what I can take from you."

"I thought she and Niall were together."

"It seems you and Niall have quite a bit in common." Fen squeezed his eyes shut with a groan and, realizing Pesha wasn't going away quietly or easily, sat up. "Whatever intentions you brought here tonight, I don't want them. I don't want your touch. I don't want your taste. I don't want…" Emotion choked the rest of the words. "Any of it. Please, just go," he pleaded weakly.

"I want to. Leaving is *soooo* easy." Pesha rolled his head upward with a drowsy laugh. "Why are you here?"

"*What*? I was sleeping!"

"*Here.*" Pesha gestured wildly. "*Here.* With me. With me on this cursed fucking mishap of a journey."

Fen clenched. "We've been over this. You've asked. I've answered."

"Yes, but…no, not really. No. No you didn't." Pesha's head shook in full, stubborn passes.

"Pesha, what on earth are you on about? Never mind. Stop. I don't want to know. You're drunk, and you're not…coherent."

"Nope. Nope, because what you never explained, what you *failed* to explain…" Pesha tapped the air. "Is why you would ever… *ever* want to do something this big for someone like…" He visibly deflated, slumping low. "Like me."

Fen's heart swelled with a dull ache. "What do you…Why would you say that?"

"I'm rotten, Stiofen." Pesha slapped his chest. "*Rotten.* To the core. Broken. Love didn't create me. Lust did. Lust."

"You're not saying…Are you? You believe what happened between Ludwik and your mother means you're not allowed to be happy?"

"LOOK AT FARREN!" Pesha leaped up and began a frenetic zigzag of pacing. "*Look* at what happened to her, what *is* happening to her! They're going to kill her, tomorrow, the next day, I don't know, and I see now it's because…" He made a strange gurgling sound, followed by choking sobs. "Not every creature is meant for this world."

"Wait, wait, wait." Fen waved his hands, catching up. "What did you say about Farren?"

"Familiar after familiar after…familiar. Rejected. She still has a few chances, but they aren't even giving her time to…Fen, they're going to *kill* her." Pesha stopped moving. He paled, staring at nothing. "They're going to kill her, and there's *nothing* I can do about it."

Fen tentatively pushed to his feet. "You know we won't let anything happen to her, Pesha. Right?

"And how would we stop it?" Tears poured from Pesha's eyes when he turned. "What can you and I do against thousands of Medvedev, in a world we don't even know *how* we entered?"

"Then we'll go get Des. Des will round up his men—"

"You keep saying that! Even if…We'd be too late, because they'll already have returned her to their fucking Light or whatever it is they worship." He stretched his arms to his sides, his head falling back. "You're right. I shouldn't have come here."

"Pesha Trevanion! You don't get to keep whirling in like a hurricane whenever you feel like it and then leave like…like nothing happened." Fen stormed to him and reached for his hands. He gripped them at the wrists and shook them. "I know what's happening here. You push me away out of guilt. You carry *everyone's* guilt when it's not yours to carry. To atone for. You did not do this to Farren. *You* put your life on hold and at risk to save hers. But even that you don't have to carry alone, Pesha, because it's a choice. Do you hear me?" He shook Pesha's wrists. "A choice."

Pesha ripped away. His head shook. "You don't understand. No one does."

Fen's voice broke. "The world may not understand you, Pesha, *but I do*!" Fen beat his fist over his heart. "*I* do! I know every trauma carved upon your soul, every ache in your neck from checking behind yourself. Every sore muscle from clenching in anticipation of some terrible thing swooping in to replace the last terrible thing, because there's *always* a terrible thing. Always. But I *see you, Pesha.* I see you the way you see me, and it's a beautiful and broken thing, but it's not hopeless. You are not hopeless."

Pesha's shoulders shook, but when Fen tried to comfort him, he angled away. "Don't."

"Why? Don't, why?"

"Just…don't."

Fen closed his eyes. So many thoughts and feelings and sensations competed for prominence, but all he had room for was the peace of silence. The peace of letting go when everything inside of him wanted to hold on. "Then until you're ready to talk about this…to face and accept things could be different for you…I'm done. Really done, Pesha. Now, please…" Fen choked on the lump forming in this throat. "Leave me alone."

"It's for the best," Pesha agreed and left without another word.

Pesha raced through the forest blindly, tripping over branches and bouncing off trees. Tears whipped sideways along his cheeks, scratched from brambles he was refusing to dodge. He welcomed pain, made an especial space for it. He craved it, the way he should crave love, acceptance.

When he reached the cliff's edge, he came to a stuttering halt, but one look at the raging river below gave him another idea.

He wiped his face on his arm and jumped.

The water was shockingly cold. He breached the surface, gasping. Laughing.

Sobbing.

Confident he could manage the current, he let his legs float upward, and he fell back until he was looking at the stars. Guardians. The Light. Gods. Ancestors. Everyone had a name for them, but no one had ever touched them. Seen them up close.

Somewhere nearby, Eshe had caught his distress and absorbed it for her own. She wasn't capable of crying, but her anguish was his anguish, and he should know because he'd been the one to give it to her. What joy had his familiar ever known, living her life at the bottom of a frozen lake? All he'd ever done was "manage" everything. Neat. Tidy. Clean. No room for joy, for light, or for happiness in managing. No cracks where the light might make its way in and offer false promises of a life that could never, ever be his.

But Fen?

Fen *could* be happy.

He should be happy.

But there was no chance of it happening if Pesha couldn't let him go.

"I'm sorry," Pesha whispered. The moon and stars blurred. The cold chilled his bones. "I'm sorry. I'm sorry, I'm sorry, I'm sorry, I'm sorry, I'm sorry..."

WHEREVER YOU ARE, THERE I'LL BE

FARREN

Wulf. Wulf.

EIGHTEEN
A CRY FOR JUSTICE

Fen pushed his foot against the boulder to keep his rocker in motion as he nursed his water. Sweat poured down his brows, satisfaction from another day's work. Beside him, Ruairi—or Air, as he preferred to be called—rocked Kaia's infant, Maia. For such a young boy, he was a natural with the infants, something Fen couldn't have imagined having had the maturity for when he was that age. Another mother, Fayda, was nursing the little boy they'd delivered that afternoon.

Fen, Air, and the others had been winding down the day in the small gathering area outside the Hatchery for close to an hour. The air had a welcome nip that cut the humidity and made the waning heat almost refreshing. Dusk would settle soon, which meant supper.

"Almost two weeks old already," Fen mused with a whistle. He mopped his face with his sleeve, soaking up the light breeze moving through the Hatchery. "Time has sure flown, hasn't it?" It was already time for them to select a new chore at the Dusktide Gathering, a relief for more than one reason. Not the least was how he'd been hauling all the water himself since his fight with Pesha.

"What does that mean?" Air asked. His brows fused in earnest interest. Anytime Fen said anything the little boy didn't understand, he wanted to know more. He loved to ask questions, and Fen was surprised to discover he enjoyed providing answers.

"It's an expression men use," Fen answered. He caught Mairead's eye from across the terrace, and they exchanged comfortable smiles. They'd spent most nights in a comfort cocoon, which was both the strangest and most heartening thing. He'd never have imagined he'd be sleeping wrapped in the arms of a woman he wasn't interested in sexually and, more, that it was helping heal his injured heart.

"Did you forget you were talking, Stiofen?"

"Yeah. Yeah, I did, Air, sorry." He shook his head and returned his focus to the boy. "It means that time often seems to pass faster when we're busy."

"Does it?" Air's face lit up. He stopped rocking.

Fen was tempted to lie just to keep the boy smiling. He'd turned it into a challenge of sorts, plying him with jokes and barbs at inapt times. It was especially delightful when he caught Air by surprise and the boy flushed with exhilaration of the unexpected. "We should all be thankful it doesn't. Life is short enough without time deciding it wants to move faster on us."

Air giggled. "What a strange thing that would be!"

"Indeed." Fen set his waterskin on the small stump between them. "I can take Maia if you're tired."

Air recoiled in clear offense. "I'm not tired."

"Of course not. You're an endless font of vigor, aren't you?"

The boy beamed and puffed up in his rocker. "I am an endless font of vigor," he whispered to Maia. "And don't you forget it."

"Watch, her first word will be 'vigor,'" Fen teased, laughing.

"I hope it's Air. Because of me, but also the sky." Air cocked his head with a dreamy look that made him seem even younger. "If I had a familiar, I'd want it to be a falcon, like Atio."

The boy's answer hit Fen in the chest like a punch. "Would you…like to meet Atio?"

"Meet your falcon?" Air lowered his chin with an astounded stare. "You'd introduce us?"

"Nothing so formal." Fen chuckled. "Besides, Atio already knows who you are."

"She does?"

Fen nodded. "She knows all about you."

"How?" In Air's arms, Maia cooed and squirmed, but the boy repositioned her, and she settled back down right away.

"Atio knows everything about me." When the answer didn't seem to mollify the boy, he said, "And, of course, I talk about you all the time."

Air beamed a smile at Maia. "Just me?"

"Well, you and Mair."

"Aww. I suppose that's all right."

"If you suppose, then it must be," Fen teased.

Mairead emerged from the hut again, waving. He nodded back, smiling in anticipation of breaking bread with her, cuddling with her. It was nice having a friend, he thought as he watched her return to the Hatchery.

But any thought of how comfortable and at peace he felt with Mairead was eclipsed by the pain of Pesha's absence. His silence. *Until you're ready to talk about this, I'm done* was as much an invitation as an ending, and Pesha had made his choice. According to Mairead, Farren was down to two more familiars to try bonding with, and after, there were no others. Fen still hadn't determined how they were going to get Farren out of Asgill without tipping off the rest of the clahnn, but he was working up the courage to ask Mairead for aid in the endeavor.

Then again, maybe Pesha already had a plan of his own. Fen wouldn't know.

Mairead appeared in the gathering area, but this time, she wasn't smiling. She nodded at him to follow her.

Palpitations fluttered in Fen's chest. "I need to go help Mair. You'll be all right without me for a bit?"

Air made a *pfft* sound. He rolled his eyes at Maia.

"Well, sorrrry for asking," Fen said, ruffling the boy's hair as he stood. Once Air could no longer see his face, though, any mirth died. It continued fading with every step, and as he approached the cluster of trees where Mairead was waiting for him, he held his breath.

"I will not make you wonder," she said quickly. She nibbled on her lip, and he realized he'd not seen her do it before. "I do not have good news, Stiofen, and I cannot foresee how you will react, but I knew you would not want to hear this in front of Air."

Fen shifted his weight between his feet, crossing his arms over his chest. "You're scaring me, Mair."

She sighed and nodded. "You already know how tense matters are in the encampment."

"I know the Medvedev aren't above prejudice," Fen answered, grinding his jaw.

"You know it's more than that."

"Yes. And I also know the only reason someone hasn't taken a knife to my throat is because I'm always with *you.*"

Mairead's face flushed with heat. "I would take the same knife to their own throats if they tried."

Fen almost smiled. "I know. But that isn't what you wanted to tell me."

She hung her head, but by the time she spoke again, she'd locked her eyes to his. He liked that about her. The way she spoke with respect, as though there was no one and nothing else in the world that mattered in the moment. He'd noted she did it with everyone, even those she wasn't fond of. It was her most endearing quality. "There's been a Cry for Justice sounded against Pesha."

"A what for what?"

"A Cry for Justice is when one Medvedev raises a claim of crime committed by another Medvedev. Anyone can declare one. For any reason. But for it to hold, there must be evidence." Her whole body lifted with her breath. With every word, her speech was faster, more harried. "Gellais was the one who made the cry."

"One of the assholes bullying Pesha?"

She nodded. "He was furious after you corrected his behavior. I can only assume any evidence he presented to my mother was forged, but...but, Stiofen, she *believes* it and has called for his confinement."

"Confinement? Is that..." His neck throbbed.

"Imprisonment. Yes. But it is not..." Mairead again breathed deep. "It is not like the confinement you experienced upon your arrival. They'll take him where we send those who are to be given the Trials and sentenced." She lowered her voice. Tears glossed her eyes. "But there is only one crime requiring confinement or sentencing. Only one punishment for such a crime."

"Murder?" But that didn't make sense, because he was reasonably sure Pesha hadn't been on a killing spree, even if Fen hadn't seen him more than in passing.

"Treason, which can only be charged if there is a murder or an attempt at one." She swallowed. "Death is the sentence. He's been accused of conspiring to overthrow the clahnn by assassinating my mother."

"Death?" Fen staggered back. He rubbed his neck. "They wouldn't...She wouldn't *actually*...right?"

Mairead's silence told him all he needed to know.

"Tell me." Fen coughed again to clear his throat, which was slowly closing. "Tell me *exactly* what they claim he did, with their so-called evidence."

"Gellais says he found a letter in Pesha's hut."

"What the *fuck* was he doing in Pesha's hut? That would be my first question, if I were Aoife."

"We do not recognize the same boundaries on space and property that you're accustomed to. Gellais has many faults, but he perpetuated no crime entering Pesha's hut. What he found—what he *says* he found—was a letter, purportedly written by Pesha, to his brother. It spoke of an uprising. It seemed to imply *he* was at the helm of it, carrying the legacy of Forsaken into a new…a new era. He requested an army."

Fen burst out laughing, caught in a wave of relief. "But that's ridiculous! We know nothing *about* the Forsaken, and your mother knows this!"

"I cannot speak for her. I only know they are on the way to the Hatchery to apprehend him and take him to the Twilight Grotto."

"Is that…" Fen dug his hands in his hair and screamed inward. "This is not good. This is not, *not* good. How long do we have?"

"Until he's taken?"

Fen nodded furiously.

Mairead glanced at the sun. "Not long. It will happen before evening meal."

"Then we still have time." His heart spurred into purpose. "There's still time." He clapped his hands, working through the plan in his head even as he was nodding at Mairead. "Tell Air… He's good with Maia. He's good at what he does. And I'm proud of him."

Mairead's eyes reflected fear. "Stiofen, I do *not* like what I am hearing in your voice right now."

Fen grabbed her by the shoulders and kissed the edge of her mouth. He squeezed, released, and tried to smile. "Everything will be all right. I know what I have to do. It will be all right."

"Stiofen!" she cried, but he was already running.

He didn't stop until he neared the hill at the north end of the Hatchery, pausing only long enough to scan the area for signs of Pesha. He spotted him on a raised platform with Niall. They were watching something in the field below.

Fen started toward them when he felt the earth move. He turned and saw a dozen Medvedev marching down the path, stoic with purpose.

He whipped his head toward Pesha, but Pesha was still watching whatever was happening in the field, as was Niall. It was better that way. If Pesha knew what he was about to do, he'd stop him.

"Aye! Over here!" Fen called. He jogged back up the path, putting Pesha and the Hatchery behind him. "It was me. I wrote the letter!"

The Medvedev stopped. A male in front whispered something to a female beside him. They nodded at each other.

"You claim responsibility for the seditious words?"

"All of it." Fen raised his chin bravely—or what he hoped seemed brave. Inside, he was a mess of nerves and chaos. He had no idea if he was doing the right thing, but Pesha wouldn't survive whatever they had planned for him. "I wrote it. I left it in Pesha's hut. It's mine."

"No!" screamed a small voice. "It's mine!"

Fen froze. All the blood in his body plummeted toward the dirt. "*Air*. Go back to the Menagerie. *Now*."

"I wrote the letter!" Air cried. "It was me!"

"Ruairi, you come back here, now!" Mairead yelled.

"It was *not* him." Fen pushed his words through gritted teeth, storming up to the sentries, his head shaking. "He's a little boy. He probably doesn't even know his letters."

"I know my letters," Air said in a haste of flushed pride. "I know them all."

Fen seized the boy by his shoulders. His hands shook as he said, as firmly as he could, "Air, you listen to me right now—"

"I wrote it! I wrote it! I wrote it!"

The Medvedev again whispered. The male pursed his mouth, sighed, and said, "There is only one answer to this. You both go."

"What? No!" Fen released Air and staggered to the sentry. "Listen to me. He's just a boy!"

"And it will be a matter for the chieftainess to determine what is to be done about it," the man said, still and emotionless. In his eyes, though, was a twitch. Was it anger? Regret?

Fen gasped when his hands were shoved together, tethered by invisible bindings. Beside him, Air yelped.

"You will have a garden for food, a stream for water, and flint for fire. Blankets and pillows have already been placed for you.

You will remain in the Twilight Grotto until you are given the Trials."

The man raised his hand, and Fen and Air both stumbled forward, pulled by their hidden magic. Air was sobbing, and Fen wanted to tell him what a foolish boy he was, to scold him and shake him, but he felt the sobs straight to his soul. He recognized them. Suddenly *he* was a boy again too, holding the world at bay so his sister could breathe.

"I'll protect you," Fen swore, looking into Air's terrified eyes. "I promise."

Air whimpered and closed his eyes. Tears rolled down his cheeks. "I'm not afraid."

Hot tears burned Fen's eyes. "I know you're not. I know you're not, Air."

Somewhere in the distance, Mairead was screaming.

Fen swiveled his head to catch one last glimpse of Pesha. This time, Pesha was looking directly his way. He started forward in alarm, but Niall grabbed him and jolted him back into place.

And then he, and the rest, were gone.

NINETEEN
YOU ARE I AND I ARE YOU

The day had started like any other. There'd been no sign it would end with Fen being hauled away by sentries.

Pesha and Niall had been doing what they did every day. Heat wavered the air, obscuring the lethargic standoff between Farren and a hare in the valley. It had been the hottest day of their visit so far—the hottest day ever for Pesha, who had spent the entirety of his sheltered life in the cool Northerlands.

The temperature was a match for the frustrations brewing in the encampment. Every hour Pesha spent in the beautiful but cursed place offered a new threat, a fresh glare. Every walk from the Menagerie to the camp had become a nerve-wracking march of doom, every taste of his food, a roll of fate.

Say nothing, Niall had coached Pesha after Gellais had left the remains of a deer's carcass in his hut, swarming with flies and rot. *Give them nothing.*

It almost seemed like Niall was on his side, but Pesha knew better.

Pesha mopped his brow and shifted his weight, transferring his exhaustion. Like every day in Asgill, Pesha had risen at dawn, shoveled fruit in his mouth in a daze, and followed Niall to the Menagerie without a single word exchanged, where he'd watched Farren do exactly as she'd done the day before and the day before that. And now she was down to two. Two chances to bond before they declared her unfit for rehabilitation.

Even Niall had started to show signs of worry. The smug self-importance of the intractable Medvedev had cracks in it. Sometimes he'd tap two fingers against his palm, mouthing the word *two* like a silent war chant.

Pesha had no reason to believe the next two attempts would be any different than the first eight. Niall might rue his next professional failure, but Pesha had been searching, for days, for a way to secret his sister out of the Hinterlands. Night seemed best, but detection was the least of his concerns when he didn't even know *how* to escape the clahnn lands. There'd been magic involved in their entry. That much he knew.

Fen would have a plan. Maybe he already did.

Fen.

Pesha had had almost two weeks to rise to Fen's challenge, but time had only separated him from the words he needed to say. It had eroded his courage and filled him with a thousand reminders of why his and Fen's separation was the best thing for Fen. The only thing.

"Coming on dusk," Niall said. He rolled his hands over the railing.

"Not hungry," Pesha muttered. "I'll stay here and watch over Farren."

"The day ends at dusk." Niall tapped the railing, his face shifting into some new sour look while his eyes widened. His chin tucked back in surprise.

Pesha turned. The air left his lungs.

A hundred yards to the east, Fen was being carted away by a dozen Medvedev sentries. Beside him was a small boy, whose eyes were trained on Fen.

Screams echoed from somewhere.

"What are they doing to him?" Pesha demanded, starting forward, only to be jerked back by Niall's iron grip. He tried to rip away, to no avail. "Get your hands off of me! Can't you see something terrible is happening?"

"I will find the truth of the matter," Niall said, almost kindly, but it was the uncharacteristic fear in his voice Pesha latched onto. Whatever was going on, the chieftainess's own adopted son had been caught by surprise. "*Stop* resisting."

His insides felt touched by fire. Belly churning and chest aching, he could do nothing but stare, powerless, as Fen was dragged down the path. Fen glanced back, their eyes catching, but then he was gone.

"Let me *go*!" Pesha screamed and jammed an elbow into Niall's side. The Medvedev yelped but didn't relent.

"I will release you when I am certain you cannot trace their path."

Pesha twisted hard enough to send a sharp bolt of pain tearing through his shoulder. "What? Why? Why?"

Niall leaned in. Through gritted teeth he said, "I know where they'll take him. If you follow, they will take you too."

"Where are they taking him then? Why are you just staring at me like that? Niall, we have to *do* something." Pesha's breathing became labored, forcing him to pause and refocus. "Why are you people so enamored with your secrets?"

"Forgive me," Niall whispered, and Pesha immediately learned why.

He was tugged to the railing. Looking down, groaning, he confirmed his suspicion that his hands had been bound and tethered by invisible magic to keep him from running. "You're not serious." He jerked his hands, accomplishing only pain. "Niall!"

"I'll return with answers." Niall tossed him a glancing look of apology. "Mair!" he cried and raced away.

Finding his way to Eshe hadn't been a conscious decision. In fact, it had been the opposite of one, for he'd been consciously *avoiding* visiting his familiar.

When Niall had returned with the news, Pesha had only heard half the words. *Fen. Imprisoned.* Except that hadn't been the word Niall used.

Took your place was the phrase haunting Pesha's steps as he staggered over underbrush, swatting branches and scooting over damp, mossy logs. What had Fen been thinking? But of course, this was typical Fen, Pesha thought, leading with recklessness. *Act before apology* was something Ludwik used to say, and though it burned Pesha to be thinking of his late monster of a father when his heart was so weak, the saying fit Fen to a T.

"You fool," Pesha muttered over and over, sweat stinging and blinding his vision. It poured down his chin and disappeared into the forest, leaving a wake of angst and rage. "You fucking fool, Stiofen. If they don't kill you first, I will."

He collapsed on the riverbank. His eyes closing in exhaustion, he flopped onto his back, arms flung wide, and exhaled through a small gap in his mouth.

I'm here.

They weren't words but a sensation, a flood of warmth and comfort formed into a message he understood. He propped himself on his elbows, searching for what might have caused it. But he already knew. He'd always known. He'd been hearing it his entire life. He just hadn't been listening.

That's you, Esh. Right?

It was, the sensation confirmed. He clapped his hands over his mouth in a sob. How had he…but he didn't deserve it now any more than he'd deserved it then, leaving her to wither in stasis for years and years. *No other choice*, he'd told himself, even when

Des had offered to bring in skilled tradesman from the guilds of Whitechurch to engineer a better solution.

Do not despair.

The message was a catharsis, seizing Pesha. He rolled onto his side, shaking with tears. *Esh, I don't deserve your comfort. I don't deserve your understanding. I don't know how I let myself believe leaving you alone was the only way.*

You are I, and I are you.

Pesha stilled. The message was simple enough, but there was something more to it, just beyond his reach. *I want to understand, Eshe, but I don't.*

You are I, and I am you.

I don't...I'm sorry. I'm failing you again. Pesha sat up and wiped his tears. They felt too much like self-pity. *How are we...Is this talking*? He winced, the weight of his failures closing in. *Like the way Fen can talk to Atio?*

Eshe's response was affirmative.

Pesha choked out a laugh. *Really? After all this time*?

I've always been with you.

That's not true. Pesha's head shook in defiance. *I abandoned you.*

Always with you.

"Pesha."

He swiveled on the ground, turning toward the sound. Mairead emerged from the forest. Her violet hair was snarled, her eyes shot with red.

"Oh, it's you." Pesha scrambled to his feet. "Niall told me next to nothing."

Mairead's arms were crossed so tight, she was practically hugging herself. "Gellais claimed to find a letter in your hut confirming you are leading a coup on behalf of the Forsaken." She leaned down and wiped her tears on her arm. "And Fen..."

Pesha was speechless. Gellais. The ruffian Fen had humiliated. "He said he did it?"

She nodded.

"But..." He scoffed, scowling. "This is simple to clear up. I wrote no letter."

"I know." She stared at the river.

"Then that's all we have to say." Pesha frantically dusted his pants off and started toward the path. "We just have to go to your mother..."

Mairead's bowed head slowed him.

"What? What aren't you saying?"

"My mother ordered his confinement."

"Mairead, all I have to do is offer a sample of my writing, and it will be clear it was not me! Nor Fen. This is ludicrous, easy to disprove, so why..." He trailed off with a slow breath out. "They're going to martyr him, aren't they?"

"I do not know, Pesha. Nothing feels as it should right now." She cleared more tears and pinched her shoulders back, letting her arms swing to her sides. "We must be at supper, or it will rouse suspicion."

"Supper? Are you kidding?"

Mairead shifted her gaze to the side.

"Mairead, you *know* this is wrong! You know I...Well, perhaps you don't know me, but I *know* you know Fen. I know you care for him."

Her throat moved.

"I know you care for him," Pesha said again, the desperation from earlier taking hold. He flexed his hands, laughing. "Why would we be beholden to a cause that has offered us nothing but exile? One we know next to nothing about?"

"You speak with rationality, but I fear none exists in this matter." She again turned toward the path. "We must go."

"No." Pesha crossed his arms and planted his feet. "I'm not sharing another meal with any of you until we fix this."

"Then you may eat in your hut alone."

"Mairead, why are you so calm about this?"

"I am not calm!" Mairead's scream bounced off the trees, startling them both. "Powerless is what I am. What you are. So we must return, perform as expected, and then perhaps, we can find a way."

"Perhaps? *Perhaps*?" Pesha sneered at her and turned back toward the river. "Then tell me what really happened with the Forsaken. You owe me that."

"I cannot." Her voice sounded small. "I'm sorry." She began to leave.

"Wait!"

"I cannot, Pesha. I'm sorry. There are some things..." She secured her bow and ran, disappearing between towering pines and marigold flowers.

When she was gone, Pesha thrust his hands to the side, tilted his head back, and screamed until his voice went hoarse.

"Aoife," he muttered when he was spent.

If Mairead and Niall were too neutered to do what was right, Pesha would go to the source of the problem herself.

TWENTY
THE TWILIGHT GROTTO

Their prison was more accurately a cave. A system of caves, if Fen was being pedantic, and despite his foul mood, he still cared about details.

When imprisoned or otherwise imperiled, details could save or cost a life.

Fen and Siofra had spent almost two decades hopping from cellars to dungeons until finally landing in a town jail, and those places all had one thing in common: danger upon danger.

The Twilight Grotto, as he'd heard one sentry call the place, was one of the most beautiful places he'd ever seen. The system of smooth tunnels had been carved into elaborate arches and smooth pathways. Walls were covered in chiseled drawings, the styles all unique enough that it was clear they'd been done by not one but many people. Ferns peeked from cracks, but they were not the source of the delicious floral scents he couldn't identify.

Fen and Air followed the roar of running water down fork after fork, until they emerged in a clearing of sorts.

"A garden," Air whispered. "Look, Fen, look! There's strawberries and cabbage and carrots and…" He went on, naming everything he saw.

Fen marveled at the lush hideaway, not part of the cave but encircled by rock walls that didn't, at first examination, seem remotely scalable. There were several archways around the perimeter, but they led back into the same labyrinthian system.

Atio's caw overhead drew his notice. Emotion welled in his chest as he waved at her, knowing she could come no closer. He was relieved to see her flying free, a lone consolation amidst uncertainty.

While Air entertained himself with an inventory of the garden, Fen stepped across the small stream—a fresh water source, as he'd been promised—and stared up at the waterfall streaming from the top of the cavern. It rained down over the edges, covering one of the doorways back into the caves. He had a strange urge to go stand under it and let the force of it sweep him into the stream and out to sea.

"Why would you use this as a prison when it has so much more to offer?" Fen joined Air, who was picking blueberries and popping them into his mouth with aplomb.

Air shrugged. "What is confinement like where you live?"

"Ugly. Dark. Cold. Not a place you want to end up."

Air shivered. "I wouldn't like that."

"No." Fen mussed the boy's hair with a stilted sigh. "You wouldn't. Were you by chance listening when they explained where the flint is stored?"

Air dug into his pocket and withdrew two charcoal sticks. "They gave it to me to hold."

Fen smiled. "The sun is waning. We'll want warmth before it fades."

Air fanned himself. "But it's so *hot*."

It was indeed hot. Almost as hot as late springtide in Newcarrow. But there was a storm building on the horizon, and the rain would cool the earth. "It won't be when night falls. It will also be too dark for us to navigate these passages."

"It will be completely dark?" Air's brows knit in concern.

"I can only assume so, unless the Medvedev's magical light show extends to us here," Fen quipped. "Hey, look. It will be fine. We just need to be ready is all." He twisted his mouth in thought. "Blankets, they mentioned. Pillows. They didn't pass you anything to cook with?"

Air was well acquainted with fear, but the caves didn't scare him. They were like puzzles, and he liked puzzles. He told Mairead delivering babies was a puzzle of sorts, and she'd understood him fully, which was part of why he loved her so. She was also kind when others were not. If he were to die in the cave, she'd be the only one who would miss him.

The doorways and corridors were the most freedom he'd ever had. He could run down one and then another, and no one was there to yell at him or look him over like he was rotted meat.

All his favorite foods grew in the garden. With no one to stop him, he could eat until he was stuffed silly. He didn't think Fen would stop him. Fen was like him.

He couldn't wait to show Fen all he'd found in his effort to mind-map the cave: blankets, pillows—both things expected, of course, but that wasn't all—and also a rusted cauldron for stews. Air could live off blueberries for the rest of his days, but Fen would want proper meals, and they could have them.

A place to sleep, to eat, to bathe, and to languish. Why, it wasn't confinement at all!

"Look at all that," Fen said, his voice filled with the same wonder brimming in Air's excited heart. "Send you off for an hour, and you come back with everything we need."

Air swelled with pride. "Tomorrow I'll find more."

"I don't doubt it." Fen examined the cauldron, smiling at Air. "I can sand some of this off with a rock. Will be fit for food in no time."

"Will you show me?"

"Of course I will." Fen wiped his brow with a faraway look he cast down one of the passageways. "You all right, Air? Feeling okay after everything that happened?"

Air balked to show he was brave. "I told you I wasn't afraid."

"Oh, I know you're not. You're the most courageous person in this cave."

Air giggled at the joke. "*You're* not scared…Are you?"

"Not scared. Concerned," Fen answered, after what seemed like forever. "But we have all we need here, and we have each other. So let's make the best of it."

Air followed him to a pile of vegetables and fruits Fen had gathered from the garden while Air had been conducting his search. He nodded, mesmerized, dreaming of all the ways they could cook everything up. But then he realized he wasn't hungry. His face fell. "Maybe I'll just eat berries tonight."

"Yeah? Me too." Fen smiled, and Air's mood healed instantly. "Come on."

Air helped him lay out the blankets and pillows, and by the time they were done stacking everything, it looked more welcoming than his own bed. He nodded approvingly. "This will do."

"This will do," Fen agreed.

After starting a small fire for warmth—Air didn't quite believe they'd need it, but he trusted Fen, and Fen had more experience than he—eating handfuls of berries, and filling their skins with water from the stream, they lay down together on the mound of quilts.

Air had never trusted the quiet. The fully grown Medvedev whispered about him. Joy left a room when he entered one. But with Fen, it was nice. It was safe. And he knew he shouldn't feel happy about being in confinement, but he did.

"How long have you been aiding Mairead?" Fen asked from beside him. They were both staring at the protrusions on the cave ceiling, but Air doubted Fen was naming each of them the way he was.

"I don't know how to..." Air flicked his fingers in the air. "A while."

"You're good at it." Fen propped his hands behind his head, wiggling a bit. "You've taught me a lot."

"Me?" Air was stunned.

"I've never been around babies, let alone delivered them," Fen said with a soft chuckle. Then he sighed. "My sister—my twin sister—is with child."

Air knew this, but not because Fen had told him. He'd heard others whispering about Fen, the same way they whispered about him. "Is that why you want to learn midwifery? For her?"

Fen nodded. "Not that I was given much of a choice, but yes. Out in the world, Air, there's no one to tell us what to do, how to do it. No one to teach us about ourselves. My sister is carrying a child that no one knows how to protect, or when they'll even come."

"What is it like having a twin?"

"The best." Fen grinned. "Siofra and I didn't have the easiest life when we were younger, but we had each other. Always."

"And your familiars."

Fen didn't answer at first. He rolled to his side and planted a serious, thoughtful look on Air. "There is *nothing* wrong with you, Ruairi. You are no less Medvedev than anyone out there with birds or fish or cats or whatever."

Air wished he believed that. He almost could, lying next to the only person, aside from Mairead, who'd ever spoken to him like he mattered. "Sometimes... When I can't sleep..." Air pulled one of the quilts tight to his neck. "I change my story."

"Change your story?" Fen tucked his hands under his cheek, offering his full attention.

"I like to tell stories. I like it even more than delivering babies," Air explained, with some reluctance. He hadn't even told Mairead. She was kind and understanding and everything he could have ever wanted in an older sister, or even a mother, but that was precisely the reason he never bared his heart. Losing her would be too painful, and now…now he was taking that same risk with Fen, his new friend.

"Oh, yeah?" A slow grin spread across Fen's face. His eyes sparkled with interest. "Will you tell me one, Air?"

Air frowned. "You want to hear a story?"

"I'd *love* to hear a story."

It was almost too much to absorb. He didn't think Fen was putting him on, but it would break Air's heart if he was wrong. "Will you…tell one with me?"

"You mean together?"

Air nodded, his breath held tight.

"Sure. All right." Fen nodded at him. "You're the expert, so why don't you lead us?"

The expert. Air swelled with purpose. When had anyone called him an expert in anything? "Let's tell a story about the cave."

Fen gestured for him to go on.

"All right." Air took a deep breath and puffed it out. "There was this cave. *This* cave. It was very magical."

"Of course."

"*Everyone* wanted to live there, but they weren't allowed." Air bit his lip and nodded at Fen, showing it was his turn.

"Oh, ah, well…" Fen screwed his mouth, squinting in thought. "Everyone wanted to live here, but the honor was reserved for the most special—" He abruptly stopped when a screeching sound echoed off the cave walls in the distance.

"Only a bat," Air said lightly. "They won't hurt you."

"Ah. Right." Fen didn't look convinced, but he cleared his throat to continue. "You see, the cave wasn't just magical. It was a portal to another world." He nodded for Air to take over.

Air's eyes widened. "And even if others found their way to the Twilight Grotto, they wouldn't see this whole other world. Because only the most special could. But this boy and his friend were special enough. They go to the cave together and find…"

"A bat!" Fen cried, and they both laughed. "But this was no ordinary bat, screeching in the darkness and scaring people silly. This bat could talk. And it said to them…."

Air's heart was racing so fast, he almost lost his words. "It said, 'You must pass three trials if you are to enter. If you pass, you can live here. If you fail, you die.' The boy and his friend were not afraid of any trials. Their lives were hard before they'd come to the cave, and the world had been very unfair to them. They knew if they stayed…if they stayed in their world, they'd probably die anyway."

Fen swallowed and cast his eyes away for a moment. "The first trial was they had to name every single plant in the garden. The man was utterly lost, but the boy was a natural, and he got every one of them right without stumbling at all."

Air giggled in delight. "The bat was very impressed. He'd never seen anyone pass the trial so fast! But he was secretly feeling quite devious because the second trial would be harder, and he knew the boy and his friend would fail. He made them blindfold themselves and said, 'If you can find me, you pass.'"

Fen whistled through his teeth. "Ooh, and this was a tough one for them, wasn't it? Because bats are—"

"Bats can see in the dark!"

"Right. Bats can see in the dark. Of course. So the bat had *aaall* the advantages in this situation. What he did not tell the boy and his friend was that if they were to fail, he would make a meal of them."

Air gasped.

"And our bat was starving on that particular day, so he was *very* invested in making the trial impossible for them to win."

"But the boy's friend had excellent senses. The best." Air fought a yawn. He wasn't ready to sleep. There was still so much left to the story, and it was just getting good. "And after several hours of wandering, he found the bat. The bat was *very* angry. He felt tricked. So he changed the last trial and make it a hundred times harder than the one he was going to give them."

Fen chewed his lip, nodding. "Very hard..." He seemed to be thinking. "No, it wasn't simply very hard; it was impossible. The bat knew they could not pass the trial, but there was something else at play here. The bat could proctor the trials, but he was not the master of the caves. There was another who decided the wins and losses, and they were not hungry, like the bat. They wanted the boy and his friend to win. So when the bat told this other entity what trial he had planned, the entity was pleased, for he knew there was more than one way to win."

Air squirmed under the blanket, fighting the call for sleep. They had to finish. He already had an ending in mind. "The bat said to the boy and his friend, 'You must climb the garden wall and escape if you want to live.' And the boy's friend was scared because he knew the wall couldn't be climbed."

"The boy's friend tried anyway," Fen said. "He tried and tried and tried, not for himself...but for the boy, who still had his whole life ahead of him."

Air swallowed a lump. As he readied for his grand finish, he worried Fen wouldn't like it. That he'd find it silly, and the story would be ruined. But he didn't think Fen would find it silly or declare the story ruined. "He watched his friend climb and fall and climb and fall for hours, but the boy didn't want to leave. He wanted to stay. When his friend fell for the last time, unable to go on, the boy turned to the bat and said, 'I don't want to escape. This is my home now.'"

Fen lowered his eyes. When he spoke, his voice was strained. "That's exactly right. And when the boy said the words, the bat knew he'd been duped. He knew the boy had outsmarted him, and he had no choice but to accept his loss and follow through on his promise to allow the boy and his friend to stay."

"The boy and his friend lived there for many years. For the rest of their lives even! Which were very, very long because the cave was magical, but also because they were happy, and happiness makes you live longer." Air's eyes fluttered closed. He smiled. "Story ended."

"Story ended," Fen whispered. He reached over and patted the blanket around Air's body. "Rest well, Air. We'll have more adventures tomorrow."

When Air was fast asleep, Fen wiped his tears and let his mind drift into peace, clearing a path for Atio.

Have you found us a way out?

Atio's answer made his heart sink.

Then I need you to do something for me, and you cannot refuse. No matter how much it will pain me, I need you to do it.

Atio listened. Refused.

I'm telling you to go back to Shadowfen Hall, that I'll be fine! Siofra needs to know...Des needs to know. We're never leaving here, Atio, but you *can. You can go, tell them what happened, and still have a life left to live when I'm gone.*

But they both knew that wasn't true. If Farren wasn't proof enough of what happened when a familiar and Medvedev were eternally severed, there'd been plenty of other examples of it in the Menagerie.

I cannot, for we are not in the same world as Siofra anymore.

Fen felt her message stab him like a dagger. *Not in the same world anymore.* And hadn't he already known that? Was her confirming it a comfort or a loss?

The only way out was the way they'd come in: at the mercy of Aoife and her sentries.

Mercy, though, was the last thing he expected.

He'd have his trials, whatever that meant, but the outcome had already been decided.

His only hope was to convince them to let Ruairi go.

TWENTY-ONE
THE OPPOSITE OF JUSTICE

Pesha paced outside Aoife's hut. Other than the sentries staring gravely ahead, no one knew he was there. Niall certainly would have stopped him, and Mairead would have tried to talk him out of it. Neither would have helped, and he had no time for obstacles. No time for anything, if Niall had been right about the "trials" happening in three days.

"You may enter," a sentry said.

Pesha allowed himself a moment to gather his wits and stepped inside.

Aoife was standing beside a table on the far end of her tent, pouring a garnet liquid into two wooden mugs. Spirits, he assumed, until she turned and handed him one. Steam rolled off the top. Tea.

"Thank you for meeting with me," Pesha forced himself to say, accepting the mug with no intention of consuming a drop. He didn't think the chieftainess would poison him, but yesterday, he hadn't believed she'd imprison Fen on false charges either, yet that was precisely what she'd done.

"It is our way of hearing what others would speak." Aoife gestured toward a chair, but Pesha was too anxious to sit.

"Then you'll hear Fen when he tells you he had nothing to do with this supposed letter."

"He was never suspected of it. You were. Yet we do not deny anyone the right to stand in judgment for another." Aoife sat and sipped from her mug. She breathed deep and sighed into a smile. "You should discard your fears and try some. I made it myself."

Pesha grimaced and set the mug on the table, then backed away and crossed his arms. "Respectfully, that makes me less inclined to drink it."

"We do not weaponize nature to serve us. The only way you'd consume poison in Asgill is if you sought it out yourself." She took another deep swallow. "There are many plants that would suit, should you decide this is appealing to you."

"Should I decide…" Pesha tilted his head, approaching in disbelief. "Are you *encouraging* me to eat hemlock, or have I misunderstood?"

"I am not encouraging you to do anything. Nor forcing you, as is your implication." She gestured around. "You have been moving about our land freely for weeks."

"I wouldn't have been for much longer, if your lackeys had gotten to me before Fen did something foolish." Pesha steadied himself. He breathed deep, remembering why he was there, and grudgingly sat. "Fen has done nothing wrong."

"We are not in disagreement." Aoife watched him closely, wearing a placid, even look. Her hands, wrapped around the mug and white at the knuckles, seemed to reveal another side to her. "Fen has taken your place in judgment."

Pesha flattened his palms on the table to restrain his anger. "And I do not *accept* him taking my place. He had no right to. I'm asking you to release him and confine me instead."

"And I am refusing." Aoife's thin lips disappeared in a scowl. "Our laws may not make sense to you, but they have served us for many, many eras, and they will serve us for many to come."

"All right, but…" Pesha closed his eyes. Breathed. "*I* wrote no such letter either. So if Fen is being punished on my behalf, then you're speaking of the opposite of justice, Chieftainess. I am not guilty, which means Fen cannot be guilty."

"We do not decide guilt, but intent." Aoife's hands moved to her lap. "A letter stirring rebellion can only have ill intent."

"But I *have* no intent toward you! I did not write the letter!"

"That is not for me to decide."

"Aoife—Chieftainess." Pesha was losing his control. He felt what little power he brought to the exchange slipping away. "Why would I write such a letter? I came here to save my sister, and how does…does inciting a coup help me do that?"

Aoife's shoulders lifted. "Your motivation is your own. Your parents—"

"Told me *nothing*. Told Fen *nothing*. We don't even know why they turned on you. We know nothing about those days because neither they nor you will tell us."

Aoife seemed to consider this, but her response made his heart fall again. "I had my concerns when you arrived, but even I did not foresee you would seek to continue the work your mothers and fathers started."

"But that's not what's happening!" Pesha's hands slipped from the table. He trapped a groan in his throat. "I have no ill will toward you or anyone here. Nor does Fen. We only want to make Farren whole and then return to our home, where we belong. Because…I see we don't belong here. I know we do not. So *please*, let us finish the work with Farren and then leave quietly, and you'll never have to see or hear from us—"

Aoife abruptly shot to her feet. "You may plead your cause at the Trials."

"But—"

"We are done." She whistled, and the hut flap opened. Sentries waited on either side. "Unless you would like to join Stiofen in the grotto?"

"I'm not leaving. I want to see this evidence—this letter."

"And you may. At the Trials."

Pesha shook his head, bewildered and more lost than before he'd endeavored to sway her. He studied the flex under her cheekbones and the strain in her smile, and the answer was suddenly painfully clear: she'd never intended to hear him out. And these "trials" would be only a farce, a means to carry out the intention she'd borne all along.

There was but one crime among the Medvedev requiring punishment, and only one punishment for the crime. Aoife wasn't the one he needed to appeal to, because her resolve was set. But there had to be someone else.

He grudgingly thanked her for her time and left. Something else about the exchange was nagging him, but it wasn't until he reached the river, and Eshe, that it dawned on him what it was.

Unless you would like to join Stiofen in the grotto?

The grotto. It was the first indication of where they'd taken Fen. Had she assumed he already knew, or had it been a slip? Without knowing, he could hardly trust the information. He'd not made the mistake of thinking Aoife was their friend, but he'd not thought of her as an enemy either.

Pesha curled up by the riverbank, his face close to the water. He examined his distorted reflection with disdain. Eighteen years he'd lived, and he didn't even know himself—who he was. The face staring back at him, however muddled, was unrecognizable. It could have been anyone. Having found no value in his life beyond service, his features—his desires, his needs and wants and loves and dislikes—had blended into a caricature of a man.

Peace.

The flood of comfort had him sobbing into the muddy bank. He rolled his face through the sludge, inhaling. *Eshe, they're going to kill him.*

Peace.

Where could I ever find peace in this?

Mairead.

Pesha laughed bitterly, spitting mud into the water. He coughed, expelling more wet dirt, and rolled onto his back. The morning sun broke through the trees, bathing him in light. *She claims to care for Fen, but when it mattered, she ran.*

Mairead.

Eshe, listen to me. She cannot help us. She will *not help us.*

Listen.

Eshe—

Listen.

Pesha listened. And, for the first time in their entire lives, her communication was one he fully understood.

When she was done, he closed his eyes and cleared his mind to make room for all she'd imparted.

Fen was in trouble. Fen would die if Pesha couldn't find a way to intervene in what the Medvedev were determined to do.

But there was more.

The boy, the one who had been with Fen when he had been apprehended, was also in trouble. Pesha didn't know his name, but he thought it might be the orphaned halfling Fen had taken a fondness to. Fen's energy would be spent protecting the child, even at his own expense.

Pesha couldn't count on Fen to be working toward the same aim as he was, but according to Eshe, he didn't need to be. Because there was someone with the influence to alter the path they were on.

Mairead can be turned had been Eshe's message.

"Are you sure, Esh? Absolutely, positively certain? Because I may only have time for one plan, and if you're wrong, Fen pays with his life." Pesha immediately wished he'd kept the words inside, instead of giving them life.

Sleep. You will see.

He felt Eshe turn in the water, curling up into her sleeping position. Pesha mimicked her movements on land, drawing his knees to his chest.

With no better choice, Pesha breathed deep, closed his eyes, and slept.

The afternoon was shrouded in fog and an eerie calm. It was the type of quiet that made Pesha want to start hollering and jumping around to break the fugue and shed the unease stealing over him. But his unease came with good cause, because it was the day of Fen's execution.

Fen and the boy stood proudly along the forest line. The boy made himself seem taller, chest puffed and shoulders back, and occasionally glanced up at Fen for a proud nod, which Fen was generous in offering.

Pesha surveyed, with his heart racing, the growing crowd. There were hundreds of Medvedev, at least twice the count he'd seen since their arrival. He searched for the face he knew he would be there and was not disappointed.

Gellais, grinning in smug satisfaction. He was the only guilty party in the clearing that day, but the Medvedev had a different idea about justice than the one Pesha had been raised with. It was apparently fine in Asgill to frame someone for a crime and execute the accused without reasonable proof.

Pesha spotted others he knew. Cassair. Fiachra. Niall and Mairead. And of course Aoife, trussed in elaborate finery for the occasion.

They will simply spell them into eternal slumber, *Mairead explained. She was a wreck of tears and angst, but Pesha struggled to feel anything for her but bland contempt. If anyone could have swayed Aoife, it would have been her daughter, who had instead opted for tearful silence.*

Eternal slumber. They had a way of making even murder sound peaceful. And that was what this was. Murder. Execution without cause had but one name.

As Pesha perused the crowd once more, his eyes passed over Fen and the boy. Fen was watching him with a sad but otherwise placid look. At peace, Pesha would have said, if not for the rage tearing through his own heart, which hadn't beat properly in days.

I love you, *Fen mouthed. His shoulders jerked, as though he was going to use his hands to complement the message, but they were bound by magic.*

Pesha locked up. His mouth opened, but all that escaped was a desperate sob. He had to say it. It was the only chance—his very last chance because he was going to fail. That much was clear. He was out of time. There would be no final-hour rescue. No change of heart.

When all Pesha did was stand and stare, Fen smiled sadly and turned his attention back to the boy. He said something that made the boy nod and beam. Pesha couldn't put words to what he was seeing, but he was witnessing something he'd never been a part of but should have. There'd been a place for him in this triad, and even now, Fen seemed to hold Pesha's spot. But he was a coward and had chosen the coward's way.

Even now.

At the end.

Soon he'd have to explain this to Siofra, and imagining her face was what broke his daze, sending him crashing to his knees in tears.

The ground was ripped away and so was Pesha, and suddenly he was whirling through time and space, rushing past Fen and the boy and into the forest. He flinched as he flew past trees and brambles, but even when they connected, he felt nothing. Whatever was happening to him was both real and not, tactile and ephemeral. When at last the dizzying voyage ended, he was back at the riverbank, near Eshe's favorite spot.

Mairead stood staring away from him, her arms crossed in the same despairing pose as the last time he'd seen her there. When she turned and saw him, she wilted in relief and rushed over.

"Pesha. There's still time. We can—"

Pesha lunged forward with a wheezing gasp. The sensation of falling sent him plummeting back into the leaves, and he clawed at the air as though he could climb it.

His panic subsided. He closed his eyes, breathing in and out to find his calm.

It had been a dream…but more.

Mairead had turned him down before, but Eshe had known what Pesha could not: if pushed, she would cave. Whether her impetus was her love for Fen or her rage at the injustice, none of it mattered.

For the first time since Fen had been taken, Pesha had hope.

"Thank you, Esh. For everything," he said and jogged back to the path, aimed for the Hatchery.

TWENTY-TWO
CHAOS IS NOT YOUR ENEMY

Sleep had come grudgingly. Every time Fen had drifted off, a sound would have his eyes flying wide, his ears listening for danger. Between the steady patter of water coursing down a wall somewhere and the echoes of voices, sometime in the night he'd accepted he was imagining things.

But none of it prepared him for the slamming reminder he had slept in a cave as a prisoner, alongside a boy he'd come to care about.

Air had complained of the chill that had appeared and disappeared randomly throughout the night, which Fen had noticed too. It was nonsensical; there was no place for a draft to carry, and yet the cave was draftier than a wind tunnel.

"To the garden?" Fen asked, trying to put a smile back on Air's face.

It worked. "Oh, I can't wait to see if I missed something yesterday. There's so much…Who do you think tends it?"

Another shiver tore down Fen's spine. Who indeed. For there was no one else except them, and it was a fair amount of work, caring for a garden that large, if no one was using it.

They got lost twice on their way to the garden. There was enough natural light slipping through cracks that they didn't need the torches they'd found, but Fen wished they'd brought one anyway. If they weren't done by the time the sun shifted to the west, they'd be wandering back in the dark.

"I think today is the day we make a stew," Air declared. He launched into a sprint when the path lightened further, teasing them with a view of the garden ahead. "You coming?"

"Right behind you!" Fen had to stop for a moment. He leaned against the wall, fighting a rush of tears. If he accomplished nothing else, he would save the boy. He would make Atio promise to look after him, to pick up the bond, offering Air the life he'd been dreaming of since he was born.

"Breathe. This is your strength. Chaos is not your enemy." Fen closed his eyes, whispering the words once more, and pushed on until he reached the garden.

Air was already gathering a hoard in his arms. He'd turned his tunic into a makeshift sling, something Fen wished he'd thought of the night before.

Fen stepped through patches of cabbage and past a long row of plump pink grapes growing tall along trellises. A haze blocked the harshest of the sun's rays, and the waterfall created a glimpse of a rainbow, which had Fen tapping Air's shoulder. "Look. Look."

Air gasped. "It's beautiful."

"It is." Fen smiled and dropped a hand onto his shoulder. "It really is."

Air leaned against him with a series of endearing sighs. He was the most unusual boy Fen had ever met, wise beyond his years and yet also still so small and innocent. Fen's urge to connect with him was equal to his need to protect him. "Mairead says they're gifts from the Light itself. She said they appear when we need them."

"I suppose that's true, isn't it?" Fen gave Air a final squeeze and released him. "Go on. I'm starving." He wasn't, but Air shouldn't witness his guardian's rolling, erratic emotions. "More of those blueberries!" he called after him.

"All right!" Air called back with a quick fist in the air.

Fen took stock of the garden in a way his stressed mind hadn't allowed the night before. It wasn't merely a food source; it was an oasis. Even the beauty of the Asgill forests didn't come close to the way the little escape made him feel like he'd been transported to yet another world. It was a peek into a place belonging to another time.

He scanned the cliff walls, searching for any patterns in the protrusions that might reveal a path out. But the rock was smooth, enough to lend credence to the idea someone had done it intentionally to prevent escape.

Later, when Air was sleeping, Fen would return with a torch and take another look.

The mist from the waterfall painted his skin in humid dots. He ran his hands down his damp face and knelt to fill both waterskins as he watched Air, his tongue wedged between his teeth in fierce concentration, move from plant to plant with firm resolve.

I think I love him. The thought stole Fen's breath.

"Right," he muttered to himself and returned to the waterskins. His thoughts drifted to Pesha. The ache that never dulled. Would he be there to watch Fen take his final breaths?

"Stop doing this to yourself. This isn't who you are." Fen slapped his face and winced. "You thrive in crises. So thrive. If not for yourself, then for the boy."

"Who are you talking to, Stiofen?" Air shouted from across the garden.

"Myself, as usual." Fen laughed. That was better. He was better. He could do this.

Water. Food. Warmth. Companionship. They had all they needed. Allowing himself to dwell on the rest was the last thing he or Air needed.

"Look at all of it. We'll never eat it all," Air declared, skipping happily at Fen's side. If the boy realized the fate awaiting him, he never showed it. Fen hoped he didn't. He wanted nothing more than Air's days in the caves to be free of worry.

I'll save him, in the end. I'll find a way.

"Says you." Fen nudged him teasingly. He did it again, but his boot caught something on the floor, and he went flying.

"Fen!" Air dropped his hoard and raced over. "Wow, look at that hole! You almost fell into it."

Fen groaned and slid along the cave floor. He planted his hands and pushed up, returning to the cause of his busted ankle. Air was right; the hole was large, and deep. Fen dropped a rock and waited to hear it land, but the sound never came.

Air gaped at him. "Do *not* fall down that."

"Absolutely not." Fen gave the hole a wide berth and helped Air collect his fallen plants. "I saw you found some leeks—those cook up real nice—and some fennel. Oh, and look at the size of these carrots! You picked some good ones." He smiled up at the boy, but the color had drained from Air's face. He stared fearfully ahead.

Fen turned and saw a man standing in the center of the path.

He shoved Air behind him, hands held out to the sides. "Don't come any closer. Who are you?"

"Who are *you*?" the man asked. He hobbled forward, stepping into the light. His dark, near-black hair was tied back, sweeping long and low. He was thin, his flesh covered in a sheen of dust and sweat, but he wasn't dirty. His clothes were fresh, not a hole or a loose seam that Fen could see.

"Prisoners," Air answered, popping out before Fen could swat him back. "We'll have our Trials soon."

The man cocked his head. Laughed. "Trials. Yes. Medvedev are entitled to those, aren't they?"

Understanding dawned on Fen. *Dark hair. Not Medvedev.*

"Say nothing else, Air," Fen said with caution. His pulse quickened. The race for control of the situation was on. To the man, he said, "We're not looking for trouble. He's just a child. We'll return to where we've made camp and go on our way."

The man's face scrunched in contemplation. He stared, wordless, swaying on his feet. "You have it wrong, young ones. I am no danger to you." He held out his bony arms. "Look at me."

"How long have you been here?" Air asked.

"Oh, about…" The man's eyes flicked upward. "Twenty-five, thirty years."

"Twenty-five or thirty *years*?" Fen stepped closer. "You've been here for over two decades?"

"Closer to three, I think. I stopped accounting for time after a spell. Does nothing, really. And who would care? You're the first people I've talked to in half that time."

Fen sensed no danger from the man. Pity took the place of his apprehension. "What's your name?"

"Ensel," the man said. He nodded at Air. "And I see you've found my garden."

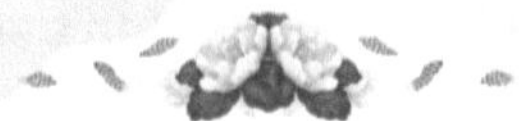

Pesha was almost to the Hatchery when Niall came racing down the path.

"There you are!" Niall doubled over to catch his breath.

Frowning, Pesha pushed past him. "I won't be coming to the Menagerie today. I have something else I need to do."

"Something more important than watching Farren bond with her new familiar?"

Pesha went stock-still. He couldn't have heard that right. The fractured sleep—the stress—was playing havoc with his mind.

"Pesha?"

"I'm sorry, did you just…Did you just say…" His mouth filled with an acrid taste.

"I said Farren has *bonded,* Pesha."

"You…" Pesha staggered off the path until he found a tree, then doubled over, retching into the fallen leaves.

"This is a good thing. She is healing. She will continue to heal."

"But she only had two left." Pesha heaved again. What was wrong with him? Why could he not feel the happiness he should be feeling?

"All she needed was one." Niall's hand hovered between Pesha's shoulders. He patted him once, a gesture as awkward as Pesha would have expected. "Don't you want to come see?"

"I do. I want that very badly." More wretched, cursed tears threatened. Guilt followed. How could he feel joy when Fen was languishing, waiting to die? When Pesha had done nothing except cry and lament?

"Then stand up and come."

Pesha followed Niall in a delirium of thoughts, past mixing with present. All of it streamed through his mind in a series of interspersed memories, the good and the bad. Des as a boy, teaching Pesha how to fish. Ludwik breaking one of his wife's beloved timekeepers when she wouldn't stop crying. Watching Des play with Wulf in the woods and carving initials upon a tree, wishing he could join them. Lotte sneaking him proper drawing charcoals when Ludwik had snapped every one of Pesha's in a fit of rage.

But the one that made his step falter was recalling the slow descent he'd made into the jail at Newcarrow, missing home and Eshe, praying his cover story would hold, and forgetting all of that when Fen's face appeared behind the bars, glowering with dark distrust.

Had Pesha ever been more determined to change a mind? From the start, Fen had resisted every offer of aid, obstinately defiant at every step, but it wasn't long before he and Pesha had found their common ground. Their respective devotion to family...their commitment to protecting their siblings, even at the expense of their own prosperity. Fen and Pesha understood one another in a way no one else did; they never had to explain their choice to forsake their own futures for Des's and Siofra's. The answer required no words.

He couldn't wait to tell Fen about Farren. To share the joy with the person who had risked everything so that Pesha wouldn't have to embark on the terrifying journey alone.

Farren healing meant they hadn't been cursed after all, that they were meant to be there. Together. Everything else would sort itself out.

It had to.

Pesha's steps lightened, pieces of his burden breaking off and crumbling away as they neared the Menagerie.

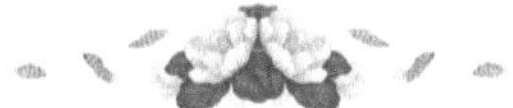

Fen was wary of the man, but Air could see right away he was going to be their friend.

Ensel helped them prepare a stew. He offered advice for seasoning and showed them other tips to add variety to their cooking. Air tried to memorize every word, excited for another chance to learn something new.

Fen said they'd only be there a few days, but Air desperately hoped he was wrong. He hoped they could live there forever, with their new friend Ensel. Of course, they'd need to sneak Atio in, because Fen needed his familiar.

They ate in silence, though Air was bursting for conversation. He had a thousand questions, but it was to Fen he looked for guidance. Fen must speak first. He was the elder, and Air trusted him to know when the time was right.

"Those walls." Ensel spooned one last bite, swallowed it, and set his wooden spoon aside. "You'll never scale them."

"I take it you've tried," Fen said. He hadn't relaxed at all throughout their meal. Air wanted to tell him it would be all right, that Ensel was a good man, but he didn't want to speak out of turn.

Ensel held up his hands, wiggling his fingers. Where once there'd been nails, he had only stumps. "Far too many times. And before you go thinking the three of us could do better than I did alone, we'd need thirty of us to reach the top." The man breathed deep. "Of course, there's another way out. Magic."

"What do you mean?" Fen probed, leaning closer.

"You look closely at the arches?"

"Close enough."

"Not close enough. If you had, you'd see one leads to a set of stairs that takes you up and into the forest, away from the caves."

Fen frowned. "Why would they want a door there when they brought us in through the main entrance?"

Ensel held out his hands in a shrug. "Now and then, I find new clothing or fresh blankets stacked at the base of the steps. I don't know who brings it, but I have my guesses."

"Who?" Air asked, unable to help himself.

"First, what's your name, little lad?"

"Ruairi, but you can call me Air. And this is—"

"Fen." Fen's hands clenched in his lap. Unclenched. "And now I'd like you to tell us how you came to be here for almost thirty years. You're no Medvedev."

The man looked down at himself in mock surprise. "Ah. So I'm not."

Air giggled.

Fen scowled.

"No reason not to tell you. If you're here, there's only one ending—" He abruptly cut himself off after a hard look from Fen. "She wouldn't want you to know, but the bitch locked me up away for half my life, so I can't say I'm compelled to protect her secrets."

"Language," Fen warned. He nodded at Air.

"I know the word," Air stated. "I'm not an infant."

"Pardon my colorful words, young Air," Ensel said with an overdone nod that made Air feel very special. "Your father is right."

"Oh, I'm…" Fen closed his mouth, his eyes on Air. "Thank you. As you can imagine…This has not been easy."

Air's heart beat so wildly, he was sure the men could hear it, if not see it. Fen had stopped himself before he could clear up the misunderstanding. He'd stopped himself before he could say he wasn't Air's father.

"You have a plan?" Ensel tipped a glance at Air, but he was looking at Fen.

"Working on one."

"If I can help, I will. But…" Ensel gestured around.

Air had no idea what they were talking about, but he listened, happy to be a part of it.

"You asked why I'm here. The answer is simple. The reason is complicated." He leaned back on his hands. "I was Aoife's mate, and as you can see, I'm no Med, which makes me a big problem for someone whose entire tenure hinges upon being tough with outsiders who meddle with insiders."

Fen rolled forward with a curt laugh. "You were Aoife'*s ma*te? Her human mate?"

Ensel's shoulders lifted. "Husband was the word I preferred, but Meds don't do marriage, not like us."

"Us. You can see I'm Medvedev, right? So is Air."

"Aye, but *you* were raised with men, weren't you?"

"What makes you say that?"

Ensel tapped his nose. "Can smell it on you."

"You can *smell* that?" Air asked. He sniffed around Fen, but there wasn't anything he could discern.

"I wasn't raised by men," Fen said slowly. "I was exploited by them. Tortured by them. Chased by them. I have no love for men." He rolled his neck and sighed. "Most of them anyway. And why would Aoife mess about with a man? That makes little sense."

"Love makes little sense." Ensel pulled his legs up to his chest and sat straighter. "We had a child. I don't know what happened to her."

Mairead, Air realized, excited to make a connection on his own.

But Fen made no comment about it, so Air followed his lead.

"We met in the Easterlands. I was a trader, traveling up from Gold Hill. Can't hear it now, I ken. This place leeched all the

Southerlands out of me. Anyhow, I'd injured myself in my travels…Ack, it's been so many years, I can't rightly say anymore what the injury was. Doesn't matter. She almost rode on by, but something compelled her to stop. She healed me. I won't tell you what happened next, since I'm watching my language and all." He winked at Air.

"Aww," Air whined.

"We spent about a fortnight together. I was late delivering my load, and she was delayed on her return home. When she left, I…Whoo, how many times now have I replayed the events of that day and wished I'd done different?" Ensel hung his head. "I followed her. I know now I could never have entered this place if I hadn't been right behind her, but I knew nothing then. Nothing at all. I wanted…It sounds foolish to say now, but I wanted a life with her. How was I to know how hated I would be to her people?"

"They didn't react well then," Fen said. He was fully engaged but also seemed to be elsewhere. Air could almost see his thoughts spinning, and he wished he could hear them.

"They never got the chance. She hid me away. At first." Ensel looked up. "Until she realized she was with child. In a panic, she stashed me here and promised to return for me. It was a year before I saw her again."

"How terrible," Air whispered. "Why would she do that?"

"It's complicated, I suppose. For her." The veins in Ensel's neck flexed. "For me, it never was. I loved her. That was all I needed."

"But why wouldn't she just send you back into the world? Send you home?" Fen asked.

"I reckon she was afraid of what I might say. Who I might tell." Ensel uncapped his waterskin and sipped, then wiped his mouth on his arm. "Or maybe she was afraid I'd take our daughter and run. She'd never tell me. Not on her first visit, nor her last."

"Which was when?"

"Three, four months ago. She comes once a year on the same day, and though I tell myself, every time, that I'll overtake her, force her to release me, I never do. I let her fall into my arms like that first night, and for a few hours, all is right again." Ensel cleared his throat. "She won't be back for a while."

The story made little sense to Air, and he could tell from Fen's stern concentration that he was struggling too.

"I have one more theory," Ensel said. "If the others knew, they'd kill me and then her. Here, she knows I'm safe."

Fen abruptly laughed. "You think she's kept you prisoner for half a lifetime because she *loves* you? Guardians, I'd hate to see what she does to those she hates."

Ensel grew deeply serious. "I suspect you're about to find out, friends."

TWENTY-THREE
THE UNEARNED CONFIDENCE OF A MAN

The enclosure was close enough that if Farren were to turn, she would see her little brother weeping, with his hands clapped over his mouth. But the lookout was glamoured, so she'd see nothing but more field.

Pesha splayed his hands on the thin glass, staring directly at his sister. She didn't know she was meeting his gaze exactly, a moment only half shared. She couldn't know the reason for his debilitating sobs was that it was the first time in over eight years he remembered how she'd looked at people when she was still herself.

Niall nodded beside him. "Well done, Farren," he whispered and tapped the glass. Then his softness was gone, and he was again the man Pesha was acquainted with. "Vaya is a lynx. A rare one. When her Med died, all of Vaya's fur fell out, and when it grew back, she was covered in silver."

"She's beautiful." Pesha swept his gaze over the gorgeous feline. It wasn't only her coat that was so unusual but her size. She wasn't much larger than a barn cat. "When can I talk to her?"

"She'll have three days of this." Niall nodded toward the frolicking pair. Farren had Vaya lifted above her head, the lynx pawing playfully at the air. "After which, reintegration."

"Reintegration?"

"She's free to leave." Niall picked up his bow, satchel, and waterskins. "Assuming she wants to."

"No assuming necessary. As soon as she's fit to leave, we're gone."

"You and Farren."

"And Fen," Pesha stated.

Niall glanced back at the window. "There's nothing you can do."

"About Fen? You're wrong."

"Take consolation…in knowing he will return to the Light and not be thrust into darkness. He's home."

Pesha palmed the glass. There was nothing to be said in the face of such blind fealty, the unflinching obedience to a leader who could be no wiser than her average citizen. Even though Desemir ruled firmly, it was always done with love. Niall could not, and would not, see that his mother's quest to vanquish all who spoke against her was not just. "What is it about your adopted mother, Niall? What is it about her that you quake at her slippers and cower at her authority?" He laughed in derision. "It's no surprise you and Mairead quibble so. You're exactly alike. How annoying it must be for you both."

"You have the unearned confidence of a man." Niall sneered, sweeping a stony gaze over him. "It is the only thing to explain your belief you have the authority to speak as one of us."

"You think *men* are overconfident?" Pesha's palm tightened as he leaned in. His peripheral gaze caught streaks of Farren and her cat racing across the field—what he should be enjoying, not arguing with a wall. "Your entire world is predicated upon the belief you're all exceptional. Where has *that* been earned, Niallan? Hm? Show me how you have come to see yourself as infallible so that I may *bask* in the glory of your enlightenment."

Niall, his nostrils flaring, a hard flush splotching his cheeks, leaned in and hissed, "You can only save one of them, you foolish man. If you keep pushing this, pushing *her*, you'll lose them both."

Pesha shook his head. Tightened his jaw. His mouth knit together. "That you believe there's ever a time when you'd choose between two people you loved tells me you know nothing about it."

"But is it love, Pesha, if you withhold it?" Niall scowled. "I have not been a perfect partner to Mair, but she has never wanted for..." He tugged at his collar. "For love."

"Fen knows how I—Niall, are you all right?"

Niall dropped to his knees, still clutching his neck. A red bloom spread up from his collar like a hand gripping his face. "Get...Mair."

He toppled face first into the grass.

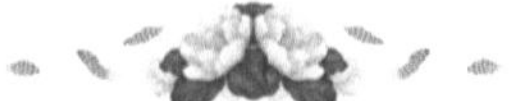

Fen and Ensel had been exchanging the same knowing glance for the past hour, waiting for the moment they could speak alone. Air at last drifted off, drowsy from a full breakfast, and Fen nodded for Ensel to follow him.

Nothing was said until they were far enough away Fen was sure Air wouldn't be able to read their echoes. "All of what you said is true?"

"And more." Ensel looked him over. "You never shared your story."

"We came to help someone we care about," Fen answered. He leaned against a dip in the wall.

Ensel, with a nod, found his own spot across the path.

"As for why Air and I are *here*, your lover thinks we were involved in stirring up a second rebellion. I think she knows it's not true, but she needs a show of faith for her people who don't want another round of Forsaken throwing their world into chaos."

Ensel's eyes fluttered downward and to the side. "Did you say Forsaken, like you're speaking of a group of individuals?"

Fen nodded. "Why?"

Ensel lowered into a crouch, cackled, and shot back up with a wild look. "That's what she called *me* when she threw me in here. She said, 'Because of you, now we are the forsaken.' I never could take her meaning."

Fen shook his head. "The Forsaken are Med who defied her and were banished for it."

"When?"

"What?"

"When did they forsake her and earn their banishment?"

Fen gazed at his feet, thinking. "About…twenty…" His head shot up in alarm. "About twenty-six years past. Give or take a year."

Ensel tapped his head and turned away, laughing. "Does knowing make it easier or more difficult to accept your fate?" The man seemed to be speaking to himself, so Fen didn't answer.

The Forsaken had turned against Aoife for her treatment against halflings, and in those same hours, Aoife had thrown her secret human lover into the grotto. But how were those two events linked?

"Did Aoife tell you anything about the uprising?" Fen asked. He ran the same set of facts over in his head again and again, but he could think of no connection between Aoife's imprisonment of Ensel and the treasonous exit of the Forsaken with the halflings.

"She never told me a damn thing about her world." Ensel dragged his hands down his face with a moan. "Or my child. What kind of mother keeps—" He pressed his mouth together.

"Mairead is wonderful." Fen pushed off the wall and approached Ensel. He squeezed one of his bony shoulders. "She's intelligent, kind, and very beautiful. She's taught me so much in the short time I've been here. I hope you get to meet her one day."

Ensel didn't seem to hear him.

It had been years and years since Fen had wished for his parents. He'd only just begun processing the traumas of his youth, but he'd never forgotten their caginess, their almost violent unwillingness to speak of a past they'd constructed on behalf of not only themselves but their children. Fen and Siofra had a right to know, and that right had been taken. Pesha's too.

Equally cruel was Aoife throwing a man she claimed to love into a mazey box she could visit over and over again.

But if Fen knew there to be one truth of the world, one key to unlocking the motivations of every terrible deed ever done, it was this:

The wounded know naught but how to wound.

The only way to take the knives from Aoife's hand was to find the one still stabbing her.

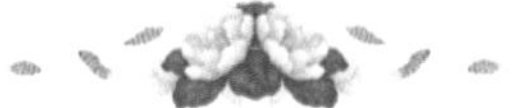

Pesha crossed his arms, one hand on his mouth, giving Mairead space.

From her chair at Niall's bedside, she looked up and said, "He'll be fine." She pulled a second quilt over Niall and patted his chest. "Rest, love."

"That's a relief," Pesha said.

"We can speak over here." She sounded as drained as she looked.

Pesha nodded, his eyes still on Niall as he moved past the bed to follow her outside. Two rockers overlooked the forest. She dropped onto one of them and flicked a hand toward the other.

"What was that?" Pesha glanced behind himself, but Niall was still asleep inside. "You didn't look surprised when you saw him."

"I wasn't." Mairead propped a foot onto a boulder and pushed off, sending the rocker into motion. Eyes closed, she tilted her head toward the sky. "Though it has been many years since he's had a tremor."

"What is it?"

"We do not know. The ones who think halflings are abominations claim it's evidence of his inferiority. Of nature being… displeased." Her face drew together in a tight scowl. "It's beyond what a healer can mend."

Pesha considered this. "What will happen to him?"

"He'll awake in a few hours with no memory of the episode, I'll drink an entire skin of wine to calm my nerves, and life will go on." Bitterness lined Mairead's quick grin. When it dissolved, she was crying. "I would take him away from here, if he would leave."

"And abandon your sanctuary?" The condescension in his tone jarred even him. "I'm sorry, Mairead. It's not you I'm angry with."

"Oh, you are. Of course you are." Her head lolled along the wooden rest of the chair. Her face turned toward him. "It isn't that I don't want to help him, Pesha. I have no lingering loyalty to anyone but Niall. But even saying this to you is a danger to both of us. Loyalty and fealty are the demands that hold our clahnn together. You and Fen coming here, with Farren…Ahh, especially with Farren…"

"Why? Why Farren?"

"Your arrival re-opened some terrible wounds of the past, for everyone. My mother believes she has no choice. Is she wrong? I'm not qualified to say. I would never strike upon that which I love, which is why it shouldn't be me who inherits the title." Mairead's face twitched. Her mouth pinched. "I wasn't born with only half a heart."

Pesha released his tension and toed the ground to push his chair. "If you were only born half-hearted, Mairead, Fen would never have taken to you as he has. He's *all* heart, Stiofen."

"Isn't he just," she replied, sniffling. "I can see why you love him, Pesha."

Pesha gripped the smooth wooden arms, curling his hands against the rounded edges. "We just want to leave here. Farren has bonded, she's found a new familiar, and we don't have to disrupt things for you any longer. We'll go and we'll never come back, but I won't leave without him. I won't."

Mairead's mouth trembled as she watched him. "Farren has bonded?"

"By some great mercy of whatever higher power is in charge here, yes."

"Does my mother know?"

"Niall may have told her. Whether she cares is another matter. She wouldn't listen to a word of my defense for Fen."

Mairead stopped rocking. She leaned over her knees. "Pesha, you overestimate my influence on my mother. She has never listened to my counsel, and I have tried, for Fen..." She pivoted toward him. "But I can do something else for you."

Pesha waited.

"I can take you to him."

TWENTY-FOUR
YOU ARE THE SUN

Mairead kept her eye on Pesha during Niall's frightened rebuke. Niall's hardship was that he was always afraid, a product of his birth and perceived deficiencies, but he failed to see that those who mattered believed he was just as he should be.

As they walked, she let him finish with his lengthy recitation of all the ways she was wrong. She heard his truth…his terror. He'd been warning her not to get close to the Forsaken ever since they'd arrived, but Niall didn't know what she did about Farren.

"Niallan. No." Mairead lifted her shoulders, sighing. *If anyone should understand prejudice, it's you. No amount of love has erased the pain. It does not have to be this way. There are other paths.* "No."

All she didn't say was tacitly understood. Their communication had been impossible to explain to Fen, or anyone who had not been raised in their ways. When one hummed along the same frequency as another, language was but a bridge across familiar water.

"Mair." Niallan crossed his hands over his chest. *You are not nearly afraid enough of the danger you keep putting yourself in. Only*

I, it seems, lose sleep over thinking of all the terrible things that might happen to you. "Ah."

Mairead waved a hand, making a *bah* sound. She had to do this. His acceptance would ease her heart, but was not required.

Telling Niallan the full truth had not been among her intentions. Secrets were anathema to peace, and her clahnn had so many, she never knew what was true for whom. This truth belonged to their mother, but not only her.

He laid a hand on her arm with a look of warning. *If you show him the way, he will find it next time without you.*

Mairead blinked. *How far simpler this would be if he did.*

Niallan's mouth curled up. Watching him watch her left her perpetually broken, knowing their love was slowly being destroyed by her mother's byzantine web of truth and lies. Would he heal or hurt to know Aoife had not merely banished his birth mother, Theta, but had had sentries follow her to the border and then take her rations and provisions? They'd then blindfolded her, marched her twenty miles away, and left her, naked and shivering, to find her way in the icy darkness. Whether Theta had lived or died was a matter for Aoife's conscience.

Aoife was the only mother Niall knew, but she was far less than he deserved.

I must, she mouthed. Her hands signed their secret symbol, fingers formed into a pair of stars. *Be with me.*

Niall's chin and cheeks dimpled. He was coming apart, for her, and trusting she would know where the pieces went. Tears pricked her eyes as she nodded, coaxing the trust she'd imbued in him for over twenty years.

Niall charged forward and gripped her braid in his hand with a firm tug. He crushed their mouths together, foregoing the last of his objections. Joining his fingers to hers, they made four stars from two, and Mairead lost the battle with her tears.

After all this time, that it was sedition closing their wounds seemed a very provocative message worth unraveling. Niall had been born in sedition, and Mairead had lived in the dark silhouettes of its limitations.

"I don't mean to interrupt, but…" Pesha nodded up at the waning light.

"Niallan and I have discussed a plan—"

"When?" Pesha balked. "How?"

Mairead grinned at Niall. "We communicate in our own way."

"We'll take you to Fen and leave you, for the night," Niall said, glancing at Mairead. It was a small gesture with big intent. He wanted her approval, and she nodded, giving it. "Mair and I will return to the encampment for evening meal so no one comes looking for us."

"And when we return, we'll tell you what you want to know about the Forsaken." Mairead didn't accept Niall's trenchant gaze this time. Pesha and Fen were not the only ones needing to prepare for hard truths.

"All right," Pesha said, looking between them as they marched along. "How much farther?"

"We're here," Mairead said. She pointed at a patch of grass growing up over a mound. "There's a system of steps that will take you to a garden on the edge of the grotto. It's the only place in the caves both the confined and the free can meet and visit. Fen will know of it, for it's the only food source in the Twilight Grotto."

Pesha surveyed the grass mound. He made his way over, tilting his head on the approach. "How do I know this isn't a trap?"

Niall snorted. "You don't."

Mairead shook her head at him. His sourness could be endearing, at times, but this was not one of them. "I'll go down with him, show him I can climb right back."

Niall shrugged and waited.

"Shall I go first?" Mairead asked, and Pesha moved aside to let her.

It had been years since she'd made the climb, but she still remembered that first rush of cool air when her head disappeared beneath the earth, followed by the peculiar warmth that stayed with her for the first fifty-seven steps. She'd counted all nine hundred and twelve enough times to be confident in her accuracy. She anticipated every crumbling spot where the carved steps had eroded away, adjusting to show Pesha how to safely descend.

Sweat was pouring off her by the time her feet touched the solid ground of the cave. She staggered a bit, adjusting, then reached out to help Pesha do the same.

Pesha dusted himself off and looked around. She grabbed him when he started down the path.

"You'll injure yourself if you hit the magic wall. Only the confined can explore." Mairead nodded the other way. "The garden is the only place that can be accessed by prisoners and visitors alike. The ward allows you to move freely about the garden, and the path back to the stairs. Test further boundaries to your own peril." She stood at the edge of the archway to the garden. Her eyes resumed old habits, scanning for her old friend Ensel. If she saw him, what would she do, apologize? Run? For years she'd been his only companion, until she'd suspected her mother was having her followed. It was for his sake she'd stopped visiting.

"Everything here is edible," she explained. "You see the stream running just there, and the waterfall and…." Mairead's words caught when she saw Ensel and Fen standing across the way, in the center of another archway. Pesha was already bounding through bushes and vines to get to Fen, but Mairead couldn't move. Ensel's penetrating gaze, brimming with pain and questions, rooted her. She couldn't even raise a hand in gentle hello.

Forgive me.

"We'll return after dusk," Mairead cried and raced back down the path and up the stairs.

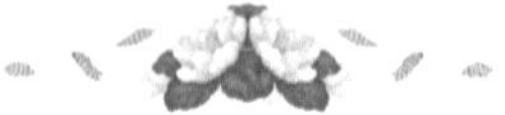

Fen couldn't have moved if he'd tried. He tilted his head slightly to the right, to ask Ensel to check on Air, but the man was already gone. The only thing he'd said at all was *that's not my daughter.*

Pesha thrashed his arms through the bushes, leaping over patches of cabbage and strawberry plants. Fen's pulse hammered with each passing second, confounding his sense of reality. Everything, from Pesha's hazy, piercing stare and his resolute stride to Fen's racing heart as he released the supports on every internal wall keeping Pesha out, was its own form of bewitching.

Fen was hurled back when Pesha barreled into him, sending them both careening into an apple tree. Pesha's hands smoothed over Fen's face, one and then the other, and then again, his eyes widening, his mouth parting, and his flesh buzzing.

Fen flattened and spread his palms over Pesha's chest, averting his gaze there, a break from the intensity. He pitched forward, burying his nose and mouth in Pesha's shirt with a splintered moan.

With one hand cupping Fen's scalp and the other skating across the edge of his jaw, Pesha dipped in to take Fen's lower lip between his teeth and scraped with a light tug. Fen rolled his head upward and breathed in the damp musk telling the story of Pesha's past days. He brushed his lips along the underside of Pesha's chin, bursting with things to say yet afraid speaking even one would reveal the reunion for the dream he feared it to be.

Pesha slid his hands until they were locked around Fen's neck. His gaze rolled over Fen's face, his body ripe with hunger. But his eyes tilted downward and his shoulders lifted in a sharp inhalation. His irises were glossy when he grimaced and forced his head back up. "Fen."

Fen's mouth twitched, watering with longing. "Pesh."

"There's nothing I can say, is there?" Pesha brushed his thumbs along the spots his eyes traveled. "Nothing except I waited too long for this."

"For what?" Fen asked, lifting to roll his forehead along Pesha's. A brief, soft laugh escaped. "For what?"

"To tell you..." Pesha's thumbs settled at the corners of Fen's mouth. He tightened his hold. "*You* are the sun, Stiofen."

"What—"

"My sky has always been dark and starless, by design. I was so afraid to be blinded, to lose my ability to thrive in the darkness. The shadows are where my true worth has always lived."

"Your true...ahh, Pesha Trevanion." Fen's hands moved to Pesha's wrists, curling around them. "I went years without seeing the sun. I *know* darkness." His toes curled as he lifted again, rested his cheek to Pesha's, and nipped down to take one of his thumbs into his mouth. "You do not have to give up what gives you purpose. You don't have to choose. You never did. And do you think it's what Des and Si would want for us?"

"And if we burn?"

"Then we burn." Fen's mouth pulled at the corner. "Then we burn together."

"From the first moment I saw you..." Pesha's head shook in silent agony. His mouth moved, his expression shifting in readiness to speak, but there was still one last barrier to overcome.

"Pesha," Fen said firmly, squeezing Pesha's wrists. "With me, you will always be safe. Sun, dark, or stars."

The first fat tear dislodged and rolled down Pesha's rosy face. Another followed, then another, until Pesha was shaking, head to toe.

Fen clasped his hands behind Pesha's neck and pulled him down, against his chest. "Shh. Pesh. None of it matters now." He buried his face in Pesha's hair, breathing deep. "You're here. With me."

They sank toward the garden floor still locked in position. Fen cleared away fallen leaves and sticks before easing them down until they were lying in the dirt, facing one another.

"I have so much to say," Pesha croaked. Tears rolled into the mud. "And I don't know where to start."

Fen smiled faintly. "In a crisis, I begin with what's the most important to surviving the situation at hand."

"Are we in a crisis?" Pesha seemed on the verge of a laugh. "I *cannot* believe those words just escaped my mouth. If *this* isn't an actual crisis, I'm certainly not built for a real one."

"This so happens to be the biggest crisis of my life too." With a glare at the sky, he said, "That's not a challenge, Guardians, you fickle bastards."

Pesha buried his face in Fen's neck as they both laughed. Fen held him tight, fighting a fresh wave of tears. It was a familiar pose. He and Siofra had been against the world for almost two decades, but now Siofra had Des, and he…He had Pesha. And Pesha had him, if he could fight the urge to withdraw.

Moments passed before Pesha pulled back. He wiped his eyes and lifted them toward Fen's. "Sun, dark, or stars," he said softly, breathlessly. He met Fen's gaze before lowering it to Fen's mouth, leaning in for a wisp of a kiss. "Stiofen. If I say what I need to say, will you pretend it's all right?"

Fen's heart caved. The tears he'd been fighting fell anyway. "I'll do better than pretend, Pesha."

Pesha nodded, averting his gaze to the dirt. He wiped his eyes, still nodding and assembling courage. Fen held his silence. This was Pesha's moment, the place Fen had come to months ago and waited for Pesha to catch up, to find him. He wanted to remember every word, every sigh, and every tic. Every brush of flesh, the precise demand applied to each kiss…

"When I was a boy, I had…two lives." Pesha's voice quaked. "I didn't know it then. That's the nature of trauma. There's what was and there's what you needed it to be, and there's no intersection. There can't be. I needed a father who approved of me and a mother who loved me, so I reformed those years to believe exactly that, while Des and Farren and Wulf—ah, and Lotte and Euric, all of them—fashioned a world for me that was safe from the strife plaguing the Hall. But they…Ah, they remembered all of it. Lived all of it. And because I believed the fantasy and not the truth, when Farren's little…When *Nera* was murdered by my father, it suited me to believe it was…" Pesha's entire face pinched in pain. "Farren's fault, for goading him. For not behaving, not listening. He was a mercurial man, and everyone knew you had to walk carefully around him. I didn't want to see what my father had really been doing with Farren, everything that had led to one terrible moment that changed everyone's life at the Hall forever."

"You were a little boy," Fen said, unable to stop himself. "A child, Pesha."

Pesha sighed, nodding. "Well, I didn't know it then, but that was the day my childhood ended. I lost my mother and father on the same day, but I'd been wrong all along about who they were. Ludwik and Arenn weren't the ones who taught me…played with me. That was Farren and Des, and after Nera was killed, Farren became what she became, and Des's heart turned to stone overnight. I never understood the guilt, the horror he carried in his heart, or the blame he felt for what happened. His escapes, his recklessness…I don't know how I didn't connect them to that day. My heart must have known though, for the only peace available to me came through acts of service, to him. Every whisper I read, every counsel I gave him that saved him grief or frustration, made me invaluable. And together, he and I existed in this fragile arrangement, unable to move forward…refusing to look back. We thought we were fine. That 'fine' was adequate. Was living. I never understood how dark our lives had been until you and Siofra came to the Hall and threw back the curtains so there could again be light."

Fen twined his hands through Pesha's, nodding to show he was listening. He had already seen Pesha's life through this view. But that was nothing compared to witnessing Pesha coming to his own understanding.

A line of tears spilled over Pesha's lids. His mouth curled upward. "But then I met you, Stiofen, and…" He exhaled slowly. "That day in Newcarrow, in the jail. You were this…this orb of fury, an incendiary waiting to explode. I remember thinking, I can break you. I can fix you. Such hubris! I was just as broken, and you were holding up a mirror I wasn't ready to look into."

"I wasn't either." Fen offered a crooked smile. "If it helps."

"It helps." Pesha returned the smile. "All this time, you've been growing and I've been wilting. I just didn't understand it was a choice."

"A choice implies intent. You were a child when your life was upended, and you're not much more than one now, Pesh. Neither of us are. You're eighteen. I'm twenty. In most parts of the realm, we're only just coming of age to be men, heads of households. And yet *neither* of us were shown the way, were we? Almost thirty years ago, our parents made choices that decided the lives *we* were going to have." Fen shook Pesha's hands in his, in the dirt. "But about a year ago? You and Desemir decided *you* wanted something different. And no matter how our time here in Asgill ends, Pesh, I will never forget what you did for Si and me. The gift of seeing her find genuine happiness…" Fen choked up. "If this is it, if this is the end, well…"

Pesha's face crumpled. "If this is the end, then I know I will have loved with my whole heart." He bit down on his bottom lip and released it. "Loved *you* with my whole heart."

Fen swallowed Pesha in a sobbing embrace. "No *loved* about it. We're still here. We're still *here,* and I won't stop fighting for every second." He peeled back to look at him, needing to *see* him—for Pesha to see Fen seeing him. "I loved you yesterday, and I love you today. Unless you piss me off again." They laughed together through a chorus of sniffles. "Then I'll probably love you tomorrow too, you pigheaded ass."

Pesha grinned. "If I can only make one assurance, it's that I'll always find another way to piss you off tomorrow."

"I'd be suspicious if you didn't." Fen spread his hands over Pesha's face, taking in every drop of his vulnerability and showing his own. "And I'd…miss you, stubbornness and all." He stifled a laugh. "*Neuroses* and—"

Pesha flattened his words with a rough kiss. Their bodies slithered against each other in response. "Saving you from saying something very mean, Stiofen."

"Oh, did I give you the impression I don't enjoy being mean?" Fen blinked. He quashed the mock offense erupting on Pesha's face with another kiss, this one softer. "Or that I don't…enjoy when you're a little mean?"

Pesha closed his mouth with a soft moan. "You don't have your daggers with you, do you?"

"Afraid not. Just these dull shears they left for pruning that are...somewhere..."

"I'm not really..." Pesha averted his eyes. "Daggers don't feel right, not right now."

"Nah," Fen agreed. He dug a knee in the dirt and pushed up and over Pesha, straddling him. "They don't, do they?"

Pesha swallowed, looking up at him, uncertainty brimming in his dreamy gaze. "Before you say anything else, I need to apologize. For so much."

Fen adjusted sideways so Pesha's distracting hard-on wasn't pressing against his ass. "I'm listening."

"You were right." Pesha looked away briefly. "About everything. I might've believed I was fearless, but my entire life...I've never *not* been afraid. As long as it was just Des and me, everything held together, because it was...It was safe, being afraid for him. I never had time to think of all I'd given up." He laughed bitterly. "The worst part is no one asked me to, certainly not Des. He never stopped trying to push me out of the nest."

Fen ran his hands down Pesha's chest, sliding until he was close enough to kiss him. "Did it ever occur to you that Desemir loves you as much as you love him?"

Pesha turned to the side, laughing. "Makes so much sense when you say it like that."

"Siofra was the same. Always trying to get me to leave. But I couldn't, not until I knew she was safe. And she is. They both are."

"I know it." Pesha nodded, smiling through tears. "I know it now. I see what he saw long before I did, that when I brought Siofra to the Hall, I wasn't just saving Des. Fen, I don't know... well, much of anything anymore. It may *look* like I do—" He swept a waggish gaze over himself, and they both laughed again. "But I know I love you." Pesha rolled his lips in as they both let the words wash over them. "And right now, that love is stronger than the fear. Right now, I'm stronger than the fear."

"My stars," Fen whispered, pulling his hands down Pesha's torso as he sat back up.

"My sun." Pesha's head lolled to the side with a sigh.

"You don't have to be stronger than the fear when someone carries it with you." Fen gripped Pesha's buckles, unlacing them one by one. "I forgive you." He tugged on the belt, freeing it, and sent it sailing into a patch of raspberries. "I release you." He ripped the buttons down the seam one by one. "From the past." He dug his hand under the waistband of Pesha's undershorts. "From the guilt." Pesha's cock sprang into his hand, and he gave it a long, gentle stroke in greeting. "From everything lying to you that you don't deserve happiness."

Pesha trembled beneath him, watching his every move—patient, for once—and trusting Fen to lead.

Fen had no idea what he was doing, whether every choice and touch would brand him as inexperienced. But as Pesha had let go of the guilt, so Fen would let go of the uncertainty. He could fail a thousand ways, and Pesha would never let him know it.

He worked his way out of his own trousers and settled between Pesha's legs, spread and fallen to the sides. He bucked, brushing his cock along Pesha's, enjoying the rise of his lover's chest when he remembered he hadn't breathed. Again and again he slid flesh against flesh, memorizing the ways Pesha's body responded to his.

Fen reared back, holding his pulsing cock in one hand and spitting into the other, and ran the spittle down his length. Pesha shuddered hard breaths, watching from underneath.

When Fen came down, Pesha lifted, his hands dug into the dirt for purchase. Fen fingered the area, making Pesha twitch with pleasure, until he found what he was looking for, then he held the spot until he had his cock pressed into place. Pesha nodded once.

Fen's eyes rolled back as soft, tight flesh squeezed his cock from all sides, an explosion of sensations that had him close to coming when he'd only barely breached. Pesha cried out, arcing higher, his thighs so rigid, so tense, it was like brushing rock.

Gathering Pesha's cock in one hand, Fen leaned close, pushed deeper, and thrust. The overstimulation was all-consuming, but he soon found his rhythm in both stroke and plunge, riding the balance between restraint and force, every widening of Pesha's eyes both a validation and a tease coaxing him to a place he wasn't ready to go.

"I've never..." Pesha moaned through a body-wide clench. His hands dug deeper into the soil. "I've always been..."

Fen's cock pulsed with excitement at the revelation. "I'm your first...like this?"

Pesha, his lower lip crushed between his teeth, nodded.

"Is it..." Fen slowed.

"Incredible." Pesha panted, lifting and spreading to support his words. "Perfect. Don't stop." He whimpered, another clench rippling through his abdomen. "Please."

Fen leaned down to kiss him, a gentle swipe of soft flesh against soft flesh. Their tongues slid together and over each other, tangling. He pulled back to study Pesha's hungered, trusting eyes and measured every flutter of his lids, adjusting his pace and his depth until Pesha was slapping the earth, searching for places to dig his hands. Through it all, Fen massaged Pesha's cock between his palms in full strokes.

All of it took every damn inch of his self-restraint to maintain.

"Feels so...Feels so..." Pesha's soft moans became a fevered grunt as he pitched forward in violent release. His seed coated everything, especially Fen's hands, which he brought to his mouth to taste, the way Pesha had done before. The flavor was surprising, warm and salty with a touch of sweetness, and soon he was spooning more of it from Pesha's shirt, slurping and thrusting until his toes were curled so tight in his boots, they nearly snapped.

Fen bore down, hooking onto Pesha's thighs as his release coursed through him. The force of it was like a blast, lifting his knees from the dirt, sending him curling against Pesha's belly to find his breath again.

When he could move again, Fen pulled out—yet another discovered pleasure, as the sensation of his cum sliding out of Pesha's ass would provide plenty of material for his fantasies—and flopped onto the dirt beside Pesha.

Pesha suddenly giggled. Concerned, Fen propped up on his elbow quickly. "What did I do wrong?"

"It's not..." Pesha was clearly trying to repress his laughter, but it wasn't working. He nodded downward, trying to speak. "Look at how sad and tired both our cocks are. Just sort of..." He made a *bloop* sound.

Fen huffed. "Did you just *bloop*?"

Pesha bit his lip and nodded. "I shouldn't have."

Sighing, Fen collapsed against Pesha's chest. "It's just all I'll be thinking of for days to come is all."

"*Bloop, bloop, bloop, bloop, bloop*—"

"You love my mean side, don't you? Because you're really—"

Pesha snuggled him close with tickles. "Really what, Stiofen?"

Fen squirmed, laughing as hard as Pesha as he clamored for air. "Testing me!" he cried.

Pesha abruptly stopped. He leaned close to Fen's ear. "I will always test you."

Fen slithered against Pesha. Was it contentment that had his eyes closing? His heart slowing? "I know. I wouldn't want you any other way."

"Don't fall asleep yet. I have something else I need to tell you."

Fen's eyes flashed open. "Uh oh."

"No." Pesha sighed. "No, this is good. This is really, really, really good."

"Don't leave me in suspense." Fen arched a brow.

"Farren." Pesha pressed his mouth tight when he took a pause. "She's bonded, Fen. With a silver lynx. Named Vaya."

Fen slowly slid until he was seated. He pulled his trousers up under his bare ass. "Farren..." Pesha's words replayed in his mind twice before he was ready to speak. "She's...She's going to be all right?"

"She's going to be all right," Pesha replied, his voice clogged with joy. "A couple more days, and she'll be ready to leave the Menagerie."

In two days, he would be dead. In one breath, he would leave this world and Farren would re-enter it.

It was the wrong thing to say though, as Pesha smiled back at him through happy tears. This was it, the entire reason for their ill-fated journey. All the strife, the terror, and the adventure had been leading to *this* moment.

"We did it," he said instead, and allowed himself to be lost to the same joy.

Old man, Pesha thought, stretching to expel the stiffness gripping him from head to toe. Hours he'd slept in the same position without moving. His shoulder still tingled in the place where Fen had lain.

Fen. Pesha searched for him, but it took several squinty passes around the dusky garden before he spotted him. He stood alone under the arch that led back to the step Pesha had come down—steps Pesha could show him but would otherwise be useless until Aoife released the magic tethering Fen to the caves.

A closer inspection revealed Fen wasn't alone. He was talking to the same man who had been with him when Pesha had arrived, who had disappeared before the reunion.

Pesha used the cover of the raspberries to shimmy back into his trousers. Sleeping nude in the dirt had been an ill-advised choice, but thinking about *why* brought a huge smile to his face.

He refastened his buckles, pushed to his feet, and started toward the arch.

Fen brightened when he saw Pesha coming, but the smile never made it to his eyes. Pesha rushed over, glancing from one to the other in a gradual return to the tense state he'd been in before Fen had calmed him.

"Pesh, this is Ensel. Ensel, this is the man I've told you about."

Ensel nodded. He had dark hair and eyes to match. Pesha, stunned, returned the nod. "But he's…"

"A man. Yeah." Fen scratched his head. "And, uh, there's more you should know about that. When did Mair say she'd be back?"

Pesha checked the sky. "Soon."

"Soon. Good." Fen crossed his arms and pivoted away. "Ensel, would you mind bringing Air back to the garden? He should be here for this. He has just as much to lose."

"For what?" Pesha stepped under the arch and reached for Fen. "Fen, last time your face looked like that, neither of us had a great day."

"She's not my daughter," Ensel said with the firmness of repetition. "It's not her."

"It has to be," Fen snapped. "Aoife has no other daughters."

"What are you two talking about?" Pesha asked, confused.

"Mairead may be Aoife's daughter." Ensel's face bloomed with red. "But I know that Med, and she is not *my* daughter." He tapped the cave wall. "Too young, for one."

"Fen," Pesha stated more firmly. He kept one eye trained on the strange man. "Tell me what's wrong."

Fen chewed the inside of his mouth, staring at the garden. "That's the thing, Pesh. I don't know what's wrong." He turned back toward Pesha. "And I won't until Mair and Niall return."

TWENTY-FIVE
HARD TRUTHS

Mairead didn't know what the deciding point had been for Niall. All she knew was her gratitude that he was there with her, plodding through the dark forest on their way to do something he didn't approve.

As was true to their relationship in recent months, they spoke only when necessary on the tepid walk to the grotto. He tugged her out of the path of obstacles twice, and she clicked her tongue when he started down the wrong path. They passed a waterskin between them. Remarked upon the strangeness of the heat.

He was anxious, but not half as much as she was. So many secrets were tied up in that cave. It would be better if they died there too.

Better for whom? she heard in Ensel's warm, soothing delivery. She loved listening to him. Sometimes she'd ask questions just to study the way his tone rose and fell with perfectly timed inflections. He was a natural storyteller…something not even nearly three decades in captivity had taken from him.

"Here." Niall thrust an arm out, and she stopped just short of barreling into it.

Mairead looked down at the protrusion marking the top of the steps, the one she almost tripped over. "Distracted."

Niall nodded, then gestured for her to go first.

He shouldn't be there. Fear struck her so suddenly, she paused midstep to look up at him in alarm. He watched her, waiting for an explanation, but the gentle patience in his eyes was worse than the aloofness he'd been offering for months. She'd been losing him day by day, and earlier that night, she'd gained some of him back.

But tonight, she would lose what remained.

Unless she didn't.

Unless he understood.

But she must be prepared for when he didn't.

"Fine," she assured him, smiling to add credence to the lie as she began her descent. After a doubting pause, Niall joined her.

Fen, Pesha, and Air were waiting in the garden. They'd cleared the old table in the corner, the one Mairead knew Ensel hadn't used in years, having arranged a bowl of fruits in the center like they were entertaining guests.

Niall was already making his way to the table when Mairead spotted Ensel standing under an arch, watching her.

She flashed a tentative glance at the others and slowly approached the arch. "Ensel."

"Mair. You're…" His eyes gleamed as he took her in. "A proper woman now."

"A proper *Medvedev,*" she teased, drawing a polite laugh from him. "I know…how long it's been…"

Ensel reached out and squeezed her arm once. He smiled thinly. "You needn't waste explanations on me. We both know how she is." His eyes flicked to the side, presumably to hide the hurt she hadn't missed.

"Will you join us?" She squeezed her hands into fists, pumping them. Adir soared ahead with Atio, both of them reminding her she was never truly alone. *Breathe.* "There are things I have to tell them. Hard truths."

"Aren't all truths?" He offered the same guarded smile as the last.

"Yes," she said, nodding. She peered over her shoulder at the other four staring, waiting. Niall's eyes narrowed in confusion. "But…There is one that belongs to you. One I have held for too long. It is your choice, of course, to hear it…"

"Mairead." Ensel inched closer. He tilted his head to catch her eyes. "We are friends, you and me. Even with the years behind and between us, you must know I'll die here. Perhaps not tomorrow or even soon. Shh, shh, no need for tears, love. I didn't tell you that to upset you. Only to ease your mind a bit. There's no secret that can hurt me anymore, not in here. Not the man I've become in here."

He was wrong, but there was only one way for him to know it. "Then please join us. If for no other reason, because it's been far too long since we've shared a waterskin."

Ensel tipped her a nod. "After you, my lady."

Mairead pinched her shoulders back and made her way to the table, not thinking of the man behind her nor the one waiting and full of questions. She had plenty to say and not much time to say it.

She slid in at the end of one bench next to Pesha, who made room for her. Ensel picked a spot on Pesha's other side. Air, Fen, and Niall all watched, waiting.

"Isn't it beautiful, Mair?" Air said with a smile bigger than her doubts. She would do anything to free Fen, but Air never should have been in the grotto. All the years she'd protected him amounted to nothing when she'd failed to save him from this.

"Stunning," she agreed, smiling back at him. "You've been eating well?"

"Don't you come here and steal our fruit!"

Mairead chuckled, as did some of the others, though the gesture was more polite than anything. They were *all* anxious. She'd repressed her empathic ability for so many years, she could hardly count it as one, but apprehension was rolling off her friends in waves.

"I would *never*," she said and stretched across the table to tweak his nose. "Stiofen, be sure this boy is eating a balanced diet as well. There are nuts just there." She pointed. "Wouldn't want him to get spoiled in prison."

"I've been imprisoned before," Fen said. "*This* is a holiday."

Wonder brightened Air's face. "Now will you tell me stories about the prisons in your world?"

"I have lots of stories, kid." Fen nudged him, winking. "Stick with me long enough, I'll bore you with all of them."

Mairead observed their need for introductions and that other bizarre custom of man: pleasantries. She waited, not-so-patiently, for the cross talk to die down, for everyone to settle in with their handfuls of berries, before jumping in.

"I will tell you what I know." Mairead tried to meet Niall's eyes, but it wasn't possible, not yet. She'd try again when it was fair, after he'd heard her confession. "But it remains unknown whether any of it will change what is to come."

Fen stretched a hand across the table and squeezed hers. "No matter what happens, Mair, you have been a loyal friend to us, and we won't forget it."

Mairead smiled sadly. "That remains to be seen."

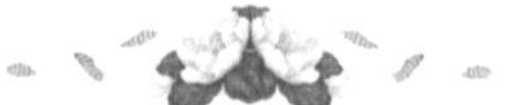

Several years before I was born, my mother met this man here, Ensel, when she was traveling through the Easterlands. She was only newly chieftainess by then and was facing a great deal of pressure from the clahnn to banish the growing number of halflings being born. Some called it an epidemic. Others opted for worse appellations.

This part of the story belongs to Ensel, who told it to me. What should never have happened did, and when it came time for my mother to return to Asgill, unbeknownst to her, Ensel followed. He should not have been able to enter the portal with her, but her guard was down, and the veil between your world and ours remained thin long enough for him to step through.

If we are tough on halflings, we are unrelenting toward men who seek to know us. Even as chieftainess, she could never keep him safe amid such growing enmity. She pleaded with him to leave. Leave our land. Leave her. But all of us here have known love. The power of it. The senselessness of fighting it. So she hid him away until the secret could no longer be kept.

She was soon with child and filled with shame. She crafted a story about meeting a Medvedev in Clahnn Mayke who broke her heart, and everyone believed it, but for many months, she agonized over what her child would become. Would they be born with a familiar, or would her lie unravel the moment her child came into the world?

It was Niall's mother, Theta, who deduced something was amiss with her dear friend Aoife. Scared and desperate, Aoife unloaded her truth, and Theta withheld judgment. She fed, bathed, and comforted Aoife, and when she felt her friend was ready to hear it, she told her what she must do.

Just until she had a better plan. These were the words my mother gave Ensel when she brought him here in the beginning, and as the time between her visits stretched from days to weeks to months, it remained her constant refrain. A promise she was unable to keep.

Meanwhile, tensions worsened in the clahnn. A small uprising, resulting in the deaths of four of her friends, pushed her to do what she'd sworn never to do: order the halflings to move to a smaller, more contained part of the forest, where they could be guarded at all hours, lest their tainted blood drive them to bad deeds. She'd never intended it to be more than temporary, just like Ensel's tenure here in the grotto, but soon, another group emerged loudly, declaring her a tyrant. They offered an ultimatum: take back her decree or face civil war.

Theta was there, again, advising her. They'll never follow through, she claimed. Call their bluff.

And so she did. And one terrible night, while the clahnn slept, over fifty Medvedev assembled. They stormed the halfling camp and took with them anyone who would follow. Most did. The ones who did not would come to wish they had.

But they weren't done. They went next to the Hatchery, where all children under two were kept. They went to the cradle where Aoife's child slept and took the child.

They also spelled Aoife's familiar, Fae, causing her to become lost in the forest, never to return. This is why my mother can be both full-blooded Med and still survive without her familiar. Fae is still out there somewhere, alive, or my mother would not be as she is now.

The next morning, the encampment was chaos. Mothers screaming for their halfling children...halfling mates. Calling for Aoife's head. It was Theta who calmed them, reminding them the Forsaken had done them all a great favor in ridding their land of the half-breeds. By then, she'd taken to using the word Aoife had forbidden them from saying, but Theta was beyond the law. She'd moved into Aoife's hut, whispering in her ear, the real mind behind everything that happened for the next few years.

Theta whipped up support for Aoife by turning the Forsaken into villains. It wasn't hard to do. Even those who had been staunchly against anyone but pure-Med living in Asgill were horrified that they'd lost so many of their own so suddenly. And worst of all, Aoife's heir had been stolen from her cradle, sent into a dangerous world, where her fate was never discovered.

The clahnn was again united, joined by their hatred of a common enemy. Slowly, halflings were accepted again, if grudgingly. It became a crime akin to treason to bring harm to them—the children anyway, for no child is accountable for the circumstances of their own birth. As for the mothers, the answer for their crime was banishment.

Several years after, in a period of calm, I was born. I do not know who my father is. I may never. Many, many times I've wished it was Ensel, but I would know, wouldn't I? I would know my own father if I looked into his eyes, and I've shared far too much with this kind man not to know if he was more.

I used to play near the grotto, never knowing there was someone inside until I climbed down into this very garden and saw him. I came back the next day, and every few days after. We'd share meals and stories. He taught me games, and I taught him about our customs. Everything I know about Ensel and Aoife I learned from him. Everything I know about what happened beyond the grotto came from others whose word I trust.

But I get ahead of myself. Years before I stumbled upon my friend here, Theta found herself in a very familiar trouble after an affair with a man. I was very young, perhaps two years along in the world, but I remember the rows my mother and Theta had in those months. I didn't understand at the time that they'd become lovers, and that Aoife viewed Theta's transgression as not merely a matter of banishment but the catalyst for a still-broken heart.

It was in one of these colorful rows when Theta blurted a terrible truth: she'd kindled the rebellion herself to create an event capable of uniting the clahnn under Aoife. When my mother had been sobbing in fear, desperate for answers, Theta had been slipping into huts and stirring dissention.

And then Niall was born, and he was...perfect, in Theta's eyes. But not in the clahnn's. Even if my mother had wanted to spare her, there was no pretending Niall was not a halfling, not when he entered the world without his sacred familiar. She ordered Theta banished, and... Niall, forgive me, but your mother was blindfolded, marched deep into the forest, and abandoned, her supplies stolen and scattered. She was left to die. And it was my mother, Aoife, who ordered this, broken with rage and heartache. Gellais was the one who followed the order and then bragged about what was supposed to be a secret over spirits with others.

Whether it was love or guilt that bade her take you in, only she can say. She does love you, as she loved your mother. But my mother's love is a complicated kind, and we all now know how she wields it.

But I have saved the worst of it—a secret she spilled to me in a moment of weakness, the night the sentries found the three of you wandering the Hinterlands—for the end. It will be hard for you to hear, but it may also be the final missing piece in the terrible puzzle that has shaped your lives and hers. All of ours, really.

Everyone remembers the individual who changed their life with a truth. I beg your forgiveness in advance, though it is not mine to request. It is hers, and always will be.

Because the child stolen from Aoife twenty-eight years ago was Farren.

Fen's gaze followed Pesha as he wandered the garden alone. His last words, as Mairead brought her story to a close, stayed with Fen. *I want to be surprised. I should be surprised. But so much that never made sense before does now. All the pain, and for what? Arenn wasn't even Farren's mother.*

Mairead sighed. "Farren wasn't her name at birth. It was Tera."

"Which explains why her familiar was called Nera. I'd guess Arenn and her mate, Naos, chose Farren because it was close enough to be believable, should they ever encounter other Medvedev." Fen shook his head. His gaze never left Pesha, who was kneeling near the stream, his back toward the group. "It also means Farren isn't Pesha's sister after all, and that's going to be harder for him to accept."

"We don't choose our blood," Ensel said, "but we choose our family. Nothing Mairead has said changes who Farren is to Pesha." He tapped his fingertips on the wood with a sideways glance. "But...She's *my*..." He brought his fist to his mouth and bit down. "It's her."

Mairead reached for Ensel in comfort. Fen peeled himself from the bench to give them space. He traded glances with Niall as he walked away. The Medvedev had gone as pale as Ensel, and he hadn't said a word since before Mairead had started her story.

Fen dropped down beside Pesha. "Hi."

Pesha gave a halfhearted smile. "Hi."

"Let me in?"

Pesha swayed sideways against him. "I'm not even sure what to say. I feel...relieved? Is that strange?"

Fen shook his head. "There's comfort in truth, even when it's tough."

"All these years, Des and I tried to save Farren when we knew so very little about her. Even Des, who was closer to her in age—her playmate. He told me once that *Farren* didn't even know her own history. She certainly didn't know Arenn wasn't her mother." Pesha, elbows on his knees, folded his hands over his mouth. "It explains why Arenn was so indifferent to Farren's suffering, until things had gone too far. But to me, that's even worse. You steal a child from their parent, you owe them so much more than whatever negligible care they offered Farren. I see you with Air. You'd die to protect him, and he's not even your son. Farren *needed* a mother, and instead every single person responsible for her well-being failed her."

Fen nodded at the dirt. "Many failed Farren. But 'everyone' doesn't include you and Desemir. I'll keep saying it until you believe it."

"Knowing doesn't...doesn't absolve anything."

Fen tilted his head, brushing it against Pesha's shoulder. "I know."

"But what's really weighing on me..." Pesha winced and peered at the night sky. "For years we believed her parents were dead, and now we know both of them are alive. They're *here.* But one of them is a monster, and the other will never walk free again. So which is worse, Fen?"

"I don't believe that's for you or me to answer," Fen said gently. He inched closer and cupped a hand over one of Pesha's knees. "And I do not believe in coincidences, love. Farren recovering just as we learn where she comes from?"

"But what..." Pesha squeezed his mouth and eyes tight. "Aoife will never let her leave. She'll never let us walk out of here with her daughter, and the worst...the worst part...I wouldn't have the heart to stop her. It's Farren's choice, not mine. We've been deciding the course of her life for over eight years, and now it's her turn, and what if she doesn't choose us?"

And there it was. Fen had assumed it would take Pesha longer to say it, but everything was different now. What had passed between them in the dirt had been a turning point, not a fork but a joining of two roads to become one. "Whatever happens, I love you."

With his eyes full of tears, Pesha turned and buried his face against Fen's chest. Fen wrapped his arms around Pesha and held him there, sliding a hand up and down his back as he sobbed. "I love you."

Fen's top-of-the-head kiss was a long, lingering one. He held the pose until his own tears dried. "I'm going to say it, because you're afraid to. You need to go see her."

Pesha whipped up. "I can't leave you here."

"You can," Fen said, stuffing his own feelings down deep. He already imagined Pesha climbing away from him, perhaps forever. "And you will. She needs to see the face of someone she knows. Someone who loves her."

Snorting, Pesha rolled his eyes upward. "Oh, and you think that's me? The one responsible for keeping her magicked and bed-bound for over a third of her life?"

"The one responsible for keeping her safe from harming herself or others until you could bring her *here*," Fen said gently. "Pesha, don't do this to yourself. Not now. There's nothing to be gained except misery you don't deserve."

Pesha reached for Fen's face and cradled it. His head shook through failed attempts to speak.

"Not convincing enough?" Fen asked. "How about this, then? I've already been here two full days and one night, and they could come for Air and me at *any* time. And I don't—" It was his turn to choke up. "I don't want to *die* in here, Pesh. I don't want the last thing I experience to be my failure to save that boy. So please, go to her, make it right, and then come *back* to me, because I do need you. I need you a great deal."

"Do you?" Pesha breathed deep. "Say it one more time."

Fen touched his forehead to Pesha's and pressed hard, wincing away more tears. "*I need you.* So go, before I lose my courage and beg you not to."

Pesha swept down and kissed him softly, gently. "All right, love."

TWENTY-SIX
THE BONDING ROOM

The Menagerie was silent. The displaced familiars were asleep when Pesha and Niall passed through, on their way to the bonding room. Farren was curled up on a large plush blanket that had been swirled and bunched around her in the perfect tuck. Vaya, the lynx, rested in the bend of Farren's knees, snoring softly.

"Outside," Niall murmured, jerking a thumb toward the door to show where he'd wait.

Pesha nodded dazedly and continued his slow approach until Vaya poked her head up. Her eyes turned to slits and a low rumble came to life.

"Vaya," Farren chided. She moaned and twisted atop her blanket. Pesha's heart twisted to hear her sound so…so normal. "What is it?"

Vaya's jaw elongated to reveal long, sharp teeth that Pesha did not want to feel sinking into his flesh—ever. But if he didn't figure out what to say, and quickly, he'd find out soon enough.

"Farren?"

Her slithering stopped. All ten toes curled inward as she drew her legs toward herself and turned.

She rolled over until she was facing him. Her eyes searched him in wild passes, but she stretched a hand down to Vaya, to calm her. "It's just Pesha," she said. Tears formed and fell. "Just my brother."

"Far," he whispered, tripping on his way toward her. He dropped to his knees and reached for her but quickly withdrew his hands, second-guessing himself. "How are…How are you?"

She watched him from where she lay, her hands wedged under her head. "Tired."

He tried to smile. "You've been sleeping a long time."

Farren's eyes blinked closed and stayed that way for a long time. "Where's Desi?"

"At home, at Shadowfen. We're…Well, we're a long, long way from there, Farren. We came a long way for you to find Vaya." Pesha settled and crossed his legs. "But we'll see him soon."

Farren's eyes fluttered toward the ceiling. "And Wulf?"

"Wulf?" A bolt of fear struck him. Was she thinking of that night in the forest? Reliving it?

"Wulfhelm."

Pesha was even more confused by her clarification, but she'd been in her own head for so long, it was understandable that she'd be reaching for her thoughts out of order. For a mind as fractured as hers had been, the Hall appearing as a series of random memories seemed understandable. "Well, he's still with us at the Hall as well. Euric too. And Lotte. And Des. Ah, he's *married* now, to this wonderful Medvedev named Siofra. You'll love her, as we all do. They're going to have children soon, if you can believe it. Des, a father. Siofra's brother, Fen, he…" He shook his head. "I'm really prattling on now, aren't I? I'm just so happy you're back, Farren. I've missed you so damn much."

"Talkative boy," she said wistfully, smiling with her eyes closed. "Answer for everything."

Pesha sniffled, laughing. "Des would say nothing has changed."

"I know…" Farren retreated into another long silence. "Ludwik. Arenn. I'm so tired, Pesha."

Pesha scooted closer and chanced reaching toward her to brush her emerald hair back off her face. "I know you are. And if more sleep is what you need, then sleep." He brushed a thumb across her temple. "I'll be here."

"Yet you shouldn't be," said a voice he recognized. "After nightfall, only Niall is approved to be here."

"Chieftainess," Pesha said. He didn't turn or stop his gentle ministrations. Farren was snoring softly. "We can have this conversation here, in front of her, or we can step into another room, but I'm not leaving."

Aoife's footsteps trailed away.

Pesha leaned in to peck a kiss on Farren's temple and then followed.

"You flaunt our rules," Aoife stated the moment he stepped through. "You respect nothing. No one."

"By your own rules, no child should be judged by the actions of the mother or father." Pesha took another step, ignoring the disgusted turn of her nose as he neared. "You know nothing about me, Chieftainess. Nothing about Stiofen. Nor Farren, even if she is your blood."

Fury spread over her features, hardening them. "You know nothing. You were not here." Aoife's upper lip peeled back. "And you cannot have her."

"I'm not her master. I'm her brother."

"You're not even *that*, halfling."

"I am," Pesha replied, lifting his chin. "In every way that matters. She was never a Wintersin, but she is a Trevanion. And when we take her home, she'll share equally in all that is ours. She will never want for anything ever again."

"Farren is going *nowhere*." Aoife enunciated the last word slowly. "You can leave without her, or you can stay and die, like your lover."

Pesha reared back. "Even after you've watched a miracle take place, you would still lead with jealousy and anger. Why? Why should not one beautiful thing lead to more beautiful things?"

"Beauty." Aoife gestured around with a sour glare. "You see what we have, but not how we've kept it. How we save it. The Forsaken tore our land and people apart, and they must never, *ever* be allowed to take a single inch more."

"Arenn and Naos took your daughter." Pesha tightened his mouth in a sad smile. "I'm sorry for that. It was wrong, and everything that's happened since is proof of what follows bad choices. But no one has suffered as much as Farren has. No one has lost what she's lost." He thrust an arm behind himself. "And that lover of mine? He had no reason to risk his life to come here, but he did it anyway. I wouldn't be here if not for Stiofen, which means *Farren* wouldn't be here if not for him."

"An act of goodness," Aoife said slowly, drawling her words, "does not erase an act of badness."

Pesha bit his lip with a bitter laugh. "Are we speaking of Fen, who stepped forward to answer for a crime he wasn't responsible for, or Gellais, for forging a letter knowing it would cause another's death?"

"Their blood is in your blood." Aoife glared him down before moving to the flap that led into where the displaced slept. "Halflings are an abomination of the Light's promise."

A horrible realization struck Pesha. "You... *You* were the one who told Gellais to plant the letter. It was your idea. You never intended to let us leave. And Farren... What about her?"

Aoife peeped through the flap. "Did Niall share with you how many rehabilitations are successful?"

"Not many," Pesha answered warily. With one eye on the room where Farren slept, he moved closer to the chieftainess. "But you have not answered *my* question."

"One in ten." Aoife released the flap. "And almost never if it's been more than a year since their mate perished."

"You know it's been eight for Farren."

"Eight," Aoife replied. "An impossibility. Viable only with the darkest magic."

Pesha couldn't help himself. He laughed. "You mean, all this time, all I needed was dark magic and we could have fixed her ourselves?"

"There is no humor in what has been done to her."

"And no one understands that more than someone who was there when her bond was severed."

Aoife sneered, passing a look over him. "An abomination in the eyes of the Light, you are. Who could believe a thing you've said?"

Weariness struck him like a sack of flour to the chest. He'd lost sense of how long they'd been there, and he was even struggling to remember how long ago he'd left Fen in the grotto. Arguing with someone as far gone as Aoife was futile, but Mairead had told them the story for a reason. She must have believed her mother was still reachable. "You. My mother. Both of you made a choice. *You* chose to lay with a man and create a child. Farren? Me? We had no say in our birth, something you yourself recognize in your laws. So we are either innocent of their machinations or it's in our blood, but it cannot be both. And if it's in our blood..." Pesha took a pause before he took the gamble. "Then any bad in Farren comes from you."

Aoife's face distorted in the dim light. It crumpled into anger, then dissolved into fear. But the fear lasted only long enough for the anger to return, and within seconds, she had settled on fury. "Sentries!"

"Aoife, wait." Pesha slowly backed toward the bonding room, his hands out in surrender. "I know you don't want to hurt Farren. I know you love your daughter."

Cassair and Fiachra stepped inside. "Chieftainess?"

"Aoife. *Please.*" Pesha pleaded with his eyes.

She snapped her gaze away from him and planted it on the sentries. "He is to be taken to the Twilight Grotto to join the seditionists. Judgment for all three will be at dawn. Tomorrow. The next day. I have not decided."

"Aoife!"

"*Chieftainess*, frog." Cassair shackled Pesha with a flick of his wrist.

Fiachra raised her hand, and Pesha came hurling forward.

"Promise you won't harm her. Promise you'll think about what I said!"

"You'll see her again," Aoife said distantly. "When she watches you embrace the Light at the forest's edge."

"Chieftainess—" Pesha pleaded as he passed, but Fiachra silenced him with an *ah-ah* sound, sealing his lips with a trace of her finger.

"I'll release it when we reach the caves," she said close to his ear, marching beside him. "For what little good it will do you."

Fen needed to get word to Mair. She'd promised to return after the morning fast breaking, but everything had changed the moment Pesha had become a prisoner.

"No. Like this." Air banged the spoon against the cauldron.

Pesha, flustered, shrugged in apology. "And what, exactly, is that supposed to do?"

Air grunted in disappointment. "It sends a message to the broth to thin out, so we can eat it without putting it back on the fire."

"Sends a message, does it?"

"You don't believe me." Air crossed his arms. "You think I'm a liar."

"No…not at all. If you say banging on the pot sends a message to the broth, then who am I to disagree?"

"Told you," Air murmured, and Pesha laughed.

"This isn't the most helpful thing to say at a time like this," Ensel said, joining Fen against the wall, where he was watching

Pesha adjust to Air's spirited ways. "But you both would have made wonderful fathers."

Fen closed his eyes and wilted against the wall. "You're right. Not the most helpful."

"There's still time."

Fen glared from the side. "For the man she can't bear to kill, sure. For the rest of us…" He slid to the floor with a sigh. "Apologies. I'm a mess."

Ensel was slower on the way down, wincing as his joints popped and cracked. "Bah. No, *you're* right. I've forgotten the art of communication. I was once more than fair at socializing. Commanded an audience or three. Hard to imagine it now as I am, I know."

"Frankly, I'm impressed you can speak at all, after almost thirty years of wondering when she was going to come to her senses." Fen's eyes glazed as he watched Pesha and Air playfully spar. A beautiful future stitched together in the haze. Fen wished more than anything he could send the thought to Siofra, where she could see that, for a short time anyway, he *had* been happy. He'd had love. Purpose. Friendship. Many lived four times as long and never had half of those things, so how could he be angry that he'd had it all, however fleeting?

"If anyone can solve this, it's Mair."

Fen rolled his head to face Ensel. "Did Aoife ever learn Mair was coming down here to see you?"

"Not as far as I know." Ensel shook his head. "No, she couldn't have. If anyone else living knew I was here, one of us would have to die, and for all her faults, Aoife loves Mairead. She loves Niall too. And Farren…"

"Pesha thinks she's sworn off Farren. That she'll harm her."

"*She* may think so as well, but she carries more than pain, Fen. A mother's guilt…She has always blamed herself for Farren's abduction. For not doing more to bring her home. It's been twenty-eight years since she last laid eyes on her daughter. It should not be surprising she's still working through her feelings on the matter."

"I hope…I hope Aoife doesn't figure out Mair has been helping us, and punish her."

"Mairead and her mother have a complicated relationship," Ensel said. He glanced at Fen. "I worry more for what her confession has done to her bond with Niall."

"Do you think it's hurt their bond?"

"Yes." Ensel groaned and pushed himself to his feet. "Thin or thick, my belly is too old for late-night stew. Fair rest to you all. I'll see you on the morrow."

"Good night," Fen said.

"Good night."

When he was gone, Fen pulled himself up and dusted himself off. "Air, it's time to get some rest."

With his spoon clutched in his fist, Air turned, his face crumpling in disappointment. "It's not done thinning."

"You eat this late, you'll get a cramp anyway. Come on."

"But now Pesha will never believe me."

Fen burned Pesha with a knowing look. "That's not true. He absolutely believes you. Isn't that right, *Pesha*?"

"Oh, yes. No doubts whatsoever," Pesha said with an over-exaggerated nod. He scrambled to his feet. "I'll be thinking about your culinary wizardry all night."

"Really?" Air asked.

Fen rolled his eyes at Pesha and waited for him to step aside before kneeling and gathering their supplies, then moving them back to the corner. He tucked Air into the pile of blankets and smoothed some matted hair off his forehead. "Dream pleasant dreams for me."

Air closed his eyes, but his smile persisted. "I will."

"Night, kid."

"Night, Fen."

"Night, kid."

"Night, Pesha."

He stood and nodded toward the leftmost passageway. Pesha waited for him, to walk together.

"Will he be all right in there by himself?" Pesha glanced behind him.

Fen smiled to himself. "Paternal instincts kicking in, are they?"

Pesha scoffed. "Neither one of us had great examples of what a father should be."

"We had examples of what not to do," Fen replied, rounding a corner. "So we just do the opposite."

Pesha laughed. "Parenting is that simple, is it?"

"Maybe so."

Pesha offered a joyless smile as he reached for Fen's hand and linked it in his. "The garden?"

Fen swallowed the lump that had been forming since Pesha had returned as a prisoner. "The garden."

The stream was deepest where it met the falls, enough for Pesha and Fen to submerge until everything below their chest was underwater. Fen leaped in first with a playful shriek—without so much as a pause, Pesha noted with a scowl, thinking of the temperature differential and the potential for poisonous aquatic nightmares, serrated rocks, and all other manner of ways the jaunt could have gone wrong. Pesha, sighing through his reservations, eased in behind him.

The water was tepid, neither frigid nor especially warm. But the moment Pesha sidled up behind Fen's nude body, he was as warm as he needed to be.

Fen craned back and kissed him. Pesha reached around and clasped Fen's face, pulling him closer and moaning into the slide of tongues.

"Why aren't you inside of me?" Fen purred, lifting onto his toes.

Pesha felt something feral rumble from deep within him, turning to a growl he buried in the back of Fen's neck as he searched underwater.

Fen screamed into his bare arm when Pesha pushed in without preparation. He felt every inch of resistance and started to withdraw, afraid of hurting him, but Fen clawed underwater until his hands found Pesha's thighs, and he tugged.

"Harder. Harder, Pesha. Fucking *harder.*"

Pesha braced on the bank and thrust as hard as he could. Fen's entire body pitched forward except his head, which fell back to collect more sloppy, ardent kisses.

"You're so tight. It feels so good." Pesha reared back and plunged again, this time sending Fen onto the tips of his toes. "You feel so good."

Fen looped a hand backward and clasped it behind Pesha's neck to hold their kiss. He whimpered in place of words, his mouth falling wide with every generous spearing. "I need more. Give me more. Give me…" His hand traveled toward his cock. He stroked the length underwater, something Pesha wished he could see. He decided in that moment he'd make Fen pleasure himself later, so he could watch. He added it to the list of the other fantasies he was determined to play out with him before the end.

Pesha's knees locked when the release hit him, and he bit down on the soft flesh of Fen's neck. Fen cried out moments later, pinned aloft by the force of the bank and Pesha.

Fen spun in the water and buried his face against Pesha's chest. Pesha wrapped his arms around him and held him, letting the roar of the waterfall drown all other thoughts but the ones connecting them in the moment.

Pesha wound his hands through Fen's wet hair and tugged. "I love you, Stiofen."

"Pesha." Fen's lips curled inward. "I love you. My stars."

"My sun." Pesha smiled and traced his tongue along the ridge of Fen's mouth. "Shall we…"

"All right."

Pesha watched Fen climb out first, admiring the tight flex of his ass as he went to retrieve his clothes. He had a sudden, primal urge to crawl to Fen on his hands and knees and take his cock in his mouth, tasting the remnants of his spend and the minerals of the stream water.

"What?" Fen asked, turning as he shrugged his tunic on. Tragically, it covered his cock.

"Nothing," Pesha said, smiling, his face tilted sideways over his crossed arms. "Just admiring how beautiful you are."

Fen flushed in embarrassment. He swatted the air and bent for his trousers.

"*No.*" Pesha was taken aback by the command he heard in his voice. But Fen's reaction—his back straightening, his hands moving to his sides—unlocked yet another fantasy. "You put them on only when I say you can."

Fen's trousers dropped to the cavern floor in a swift, echoing whoosh. "Yes, sir."

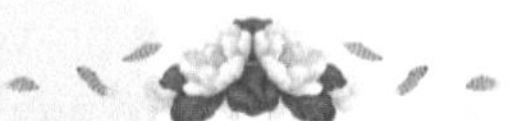

For hours, they talked. About everything. The conversation began with comparing stories of their childhoods, some they'd told no one else, and eventually returned to the matter at hand.

"I need to ask you something," Pesha said during one of the perfect silences, in a way that seemed he'd been working up to it for some time. "I want you to know you can be honest. I won't be hurt either way." He smirked. "I might be hurt, but I won't be angry or resentful."

Fen propped himself on his elbow, losing his warm spot. He was grateful he'd had the foresight to take a blanket with them, because waterfall sex and loose soil were not a great pairing. "Ask then."

"Mairead." A cloudy look passed over Pesha's face. He lay on his back, staring upward. "I have no right to be upset. You did nothing wrong. I just want to know."

"That's not a question," Fen said carefully. He could guess where it was heading. "But it wasn't like that with us, so there's nothing to be hurt by."

"I've seen you kiss her, Fen."

"Yes, and it's not…not like it is with us."

"So you're not attracted to her?"

Fen thought about his answer for a moment. "I am attracted to her."

Pesha shook his head against the blanket. He turned his head slightly but wouldn't meet Fen's eyes.

"You've only ever desired men." Fen craned over, looking down at him. "I've always fancied both."

"Always?" Pesha looked skeptical.

"There's plenty to desire about Mairead. She's beautiful. Kind. Clever. Puts everyone else's needs above her own. Is an incredible kisser." A devious grin spread over Fen's face right as Pesha got worked up. "But she's not you, Pesh. She could never be you." Fen dropped back down, nestling beside Pesha, and planted a kiss on his bare shoulder. "She taught me the power of touch. The inherent value in closeness." Fen kissed him again. "How it restores us, not to who we were but who we should be."

Pesha scowled. "Taught you that, did she?"

"I love you." He pecked another kiss. "And I don't begrudge you the men you were with before me." Biting back a laugh, he said, "Even crusty old Euric."

"You swine." Pesha rolled over until Fen was pinned beneath him. He gathered Fen's hands and locked them above his head. Fen growled and thrust upward in insolence. "Did you fuck her?"

Fen grinned.

"You did."

Fen shrugged.

"Stiofen Thornheart, you'll use your words when I ask you a question."

He bit down on his lip and winked.

Pesha reached down and cupped his balls with a warning squeeze.

"All right! No…No, I didn't. You were my…first." Fen wriggled out from under him when the embarrassment hit. He turned and faced away. "My only."

Silence followed. Pesha's hand slid over Fen's hip. "I didn't mean to make you feel ashamed."

"You didn't. It's not you." And it wasn't. It was everything, every awful thing colliding with every wonderful thing that had ever happened to him. It was realizing he'd known happiness—in the form of love, with Pesha, in the form of purpose, with Air—but also the bittersweet ache of knowing how and when it would end.

Pesha swallowed him in a hug from behind. "You won't let me retreat into myself, and I'm not giving you any pardon either. I can hear it in your voice, Fen. You've already given up."

"No...No, I just..." Fen melted, rolling back against Pesha. "Is it still giving up when you see no way out?"

"*See.* That's the key."

"Huh?"

"The answer isn't what we know. It's what we don't."

"Studying philosophy now, are we?" Fen squinted at him.

"Or your influence is showing." Pesha smiled, planting a soft kiss along Fen's hairline. "Mairead will be here in a few hours, but until then...Why waste the time we have with worry?" Pesha tugged him until he was on his back. "I waited for my whole life for you, and I won't surrender a single second that hasn't been taken."

Fen tilted up to kiss him, sighing. "I'm sorry. You're right."

Pesha grew solemn. For a moment, it seemed his words would die there. "There's something I want to do in the morning, with you, and you don't have to...to do it. But it would mean the world to me if you did."

Fen peered up at him. "You aren't going to tell me, are you?"

Pesha, grinning deviously, shook his head.

"And you expect me to trust you're not up to no good?"

"Actually, I do."

Sighing, Fen closed his eyes. He breathed in the heady musk of lilac...the waft of grapes and berries so well-tended, they could sustain the four of them for a lifetime. And would it be so bad, for *this* to be their life? Fen and Pesha raising Air to be a thoughtful man, Ensel taking on a sage-uncle role. Every day would be bliss, as long as they never thought of all they'd been forced to leave behind.

"The answer is yes. Doesn't matter what it is." Fen snuggled against Pesha, yawning. "Wherever you are, there I'll be."

TWENTY-SEVEN
TAPESTRY OF LIFE

Until the moment everything was in place and there was nothing left to do but the thing itself, Pesha was convinced Fen would think the idea was silly. A *no* he could handle, but Fen only going along with it because he assumed it was a jape would be a personal failing of Pesha's.

Because prison or no, Pesha's one lingering desire was for Fen to make him an honest man.

Craning down, he inspected every stone Mairead and Air had made into a circle. He adjusted one, then another, ignoring the exasperated look Niall shot at Ensel. Pesha didn't care what Niall or any of them thought. If this was the last truly joyous thing Pesha ever did, he'd ensure every detail was worth taking with him into the afterlife.

"Is this really what you want? You're not just scared?" Fen folded his arms around Pesha from behind, resting his face between his shoulders.

"I'm plenty scared, Stiofen," Pesha replied. "And if you think… If you think I wouldn't do this if we were home, at the Hall, you're wrong. I'm only suggesting we do it now in case we don't get that chance."

Fen nodded against him, wrapping himself tighter at Pesha's back. "Then I need to tell you my own intentions."

Pesha spun, holding the embrace. His pulse skipped. "What?"

Fen nodded at Air. "Either I can save him or I can't, but he isn't staying here."

"I don't follow," Pesha said, shaking his head.

Fen's hands fell away before traveling up Pesha's chest. He looked up. "This has been…" His face scrunched in a wincing laugh. "The absolute *worst* holiday of my life."

Pesha laughed too.

"But I discovered my three loves here, and that has to mean something."

Pesha laid his hands over Fen's and nodded for him to continue, his mind already skipping ahead to predict what he'd say. Even though he *knew* where he stood with Fen and had made it clear, for Fen, where he stood, it didn't erase the fear that Fen's confession would come with a loss.

"You. Of course." Fen grinned. "*Midwifery*, of all things…"

Pesha balked. "Really? You enjoy delivering babies?"

"Bizarrely, yes." Fen's head shook. "And the third is him. Air. Pesh, he's more than just a boy unfortunate enough to cross fates with a man condemned. He's so much more. Mair sees it, but she's special. She sees everyone for who they are. But you see that light in his eyes? The way he sparkles with curiosity at every little thing?" Fen bit his lip. "They'll crush it from him, Pesha. They'll grind it out of him until he passes for 'normal' and there's nothing unique left about him. The same way they'd have done to you and Farren, had you been raised here."

Pesha shifted from one foot to the other. He forced himself to listen instead of jumping ahead. "What are you saying then?"

Fen swelled with a deep breath. "I'm saying that boy is already my kin, and…I think he could be yours too."

"Ah." Spots split Pesha's vision. He released Fen and backed away, his eyes trained on the ground, on the rows of strawberries.

"Pesh?"

"A moment." Pesha whipped a hand out, and it struck the apple tree. He dug his fingers into the bark. A son. A father. Even as a boy, before tragedy had changed everything, he'd never *actually* entertained having a family of his own. From a young age, he'd learned to see the world through the safest lens, one where he absorbed all he needed from life through acts of service. Service to Des, to the Hall, to their people. A life where he could give everything and need nothing, knowing his gifts would never harm another—an existence free of risk yet full of reward, as long as he never peeled back the rib to examine the heart and learn what really made it beat.

There was nothing but patience in Fen's expression as he honored Pesha's request.

"What if we…What if *I*…" Pesha wedged his fist between his teeth and grunted. "Even in what little time we have let to us, what if I can't help but hurt him as well?"

Fen sagged with a tender smile and slowly approached. "You are not Ludwik, and I am not Rohan. We've had all these years to ponder the ways they've messed our lives about, and we *know* what not to do. Getting it right every time…That's not the aim, Pesha. Even if we get it right half the time, and the other half we never lose sight of the love at the center of it all, he'll still turn out all right."

The way Fen could still speak of the future with such optimism was infectious, and Pesha was soon smiling despite himself. "You're assuming he even wants us."

Fen glanced at Air and waved. The boy returned the gesture with enthusiasm, working both hands into it.

"See?" Fen laughed. "It will be his decision in the end, but I don't even want to make the offer unless both of our hearts are fully invested." Fen reached up and brushed Pesha's cheek with his palm. "I'll marry you either way. I don't want you to say yes for the wrong reason. I don't want you to say yes at all, unless you could learn to love him as I already do."

"Love…That's not the problem." Pesha angled his face into Fen's palm. He breathed him in. "I could love him. I love you even more when I see you with him, and I realize how much this place has given and taken with the same hand, in the same breath."

"Then love him," Fen said, leaning up to kiss him. "Love him and love me, and love whatever threads we have left to weave in this tapestry of life. No matter what comes, few will have known such wealth as us."

Pesha nodded. He tried to speak but couldn't, so he kept on nodding.

"Then let's not keep our guests waiting."

Fen had never been to a handfast, nor even a wedding. He'd missed Siofra's clandestine dawn wedding because he'd acted so poorly about it she'd had to do it in secret. Few regrets gnawed as deeply as that one.

"The circle of stones represent the eternal nature of love and partnership," Mairead said. She traced a burning bundle of herbs through the air to cleanse it of the past, she'd explained, so that no troubles carried into the union. "Once you step inside, you remain inside. The circle is unending, with no beginning, no end. Within it, you hold eternity. If you ever choose to step beyond the ring, to break the unending nature of the circle, you must leave something behind—something you would miss, a symbol of your abandonment of one season for the next."

"Leave a part of ourselves behind?" Pesha squinted. "Is this a literal or a metaphorical exercise?"

"A hand," Niall said with a flippant shrug. "Or a foot."

"Pardon?" Ensel coughed. He stood several feet away, aiding Mairead as she needed it.

"Niall." Mairead sighed, shaking her head. "He's right. You must decide now what you will leave in the circle, should you ever choose to step outside without the other. A physical part of yourself to remain alongside the piece of your soul you surrender. Like the loss of love, the loss of limb is a reminder of the fragility of choice."

Fen sucked in through his teeth, wincing at Pesha. It sounded ludicrous, even in Mairead's dulcet delivery. But what was commitment without cost? "I would very much miss my right hand. I use it for everything."

"I'd miss your cock more," Pesha said through a small gap in his mouth.

"Pesha!" Fen felt a flush darken his face. He immediately searched for Air, who was mercifully squinting in confusion.

"Fine." Pesha smirked. "My left hand then, as a complement to your right one."

"You only lose your hands if you leave each other," Air said wisely. "So don't leave."

"It is that simple, isn't it?" Pesha teased, smiling at Air, and Fen's heart melted into the dirt.

"Sure is." Air beamed.

"Can we bring him in with us, into the circle?" Pesha asked. "Air? Not, of course, if he has to agree to chopping off a foot, but if he *wants* to be in here, with us?"

Fen tapped his chest where a well of emotion gathered. "Really?"

"Really." Pesha nodded. "Air, would you like to join us on whatever adventure awaits us?"

Air's chin quivered. His dark eyes, full of tears, widened as he nodded. "I can come?"

Fen couldn't stand still a moment longer. He rushed to Air, lowering to the boy's height. "You don't have to do anything you don't want to do, Ruairi, but if you'll have us…" He cleared his throat. "If you'll have us, Pesha and I would be honored for you to join our family."

Air's voice dropped low. Tears spilled, and he buried his head. "But I'm an abomination."

Somewhere nearby, Fen heard Mairead cry. He hoped Niall had the good sense to comfort her before he, too, lost what mattered most.

"You are *not* an abomination. You are Ruairi de Medvedev, the best birthing assistant I've ever met, a captivating storyteller of no compare, and one of a kind." Fen tilted the boy's chin upward. "If anything, I'm a little worried you wouldn't want *us*."

Air's little face softened. "You don't have to worry anymore, Fen."

Fen wiped an eye. "No, I don't, do I?" He reached for Air and crushed him in for a hug. Pesha soon joined them, wrapping his arms around them both.

"Shall we?" Pesha asked, standing and holding both hands out.

Air glanced at Fen, who nodded in gentle approval, and the boy took Pesha's left hand. Fen, smiling, took his right. Together, the three stepped into the circle of stones.

Mairead smudged the circle once more before handing the bundle to Niall. "You have taken the first and most crucial step. You have left your old life behind for a new one, knowing the risk you take, body and heart, believing they are worth it. And now you are here." She smiled down at Air. "The three of you. This is not only a handfast, to seal a commitment of lovers, but a pact between a fresh family of three. And all three of you have suffered so much, for so long. When you leave this circle, you do not leave behind suffering. No one could. But you leave behind the past that has opened your wounds, and submit to a future where, together, they can be closed."

Fen glanced at Pesha when Mairead turned away. But Pesha had his eyes on Air, smiling at him in reassurance. Fen's heart swelled so full with love and joy, he feared it would burst right there, littering the circle with its parts.

"All three of you will now close your eyes and join a circle of hands. Together, you will say, 'We are one, always in eternity, until the earth shrivels.'"

"Would it ever do that? Shrivel?" Air seemed genuinely concerned at the notion. "I can't imagine it."

"Not today anyway." Mairead smiled. She nodded at Fen, who curved in toward the other two, joining his hand to Air's to complete the circle.

"We are one," Fen said.

"Always in eternity," Pesha said.

Stifling a giggle, Air finished them off. "Until the earth shrivels."

"We have honored the earth by committing to your circle," Mairead said. "Now we honor the sea, by sharing sacred water from the Light's bowl."

"The same bowl we pick our chores from?" Pesha asked.

Niall groaned.

Mairead flicked a warning look his way. "No, there are many fonts for the Light. But they are all, each of them, blessed." She reached behind her and lifted a broad mug, cupping it in both hands as she showed it to the three of them. "The sacred waters of the Light are for but few purposes. Births. Deaths. The cycles of rebirth and renewal. And the union of souls. To accept this bountiful gift is to believe in it. To know, with utter certainty in your heart, that the water washing down your throat, through your body, is a blessing of beauty. If you accept the water from this cup and do not believe in the blessing, it will turn to liquid fire and burn you from the inside."

"Fuck," Pesha whispered with a sidelong glance at Fen. They both checked on Air to make sure he wasn't too disturbed by the words, but he seemed just as excited as he'd been to learn the earth might shrivel.

"This one is a bit more metaphorical," Mairead said with a short laugh. "But keep your hearts open for this. When you accept this cup, you bathe in the gift of the Light, which will sustain you for the rest of your years."

Pesha nodded and reached for the cup, but Mairead shook her head and lifted it to his mouth herself.

"Hold the circle until we are done." She lifted the cup to Pesha's mouth and placed a hand on the back of his head as she tilted. Pesha swallowed, nodding, and she moved on to Fen, who swallowed the mouthful her pour offered.

Air was last, practically bouncing in place for his turn. It dripped from his mouth, and he tried flinging his head to clear it, but Pesha, grinning, lifted an arm high enough and nodded for him to use it. Air, with a matching smile, swiped his face along Pesha's sleeve and then returned to his formation, his shoulders back.

"We are one, always in eternity, until the sea runs dry. Air, you are first this time," Mairead said.

"We are one," he said, his eyes flitting between the men.

"Always in eternity," Fen said.

Pesha grinned. "Until the sea runs dry."

Mairead handed the cup to Niall and returned with a tiny feather. "This belongs to Adir, who graciously offered one of his for this last part."

Adir screeched, a far cry from his usual beautiful singing.

Everyone laughed.

"Or not so graciously." Mairead twirled the light-pink feather by its shaft. "I'm sure Atio would have loved to offer one of hers, but it must come from a familiar of one who is not in the circle."

Holding the feather aloft, she continued. "Just as the earth gives us sustenance, and the water makes us whole, we are nothing without the breath air gives us. This is why the Light imbued the earth, the sea, and the sky into each one of us when we are made. There is no predicting which the Light will choose for us, and for some…" Mairead smiled at Air. "And then there are those who are far too important to be given just *one* bequeathment. They have all three, and that would not be fair to any familiar, who can only be one."

Fen knew she'd made up the last part just for Air. When she lifted her gaze again, he met it, sharing a grateful nod.

Air tapped his feet in giddy anticipation, his smile growing bigger and broader.

"The air carries breath, scent, pollination…Its clouds deliver needed rain. Its gusts remind us to be vigilant, always. I place this feather, a symbol of the air, between the three of you in the circle. You will clear your minds and imagine the three of you are one of the barbs along the shaft. You will feel the security of it. The promise of the air to carry you wherever you go. The distant but powerful connection to earth and sea."

Fen closed his eyes and attempted to follow her instruction. He knew the security of the shaft, the call of the wind. He felt the flutter of liftoff, of climbing toward home, and the keening desire to be free to fly. Tears burned behind his lids as he thought of Atio doing this every day of her life. He'd never understood her before, and until he'd visualized what a moment of time for her was like, he hadn't realized there was still so much discovery left between them.

"Should you lose your sight of the feather, of the ephemeral but capricious nature of the wind and sky, you will fall, cratering the earth…changing the tides." Mairead breathed deep. "You may open your eyes. Pesha, this time you will lead. 'We are one. Always in eternity. Until the sky falls.'"

"We are one." Pesha's grin couldn't be contained. It spread so broadly across his face, Fen mimicked it.

Air squeezed both their hands, hardly able to stand still. "Always in eternity."

"Until the sky falls," Fen said.

"Once more, all together," Mairead said. She accepted the cup back from Niall and started circling the outer edge of the stones, dripping a trail around Pesha, Fen, and Air. "Until the sky falls, the earth shrivels, and the sea runs dry."

"Until the sky falls, the earth shrivels, and the sea runs dry," all three replied, repeating in perfect concert.

Mairead returned to her place and, shuddering into a soft laugh, clasped her hands and said, "You are now one in the Light.

Your season has begun. Only you decide how long it lasts, but there is nothing but yourselves standing between your triad and eternity."

Pesha snaked a hand behind Fen's head and pulled him in for a crushing kiss. With his other, he tugged Air toward them, and the three held each other, laughing and weeping until Niall coughed.

"You may leave the circle safely now," Mairead said with a weary glance at her lover.

"Blessings to all three of you," Ensel said. He clapped hands around Fen's and Pesha's shoulders. A shine appeared in his eyes. "This was a gift for me too. I've become an old man in here, and I'd forgotten…" He choked down emotion. "Doesn't matter. I'd just forgotten is all. Thank you for reminding me. For including me."

"You don't belong here, Ensel," Fen said. "And you're not an old man. Not yet. If tomorrow…" He tapered his words, thinking of Air. "Then we will all do what we can for you as well. It's not a secret anymore, is it? Niall knows now. We know."

Ensel nodded at his feet. "Where would I go, in a world that has moved on? My parents are probably dead. My brother would have taken over my homestead, claimed my birthright…and how could I take that from him? I've made peace with being here, because everyone out there has already made their peace with the loss of me."

"You'd come home, with us," Pesha said, surprising everyone.

Ensel frowned. "You would invite me into your home, a man you just met?"

"If you wanted to, that is. We're all orphans at Shadowfen Hall, but we're a family. A proper family. Stronger than most because we chose each other." He pulled Fen and Air tight. "The offer stands, Ensel. We'd all understand if you said no. But we'd be honored if you said yes. And it might be your one chance to get to know your daughter."

"Say yes," Air pleaded, peering up at Ensel.

"Something to think about," Ensel muttered and wandered away.

"Is that…" Fen glanced around. "Are we…"

"You are now a union." Mairead smiled at all of them. "And Niall and I must away. We'll return in the morning, after we've checked in on our respective charges."

"Farren, you mean." Pesha sucked his teeth. "I don't know what Aoife's intention is for her. I can't read your mother. But she can't…"

"She won't." Mairead held a hand toward Niall. "Right, Niallan? We'll keep Farren safe until all this is resolved?"

Niallan tentatively nodded, looking at her hand. "Safe."

Fen read the exchange between the words. Mairead was extending an offer of peace between them, giving Niall a way to redeem himself and restore their bond.

"Good." Mairead hugged Fen, Pesha, and Air, whose nose she tweaked before she stood. "I cannot see the future, my friends, but I know myself. I know what I will not do and what I will do to see this wrong restored to right."

"What time will they come for us tomorrow?" Pesha asked, his eyes on Air as he selected each word carefully.

Mairead shook her head. "I do not know. It could be…" She looked down at Air, but he was turned away, watching Ensel. "Tonight even. No second should be taken for granted."

"No matter how this ends, that's a lesson I needed to learn," Pesha said.

"And me," Fen replied. He kissed Pesha's shoulder. "Until tomorrow."

TWENTY-EIGHT
THEIR OWN ETERNITY

Painless.

Quick.

Final.

The words were whispered, shouted, debated on the dawn march up the stairs, sentries leading and taking up the rear. It almost seemed like they were trying, in their own strange way, to comfort the damned.

Pesha didn't relinquish a single moment to fear. He was plenty scared but would allow nothing to steal his opportunity to examine the depth of color in the rare blooms along the path—or guess the heights of the conifers shimmering in the innocuous breeze.

It certainly didn't stop him from memorizing the way Fen's and Air's hands felt in his, the way Fen's was his equal but Air's disappeared into his palm, the ultimate symbol of trust.

Mairead came streaming from the forest. Her hair was down, wild in the breeze. Niall was right behind her.

"No! You believe you can secret them away to be executed quietly?" she demanded, running alongside the procession. "You will answer me, sentries!"

"We come by orders of Chieftainess Aoife herself." The female sentry never broke her forward gaze. "And we are to subdue any interference."

"I dare you to strike her own daughter." Mairead's face was ablaze with rage. Her nose flared, her neck flexing. "And then we'll see what the chieftainess says about interference."

"Mair," Fen called.

She whipped around until she spotted him, her flusterment softening.

"Oh, Stiofen. I didn't know." She fell into pace beside them, offering a brief smile to Air and Pesha. "I didn't know, or I would have been there when they came for you." With a gasp, she looked down and then back up. "They've bound you together."

"They gave us a choice," Pesha explained. "Fen and I..." He caught Fen's eyes over Air's head. But they were past the point of dulling the danger for the boy. He would be asked to renounce his place with the Forsaken, and the only way he'd make the right choice was if he knew what would happen if he didn't. "If we're going to leave this world, we want to leave it as we chose to live it. Together."

Fen lifted one hand, and Air's came with it. "It's really not so bad. Lucky for these two, I'm not tired of them yet."

Mairead was stunned. She seemed lost for a response, shaking her head slowly. "I tried to see my mother..." She glanced around. "But she wouldn't see me." She winced. "She sent me away. Didn't want to see me, I was told, and from now on she would prefer if I made proper arrangements ahead of time."

"I'm so sorry," Fen said, sighing with her. "I never meant to drag you down with us, Mair. You don't have to come today. Might be best for you if you didn't."

"I would not be a true friend if I left you in your darkest hour." Her mouth knit into a scowl, which she pointed forward. "This is truly madness. If she does this, I will tell…I will tell the clahnn about Ensel. I will tell them *everything*. They all deserve to know their leader has exempted herself from the same rules she wields with such rigidity."

"Don't do that, unless you can protect yourself," Pesha said, leaning across to catch her attention. Across the space of the visits Mairead had made to the grotto, he'd come to understand Fen's care for her. In a dark but brief moment, Pesha even wondered if the right thing to do would be to take the fault for everything and let Fen pick up the pieces with Mairead and Air. But Fen wouldn't want that, and neither would Pesha. In life and in death, he chose Stiofen, and he would keep choosing him no matter the alternatives placed at his feet. And together, they would choose the boy and show him he was perfect, as all creatures were in the eyes of those who loved them.

Pesha would never surrender what he had fought so hard to gain.

So their death might be quick. It might even be painless, if they were fortunate.

But it would never be final.

Wherever they ended up when the day was done, they would find each other.

They would find their own eternity.

In this life or the next.

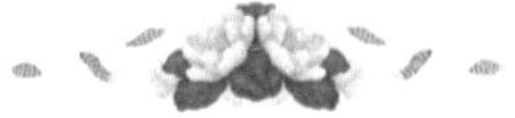

What would happen to Atio? To Eshe? And where *were* they? Eshe was hopefully still swimming in her stream, but there hadn't been even a glimpse of Atio in the sky.

Fen tried to get even one sentry to answer as they positioned the prisoners along the forest line, beyond which onlookers streamed in from all sides. There were at least a hundred watching, more coming.

Mairead and Niall had disappeared to head Aoife off before she arrived, but Fen no longer held any hope for a last-minute save. Their so-called crime wasn't about them at all, but about a betrayal that ran so deep, the only apparent cure was to make them a sacrifice.

Fen wasn't ready to die, but his many years in flight with Siofra had taught him acceptance. There were times to fight, and there were times to set down the sword. Siofra's sweet optimism sometimes had him continuing past what was reasonable, but they were comforts for her, nothing more.

There was peace in knowing he'd done his best. That Pesha had done his best. Farren was healed and would continue to heal. And, however briefly, they'd taken a beautiful little boy into their hearts and shown him a place where he belonged.

Those watching from the field were unusually quiet. A few exchanged whispers in clusters, huddling close in the chill, dewy morning, but most just stared at the condemned in terse examination.

He caught the eyes of the one who had orchestrated the entire farce, Gellais, expecting to find him gloating. All he saw was a bland curiosity, marred with a touch of cautious fear.

A man who can so easily condemn can himself be easily condemned.

"Be careful what you wish for," Fen whispered. He closed his eyes to enjoy the smooth breeze.

"What's that?" Pesha asked, tilting slightly.

"Just thinking is all." He nodded at the crowd. "They don't look bloodthirsty, do they?"

"The Medvedev I've interacted with here are not much for overreaction." Pesha snorted. "A lot of Nialls out there. Count the scowls if you need something to keep your mind busy."

"Or they're imagining themselves up here." Fen turned toward Pesha. "They're seeing how easily it can all end for them if they anger the wrong person."

"And yet it's not them up here. It's us. They don't see themselves in us at all, Fen. They see outsiders."

"They don't like change." Air glanced up at both of them, one by one. "Fanne told me there hasn't been an execution since the

Forsaken were banished. The chieftainess made them a promise that there wouldn't be any more. Just banishments. Maybe they're mad because she lied."

"You're onto something there," Fen said, softly musing. Air could have been describing anyone but especially Fen and Pesha, whose resistance to transformation had shaped their entire lifetimes. "Air, Pesha and I had time last night to talk about how this day might go. And we have something very important to ask of you. I don't know how much time you'll have to think about your answer, but I wouldn't guess very long." He nodded at Pesha to continue.

"It's a decision a boy your age should never be forced to make, and if there was a way we could take the choice from you, make it easier, we would. But we can't." Pesha's eyes squeezed close as he breathed deep. "They're going to ask you to confirm or renounce the charge that you were involved in this crime."

"But there *was* no crime, Pesha," Air whined. "She has to see that! She will see it after we talk to her." He nodded as if to reassure himself.

Pesha pursed his mouth with a pained look at Fen. "But if she doesn't, Air, then you need to be prepared to answer the question. Fen and I, we won't make you answer any way you don't want to. But we won't...We won't love you any less if you renounce your part in all of this. In fact, we would love you more, for we'd know you'll still go on to live a life when we're gone."

"We made a promise in that circle." Air didn't understand. His face was all confusion.

"And we intend to keep that promise," Fen replied. "We meant every word. All of them. It will not be Pesha and I breaking that vow if they follow through on executing us. Nor you."

"Then I'd chop off my hand *and* my foot."

Fen willed his tears to stay. "That's very brave of you, but please don't. You'll need them."

"I need you." Air turned toward Pesha. "And you."

Pesha looked at the sky with a shuddering sigh.

Fen's heart squeezed a little tighter. "I know, kid. I know."

A deeper hush fell over the gathered. They passed glances between them. A few seemed excited, but most were pale, nervous.

Aoife emerged with a retinue of sentries. Fen recognized two, Cassair and Fiachra, from their first day. Neither betrayed in their expression how they felt about the day's events.

Fen squinted when the clouds cleared and the sun beamed down. Others peered up, using the change to remark on something innocuous. Rain had poured from the skies the day his mother and father had died. At least he was going to die on a nice day.

What the fuck is wrong with you? You've just given up? Accepted it?

He glanced down at Air, who was staring at him. "It's all right, Air. We'll be brave together."

"I'm not afraid," Air pronounced with a swell in his shoulders. "I'm with you and Pesha."

"Until the sky falls, the earth shrivels, and the sea runs dry," Pesha said with a smile that looked genuine enough, if Fen didn't know him so well.

"I know it isn't real." Air shifted, tugging on his invisible bindings with a light, frustrated sigh. "I know there was no rebellion. But I wish there was. I've heard others say it too."

"Say what?" Fen asked.

"That things were better before."

"I imagine she did what she felt she must for the good of her people," Fen said charitably, suppressing a sneer. "I wouldn't want her job for anything in the world."

"I don't think she wants it either." Air twisted his mouth and nose. "She doesn't look thrilled to be here."

"I'm sure she'll sleep just fine after the deed is done," Pesha said. "Why is she just standing there?"

"I don't know..." Fen watched as Mairead came running from the east path. She flew across the clearing, dodging Medvedev until she reached her mother.

Aoife's cool demeanor disappeared, replaced by a furious flush as the women traded words, their hands flying.

"Dammit, Mair, don't get yourself thrown into prison too."

Aoife thrust a hand forward. The sentries swarmed a confused Mair, who glared at her restraints with a deep hurt on her face. Fen saw her mouth the words, *Why, Mother*?

She was dragged away.

Aoife stepped forward.

Fen and Pesha both squeezed Air's hands.

"We in Clahnn Asgill have known strife. We have known treachery. And almost all of it, from within." Aoife was facing her people as she spoke. "And yet there are far greater dangers beyond our borders. It is for this reason we forbid mating with men. Why we discourage sojourns into the White Kingdom, which is not now, never was, nor ever will be a safe place for anyone called Medvedev. And yet…We know these things happen. We are no more or less fallible than men in matters of the heart. The names of the Forsaken are not written in our histories only as villains. Before they caused so much damage, they were our friends. Our chosen mates. Our peers. This makes what they did even more dangerous, for no one ever thinks to look in bed beside them when treason calls."

Most of the gathered nodded. Some looked at each other.

"She's good," Pesha grumbled. "Des would probably hire her."

"Even considering all of that, we still loved our foundlings. Our halflings. For they did not choose the manner of their birth, the mix of bloodlines that made them what they were. There was strife, yes, and confusion among the clahnn, but no one wanted them disposed of. We were working on a way to protect them. To integrate them. And then the Forsaken *stole* that from us when they stole our children."

More affirming murmurs rumbled from the crowd.

"She didn't bring Farren with her," Fen noted aloud. He locked eyes with Gellais, who swiftly looked away. "Do you think it's because the others might recognize her as the child that was stolen? And then they'd know she was guilty of breaking her own law?"

"She didn't bring Farren because she can't bear to face her own shame. She's a filthy liar." Pesha ground his jaw. "If I didn't think she'd punish Farren for it, I would declare that truth for all of her little sycophants to hear. Even thinking about her shocked face, their stunned gasps, makes me a little hard."

"Maybe they should hear it. They deserve to know who they follow."

"No one would ever believe it coming from us, Fen." Pesha eyed him from the side. "There's a reason she had Mairead carted away."

"The Forsaken have returned to us on occasion." Aoife nodded. "A few have found their redemption in labor and atonement. We can see in their eyes that they were easily swayed by terrible creatures bent on destruction, and we have all, in our lives, listened to the wrong voice. Most, however, proved they were exactly who we knew them to be. Monsters. Devils. Miscreants. Malcontents." She turned and thrust both arms toward the prisoners. "And now they send their children to finish what they started!"

"Abominations!"

"Murderers!"

"Forsaken!"

"Yeah, Des would love this bitch," Pesha said.

"And so we will call the Trials. It has been many years since we have had a crime worthy of such. There is but one crime that we do not abide in the Territory of Asgill, against the clahnn or against each other." Aoife pivoted back to face her people. "So our offenders will be given the Trials. I will ask you three questions. Your answers will determine their fate."

"I ask you now, are the Forsaken welcome here?"

The gathered erupted in a healthy chorus of *noes*. Only a few rogue *yeses*.

"What a leading question." Pesha groaned.

"You have decided the accused guilty in their first Trial," Aoife said with a pleased look, which she tossed back at Fen, Pesha, and Air before continuing. "I ask you now, do you believe it is just and fair for the children of the Forsaken to return here and plot against us?"

The answer was more resoundingly no.

"Is this how it happens where you're from?" Air asked. "When someone does a bad thing?"

"We have done nothing wrong, Air," Fen assured him.

"If you mean, do we have farcical trials instead of real, actual ones...sometimes." Pesha breathed in. "As for whether justice is ever truly served, I don't think any society gets it right."

"Our accused have failed two of the three Trials. No matter how you answer the third, their fate has been decided. But first I must ask the child, Ruairi, where he aligns himself. He is too young to be held to our laws, but he alone can choose whether he leaves their side and returns to us, where we can hold him close and offer him love and compassion. Or he can remain with these seditionists and die with them." Aoife turned and leveled a hard look on Air. "What say you, Ruairi? Will you die for these men you just met? Or will you return to us, to your home and your people?"

Air glanced at Fen and Pesha before speaking. His voice was loud and clear, carrying over the breeze. "I like my days in the Hatchery, with Mairead. She's very nice and has taught me so much. She looks after me when no one else does. But I didn't know what love felt like until I met Fen and Pesha. I don't know much of anything, but I know I want to be with them. Forever."

Aoife's unruffled gaze flickered for the briefest moment. The Medvedev in the field murmured, wondering if she was really going to murder a little boy.

"You have made your choice," she said and spun back toward the field.

Fen suddenly couldn't breathe. He reached for his neck on instinct, nearly tearing his shoulder in the effort. He could turn just enough to see Air and Pesha enduring the same strain.

He sputtered, tripping to his knees. Air tripped and fell on top of him, tugging Pesha with him. His lungs were full of breath, but it was as if someone had closed a valve in his chest, allowing nothing in or out. Dark spots floated across his vision, and he fell onto his back, his eyes burning from the morning sun.

"She's lying to you! She's lying to you all, and she would have you murder innocents to keep her secret!"

Gasps rippled across the crowd. Fen vaguely heard someone say the name *Niallan* before everything went dark.

Fen came to, heaving and wheezing though his windpipe was clear. Air was crying, and Pesha was flat on his back, panting for air.

"Niallan. If you cannot…" Aoife faltered. "Go to Mairead. Be a good boy."

"I have always been your good boy, Aoife. Your little pet."

Fen managed to sit up, Air and Pesha doing the same. Their bindings made the effort awkward as they twisted and contorted until they were again in proper formation.

Only then did he allow himself to absorb what was happening.

"Did he just—" Pesha was interrupted by a coughing fit.

"You all right?" Fen asked Air, who nodded despite the tears in his eyes.

Aoife's voice thundered over the plain. "Go to Mairead, Niallan. If you will not take part, then you are not welcome."

"Who am I, if not your chief participant?" Niallan asked in challenge. "The very symbol of your entire reign." He swept his arms toward the gathered. "I see other halflings here watching, listening, but none of them were given the privilege of rehabilitation. None except me. And they deserve to know why."

Fen pushed to his feet, helping Air, who aided Pesha. "Pesh, what is he doing? He's going to get himself killed."

Pesha whistled an exhale. "I'm the wrong person to ask, because that is *not* the man who has been glaring and grunting at me for weeks."

"We have to do something." Fen's voice scratched from the trauma.

Pesha lifted his hand, tugging Air's with it. "What exactly are we supposed to do?"

"Niallan, if you do not return now, I will..." Aoife's face contorted. "I will hold you to account for your seditious words."

"Seditious?" Niallan charged closer. "Seditious? Is truth now forbidden from our lands, Mother? Or do our laws apply to everyone *but* you?"

The mood of the gathered Medvedev shifted fast. Murmurs of dissent became shouts in defense of Niallan's right to speak.

"So I thought." Niallan leaped up onto a log and faced the crowd.

"Niallan, come down from there! Sentries!"

"Don't you dare touch him!" Mairead cried, streaming from the forest with her hands at her sides. An onerous boom shook the earth, sending everyone scattering. "I can corroborate every claim Niallan makes, and if you kill us both, they'll know you would murder your own kin to protect your years of lies."

Mairead stopped between Niallan and Aoife, then snapped her hand, and Aoife's eyes widened, her hands traveling to her throat in a panic.

"You can breathe, Mother, but until Niallan has said his piece, you will not again speak."

Mairead nodded at Niallan, who gave her a short, relieved one in return.

"Aoife did not just banish my mother," Niallan said to everyone watching. "She had her supplies ripped away, and ordered the sentries to leave her somewhere she would never find her way out of. She left her to die for a crime..." He looked at Mairead, who crossed her arms over her chest. "The same crime she committed when she lay with a man of the realm and birthed an infant of his blood. An infant stolen by the Forsaken, who feared what she might do to the poor halfling." Niallan breathed deep. "That same man has been living in the Twilight Grotto as her prisoner for almost thirty years."

Mairead released her mother's stranglehold. Aoife bowed forward, sputtering.

"Everything Niall says is true," Mairead declared. She joined him at his side, slipping her hand into his. "I have not only met the man, Ensel, but I call him friend. And he has committed no crime but loving a Medvedev. He should be watching his children and grandchildren grow, and that has been stolen from him. And the Forsaken? All they ever wanted was to protect *all* and not just some."

Pesha breathed out in relief. "They left Farren out of it."

"It was the only way. They knew that," Fen said.

Sentries swarmed the perimeter, closing out the agitated crowd before they could reach the chieftainess.

"If you execute these three today, Aoife, you will not just be a murderer, you will also have committed sedition yourself." Mairead approached her mother, dropping her voice low. Fen had to strain to hear. "Or you could let them go, Mother, and put an end to three decades of sadness and strife. You could make amends with the man who loved you so much, he let the years pass instead of taking his life and ending his misery. Because he didn't want *you* to find him like that. Imagine that kind of love."

"You speak of truth and lies, but you know so very little, Mairead." But the venom was gone from Aoife's voice, replaced by tears on her cheeks. "You have never walked my steps. You do not know the burden I carry, for all of us."

"But I do." Mairead reached forward and held her mother's arms. "I do, because I have been here with you for so much of it. I have heard your tears when you think no one is listening. Your lamentations as you speak to a man who cannot hear you. Why spread suffering when you could slow it? Please. Everyone knows now, and if you do not renounce your sentence and all you've done to confound and repress our clahnn, you know what will happen. You know, because it's the law you created."

"You've…seen him? You've really seen him?"

"I *know* him. He's a good man, and he does not deserve what you've done to him."

"They would have killed him!"

"No, Mother. They would never have known, because all you had to do was let him go home to his family. Instead, you kept him for yourself, like a child with a toy she's only interested in when she's bored."

Aoife lowered her head. "It's too late."

"It is not. You are loved. Even now, they don't understand." Mairead let go of her mother and stepped back. "But even if it is too late, the result is yours alone to bear. You either release Stiofen, Pesha, and Ruairi, or others will do it for you, and you will lose everything. You can still salvage this. I'll say no more."

Mairead backed away, joining Niall again. He leaned sideways and kissed the corner of her mouth.

Fen gasped when his hand popped free from Air's. Pesha did the same, all three of them rubbing their wrists in surprise.

"I can no longer continue as your chieftainess," Aoife said, her shrill voice carrying over the plain. "The Trials have ended. Our prisoners are freed. There will be nothing more said on the matter."

She wrapped her vest tight and stormed into the forest.

Mairead and Niall rushed toward the prisoners.

"I don't know what to say," Fen said, breathless, as he embraced Mairead and then Niall. He waited until the hugs were finished. "Except thank you. Thank you… *Thank you.* You risked everything for us, and I don't know if there's anything sufficient that could ever repay this."

"I didn't do it for you," Niallan said, glancing in the direction Aoife had run. Others in the crowd were already following her path. "There can be no peace. No healing. Not until the secrets are suffocated."

"Did more than suffocate them, my friend," Pesha said with a gentle, playful wince. "It hasn't hit me we're still alive."

"Me either," Fen said. He hoisted Air into his arms. "You're heavier than you look."

"I'm a growing boy." Air shrugged.

Pesha leaned in and ruffled his hair. "That you are."

"Now what?" Fen asked. A tremor began in his shoulders and traveled down his arms. *No. Not yet. You can fall apart later.* "Do we…" He wasn't sure how to finish.

"I believe she's gone to the grotto." Mairead bowed her head. "I do not know what the others will do when they see, but there is little we can do now. We eliminated the secrets because they were dangerous and more blood would have been spilled. But I cannot save her from herself. I hope there can be forgiveness for her, but it is not…"

Niallan pulled her into his arms and held her through her tears. "You have done all you can, my heart."

Fen grinned at Pesha, who waggled his brows.

"I'm tired." Air buried his face in Fen's neck. "I lied earlier."

"Oh?" Fen brushed the boy's hair back and kissed his temple.

"I was very scared. But I tried to be brave."

"And you were," Pesha said, cuddling Air from the side. "So brave. It was because of you I could be brave when I was very scared as well. Fen too."

"Really?"

"Really," Fen and Pesha said together.

"No one will harm you now," Mairead said. "In accordance with our customs, I will take up my mother's mantle until a replacement is chosen. And I, Mairead de Medvedev, declare the three of you innocent of all charges, and free to move about our lands without restraint or prejudice." She bowed. "Let me welcome you now, in the way my mother should have the first time."

TWENTY-NINE
THERE ARE WORSE WAYS TO DIE

"I want to introduce the two of you properly." Pesha held his breath, his eyes traveling between Fen and Farren with fearful anticipation. Did Farren remember? Fen did. And no matter what he said, he would never forget it either. "Farren, this is my…" A grin spread over his face. "Husband, Stiofen. Fen. And Fen, you know who my sister is."

Fen tentatively reached for her hand and brought it to his mouth. It was a gentleman's greeting. "I've been waiting a long time to say hello to you, Farren."

Farren's mouth trembled. A cascade of emotions played out over her face. "Hello."

Fen smiled. "Hello."

They'd agreed it was too soon to tell Farren any of what they'd learned about Aoife and Ensel. They'd given her a few extra days of rehabilitation, but even the following morning, when they would return to the wagon and head for north—and home—would be too soon. Niall had warned that revealing these difficult truths should be a final step in her recovery or not at all. *She may never be ready.*

When the time came, they would have to decide how to respond if she wanted to meet her parents. Aoife had officially been dethroned as chieftainess—though *dethroned* wasn't the word they'd used, and Pesha, in his delirium, couldn't recall it now—and Mairead had been unanimously hailed as her replacement. Her first act in the role had been to undo any law forbidding relations with the outside realm or relating to the rights of halflings. She declared rehabilitation a right for all who had been displaced or born without, and for those who never bonded or struggled in any other way, she vowed to explore ways to protect and nurture them.

As for Ensel, the man had been finally freed and was presently enjoying his own rehabilitation as an honored guest of the new chieftainess. He was still considering the offer to travel home with Fen and Pesha to Shadowfen Hall, and there were only a few hours left for him to decide. *I'm not ready,* he'd said, watching Farren from afar. *Neither is she,* Pesha had answered, *but don't you want to be there when she is?*

Farren traced a hand down her jaw with a solemn nod at Fen. "I'm sorry."

Fen wilted and slowly leaned in. His hand hovered near hers, Farren hesitating briefly before peeling hers away. "It's not your fault, Farren. I forgive you, but it's not your fault."

Pesha had to turn away. Tears stung his eyes, hopefully the last of them for a while, but probably not. There'd be a wealth of them the moment they pulled through the front gates of Shadowfen Hall. He'd need to prepare himself for Desemir's reaction—and for the aftermath, where his brother would undoubtedly fall apart. Hopefully, Pesha prayed, in a way that allowed him to finally move forward and heal.

It was for Desemir and Siofra they'd decided to leave tomorrow. There'd been no opportunity to send a raven before they were kidnapped and whisked into the Territory of Asgill, and there was no telling what Desemir might have done about that.

He turned back in time to see Farren and Fen wrapped in a hug. Pesha's hand traveled to his throat to trap his own sob, but there was no point in holding back anymore. He let it happen, crying along with them.

"There's someone else we want you to meet, Farren." Pesha dipped back and peeked a head through the flap, waving. Air trudged forward, his head cast shyly down. "This is our son, Air."

Air peered up with a tearful smile and then joined Fen and Farren on the rug. Farren stared at him without speaking, looking up at Pesha in bewilderment. "He's yours?"

"Not by blood," Pesha said, this time looking at Fen. "By choice."

Fen mouthed *I love you* before taking Air into his arms. "He does not have a familiar, but he isn't eligible for rehabilitation like you were," he explained to Farren.

"Why?" A troubled look squished her face together.

They'd only learned it the day before, from Niall, whom Pesha had begun to understand a bit more. Niall had secretly ushered little Air into the Menagerie for months, day after day, early enough to not draw notice. After twenty-two attempts, Air had decided he was done.

"He's already tried. And it's okay, isn't it, Air?" Fen said, squeezing the boy tight. "Atio and Eshe will look after him, same as they look after us."

"And Vaya," Farren said. Her head was tilted to the side as she watched Air. She yawned and stretched, gently falling down on the rug. "Tired."

"I know," Pesha said, approaching into a crouch. "Tomorrow, we go home, Farren."

She smiled sleepily, slithering on the fur. "Home."

"Home." Pesha smiled. His heart was full, though so much of their strange visit hadn't yet hit him. To think, three days ago he had nearly died, alongside the man and boy he'd chosen to spend his life with. He should feel…*something* about it.

Later, maybe he would.

But for now, he would lean into the joy, for however long it lasted.

Fen bounced on Pesha's lap, gripping his lover's clenched thighs. Pesha had both hands wound in Fen's hair, half tugging and half shoving as he filled the air with half-formed grunts and moans. Fen slammed down, driving a shock of pain straight to his head, enjoying the desperate little whimper it earned him so much that he did it again and again.

"Are you…" Pesha said through gritted teeth. "Trying to kill me…"

"There are worse ways to die." Fen quickened his pace. He slid his clammy hand down to his cock and stroked, already close before flesh closed over flesh. "But few better ones."

"You're asking for it…" Pesha closed his hands around Fen's and peeled it away from his cock. "Mine."

"Yours," Fen agreed, baring down for another hard slam. This last one had Pesha's entire body lifting into a violent release, jerking wildly as his seed flooded Fen's ass. Fen stroked his own cock faster, harder, until his eyes exploded with stars.

Fen fell to his knees and crawled several feet before he collapsed.

Pesha, laughing, slithered along the floor until he was lying beside him. "Exhausted yourself there, Fen?"

"Mm" was all Fen could manage.

"You must be very sore."

"Mm." He would pay for it later.

"Later tonight…" Pesha tenderly flicked the hair dangling in Fen's eyes. "Before you fall asleep, I'll kiss it until it feels better. Lick it even. Suck—"

"Shit." Fen's cock thumped the floor. "You said the magic words. No putting this gift back in the box."

"Oh, my cock approves?"

"*Your* cock?" Fen made a playful *harrumph.*

Pesha snaked a hand forward and grabbed it. "Mine."

Fen's eyes fluttered back. He panted. "Yours."

"Good. So you understand." Pesha opened his hand and pulled it back.

"No fair," Fen whined. He counted to three and pushed himself up off the floor. Before Pesha could taunt him again—alluring though that was—Fen shimmied into his trousers, bouncing as he fastened the ties. "You think our carriage will still be there?"

Pesha snorted with laughter. He was still on the floor, his hands linked under his head. "That's a sobering question." He glanced down. "Very sobering."

"Isn't it? How far is the nearest village, if it's not there?"

"You really want to know?"

Fen winced. "Maybe not."

Pesha's eyes turned upward as he seemed to perform some rough calculations in his head. "Maybe two days' ride. *Ride.*"

"What are you saying exactly?" Fen tossed him his shirt.

Pesha caught the tunic and let it fall to the side. "I'm saying if that carriage isn't there, we're fucked."

"Not a good fucked, I take it."

"No, not the good kind, Stiofen."

Fen moved to the table and poured a mug of mead, then took a swallow. He stared at the light-amber liquid. "I haven't really thought about everything that's happened here. Not sure I want to."

Seconds later, Pesha came up behind him, cradling him in a soft embrace. His breath warmed Fen's neck. "The only thing I want to think about right now is how I came here a broken man and am leaving whole."

Fen stretched a hand back and cupped it behind Pesha's head. "I love you, Pesha. We'll figure out the rest."

"Yes, my love." Pesha breathed into his scalp. "I hate to even suggest such blasphemy, but should we consider getting some rest? Long day tomorrow."

"Long days for a while." Fen wasn't looking forward to the grueling ride home. And though he was eager to return to Siofra and the Hall, thinking about everything still ahead—including the very real threat to Siofra's life when her child came—was daunting.

For all he knew, she'd already delivered. He couldn't think about it though, not until he could be useful.

Pesha nodded, nuzzling his face between Fen's shoulders. "You think Air is all right tonight?" He'd asked to stay with Ensel, who had taken Pesha's hut.

"Better question is, is our friend Ensel all right?"

They both laughed.

"Do you think he'll come?" Pesha asked.

"I hope so, but it's not a choice we can make for him." Fen turned to help Pesha into his clothes. "Wait, why am I dressing us?"

"Because you know if we sleep naked, we won't be able to keep our hands off of each other?"

"And we need to sleep..."

"We need to sleep." Pesha kissed him. "We have our whole lives ahead, Fen. I can...*maybe* resist you for a few more hours."

"Stronger man than I, Pesh," Fen teased, wrapping himself into his husband's arms with a contented sigh.

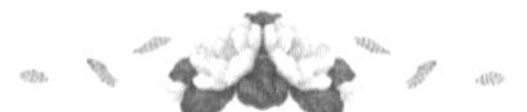

"This is where we leave you," Mairead said. Her arms were wrapped around herself. She kicked at the ground. "I would come with you, Stiofen, if I could. Perhaps one day. But you can do this. You can deliver your sister's child." She grinned at Air. "And you have the best helper you could ever ask for."

"I understand," Fen said, searching for a smile. "You have more than enough to keep you busy here for years."

"I know what to do," Air said with a confident tilt of his chin.

"Do you have all your belongings?" Niall asked the boy.

Air lifted a small satchel, half full. "I don't have many."

Pesha knelt in front of him. "You'll have anything you could ever need or want at Shadowfen Hall."

Air grinned and secured his bag on his back. "I don't need much."

Mairead cast a wistful look to the side. "Be kind to him, friends, and to yourselves. You may not see it this way, not at first, but your arrival here *was* a blessing. Not only for Niall and me."

Niall nodded.

"If you hadn't come…" She glanced at Ensel, who raised both hands.

"I *really* don't have much," he joked.

Fen was so glad the man had decided to return with them. They'd all agreed—even Air, who made it known he took secrets very seriously—that Farren would know him as nothing more than someone they'd invited back to Darkwood Run to work at the Hall. When they'd told her, she'd nodded, saying *where else would he go after all this time?*

Whatever life Ensel had left behind, it was unlikely it would still be waiting for him. But ahead…

We're all orphans at Shadowfen Hall.

Fen embraced Niall, quickly yet stalling to avoid the goodbye he was most dreading. Mairead ended his debate when she stepped up to him.

"I will miss our palavers," she said, her mouth turning upward. "And our comfort cocoons."

"Me too." Fen turned a smile on the ground, trying not to cry.

"You're always welcome to come back to us. There are no Forsaken. Not anymore."

"I know. Thanks to you."

"You opened our eyes, Stiofen." She gestured toward Niall. "And helped us understand each other better, so that we could find our way back to where we belong."

"You deserve all the happiness the world can offer you, Mairead. And I will—" Fen's voice choked. "Miss you very much."

Mairead threw herself into his arms with a powerful squeeze. "This is not good-bye."

Fen, sniffling, held her tighter. "Never."

She kissed him when he pulled away, drawing a cough from Pesha. "You have not explained comfort cocoons to your husband then," she said, and they both laughed.

With a wink at Pesha, Fen whispered to her, "Let him wonder, eh? Certainly made me wonder long enough."

Mairead winked back, grinning. She gave him one last lingering appraisal, sighed, and went to say good-bye to Ensel and Air.

Fen passed Niall and Pesha on his way to Farren. Pesha was shaking his head at the Medvedev, laughing.

"You ready to go home?" Fen asked her. Her pale lynx, Vaya, snaked around his feet with a rumbly purr.

Farren nodded. "It's all…" She pointed at her head.

"Yeah," Fen said. He reached for her shoulder but remembered she was still sensitive to touch. "We'll all be there to help you."

She dusted her hands down her chest. "I look…" She squinted at him. "No older than you. But I shouldn't."

"The magic preserved you to who you were before that terrible day," Fen said. He watched Niall and Pesha hug before turning back to her. "I know you've lost so much time, Farren, but you've gained some too. You have your whole life ahead of you."

Farren twisted her mouth, staring away. "Is Desi mad?"

"Mad? At you?"

She nodded.

"No. No, definitely not. He's mad at himself."

Her eyes narrowed. "Why?"

"For not…" Fen breathed deep. "For not knowing how to save you from what happened."

Farren scoffed but said no more.

Pesha approached, followed by Ensel and Air. Mairead and Niall hung back, watching.

"Shall we?" Pesha asked. He waved at their friends. "I didn't expect leaving to be hard."

"Me either," Fen said, laughing and crying in unison. "And they said just keep walking straight and we'll eventually come out where they found us?"

"Makes no sense to me either, but..." Pesha blew out and lifted his brows.

"Because it's magic," Air said helpfully. "The doorway will appear when we need it."

"An actual doorway?" Ensel asked, shaking his head. "I hardly remember anything from the day I came here. Maybe I don't want to."

Fen clapped him on the back. "Come on then. Before we change our minds and stay here forever."

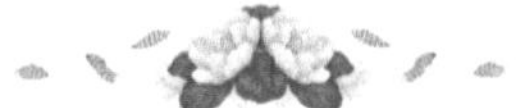

"Is that it?" Air asked, leaping in the air of a forest that was definitely *not* the forest they'd emerged from. But that was not what had Pesha speechless.

It was the hundred men gathered around the carriage.

"*Wulfhelm*?" Fen rushed forward, stepping in front of Air. He swung an arm around, at the mounted guards awaiting Wulf's command. "What...What is this?"

Wulfhelm descended his mount and took slow steps as he examined the party from afar. The look he wore suggested he wasn't quite sure he was looking at who he thought he was. *Probably because he just watched the five of us appear out of nowhere.*

"*Where* have you *been*, Fen? Pesha?" Wulfhelm broke from his daze, hurrying over. "Des sent our relay raven, and it brought us here, but all we found was the carriage. And I don't..." He searched around. "See anything except forest."

"It's hard to explain, even harder to understand," Pesha said. "He really sent the relay?"

"Of course he did!" Wulfhelm regarded him with astounded annoyance. "You promised a raven when you arrived, and you can imagine what your brother thought when none came."

"Things were not exactly cordial when we got here," Fen said. "We're sorry for worrying everyone."

"And who are…" Wulf's breath caught. Both of his hands flew to his mouth. In the span of a moment, his eyes filled with tears and they streamed down his cheeks. "Far…Farren?"

Farren rushed forward and launched herself into his arms. He lifted her, spinning them around, and then clamped both hands to her face.

"Wulfie?" Farren cried. She started to sway and Wulf caught her, whisking her into his arms like a bride on her wedding day.

"My heart," Wulf cooed. "You've come back to me."

"My heart." Farren buried her face in his neck.

Pesha exchanged a dumbfounded look with Fen.

"What the fuck?" Fen whispered. "What the *fuck*?"

"Whatever *that* is…" Pesha struggled to find the words. "We have about a fortnight to figure out how we're going to keep Desemir from murdering him and scattering his parts across the Darkwood."

SUN, DARK, OR STARS

THIRTY
A NOT-QUITE INTERROGATION

For the past hour, Desemir and Siofra had listened to Pesha and Fen recount a fantastical tale that almost beggared belief. Wulf was there too, offering his own stories from the road. Farren sat in the corner of the small parlor with her legs drawn up, her new familiar, a silver cat of some sort, balanced across her knees like a lithe acrobat happy to be free of the carnival.

Desemir had asked the old man and the boy to wait in the sitting room. *The old man and the boy* was how he would think of them until Pesha had a chance to explain himself, but the man was not actually old at all, and the boy was half Medvedev, like Pesha, except somehow he had lived a normal, non-feral life *without* a familiar.

He'd almost asked Farren to sit out the meeting as well, not because she shouldn't be there but because she'd already, in only a handful of glances, reminded him of every one of his failures.

"All right," Desemir said after they'd finished their recollections. He threaded his hands together to keep from fidgeting, fighting an onslaught of uneasiness. "I'm going to repeat this back, make sure I understand."

"Of course," Pesha said with a harried nod. Beside him, Fen stared at his lap.

"You're traveling through the forest when suddenly you're... jumped by a bunch of assholes Medvedev, who proceed to *kidnap* you, imprison you, interrogate you—"

"Wasn't quite an interrogation," Fen muttered without looking up.

"What's that?"

"Nothing. Go on."

"By all means, Stiofen. Enlighten us." Desemir dug his tongue to the roof of his mouth. Why could he not shake the disquiet? Siofra was watching him closely—had been ever since the carriage had rolled up just before midnight. She shouldn't even be awake at the late hour. The past week she'd shown signs that delivery was imminent. With every passing day, Lotte's brows threatened to join permanently. The others had made it home just in time, but he wasn't ready to trust Fen's newfound midwifery skills just yet.

"It's nothing...It's..." Fen sighed.

Pesha smiled tightly at him in gentle but strained encouragement.

"They just asked the same question over and over. Wasn't an interrogation."

"Why?" Siofra asked. She was stretched across the chaise, her hands resting on her mountainous belly. Every day, Desemir marveled at how she could even walk with that boulder attached to her at all times, but his wife was the strongest person he'd ever known, and there wasn't a day that went by that he'd let himself forget it.

"They wanted a different answer."

"Did you give them one?"

"They wanted to know why we'd come," Pesha said, sighing. "No matter how many times we both told them we'd traveled there to help Farren, they wouldn't accept it."

"But they eventually relented. Why?" Desemir asked.

"I'm not sure." Fen dug his thumbs along the arms of his tall-backed chair. "But I think it had to do with the Forsaken."

"Explain."

Pesha chewed the inside of his mouth, his eyes on his hands. "Maybe they understood about us what we could not understand about ourselves. That we needed closure for what happened there between our parents and the chieftainess. And I guess we did."

"Mm." Desemir fingered the bare spot on his finger where his father's ring—which had taken residence at the bottom of the lake—used to sit. He'd rid himself of the cursed jewelry but not the habit. "So they finish their interrogation-not-interrogation, give you each a place to live, and then put you to work."

"It wasn't exactly slave labor," Fen replied. "We each learned something."

"Fen learned something invaluable." Pesha glanced at Fen with a nod of pride that sent a bolt of warmth through Desemir. He'd prayed his little brother would open his heart to the possibility of happiness, but until neurotic, chaotic Stiofen had come to the Hall, he'd not seen the path it might take.

"I'm sure you'll be an excellent consultant to Lotte when the time comes, Fen," Siofra said. Her lids had gotten heavier and heavier as the hours wore on. Desemir knew better than to tell her what to do though, not that she'd listen if he did. The same traits that in him had made full-grown barons piss themselves made her giggle and tweak his chin, like he was a child who'd said something silly. The only place his ferociousness still had any effect on her was in the privacy of their bedchamber.

"Right. Fen the midwife." Desemir shrugged his shoulders in a dismissive lift. "So you ate some weird shit, made some friends, pissed off some others, and were thrown into prison with a strange man who claimed he'd been stuck there thirty years ago by a vengeful lover, who also happens to be the one responsible for the clahnn. I'm on the right path so far?"

Fen groaned, and Pesha nodded.

Desemir caught Wulf watching Farren intently and remembered the strange dream his old friend had had the same night as Siofra's. The guard had said nothing in over an hour, probably fascinated with Farren's transformation. So was Desemir. But the same thing prompting Wulf's staring was keeping Desemir from glancing her way.

He slowly peeled his gaze away from Wulf, returning it to the others. "And in this prison, you…" Now he grinned. "Wed each other."

Neither man could restrain their smiles. "A handfast ceremony, but…" Pesha tilted his head at Fen, tugging his lower lip between his teeth at the corner. "It's binding for us. And that's all that matters."

"We don't need the law to define our commitment," Fen said, his eyes on Pesha as though no one else in the room existed.

Desemir smirked, remembering the way Pesha had turned his nose at the very idea of romance.

"I cannot tell you…" Siofra shuddered in a breath and clapped her hands together. "Fen, Pesha… You were both created for one another. For *this*. I've grown maudlin in my confinement, so I'll say no more, except…" Tears rolled down her flushed cheeks. "I love you both so dearly, and I wish you all the happiness you deserve."

"What Si said." Desemir jammed his tongue harder against the top of his mouth. He reached for his wine and swallowed a generous sip to subdue his own maddeningly maudlin inclinations. The months of worry had done a number on him, and he looked forward to things returning to a semblance of normalcy. "We couldn't be happier for you both. I mean it."

"Thank you, Siofra, brother," Pesha replied with a long nod.

"Thank you," Fen said.

"But then there's the matter of the boy…"

"His name is Ruairi," Farren said. It came out like a hiss, her s's dragging. "And he is not any boy, Desi. He's their son."

Desemir chortled, more from discomfort than anything. He might have been responding to Farren, but he still couldn't look at her. "Right, but not *actually* their son, unless the land of Asgill is even more fantastical than you'd have us believe." He didn't know why he was challenging the matter. He'd never turned away anyone who needed a home and family, and to Pesha and Fen, the boy was already family.

The looks in both of their eyes suggested he was way out of order, but it was Siofra's stone glower that had him remembering himself. "Forgive me. It's late. This is a lot to take in. Ruairi is welcome here, obviously. Whatever he needs."

"I need him to be more than welcome, Des." Pesha's face had gone deadly pale, and in his eyes was a look Desemir hadn't seen in years: the intensity of purpose. "Fen and I made a commitment, not only to Air but to those who loved him in Asgill. He's not here to work, beyond what we all do for the family. He's here as our adopted son and should be treated with the same respect and importance as Siofra's children."

Fen stared at his lap, tears running down his cheeks.

Desemir's heart melted. It had been doing that a fair bit lately, a hopefully temporary affliction he could only assume was related to his impending fatherhood. "You're right. Whatever he needs. Whatever he *wants*."

Thank you, Pesha mouthed, too overcome to speak.

There was more they weren't telling him. It had to do with Farren, and they wouldn't say it in front of her. Whatever it was, he wouldn't sleep until he heard it. "It's been a long night," Desemir said finally. "We're all tired. Pesh, why don't you and I finish up here and then you can join Fen in bed."

"We should probably discuss where we're sleeping," Fen said with a short laugh. "And Air."

"You don't have to make any commitments tonight," Siofra said sweetly. "But, Pesha, after you're done with Des, there is something I want to show you. It won't take long."

"You're swaying on your feet, darling." Fresh worry peppered Desemir's words with agitation. "Can't it wait until morning?"

"I'm not on my feet, darling." She smiled and carefully pushed herself to a seated position.

"Then you go first." Desemir waved to conceal his turmoil. No one wanted to see him so unsettled. "And I'll speak to him after."

"That is a lovely compromise." Siofra waddled over to him and gave him a kiss. With a wink, she whispered, "You can punish me later for my insolence."

A growl ripped from deep within him. "Bet on it."

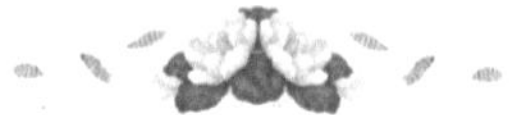

Siofra beckoned Pesha to follow her down the long hall of windows. When she'd imagined this moment, they'd been walking down to the lake, winding through the maze in the gardens, but for all her obstinacy, she truly didn't want to give Desemir more to worry about. He'd been burying his fears so deep, even she couldn't reach them, and she loved him too much to add to them.

"We can do this tomorrow, Si," Pesha said, slowing to match her pace. "Des is right. You should probably be resting."

"I know Des is right." Siofra grinned from the side. "But I've been waiting a long time to show you this, and I don't want to let it sit another night."

When they reached the center of the long hall, she chose a window at random and stopped. The entire forest was bathed in darkness, save the lake, which reflected a thin sliver of moonlight.

She'd been working up to what she was about to show him for weeks. It wasn't safe to practice her magic anywhere really, and until that point in her life, she'd practiced avoidance tactics only. But she was going to be a mother of at least two Medvedev, and if she could not learn to harness her gift, she'd never be able to teach them to do the same.

At first, she'd gone deep into the forest, where no one was around who might get caught in the wake of her destruction. Des wasn't happy about it, especially since she'd been kidnapped in that same forest not so long ago, but if he had his way, she'd be propped in bed all day, being doted upon. His compromise had been to have Euric and other men stationed at various points while she practiced singing without devastation.

A couple dozen singed trees and weeks later, she worked up the courage to try it on the lake.

"You returned Eshe to the lake before you rode to the house," she said. "Were you surprised to find it wasn't frozen?"

Pesha sucked his teeth. "Well, yes." He had one hand propped on the frame as he stared into the night. "But after the trip we had, it wasn't front of mind." He seemed ready to say more but didn't.

"Springtide is ended," Siofra said. "Autumnwhile was over in a whisper, and we're just inside the start of midwinter."

"Right..."

"So it should be frozen." She winced, straining against her exhaustion. Pesha made as if to gather her in his arms, but she shook her head. "It is not, because while you were gone, I was working on a gift for you. For Eshe too."

"I don't understand." His gaze danced between her and the lake.

"I found a way to harness my song. My melody." She swelled with pride, beaming through her exhaustion. The words opened up so many possibilities, they eclipsed a horrifying past and gave hope for a better future. "And I was able to safely thaw the lake without harming anything in it."

Pesha released the window and spun toward her, his eyes wide with disbelief. "You did what?"

"I know it sounds impossible, given..." She pulled in a sigh. "But all magic can be harnessed. When my children are born, I want them to know this to be true. We cannot know what terrible gifts the Guardians will imbue them with, but if we can learn to work with whatever they are, nothing has to be a curse."

Pesha shook his head, wordless. He turned back toward the window with a sharp inhale. "There's nothing I could say...nothing remotely..."

Siofra sidled up behind him for a hug, pressing her face to his back. He wrapped his hands around hers and squeezed. "You need say nothing, brother. I love you. My only ask is that you be kind to yourself. See yourself as Fen sees you. As we do. I will sing warmth into our lake however much is necessary. Eshe will never have to retreat inside herself again, and neither will you."

"Talk to me, Pesh."

Four words had never been so terrifying. He'd been talking to Desemir for eighteen years, but *talking*?

Desemir drummed his hands on a bookshelf, not quite looking at Pesha. His eyes were hazy with deep thought, as though he'd anticipated Pesha's reticence and was debating how to break through. "I know you hate talking about yourself. You always have. Always shut fucking down whenever I suggested there might be more than being a nanny to your rapscallion of a brother."

That got a peek of a smile from Pesha.

"But...*How*? How did you make the leap from forsaking even the idea of doing something for yourself to getting *married* in a magical forest?"

"How?" Pesha repeated his brother's words back to him, stalling for time. For words of his own. What could he even say that would give Des a satisfying answer...when he couldn't even answer the question for himself?

"Yes, Pesh, it means—"

"Don't be an ass."

Des grinned and shrugged. "I could be an ass who asks thoughtful questions of the little brother he loves dearly, or I could be another kind of ass, one you're also well acquainted with."

Des was almost a full decade older than him, but there had been large pockets of time when Pesha had played the role of tempering reason into his brother. He had defused so many precarious situations that doing so had become second nature, a part of his personality. But Des was a shrewd man who had never *truly* needed Pesha's counsel, only his companionship. Desemir had only tested the limits of the bloodthirsty barons because Pesha had been there to smooth him over, but if he'd never have been born, Des would have chosen a different tactic. He would have—

"Wow, so you're a married man now, father to an orphan you just met, but nothing else has changed, eh?"

Pesha wrinkled his nose. "Pardon?"

Des waved a hand. Snorted. "I can practically *see* your thoughts working against you."

"Working against..." Pesha shook his head at the floor. "Fine. You win."

Desemir grinned. "You know that's all I ever want."

"Oh, *I know*."

They both laughed. Gradually, the vise lessened on Pesha's chest.

Pesha reluctantly gestured toward the sofa. Desemir peeled off the shelf with raised brows and took a seat on the opposite end.

"I don't know *how* it all happened." Pesha twisted his hands in his lap, pulling each finger one by one. "When I met Fen, something felt...different inside of me. I can't explain it. And I thought life would be better—*simpler* if I didn't acknowledge it. If I thought of it as...as a surprising amusement. But once we were on the road together, alone for days, weeks, it became harder to lie to myself."

"Oh my Guardians, did you...You did." Desemir leaned forward and slapped the sofa. "You said the words."

Pesha frowned.

"You *have* been lying to yourself. How many times have I told you so?"

"Uh, none?"

"Perhaps not in those exact words..."

Pesha rolled his eyes. "Doesn't matter. Once I realized what I was feeling, I started shutting down again. I took it out on Fen, and it broke my damn heart every time I saw what I'd done to him, in his beautiful violet eyes..." He had to bow his head for a moment of recovery. "I hated myself in a way I had never known hatred before. And then Farren attacked him, and... then we were separated, and...I don't know, Des. I don't know how to tell you what you want to hear. I've loved Fen from the moment I first saw him in Newcarrow, but it took a fortnight with the Medvedev to make me realize it's a matter for someone wiser than me."

Desemir nodded to himself, his whole body shifting with the gesture. "I could have told you that. In fact...I believe I did."

Laughing, Pesha groaned. "As for Air...Fen chose him. And I chose Fen. It's as simple as that."

"Having a child is not as simple as that. Even *I* know it, and my twins are still baking inside my wife."

"Lovely imagery." Pesha crinkled his mouth together. "I know it isn't. And I was initially dubious, but seeing Fen with him...All I can tell you, Des, is when you see Siofra with your babies, you'll love her in a way you never thought possible. And she will love you just as much when she sees you with them."

Desemir looked away again. "It's not like you to wax poetic."

"Why should truth be branded poetry just because it involves matters of the heart?"

"All right," Desemir said after a thoughtful pause. "Then congratulations, Pesh. I'm truly happy for you. You left here a broken man, and you're too damn young for that horseshit. Whether it was Fen or Air or both, it doesn't matter to me. You could have adopted fifty little orphans, and I'd have asked Lotte to get creative with the sleeping arrangements. All I want is your happiness, and only you get to decide what that looks like."

Hot tears pricked Pesha's eyes. Serious brotherly talks had never been part of their personal culture. The few they had, Desemir had been on the receiving end of a lecture. If matters ever veered too close to something personal for Pesha, he was good at redirecting the conversation somewhere safer.

If he'd known how incredible it would feel to have his older brother's approval, he might have kicked down his walls sooner.

"Thank you," he croaked. "For everything. For…taking care of me. Looking after me when my mother…when Farren…"

"You're my *brother.*" Desemir reached across the sofa and clamped a hand hard on his knee, squeezing. "What happened with our parents is none of our fucking business. None of our fuckin' concern. Shouldn't have been then, and there's no room for it now. *We* decide the future, Pesha. You and me, with our spouses, who could probably do a lot better than us, if we're being honest…"

Pesha chuckled, hanging his head. "You've always had such a way with words."

"My speeches work better on my enemies." Desemir retreated to his side of the sofa with a flippant shrug.

"*Adversaries*, not enemies. Remember?"

Desemir grinned. "You do listen to me."

"When it suits me."

"Right, so Air will have everything he needs. You and Fen can decide whose room you'll be sleeping in from now on. Could always take one of the empty family suites, you know. Your choice though." Desemir made tick marks on the cushion. "So—Farren. She doesn't know that the man you brought home with you is her father?"

Pesha shook his head. He loathed secrets. All they'd ever done was cause harm. Not telling Farren about her mother and father was a mercy, one he could justify by considering all she'd been through and what she would still endure before she was fully healed. But not telling Des about Wulf…That was a different betrayal. "I suggest we wait until she's settled and can handle it."

"You're right." He nodded. "I agree. But we should be prepared for her wanting to return to Asgill when she learns her mother was the chieftainess."

"I had considered that." Pesha breathed in deep. "We'll address it when the time comes."

"And Ensel. What's his trade?"

Pesha realized he'd never asked what the man had been doing when he'd crossed paths with Aoife. "I'm ashamed to say I don't know. I imagine he'd be willing to do any work you handed to him."

"There's never a shortage at the Hall. Send him to my office tomorrow after breakfast."

"Thank you. I will."

"I'm having some paperwork drawn up." Des swatted the air. "Not tonight. It's late. Go on to bed. Fuck your husband. Whatever."

Pesha grinned. "I might just do that."

Desemir rose. He pulled Pesha into his arms as he was standing. "You deserve happiness. Never forget it."

Pesha buried his face in his brother's neck and sighed. "So do you."

Releasing him, Des blew out a breath and glanced at the door. "One more thing. If you'd like, we can have a wedding here. A legal one."

"Oh." Pesha hadn't been expecting that. "What Fen and I did in that cave *was* binding. To us it was. I appreciate the offer—"

"I'm not suggesting the handfast doesn't mean the same thing to the both of you, but there are benefits to having the union legitimized by the law. Protections, if you will, for Fen *and* Air. Not that you have to worry about that with me, but it may give you peace of mind, just the same. When something is made law, it is far harder to challenge." Des cupped Pesha's cheek with a pat. "Just think about it."

"I will." Pesha sighed at the door. "I better go find Fen and Air."

"Go on then."

"We'll be *right* next door." Fen was at a loss for what to do next. His father had been a serviceable guardian but not much of a caregiver. He'd once heard another child talk about being "tucked in" by his parents, but Fen could only pretend he understood what it meant. Instead, he did what felt the most right, leaning in to kiss Air's forehead. "That's why we chose this suite, because it was made for a family."

"And we're a family." Air smiled, his eyes fluttering with drowsiness. "Right?"

"Right," Pesha said. He dropped in close. "Not just the three of us either. Now you have a *huge* extended family. Des, Siofra, Wulf, Euric, Lotte, Gisela…I could stand here all night reciting names."

"And don't forget Ensel," Fen said.

"That's right." Pesha slid an arm around his back. Fen melted against it with a lethargic sigh.

"Tomorrow…You'll wake me for breakfast?"

"We wouldn't dare leave this room without you," Fen teased.

Air smiled with his eyes closed. "I suppose that's fine then."

"Oh, you suppose?" Pesha reached down and tickled his side, drawing sleepy giggles.

"Good night, Air," Fen said from the door. Pesha joined him. "We'll see you when you wake."

Air's mouth moved with the hint of words, but he was already falling asleep.

Fen gently clicked the door closed, wincing, and listened. But there were no sounds on the other side except Air's soft breathing.

They moved into the sitting room, which divided one bedchamber from another. "There are three family suites in the Hall, going back to when the brothers of barons shared in their inheritance," Pesha explained. "This one hasn't been used since Klaus's brother—I forget his name—was alive. Klaus was my grandfather, in case you've forgotten."

"Thanks for the history lesson," Fen joked, sidling up behind him. He nuzzled his face to Pesha's back, sliding a hand around to his front. "But I have *just* enough energy left to swallow this cock. Unless you'd rather talk about Klaus and—"

Pesha spun and locked his mouth over Fen's. "Point taken."

THIRTY-ONE
ALL FOR SOMETHING

"Are you sure Lotte isn't going to scare the poor kid?" Fen stopped walking midway through the maze.

Siofra slowed and then turned back, waiting.

"Maybe I should go get him."

"You're being silly. Lotte is pleased as ever to have a child in the Hall again. The last one was Pesha." Siofra's cheeks were flush with color as she swaddled her belly with both hands. He'd been perfectly content to spend time with her inside, where she could sit and relax, but she'd insisted the exercise was beneficial and would help her labor. Mairead had said nothing about women needing exercise in their confinement, but he hadn't had nearly enough time to learn from her.

Shadows painted the maze. Fen tilted his head back to see Aio and Atio playing overhead in the cloudy sky. He smiled, imagining Atio regaling Aio with her Medvedev adventures. "Maybe you're right," Fen said distantly. He squinted when the sun glared through a gap in the clouds. "He's a good kid, Si. When I met him, I saw something in his eyes…" He sighed and pulled his gaze back to his twin sister. "It was the same thing I used to see in my own every time I looked in a mirror."

Siofra smile was thin but warm. "Sometimes those days feel like a dream."

"More like a nightmare."

She laughed. "It wasn't all bad." At Fen's dubious look, she quickly said, "All right, most of it was pretty atrocious."

Fen chuckled. "Remember what you used to say to me?"

Siofra cocked her head. Her pale-blonde hair spilled out of the array of pins.

"You would say, 'This is all for something.' It sounded like nonsense, right up there with 'everything happens for a reason.' I told you as much every time." Fen scratched his head with a half grin. "This is all for something. I never would have believed that being thrown into a moldy prison cell in Newcarrow was the best thing that could ever happen to us, but…"

She smiled. "Pesha is good for you. I can see Air is too."

"I know nothing about being a father." Fen scoffed, kicking at clumps of grass and dirt. "I don't even know if he'll see me that way. If he even wants to. His real mother and father are dead, and I'm more child than man myself."

"Fen, you and I were never children," Siofra said gently. "We should have been, but we never got the chance. We've been making our own way since we were Air's age. And that's also true of Pesha and Des, isn't it?" She pulled a hand from her belly to wave it around with a sweeping look. "The setting was better for them, but they were fighting their own wars as boys." She waddled closer. "You've been training your whole life for this moment. Air doesn't belong with some perfect family who can't possibly understand the trauma in his heart. The Guardians couldn't have chosen a better placement for him than with two men who know what it is to be exiles and outcasts."

"But isn't that the problem, Si? That's all we know."

"That's not all you know, Fen." She lifted both hands to his face and cradled it. "You're the reason I'm even still alive. The reason I get to be Baroness Trevanion, wife to a man I love with my entire soul and, soon, mother to our children. If something happened to Des and me, Guardians forbid, it would be *you* I'd want to look after our little ones. You and Pesh. No question. No hesitation." She planted a kiss at the corner of his mouth. "You've come so far. Don't look back, brother. Don't look to a past that can't hurt you anymore."

Everything she said rang true. It was a modified version of everything he'd been saying to Pesha for weeks and weeks in Fen's attempts to show him it was possible to look forward and not back…to find and embrace happiness without guilt or remorse. He'd believed himself so *enlightened* in his attempts to break through Pesha's barriers, but here he was, doing the same thing.

"I'll try," he said, forcing a smile.

Siofra released him. "Good. To that regard, have you given Des's offer any further thought?"

Fen frowned. "What offer?"

"The one he gave Pesha last night, about a legal wedding here at the Hall?"

Pesha had not said a single word about it. To be fair, he hadn't had much of an opportunity between Fen sucking his cock and Pesha returning the favor, but they *had* talked in bed after, until they'd drifted off. And then that morning, before breakfast. After. "Ah, no, we're still discussing it."

Siofra recoiled. "He didn't tell you."

Fen lowered his head and shook it.

"You've had no shortage of diversions since you came home. He'll mention it when the time is right."

"No, of course." Fen forced a smile, then remembered Siofra could read him with precise clarity. "All right, it upsets me. I thought we'd made progress in Asgill, but maybe I was right to worry that the 'magic' of those days wouldn't follow us home."

"But it *has*," Siofra said with a broad smile. "I see how he looks at you. Don't hold him to the standards you set for yourself, Fen. You'll only be disappointed. Pesha just takes longer with things."

"When did you become so damned wise?"

"Well, when you have an utterly dashing husband who breaks you every single night and puts you back together in the morning—"

"You made your point!" Fen lifted his hands in surrender, and they both laughed. He waited for the moment to dwindle. "Look, Si, I don't know if I'll be any better than Lotte at helping you when the time comes, but I learned a fair bit from Mairead about the differences in bringing halflings. Air knows even more than I do. Between the three of us, we'll keep you safe."

Siofra's eyes fluttered as she smiled, nodding. "I know you will. Perhaps you were right. I am feeling a bit peaked. Let's go inside."

Pesha sat next to Farren at the same long table where Des had made and broken alliances with the barons. It was reserved for business only, and he'd not yet been on the other end of one of his brother's deals.

Farren had her legs drawn up, Vaya wedged between her thighs and her belly. They were already inseparable, even more so than the Medvedev and familiars he'd seen in Asgill. He wondered if all rehabilitated displaced had such powerful bonds, but he'd likely never get the answer. For all he'd gained from his time with the Medvedev, he never ever wanted to return.

She'd said little since their arrival the night before. On the ride home, she'd spoken only when necessary, even when he and Fen had tried to engage her in innocuous conversation. Her words clear and crisp, a far cry from her howls of *wulf, wulf, wulf,* but whatever was on her mind, most of it stayed there.

Desemir pushed two stacks of documents across the table, one to Pesha, one to Farren.

Pesha lifted the top one, then the second. "What is this?" Farren hadn't touched hers.

Des was watching Farren closely. "That's why we're here. For me to explain. Farren, are you…Can you…"

"I can read." She shifted slightly in her chair without looking at the paper.

Nodding, Des turned back toward Pesha. "I've had a lot of time to think since you left. Too much maybe. Never a good thing with me."

Pesha grinned. "No."

"You and I, we had always said there was an unofficial agreement on your inheritance. We never wanted to document it for fear people would look into you, your past. We have too many fucking en—adversaries in Darkwood Run, and they'll look for any way to take what we have."

"I already know all of this."

"And I'm saying it again anyway, because I was wrong." Des swallowed hard, leaning back in his chair. "They'll find reasons no matter what, Pesha. They'll always find reasons. That's not a reason for me *not* to make this official." He nodded at the stack. "You'll see in there that I have split my portion of the Darkwood exports into four parts. One for Siofra and me. One for our children, who will also inherit our portion upon our deaths, giving them half the estate. The other half, I've split between you..." He looked at Farren. "And you."

Farren's mouth twitched. She looked away.

Pesha flipped through the pages again. "You don't have to do this. I'm not concerned about the money, the land...any of it."

"You should be. You're a father now." Des twisted his finger where their father's ring had once been. "This isn't just your inheritance, Pesha. It's Air's. And to that, I've officially filed paperwork to have him established as a Trevanion—and as your descendant. No matter what happens, Air will be taken care of."

Pesha scratched at his neck, searching for the right thing to say, but he couldn't organize a single thought. "Des, I..."

"Don't need to say anything." Des gestured at the papers. "Those are yours to keep. Read over them when the time feels right. I've already sent Cassius into the village to file them with the magistrate." He tapped the table and turned toward Farren.

"And yours, Farren. You are officially a Trevanion now, with a quarter of the estate. This is your home, and Pesha's, as much as mine. You should never be dependent upon anyone, ever again. Not even me."

Farren daintily stretched a hand to her documents and lifted one at the corner. "Why?"

Desemir flinched. "Why?"

"I'm not your sister. I'm not your family."

"Farren…" Desemir set his mouth in a soft line. "You *are* my sister. You *are* my family. And I deeply regret ever treating you otherwise. I regret…a lot about those years."

Guilt stabbed Pesha's chest. Farren wasn't *his* sister either, not in a biological sense. The revelations of Asgill had saved her life but had cost him another member of his small, precious family. A cost she wouldn't ever know about unless they told her.

Farren pushed the papers aside and looked up. "It wasn't your fault."

"Yes. It was. I wasn't a child, like Pesh. I was old enough to do better, and I fucking choked, I…" Des closed his eyes and breathed in through his nose. "If I hadn't encouraged you to lie to my father, Nera would still be here."

Farren stroked a purring Vaya. "It was me he wanted dead. Ludwik did not like no."

"No, he didn't." Desemir breathed deep with a quick glance at Pesha. "But he's gone. He's been gone for years. Everyone from that generation is dead, gone, buried…They can't hurt us anymore, not unless we let them."

"Years, for you." Farren lifted her gaze. "For me, yesterday."

Desemir bowed his head. "If I could go back…"

"Desi." Farren stretched her hand across the table, though not quite close enough for him to reach forward and touch it. "You were the only one who tried. I would like never to speak of it again."

Pesha and Des shared a wary glance. No words were needed. Farren wouldn't fully recover until she processed her trauma, but re-injuring her by speaking of it seemed cruel, especially when she'd bravely asked them not to.

"Yeah." Des cleared his throat. "Fine. We'll put it to bed, if that's what you want."

Farren nodded low.

"Then welcome to the family. *Officially.*"

Farren nodded again, shifting Vaya to her arms as she stood. Then she left without another word.

Desemir's eyes widened through a hard exhale. "Is that what the ride home was like?"

"I think she said more in this meeting than the entire trip." Pesha massaged his cheeks. "This *really* wasn't necessary, though—"

"It was. And I did it. End of discussion." He folded his hands atop the table with a defiant glower.

Pesha snorted. "There's the Des I remember." He pushed back from the table and dropped his hands down over the surface. "Thank you then. I already knew…I *know* you'd never let anything happen to Fen or Air, but I suppose it gives a deeper comfort to know the law agrees with you."

"I don't think the law around here has ever *agreed* with me, Pesh."

They both laughed. "Perhaps the aggravation is more that the law keeps the barons from tearing down your dynasty, piece by piece, and parceling it among them."

Desemir stood. "Mind bringing your man in here? Ensel?"

"Did you talk to him this morning?"

"Wanted to speak with you and Farren first."

"Ah." Pesha rapped his knuckles on the wood. "I'll go get him now."

Pesha exited the room and started toward the guest apartment Lotte had arranged for Ensel in the newly refurbished west wing of the Hall. On the way, he passed the apartment Farren had spent the past eight years in, under the command of the powerful magic that had kept her—and everyone else—safe. The visual reminder was the first time Pesha really understood and appreciated the miracle of her rehabilitation. Year after year, he and Des had eyed the west wing with trepidation, afraid to speak about it…to hope. Neither really believed they could save her, but they couldn't bear to let her go either.

Yet though she was saved, a different guilt was creeping in. *You might have saved her sooner if you'd believed it was possible.*

Wulf emerged from the apartment. When he saw Pesha, he startled in alarm.

Pesha's eyes narrowed. "What were you doing in there?"

"Checking on her. She's been through a lot." Wulf glanced past him. His throat bobbed.

"You don't think I know what she's been through?" Pesha rested a hand on the wall, effectively pinning Wulf into the alcove. "I was there, for *all* of it."

Wulf nodded, glancing back toward the closed door. He rolled his tongue along the underside of his lip. "You and Des. Sure. But you aren't the only ones. And you didn't know her like…" He rolled his eyes with a scoff. "What's the point? You don't want the truth, because it's inconvenient, just like it was inconvenient when Ludwik turned his eyes on her and started ignoring his wife and mistress. Just like the past eight fucking *years* have been so inconvenient to the two of you, in your quest for domination of the region." He shook his head, sizing Pesha up. "You want to protect your sister, Pesha? Then realize there's more to saving her than reviving her body."

Wulfhelm brushed past, knocking Pesha sideways. He stormed down the hall, toward the main wing.

Pesha was still reeling from the charged encounter when he spotted Ensel coming out of his apartment, with Fen. Fen's smile dulled when his eyes connected with Pesha's, which was odd, but it wasn't until Fen kept walking without so much as a shared glance that Pesha's blood chilled.

"You two having a row?" Ensel asked.

"I'm not…sure," Pesha said distantly, his eyes following Fen as he turned the corner. Everything had been fine the night before, and at breakfast, but *something* had changed since. He wasn't reading a problem that wasn't there; Fen *was* upset with him. In the past, Pesha would have stubbornly waited for Fen to come around, but things were different. Choosing a life together meant making better choices about everything.

"It will clear up. These things always do."

"Unless your lover is Aoife, you mean?"

Ensel winced with a grin. "Fair play."

Pesha matched his grin, but only one side of his mouth lifted. He was still staring at the hall, replaying the past hours for answers. "Are you ready to speak with Desemir?"

Ensel smiled and nodded. "Put me to work."

THIRTY-TWO
A WALK IN THE GARDEN

Air had never seen *anything* like the crypts at Shadowfen Hall. Even in his wildest imaginings he'd never considered there might be places one could go *underground*. He looked up at the damp, cobwebbed ceilings, wondering just how far into the earth they'd gone. He should have counted the stairs. He would on the return.

"These," Desemir said, sweeping an arm, "are our ancestors, Ruairi. Every last one who lived at the Hall."

"They're *here*? Their bodies?" Air gaped, his eyes averting to the names chiseled into the old, crumbling stone. Klaus I. Frederik. Ludwik I.

"Most of them anyway. A few died away from the Hall, in some battle or another. Take Gautier here. He died fighting for the Darkwood, and his remains were never found, just his sword. So that's all you'd find in his tomb."

"Perhaps too mature for our little Air," Siofra said sweetly. Air had liked her from the moment he'd met her. Mairead had taught him to read a person's aura, and hers was full of bright, inviting light. Desemir's was muddier, like most auras tended to be. Even Fen and Pesha had some darkness in theirs. "But you ask good questions. This must all feel so different for you."

Bonding time with your aunt and uncle, Fen had said when he'd told Air how he'd be spending his afternoon. He wasn't familiar with those terms, aunt and uncle, so Fen had patiently explained the concept of extended families and then Air wished he had a hundred aunts and uncles. And cousins. Soon, he'd have two of his own to play with. "Everything is very different, yes."

"You'll get used to it. A boy like you, all you've seen and done, you'd have to be pretty adaptable, wouldn't you?" Desemir knelt to meet Air's height. "Do you want to see more?"

"Yes!"

Siofra giggled. Desemir grinned. "Then let's continue," he said.

They moved farther into the dusty crypts. Air sidestepped a gigantic rat and reached out to touch a spider bigger than any he'd seen in Asgill. Siofra gave him a frightened, chiding look at that, but it made him brighten with unexpected warmth and gladness. She didn't want to see him hurt. Maybe she'd even come to love him.

Desemir recited more names on their walk, pausing once more when they reached one with the name *Klaus III*. "My grandfather. You would have liked him, Air. He was a stern man but a fair one, the kind of father I'll aim to be when our little ones are born. My own father was a tyrant, a terrible man who did terrible things." He fingered the names on the stone etching, tracing the letters. "There are the people in our lives who we didn't ask for and wish we could forget. But never lose sight of knowing you can choose your family. That's what Shadowfen Hall is all about. Everyone here chose to be here." He ruffled Air's hair. "Including you, yes? Fen and Pesha asked if you wanted to come?"

Air nodded. A lump formed in his throat.

"Then you belong." Desemir looped an arm around Siofra's waist and tugged her close. "We don't choose our blood. But we choose our family. And *this* is your family. Your ancestors. And if one day you decide to have children of your own, they'll be Trevanions, just as you are, Air."

"I'm a Trevanion?" Air was breathless with joy.

"Legally, soon." Desemir winked at Siofra, who pulled a small rolled scroll from a bag tied to her wrist.

"This is going to the magistrate tomorrow," she said, unrolling the paper with a smile. "Would you like to read it?"

"I…" Air's eyes welled with tears of shame. He'd lied about it before, when the sentries had come for Fen, and it had been weighing on him ever since. "Cannot read."

But Siofra was still smiling. Still watching him with that patient, loving expression he wished he could fuse to his memories for all time. "Would you like to learn?"

Air nodded when words wouldn't come.

"Lotte taught Pesha and me, she'd be happy to teach you," Desemir said. "In the meantime, the scroll your aunt is holding says that Ruairi Trevanion is officially entered into the lineage of the Trevanions of Darkwood Run. I've already spoken to your fathers about it, and they were happy to name you as their heir as well."

Air stared at them both, unsure of what he was supposed to say, or even feel. His life had changed so fast in so many ways, all of them too good to be true. He went from being a foundling to having two incredible fathers. To having aunts and uncles and all the other kind and wonderful people who made up Shadowfen Hall.

"Taking you down here is a rather morbid way of making our point," Siofra said with a pointed look at Desemir, "but men take great pride in their ancestry. Their histories. Medvedev see time and past differently, don't they?"

Air nodded. Tears rolled down his cheeks.

"This is our way of inviting you into your new world. Desemir and I…" Siofra folded her hands over her heart, tilting her head to the side. "We're so happy you're here, Air. You make Fen and

Pesha so very happy, and we cannot wait to get to know you as they do."

"My wife said it so well, I won't bother trying to compete," Desemir said. "Everything on this property, for miles and miles, is yours to explore. Pesha said you feel at home in the forest? Lots of fucking trees—"

"Des!"

Desemir braced in mock annoyance. "Lots of *trees* and…I forgot what I was saying."

Air giggled at the two of them. He had so many questions for Siofra, a full Medvedev who had chosen a man as her mate. He wanted to understand not only that but everything there was to know about the world of men, of which he only knew the foul things other Medvedev whispered over food and fire. All he'd seen so far at Shadowfen Hall was in direct conflict with everything he'd believed to be true.

He had his whole life to learn, and the revelation filled him with indescribable joy.

Air threw himself into Siofra's arms with a sob. Soon there was warmth at his back as well, as Desemir joined the embrace.

"You're home," his uncle said. "That word never has to feel scary to you again."

"Thank you," was all Air managed to say.

"And…" Desemir trailed off, peeling away. "Si, what's wrong?"

"It's…" Siofra staggered back, palming Ludwik II's tomb. "Oh, no." She looked down and so did Air and Desemir, right as a gush of water spread and pooled in the dirt.

"Your children are coming!" Air cried, whipping his gaze from her to Desemir. "That's what that means. You've broken your waters."

Siofra's eyes closed. Desemir caught her right before she lost balance.

"Go get Lotte, Air. Now!" Desemir cried. He brushed hair off Siofra's face and kissed her cheek. "You know your way?"

Air nodded, his heart racing. "I'm very good with direction."

"Find Lotte…find Fen…and…send Euric to help me carry Siofra back safely." Desemir looked up. Worry painted his expression. "We want you there too, in the delivery. You know more about bringing Medvedev than anyone here."

Air swelled with pride, with fear. "Lotte. Fen. Euric."

"Lotte, Fen, Euric," Desemir said. "Now go, and let's bring my children into this world safe and sound."

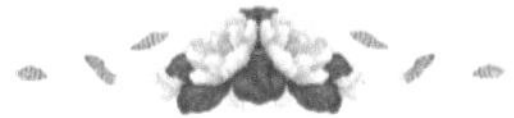

Pesha found Fen pacing the library. It was the last place he checked, and by the time he got there, Fen had already whipped himself into a frenzy. His eyes were as wild as his hair, disheveled, and his face was a splotched mess of tears old and new.

"Hi," Pesha said, closing the door and leaning against it.

Fen halted. His mouth and chin contorted briefly. "Hi." The word was forced.

Pesha took a step inside. He breathed deep and held it, then released it slowly before speaking. "Fen, I'd like to tell you what's not going to happen. You're *not* going to retreat when you're upset. You will not tell me nothing's wrong when I ask, because something *is* wrong. We're not going backward."

Fen's nose and mouth twitched. He pointed his gaze at the shelves along the right wall. "Roles are reversed now, is that it? You're the reasonable one? The *enlightened* one?"

"You want me to react," Pesha said calmly. Fen wasn't wrong. It was *him* Pesha was channeling with every step, every word. Every lesson was one Fen had taught him. "And I won't. Because the only thing that matters to me, right now, is understanding what's upset you so much that you won't even look at me."

Fen turned toward a table, leaning over it with his palms turned backward. "You're going to make me say it, aren't you? Pretend you don't know."

Pesha took another step. "I *don't* know. Not unless you tell me."

With his head tilted back, Fen snorted. "That's even worse, because if you don't know, then it means we have very different ideas of what it is to commit our lives to each other."

"What? I don't know what this is."

"You're right. It's just me." Fen sprung back and slapped his chest. "I'm the one who cares too much, who *loves* too much. It's my fault for both things."

"Stiofen, talk to me!" Pesha's voice cracked into a screech. The awful sense he was losing Fen, inch by inch, dissolved his prior calm, leaving him boneless and terrified. "I can't…I love you. I fucking love you, and I don't know how to fix what's broken if you don't tell me!"

The library doors yawned open, startling them both.

Lotte.

"It's Siofra. It's time." She clutched her waist. "Air is already with her."

Fen wiped his eyes and raced past Pesha and Lotte.

"Why do you look so scared?" Pesha asked Lotte, just as she turned to follow Fen.

"I have a sense we'll need all the help we can muster," she said with a look up and a soundless whisper. A prayer. "You should come as well, Pesha. Desemir will need you."

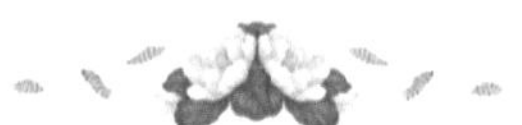

Fen walked in and found the entire apartment had already been converted into a birthing chamber. Most of the furnishings were draped in cloths; the curtains were drawn tight, candlelight the only illumination. There were dozens positioned in safe places around the bed, which had thick towels where the sheets had been. More were stacked nearby, and on both nightstands were steaming basins of water.

Siofra lay atop the pillows with her knees drawn, her flushed face tilted back as Gisela guided her through breathing exercises. Air was on the far side of the bed, his face near Siofra's. His mouth moved without sound, the way Datu had whispered to Kaia.

Desemir paced about ten feet away, practically ripping his hair out. Wulf stepped where he stepped, tasked with keeping the man from coming too close.

"Air says you may stand behind her, Desemir, once the labor begins. But not a moment before!" Lotte cried, barging in with a commanding stomp. "Stiofen, is that you? Get in here!"

"How can I help?" Pesha asked quietly, hanging back.

"I don't…I don't know. Maybe Des needs you," Fen murmured and inched toward the bed, gripped by a daze.

Lotte beckoned wildly, impatience woven through her expression. He focused on that and not the fear he'd seen in Siofra's eyes.

When he reached Lotte, she moved over to the other stool and left the one in the center for him. "You're the expert here, Stiofen. You tell us what to do."

"What?" Fen swayed. He gripped the stool, glancing only so far as Siofra's drawn legs. She was terrified, and he didn't need to see her eyes to know it. He *felt* it, same as he'd felt her joy, her sadness…her everything for almost twenty years.

"You need to get your head on straight, boy," Lotte chided. "Your sister needs you right now. We all do."

"Fen." Air's usually small voice was firm and confident. "Both babies are ready. She's not cosa. But there are signs…" He glanced at Siofra. "Of the dissonance."

Fen swallowed hard. He mopped sweat from his temples. "What?"

"I cannot tell which kind." Air's eyes flitted to the side in shame. "But you should do the whispering."

"Me?" Fen gripped the stool, guiding himself onto it. "Why?"

"What the fuck is going on over there?" Desemir cried. Fen vaguely heard Wulf trying to pacify him.

"If I don't know what kind of dissonance, then I don't know what to do." Air's shoulders lifted in a sigh. "You have the twin bond. You can sense what's inside of her. You can reach her there."

"Not like that," Fen said, struggling to meter his breaths. The room wavered. "It's not like that, Air."

Air leaned close and whispered, "It has to be. I'll show Lotte what to do."

"You and Lotte are going to deliver these babies?"

"You heard the boy. Go." Lotte nudged him off the stool. "Air, bring the towels and one of the basins. And a knife."

Fen staggered back, giving his face another wipe with his sleeve. His gaze moved across the room in slow motion, from a frenzied Desemir to a helpless Pesha—everywhere but Siofra, where he needed to be. Where he'd *trained* to be, but Mairead had said nothing about how she always stayed so calm under pressure.

Calm under pressure is quite literally your strength. Find it.

"We need a forest runner!" Air called, sounding four times his age.

"I'll do it." Pesha rushed forward. "Tell me what to do."

Fen blinked, watching the exchange as his daze slipped away.

Air swiveled all the way around, gesturing with his hands as he spoke. "You won't have to go far, Pesha. The familiars are never born far away. A hundred yards at most. There will be a light. Follow it."

"What do I do when I get there?"

"Keep it safe from predators while you wait for a second light." Air glanced at Fen. "If there are no lights…Wait until we tell you both children are here, until we know there's no hope for familiars."

Pesha nodded, locked eyes with Fen, and left.

"Stiofen, if you don't snap out of it right now—"

"I'm fine, Lotte." Fen held a hand out, steadying himself, and made his way to where Air had been positioned near Siofra's head. When she saw him, her forehead creased like an accordion, but her fear seemed to dissolve right before his eyes. And he felt, in that moment, that it was because she believed he knew what to do. She'd placed her hope in *him*.

"I'm here, Si," he said softly, gathering one of her sweaty hands in both of his as he pulled the chair closer. "I'm here."

"I don't know what's happening inside of me, Fen. Something feels strange, and—" Her face drew together in a wince, followed by a screech of pain. Fen brushed her hair back as she recovered. "I don't have the experience to understand it…to understand if this is how it's supposed to be."

There are signs of the dissonance.

At least one of Siofra's children would be born without a familiar.

Mairead had trained him *not* to force that revelation upon the mother, lest they create further dissonance and confusion, both of which could put mother and child in mortal peril. But if Siofra didn't come to that realization on her own, the result would be the same.

Another contraction wracked Siofra hard enough to shake the entire bed.

"They're close. We need her on her knees," Lotte said. "Now."

Fen helped them turn Siofra. The bed was drenched in her sweat, and the real labor was only beginning. "Si, I want you to close your eyes and listen to me. When they tell you to push, you push. But when you're not pushing, you're focusing on the sound of my voice. Do you understand?"

With her head arced low, her hair plastered to her face and neck, Siofra nodded.

"Can I be with my fucking wife now?" Desemir snapped.

"Can she, Air?" Fen called.

"Yes, if he lets you do the talking."

Desemir shook Wulf away and stormed over, snapping a chair to Siofra's other side. "I'm here, baby. I'm here," he said, gathering her hair into a knot. "I'm here, love."

"Desi," Siofra whimpered. Her face contorted in another ferocious contraction.

Fen locked eyes with Desemir, who looked more terrified than Fen had ever seen him. "Just…do that. Touch her. Soothe her. Let me do the rest."

Desemir returned a harried nod.

With a deep intake of breath and a silent prayer to both the Light and the Guardians, Fen ventured forth. "Si, do you remember how...how Mother...how she used to sing that song? The one that talked about the foxes in the grove?"

Siofra braced through another scream, but she was looking at him. She couldn't speak, but her answer was in her eyes.

Would it work? Could he guide her where she needed to go without interfering in the process and causing her harm? Questions plagued him, but he had no time to ponder any of it. The children were coming and, from the sound of Lotte and Air's scattered conversation below, soon.

"We used to tell her the song made no sense. Foxes emerging from cabbage by the moonlight." Fen laughed, remembering the way they'd roll their eyes when Moira sang the strange words. "That's how familiars are born, Si. They're born in forests and gardens. They enter the world at the same time as their Medvedev. Of course..." *Careful.* "Not all Medvedev are born with familiars, as we know. Like Air."

Desemir briefly ceased his gentle ministrations to give Fen a confused—and slightly infuriated—look.

Fen answered with a tight shake of his head. *Trust me.*

The lights flickered, Siofra's scream shaking the candelabras. Gisela and Wulf scrambled to catch them before disaster struck.

"She's crowning," Lotte said. "Siofra, I need you to push again. Can you do that?"

"I don't know." Siofra sobbed.

"You *can*," Fen replied. He drew up off the chair and leaned close, brushing the sweat from her cheek as he whispered, "You have always been the strongest of us, Siofra. I was only strong because you allowed me to be."

"That's..." Siofra howled through a straining push.

"Breathe, baby. Breathe," Desemir coaxed.

"Another!" Air yelled.

"Not true." Siofra panted. "I needed you then. I need you..." Her head lifted in a howl. "Now."

"One more," Lotte said, giving Siofra's leg a loving tap. "One more, sweet girl, and then you can rest a moment."

"I can't do this. I can't do this. I can't—"

"You can," said Fen and Desemir, in perfect concert.

"Do you see the fox in the grove, Si? Do you see the moonlight and the cabbage?"

Siofra's head tossed back and forth. Desemir struggled to keep her hair pinned back, so he stood, moving with her.

"Come on, Si. Push," Lotte said.

"It's not a fox. It's a…a wulf cub." Siofra roared like a caged lion, and Lotte made a startled, delighted gasp.

"There we are. There we are." When Lotte stood, she was cradling an infant, which she passed to Gisela. "Your first one is a beautiful baby girl, Siofra."

Desemir started sobbing in relief.

"A little girl?" Siofra swiveled her head to the side. "I have a little girl?"

A sharp cry ripped through the bedchamber, followed by the sound of everyone's gentle relief. Gisela brought the bundle to Siofra and Desemir for a brief look.

"Lidia," Siofra said, wheezing. "Her name is Lidia. For Desi's mother."

"You both can hold her when the labor is done," Gisela said. "I'll go get her cleaned up."

Desemir buried his face in his arm, crying. He wiped it and kissed Siofra's cheek, her mouth, and her forehead. "I love you, Si. I love you so much. I love you both so much."

"I know, love," Siofra said. She tried to pull her knees up, but Lotte tapped her thighs.

"Not just yet. Take a moment to breathe."

Fen did the same. He quietly pondered her words. *It's a wulf cub.* Was she seeing Lidia's familiar…or her other child's? "Si, I'll be right back. Just breathe, as Lotte said."

He rose and went to Wulf. Air quickly joined them.

"She said there's a wulf, that she saw a wulf, in her mind," Fen whispered to them both. "It has to be a familiar, but I don't know if the familiar is Lidia's or not. There's still so much about this I don't know, and Lidia seems fine, but if I'm wrong, then I need to know that. And I need to know it now."

"Tell me what to do," Wulf said. He shifted in place with nervous energy.

"You want him to go outside, don't you?" Air asked. "To see?"

"Pesha needs to stay outside, to keep the familiars safe, but we can't wait on the answer. Can you be quick, Wulf?"

Wulf nodded. "How long until the next one comes?"

"Not long," Air said, his eyes wide as he looked back at the bed. "Not long at all."

Wulf nodded and raced out of the room without another word.

Lotte cleared her throat. "Fen, Air, you need to come back."

Fen nodded but leaned in toward Air. "How am I doing? Should I change anything?"

Air seemed surprised by the question, that Fen would ask *him*. "You're doing very good. Change nothing."

Fen pecked a kiss on the boy's forehead, smiled, and went back to his place by Siofra's head. He locked gazes with Desemir, whose eyes were filled with questions he seemed to know better than to ask. Fen nodded to indicate everything was fine, though he had no idea if it was.

Somewhere in the room, Lidia cried and Gisela gently soothed her.

"Are you ready to push again?" Lotte asked.

"No!" Siofra cried, laughing. "Are you joking right now? Was that what you call a break?"

"Hey, babies choose their own time of entry," Fen said. He brushed a thumb along her cheek. "But you're already halfway done, Si. One more to go and then you can rest for a full year."

"What a lie that is. We both know mothers don't rest."

"*This* mother will, because you're not raising these babies alone. You have me. You have the entire Hall." Desemir dipped under her bowed head to kiss her. "I can't deliver this child for you, Siofra, but everything that comes after…I would and will do anything for our children. *Everything* for our children. For you."

"Focus!" Air cried.

Fen and Desemir exchanged a smirk and returned to their places.

"Tell me more about that wulf, Si," Fen said after her next contraction. "The one you saw in the garden."

Siofra responded with another guttural howl.

"Gonna need more, Siofra," Lotte coached.

"What color is he?" Fen probed.

"I don't…" Siofra's lips peeled back in pain. "I can't do this anymore, Fen. I'm so tired."

Wulf burst into the room. Fen whipped his head up. Wulf, frazzled, nodded once.

The wulf was Lidia's, as Fen had suspected.

Siofra's second child was the one in danger.

"You don't have to describe it, Si," Fen said gently, his heart racing. What if he said the wrong thing? What if *he* caused disaster with his woeful inexperience? "Maybe the wulf left the patch."

"Yes." Siofra panted. "It's gone. There is no wulf." She howled again.

"Crowning," Lotte said. "I need a fresh basin, Air."

"No wulf," Fen said. Fearful tingles seized him from head to toe. "Maybe the garden is just…empty. Because there doesn't need to be a wulf."

"What?" Sweat dripped from her face onto the bed. Desemir traced the heel of his palm along her back.

"Come on, Aunt Siofra," Air said. "Give us another push."

"I can't," she whispered. She said it again, louder. "Isn't there… another way…"

"No, there isn't," Fen said. "Women have been doing this for thousands of years. Medvedev have been doing this for thousands of years. And it's a lot more common than you think for women to bring halflings. Air here has taken part in thirteen halfling births, and he's just a child. So you *can* do this. Meet me in the garden."

"What?"

"Let's walk where the wulf was but is no longer. You and me. Together."

"Where…Where did the wulf go?"

"Lidia needed him."

"What about my other child?"

Desemir stopped his gentle kneading, waiting for Fen's answer as well.

"That's why you and I are going for a walk in the garden. Let's just see what we see. Together," Fen said carefully.

Desemir's eyes narrowed in worry.

"But there's nothing in the garden. There's nothing…" Her back arched in a powerful contraction. Fen and Desemir caught her before she collapsed.

What the fuck is happening? Desemir mouthed. The cords in his neck were so pronounced, they looked ready to burst.

Fen met his eyes. "There doesn't have to be. There doesn't have to be, Si. Just breathe and walk with me."

"Breathe and walk with you."

"Breathe and walk with me." Fen inhaled through his nose to show her. "Just like that."

"Something's…" The rest of Lotte's words faded.

"Everything's fine. Everything is fine," Fen said over and over, drowning Lotte's voice with his. "Walk with me, Si. Walk with me through the garden, which is just as it should be. Just as it needs to be."

"Empty."

"Empty. That's right." Fen swiped his sleeve over his forehead. "Just you and me, and this little one who's ready to enter the world."

"Push!" yelled either Lotte or Air. Everything beyond Siofra blurred together, becoming one.

Fen leaned closer, whispering the same words over and over. "You and me and your little one. The three of us are in the garden, where it's safe and beautiful and just for us. Can you see it?"

Sobbing, Siofra nodded. Her hands scrunched into the pillow.

"Is it beautiful?"

"It's beautiful," she cried.

"Then it's time to push. Time to bring them into the garden with us, where it's beautiful and safe and perfect." Fen held his breath.

Siofra's head curled all the way down and then back up with a toe-curling scream. In that moment, she reminded him of the wulves that had circled Farren in the forest. Wild and feral and free.

"That was a good one. That was a very good one, Siofra. Just one more good one and we're there," Lotte said, each word coming faster than the last.

"That's it, love. That's it," Desemir said through his tears.

Siofra pressed her face into the pillow and clenched for one final push.

"Oh, dear Guardians, there we are. There's our little one." Lotte expelled a heaving breath and pushed to her feet, and Gisela joined her with a blanket. "Siofra, you have another little girl."

Siofra collapsed onto her side, sobbing.

"Moira." Desemir's voice, thin and choked, rose above the bustle of excitement. "For my wife's mother."

"Lidia and Moira. The perfect names for these perfect little girls," Lotte said, cooing at the infant as she passed it to Gisela. A soft, gurgling cry ripped from Moira's healthy lungs. "Are you ready to meet your children?"

Desemir nodded, mopping a wet cloth on Siofra's flushed and sweaty body. He wiped his tears on his bicep. "Yes. Very much so."

Gisela and Lotte each took an infant to their bedside.

Fen stood to make way for them, stumbling back. A wave of dizziness struck him so suddenly that Wulf's reflexes were the only reason he didn't go down like a sack of flour.

"Easy," Wulf said as he aided him into a chair. "You need to rest yourself."

"Pesh." Fen panted. He didn't know why he'd said it, what he needed.

Air rushed over. "You kept her safe. You said the right things."

"Did I?"

The doors opened, and Pesha entered with a mewling cub in his arms. Fen laughed in delight, sitting up as everyone turned to look.

"Where's the other one?" Siofra asked, cradling Lidia against her chest. "The other familiar?"

"There isn't one, love," Desemir said, sliding in the bed beside her, Moira in his arms. "But not to worry; Moira will never want for anything. Will she?"

Siofra's eyes flooded with tears. "What will it mean for her, Desi?"

This time, it was Air who answered. "It means she's like me, and I can help her with that."

Siofra stared at him, shivering. Her expression softened. "You can, can't you?"

Air nodded, his hands linked at his back. His chest swelled with pride. "I know all about it."

"I'm going to get Siofra and the babies cleaned up." Lotte clapped her hands and made a swatting gesture. "Everyone out except the parents and Air. Go on then!"

Pesha placed the wulf on the end of the bed with a long look at Fen. Fen tensed, waiting for whatever he was about to say, but it never came.

He nodded, turned, and left.

Gisela and Wulf followed.

Fen was last, lingering long enough to cross his hands over his chest for Siofra.

Thank you, she mouthed and blew him a kiss. *I love you.*

THIRTY-THREE
NO MORE TEARS

Pesha hadn't known his destination was the lake until he was standing along the shallow bank. Moonlight mirrored in a soft ripple along the mostly still surface—a surface that was perfectly fluid, not frozen.

A hard lump formed and dissolved in his chest as he ripped his clothes from his body, tearing his shirt down the middle and breaking buttons on his trousers. He grunted through the harried unlacing of his boots and flung them into the darkness.

He waded into the water, step by step. Each one brought him closer to Eshe, to feeling her presence, her inviting warmth. The cool water didn't slow him. Nothing could. The urge had come on so suddenly, only something with equal power could stay it.

When the water reached his waist, he swallowed a deep breath and dived under the surface for the first time in his entire life.

Pesha knew how to swim. Despite having a perfectly good lake so close to the house—a lake full of his guilt and shame and failure—he'd pushed Des and Wulf to take him to the river when it was time for his lessons, unable to bear facing Eshe so close up.

The river wasn't deep, but it had been enough for him to practice his strokes, to learn when to float and when to sink.

Now was the time to sink.

He wriggled through the chill water, delving deeper than he'd ever gone in the river—in water period. Niall's face appeared in his mind, smug but not unkind. *Now you will learn to swim.*

Eshe. I'm coming.

I know.

I should have come so long ago. I should have…

And then she was there. He opened his eyes to see hers wide with wonder. Her soft snout nudged his face and then bucked upward. When she twirled toward the surface, he understood she meant for him to follow.

His lungs burned as he pushed back to the surface to join her. She'd sensed it, he realized, knowing the place for them to meet was not beneath the water but above, connecting his world to hers.

Pesha heaved in a greedy breath when he breached. Eshe barked and splashed him.

He wiped his face, and she did it again.

She's playing.

With his eyes narrowing with mischief, Pesha scooped a palmful of water and batted it at her. She flopped backward with a happy chittering sound and smashed her fins, creating impressive ripples.

Pesha laughed and swept his arms in the water to match her intensity, but she'd had many years to understand the water, and he'd only just been introduced. He splashed, she splashed, and on it went, until he was laughing so hard, all he could do was roll onto his back, wheezing, and attempt to float.

Eshe swam up beside him. She nudged him again with a soft bark and then flipped upside down, floating beside him.

Pesha glanced over at her as though seeing her for the first time. In the way that mattered most, he was. "Hi," he said.

Eshe barked and slapped her tail flipper against the surface.

Tears rolled, joining the drops of water on his cheeks, which ached from all the smiles. He indulged the instinct to reach a hand toward her, and it felt right, exactly right, when she floated sideways and laid a fin in his palm.

"The promises I made to Fen in that garden...If I could have had you in the circle with us..." Pesha closed his eyes and breathed deep. "It's so much easier to believe you need nothing when you don't have it. But that isn't the life I want, not anymore. For either of us." He opened his eyes. "Can you forgive me?"

Eshe barked and slapped her tail flipper. *Pesha. My Pesha.*

Hot tears rolled down his cheeks, into the water. *Eshe. My Eshe.*

Fen would need time to himself after the stressful births. And when Pesha came for him, to clear up the misunderstanding, he would do so with his mind clear, his voice firm and unshaking.

At peace.

Finally.

Des can't know about Wulf. He can't know about Wulf. He can't know—

Farren ran her palms along the freshly painted walls of the west wing, Vaya close at her heels. Everything that had happened since the lynx had ushered Farren's return to the world was a whirlwind of confusing thoughts and tainted memories. The eight years she'd been magicked weren't real. She was afraid they might become real and, when they did, she'd be unable to fight the grip of darkness.

Desemir. Ludwik. Pesha. Wulfhelm. They cycled through her thoughts in illogical order, blending memory with fantasy with something else...something she didn't understand. She remembered the way her fingers felt tracing the bark where their initials had been carved. *W.K.* for Wulfhelm Killian. *F. W.* for herself. W for Wintersin, a name her mother and father had dreamed up when they'd left Asgill. But she had become a Trevanion; Desemir had said so, had shown her the papers she couldn't bring herself to read.

After Vaya was a life with potential, but Farren no longer knew herself, so how could she ever find the potential without that knowledge?

"Farren."

Her hand stopped. She shifted her head to the side but didn't turn.

"I thought…I thought you might want to know that Siofra and Desemir's twins were born. They're both healthy, thank the Guardians." Wulfhelm. Wulfie. Her Wulf. He sounded so unsure of himself.

Vaya ripped a deep howl that probably sounded terrifying to others; to Farren, it was a great comfort, the only one she'd known in so long. Prior to Nera…No, she couldn't think of it now. None of it. Not even Wulfie.

"Thank you for telling me."

"Two girls. Lidia and Moira."

"Lidia," Farren said quietly. Lidia Trevanion had always been kind to her—mothered her when Arenn ignored her. How sad Farren had been when Lidia had died. All the light at Shadowfen Hall had winked from existence. Nothing good had come after.

"Moira was born without a familiar, and…and Siofra is scared. Maybe you could be a comfort to her."

Farren cocked her head. A comfort. What was comfort? Eight years of being magicked from hurting herself and others? Eight years of grief without end? She couldn't even remember it, so how was she to work through it and be of help to anyone? "She has Air."

"Air is a good boy." His boots echoed as he moved closer. "And he's eager to help." Another step. "You used to say to me how sad you were to never have a sister. Far, you would *love* Siofra. She's everything you could have ever wanted."

"You're attracted to her." Farren heard it through the extra effort he seemed to require when saying Siofra's name.

Wulf stopped moving. A strange pause followed. "I was. But there's attraction and then there's…there's…something else. It wasn't the same. It could never be."

"It could never be," Farren said. She turned. "Desemir can't know."

"About us?" Wulf breathed deep. "I know. For now. But it's not a secret we can keep forever, Far. You know that. No matter what happens from here on out, what happened before won't stay buried."

She felt his muscular hand wrapped over hers as they'd carved her initials into the tree. She wasn't even supposed to have been there that day; it was for the boys only, no girls allowed. But Wulf had found her watching from behind another tree, and when the boys were gone, he'd dragged her out and helped her make her own mark. His callouses had scored the back of her hands, his scent…deep and musky and safe. Always safe. Always safe with Wulfhelm.

"Farren…"

"Tired," she murmured, returning her gaze forward. "I'm going to sleep now."

His voice was heavy, clogged with emotion. "Of course. Sleep well. I hope your dreams are full of peace. No one deserves it more than you."

"Wulfie," she whispered after she was certain he'd turned the corner.

Farren resumed trailing her palms along the walls of the west wing.

Fen had just finished putting Air to bed. Whatever burst of energy had pushed him through the tense delivery was gone, and in its place, an exhaustion greater than he'd ever known.

Lidia and Moira were beautiful babies, perfect in every way, and he was an *uncle* now, almost as quickly as he'd become a father.

Trying to imagine a younger version of himself dreaming of such a future was daunting. Impossible. Younger Fen knew the world was hard, and he'd adapted accordingly. He expected bad things to happen, but *when* they did, he was prepared for them. He had never lost a fight for lack of trying.

Was it so surprising, then, that whatever magic he and Pesha had captured in Asgill was already becoming a relic of the past?

He paused outside the door linking Air's apartment to theirs. It would be so easy to turn and head to his old room, sleep until he had his energy back, and avoid Pesha until he had no choice but to confront what was happening.

It was Air he was thinking of when he opened the door and stepped inside—the real commitment he'd made to the boy when he'd whisked him away to Shadowfen Hall, not so unlike how Pesha had done for Fen and Siofra all those months ago.

Pesha was sitting on the end of the bed, his head bowed. He looked up when Fen entered. "I just came from Des and Si's apartment. The twins…They're beautiful. They're utterly…perfect. You did really well, Fen. If no one else has told you that, you should know."

Fen nodded. He chewed the inside of his mouth, his gaze on the window. "I can, um, take the chaise tonight, if you want the bed. Tomorrow we can figure out a better arrangement."

"I know why you're upset now." Pesha stood. "I didn't tell you what Desemir had offered because I didn't want you think…I didn't want you to react as you are now, wondering whether I really meant the words we said in that garden."

"It should not be hard to present the idea of a *wedding* to a man you already wed, unless the first wedding meant nothing." Fen's mouth puckered, trembling. The rest of his energy sank to the floor. "Because we don't need…I didn't think we needed—"

Pesha rushed to him and swallowed him in a hug. "Stiofen, I fucking *love* you. I love you, and I need you, and I should have said it before we even got to the Hinterlands. Before any of the rest happened. I'm sorry I failed you. I am. I always will be. But I'm *not going anywhere.*" He pulled back, gripping Fen's shoulders with a firm shake. "Do you understand what I'm saying? You can rage and huff and cry and accuse, and I'll take it, because you endured the same from me, for far too long. But I am *not leaving you.*"

Fen was too spent to subdue the sob rising from his chest into his throat. He whimpered and collapsed into Pesha, dead on his feet. "I don't know what's wrong with me, Pesha."

"I do." Pesha brushed his lips back and forth across Fen's head with a slow inhale. "You've spent so long expecting tragedy that when happiness steps forward instead, you don't recognize it."

"I don't want to be this broken," Fen cried. He gripped Pesha's shirt in both hands, wiping his tears on it. "I don't want to be this way. How can I raise a son to thrive when I don't know how to do it myself?"

"There are no instructions. Be glad of it, for you're not much for rules, are you?"

Fen sniffled with a half-suppressed laugh. "We don't have to get married here, Pesha. What we did in Asgill was for us. That's all I needed then. It's all I need now."

"It's not for us at all." Pesha reached for Fen's chin and tilted it up. "It's for Air, so he never has to worry about his legitimacy. About the legitimacy of the children he'll have one day—and their children. You've seen firsthand how hard Des has fought to keep those greedy barons from our doors, but the one thing they cannot disavow is the law itself. Now *I* am a legitimate heir of the Trevanion estate, as is Farren. And that means Air is as well."

"Why did you not...just say that?" Fen wiped his eyes and released Pesha's shirt. "Shit, Pesha, I'd have done it even if you just wanted to tell the world you loved me again."

"I needed time with it. Illegitimacy has defined my entire life." Pesha moved back to the bed. "But *legitimacy*? It does not make me *more.* I am no different today than I was before Desemir sent paperwork to the magistrate. It wasn't Desemir's fault. I have never wanted or needed for anything practical. But the barons... Had they known I was part Medvedev...He was so scared they'd come for me, just like men have come for you and Siofra your whole lives. I'm the *same man* now that I was before, and I never want Ruairi to believe…" Pesha screwed his mouth shut, grinding a fist against his thigh. "To believe the only thing that makes him real is a piece of paper saying so."

Fen rushed to the bed. "Then I will let it be your choice, my love. Don't force an unfair standard upon Air if you don't feel it will benefit him."

"But it will, won't it?" Pesha's eyes welled with tears. He opened his mouth wide and breathed out. "Without it, he'll suffer. Once Des is gone and we're gone, he will suffer. And there will be *nothing* we can do about it."

Fen caressed Pesha's cheek, looking up into his eyes. "This does not have to be decided tonight."

Pesha nodded, lowering his eyes. "But I need *you* to know that when I chose you, Fen, it was forever." He looked up. "Not until the magic fades or the feelings mature, but for as long as I live. I chose *you.* I chose *Air.* And this is the life I want. Together. If the past day has changed your mind, I'll accept it, but—"

Fen silenced him with a hard kiss, both hands wrapped around his face. "Forgive me. I shouldn't have reacted as I did, not without hearing you out. Old habits can be hard to shed."

"You're telling me." Pesha laughed and wiped his eyes. "I have to say, I'm dead tired of crying."

"Oh, Guardians, you and me both." Fen exhaled, whistling. "Can we perhaps…*not* for a while?"

Pesha grinned. "Can it be so simple?"

"Hardly." Fen craned up to kiss him again. "Just for tonight then. No more tears."

"No more tears."

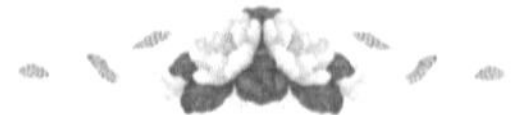

Pesha crawled backward up and onto the bed, sliding until his head was close enough to the pillow to fall back. Fen was right behind, matching his pace, his movements.

Fen seized Pesha's belt and lifted with a commanding tug that had Pesha's belly clenching with need. "I'm exhausted," he said, still gripping tight. "But I need to fuck my husband before I fall asleep, and that's what I'm going to do."

Pesha dug his hands into the sheets and peered up with a defiant, challenging grin. "Are you going to talk about fucking me, or are you going to fuck me?"

Fen gripped Pesha's hands and shoved them onto the pillow with one hand, pinning him, while the other ripped at the buttons until they all popped open. He dug his hand down and circled Pesha's cock. "And are you going to be good, or will I have to force the matter?"

"What do you think?" Pesha slid his tongue along his lips.

Fen reared back on his knees, lifting his shirt over his head. "If you move those hands, I'll stop." He shimmied out of his trousers, flinging them off his feet. "And you'll go to bed unsatisfied."

"You know just how to threaten me." Pesha twisted in anticipation but left his hands linked over his head. His cock throbbed against his belly. Guardians, how he enjoyed this side of Fen. Just rare enough to be a perfect novelty.

Fen stroked his cock, his mouth parted and his shoulders rising with every pass. "Or maybe I'll just pleasure myself all over you."

Pesha licked his lips again. "Or put it in my mouth, and we'll both be satisfied."

"Riding your face is tempting. Spilling it all down your throat, watching your eyes widen as you struggle to swallow…mmm… even better." Fen's eyes rolled back as he stroked. "But I need a bit…tighter. I have a lot pent up, and I want all of it gone."

Pesha bucked his hips. Fen had never said he couldn't. "How much?"

"You'll see soon enough. It won't take me long, I'm afraid." Fen spit into his palm and slid it down the length of his cock. He did it again, working the spit around. Dropping down, he pinned one hand beside Pesha's head, and the other guided himself into place. "If you don't relax, it won't fit."

Pesha's toes curled. He nearly came up off the bed, he was so ripe with desire. "I could use a good *stretching*."

"Fuck." Fen's lips peeled back as he shoved in, building a groan through his gritted teeth. "I don't remember…" His head fell back as he pushed until he could go no farther. "It wasn't this tight before."

"You weren't this hard before."

Fen grimaced, pushing through the resistance. "I don't want to come so fast."

Pesha forced his hands to still and lifted for a kiss.

Fen took his lips between his teeth instead and dragged with a soft *pop*.

"Don't deny yourself." He spread his legs to allow Fen to go deeper, clenching through the delicious, impeccable pain. "Or me."

Fen lifted higher and quickened his pace, thrusting all the way in and out with every pass. He buried himself with a forceful slam and dragged back out, again and again.

Delirious, Pesha closed his eyes and lost himself to the pleasure. He counted every thrust, measuring them against his own need to come, the smooth swollen head of his cock threatening to burst without even being touched.

"Mine." Fen spread Pesha's legs even wider as he slammed into him with a shuddering cry.

Straining for breath, Fen bowed his head, his back arced. He slowly slid out and down, moving back to the end of the bed. Pesha's hand traveled downward, aware of how close he was to finishing, but Fen swallowed his cock before he could, guiding it to the back of his throat without moving. Without sucking. Just waiting.

Pesha bucked up, gripping the back of Fen's head as the orgasm coursed through him. His feet kicked up, the rest of him spasming wildly out of control as he poured his release down Fen's throat.

Fen peeled back and stuck out his coated tongue. With a devious smile, he closed his mouth again and made a show of swallowing.

"And I'm already hard again, you miscreant." Pesha moaned, lifting to kiss his husband's filthy mouth. "If I wasn't so tired, I'd tie you to this bed…"

Fen leaned in to kiss him once more. "Tomorrow then."

"Why limit ourselves? There's seven days in a week. Over a hundred in a season."

"And winter will be cold. So cold…"

"So cold." Pesha panted. He closed his eyes to force a recovery he wasn't ready for. But he was tired; Fen was exhausted. They needed rest, even if they didn't want it. Before he slipped away though, he had one last important thing to say. "Marry me, Fen. Only if you want to."

Fen nestled in beside him. He buried his face against Pesha's neck and slid an arm and a leg over him. "All right. Let's do it."

Epilogue

Siofra swayed to the band's lively chorales, Lidia strapped to her chest in a soft sling Desemir had fashioned himself. She sang along, whispering the words to her daughter. "And there we are, at the end again, you and me, dancing in the glen."

She caught sight of Desemir across the ballroom, speaking with Lotte and Wulf. *I do not sing, nor dance, unless it is a waltz*, he'd told her, many times, but while he was engaged in the conversation, his toes tapped in time to the spirited rhythm, Moira gently bouncing against his shoulder.

"How can you sleep through such a thing, hm?" Siofra kissed Lidia's soft, warm forehead and moved closer to those dancing. Pesha and Fen were howling with laughter about something. Both of them had consumed far more spirits than either were used to, but it softened her heart to see them so carefree for once. Fen was half draped over Pesha like a drunken tavern girl, and the look Pesha was giving him was far more suitable for their bedchamber.

"Auntie Si," Air said, walking up to her and looking a proper gentleman in his suit and bowtie. Lotte had pulled it from Desemir's old trunks. "Any changes in their development?"

Siofra smiled softly, gently laughing. "You do not need to work today, Air. Or any day really." When his solemn expression didn't budge, she sighed. "You're an excellent midwife. Both Lidia and Moira are doing exceptionally well, thanks to your unmatched expertise on the matter."

She feared saying anything more. Desemir had suggested they invite Steward Arranden and his wife, Agnes, to legitimize the wedding with outside witnesses. A few others from the village had come as well. But it meant no talk of Medvedev or familiars. They'd even left Lidia's wulf, Aida, outside with Vaya, the birds, and Eshe, for the utmost precaution.

But Air understood the balance between saying what he meant and saying it in a way only they comprehended.

"I will come see you again tomorrow," he said with a low bow. She stifled a giggle, her heart swelling in affection for the sweet little boy she'd come to love so easily.

He ran off to play with Arranden's grandchildren. Siofra watched them chase each other around the fluted columns, wondering if any of the Trevanion children could ever enjoy normal relationships with the town kids. Desemir had been companions of some for a spell, but it had ended when he reached maturity. Maybe history would break the cycle, so the next generation could open their doors more freely and with love and trust in their hearts.

Siofra peppered Lidia's soft chubby cheek with kisses, reminding herself the day was one for celebration, not pondering futures. Pesha and Fen had become legally husband and husband in the eyes of the law. Everything Siofra had wished for her brother had happened, and there was no man more perfect for Stiofen Thornheart—*sorry*, she thought, *Trevanion*—than Pesha Trevanion.

Life had behaved most unexpectedly in the year since they'd arrived from Newcarrow, scared and wondering why a wealthy benefactor had sent across the kingdom for them—assuming the worst and instead finding the happiness they'd not believed would ever be theirs to take.

Several men turned their eyes as Farren moved across the dance floor. She wore a strapless gown that had belonged to Desemir's mother, Lidia, a bold, shimmery color that reminded Siofra of forest in springtide. Her green hair had been magicked, like that of every Medvedev in the house, for the event, and she'd chosen a pale gold that had even Siofra's breath catching.

But it was Wulf's slowly parting jaw that Siofra noted with the most scrutiny. The absent-minded way he adjusted his tie… the apple in his throat jumping. In his eyes lived a competition of emotions too blurred to read.

"Well, what of it?" she asked Lidia. "Farren is beautiful. It can't be the first time he's noticed."

It was more than that though. There was a history there, one Desemir undoubtedly knew nothing about, or it would have come up already. Watching Wulf follow Farren was like witnessing a deep, dark secret Siofra wasn't supposed to know.

"Siofra." Farren nodded with a gentle smile as she approached. "Hi, Lidia."

Lidia cooed and gurgled, shoving a tiny hand into her mouth.

"I think she's saying hello." Siofra laughed. Farren did too, and she'd never looked so beautiful, mirth coloring the lines and edges of her face.

"I'm sorry I wasn't there that day. She's perfect." Farren's reach was tentative as she swiped the back of her finger down Lidia's cheek. The woman's speech had become more complete and cohesive in the month since they'd come home from the Hinterlands. They'd debated having her join the reception, worried how she might feel around outsiders, but she'd handled herself with impressive poise and grace. The only precarious moment had been when Hugh Arranden had made a snide comment about forgetting Desemir had such a beautiful sister, let alone a sister at all. But everyone had laughed, as though it were a joke, and the accusation faded into a new topic.

"I've already told you, Farren, there is nothing to be sorry for. That was a very hectic evening, and I wouldn't have realized if you were there." Siofra reached her free hand for one of Farren's and squeezed.

"Moira is beautiful too." Farren's smile lingered on Lidia another moment. She looked into Siofra's eyes. "I know it worries you about…" She tilted her head back and forth in place of the word they wouldn't say that night. "But do not let it be a fear. Do not let my experience be the one you think of. It is very different to have something and watch it be ripped from you than to never have it at all. Moira will grow and learn who she is without… but she will not be less than Lidia, just as Air is not less than any other child."

Siofra had never heard Farren speak so much in one pass. "Thank you, I…It worries me at times, but not because I fear for what will befall her but because she'll grow up in a household where others have what she does not. I never want her to feel less than."

"Then you ensure she never does." Farren's jaw slid back and forth as she looked back into the crowd. Her fingers fidgeted at her side.

Siofra followed her gaze and saw Wulf staring at them. "You don't have to tell me—"

Farren snapped her focus back in a panic.

"But if the two of you cannot resist these charged, stolen glances, then the person you're attempting to keep this secret from will soon discover it. He's a perceptive man, who has been distracted by fatherhood, but eventually he *will* see it." Siofra smiled to show Farren her words were support, not admonishment. "I know you and I are still getting to know one another. But I can be a friend to you, if you need one. Until I came to Shadowfen Hall, I had never had a friend before, other than Stiofen. I know how lonely it can be. How isolating."

Farren nodded, looking off into the distance. "I would like a friend."

"Then we are friends." Siofra shifted Lidia higher and leaned in to kiss Farren on her cheek. "Have you danced much?"

Farren's face wrinkled together. "No."

"Would you like to learn?"

"I know how." A dark cloud passed over Farren's expression. "But it is not…" She shook her head, smiled quickly, and hurried away.

Desemir slid in behind Siofra, his arm tightening around her and Lidia in anticipation of her jump. He had Moira expertly pinned in the other. "You look ravishing, Mrs. Trevanion."

"Perhaps I had designs on being ravished later." Siofra coquetted, grinning. She tilted up to kiss him, relishing the earthy taste—forest, strength, and home. Her cup was so full, it was in a constant state of overflow. "Look at them, Des. I saw something between them from the very start, but I never thought they'd see it, and even if they did…"

"They're more stubborn than us, you mean." Desemir brushed his lips along her temple.

"An impressive feat, when you consider it."

Desemir chuckled. "Mm." He leaned in and swooped Lidia from her arms, effortlessly balancing both girls. "I'm going to put them down for their second nap."

"Is it already time?" Siofra scanned the room until she laid eyes on one of the late Lidia Trevanion's precious timekeepers. "So it is." She sighed. "I never like this time of day."

"Happy to send every one of these malcontents home early." Desemir's brows lifted.

"No, love, I'm just being silly." She kissed both girls and then him. "I'll come join you soon."

Desemir snuck one more kiss, brushing it along the length of her lips before winking and leaving with the twins.

Siofra made her way to where Fen and Pesha were practically tripping over each other as they giggled. She crossed her arms and waited for them to recover.

Fen snorted with laughter, waving an arm over his face. Pesha, grinning, wore a look so full of mischief, she was concerned she'd accidentally walked in on something deeply personal.

"If you two are over here sucking each other's—"

"Si!" Fen exclaimed, and both men were cackling again.

"Desemir made that filthy mouth, didn't he?" Pesha charged with a hiccup. "You used to be so demure and innocent…"

"He makes my mouth filthy, if that's what you mean," Siofra answered with a sly grin.

"Disgusting. Make it stop!" Fen cried, pretending to claw his ears.

"I like naughty Siofra," Pesha said, his grin widening. "She's more fun."

"Well…" Siofra clasped her hands in front of her. "I only came over to tell you both, *again,* how utterly happy I am for you. I wanted to say it once more, before you both passed out from your drunken antics."

"Drunken antics?" Pesha's hands crossed over his heart. "You wound me."

"I'll wound you later," Fen muttered, drawing a sip of his wine.

"Daggers? Please say yes."

"And *that,* gentlemen, is my cue to bid you good night." Siofra pecked them both on the cheeks and squeezed their arms. "I love you both. Enjoy everything the rest of this night offers, and every night henceforth."

Fen nodded low. "Night, Si."

"Thank you, Si," Pesha said. "For everything."

"Here's to the rest of your lives, boys," Siofra said, still smiling as she turned and went to join her husband in the nursery.

The gazebo held memories. Too many. Equally bad as good. It had been there where Farren had recovered from Ludwik's abuses, safe in the knowledge he would never go to a place full of bad memories for him. The gazebo had belonged to Elaina, Ludwik's mother. She'd built it and, later, died in it. To him, the place was cursed.

To Farren, it was a sanctuary from a cruel man who had always taken whatever he wanted, never asking. Never needing to. Everyone was too afraid to tell him no, and the only one who had dared challenge him had been beaten for it. Desemir might not think Farren knew about that, but she did because she'd been there, watching, when Ludwik took a strap to his eldest son for over an hour. It had taken twice as long for Lotte to apply the bandages.

And still, Des hadn't abandoned her. All the guilt he carried was misremembered. They'd been like oil and water most of their lives, but the moment Farren had told him Ludwik was abusing her, all that had been forgotten.

But it had not been Desemir in the gazebo, holding her in his lap as she sobbed until her tears ran dry and her heart was again calloused toward what would happen again and again and again.

"I thought you might be here." Wulf braced both hands on the archway but didn't enter. "You must be overwhelmed after all those people."

Farren nodded, bowing her head over her lap. "It wasn't the people. It was the memory."

"That last ball." Wulf exhaled in understanding. "Is that the last…thing you remember, before…"

"My memories stopped when Nera was killed." She pulled her knees up onto the bench, circling her satin dress with her arms. "Everything after becomes something indescribable, even to me."

"Far, I know you need me to keep my distance, and I will. But you need to know, eight years, ten years…twenty…None would be long enough for me to forget my care for you. The commitment I made to you." He took one step and held it. "It stands today. It will stand forever. When you need me, I *will* be here. I will hold you or listen to you or laugh with you. Cry with you. You need never wonder where I stand."

Farren bowed her head and squeezed her eyes closed, though the tears fell anyway. One day there would be no more to cry. And who would she be when the grief ran dry? Would she know herself?

Wulf knelt and set something on the stairs. "Good night then, Farren. Be kind to yourself."

She waited for him to leave before retrieving the item she'd already guessed he'd left behind.

Farren knelt and lifted the stone, shaped like a crooked heart. Wulf had found it in the forest when he was a boy, keeping it in his pocket over the years to rub when he was stressed or worried. The deep, soft groove where his thumb stroked had grown more pronounced in the intervening years. It was as much a part of Wulfhelm as his sword and armor, but it belied a side of him no one but Farren had ever really seen.

"This is yours. You shouldn't give it to me," she whispered, but he was gone, and he wanted her to have it.

Farren closed both fists over it and brought them to her heart. Vaya appeared from the grass, slinking in, and winded herself around Farren's legs with a deep, loving purr.

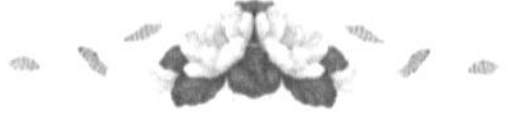

"Perfectly dapper."

"Astoundingly handsome."

"Exquisitely tailored."

Air beamed as his fathers plied him with silly but welcome compliments. He'd needed their help putting on and taking off the suit, which he was told had belonged to his Uncle Desemir. Lotte had tailored it around his shoulders, but it had been otherwise a near-perfect fit.

Just right for the day his fathers became legal husbands, and he became their lawful son.

Pesha lifted him in a playful swing and carried him to the bed in his brand-new pajamas. He hadn't even known that word before coming to the Hall. He'd never even been in a *home* before that wasn't a hut. It was one of many brand-new experiences, and every single day was full of them. "I saw you cutting a rug out there, Air. Some of the, ahem, younger ladies did as well."

"Mhm," Fen said, wagging his brows. "Proper dancer, you are."

Air didn't know what *cutting a rug* meant, but he could guess. "I was not." His face washed with heat as he pulled the covers tight around his neck, Fen and Pesha smiling their knowing smiles.

"Little Ella Arranden might have something to say about it," Fen answered with an embellished nod at Pesha.

"Three dances with her," Pesha said. "You're practically betrothed, Air."

"One is polite." Fen nodded. "Two is intention. Three requires paperwork."

Of course he'd danced. Everyone was dancing. It seemed the thing to do, and it *had* been fun, especially when pretty Ella with her bright-red curls had shyly asked if he could save a spot for her on his card. He didn't know what a card was, so he'd said yes. "Do I have to marry her now?"

Fen and Pesha laughed with him, both lowering to kiss him good night. "You'll marry whoever you want to marry," Pesha said.

"*When* the time is right. Bit early to be talking about this, don't you think?" Fen flashed Pesha a gentle look of warning.

Pesha winked at Air. "Of course, dear. Whatever you say, dear."

"Oh, you're asking for it now."

Air loved hearing them spar. Flirting, Mairead had called it, but whatever it was, it left him feeling happy and safe. Part of something bigger than himself. He finally belonged—here, with these men who had not only whisked him away to a new life but had put *in writing* their intention for him to be their son.

"Fen...Pesha..." Air ventured shyly. The creeping fear of rejection was back. "You said I'm like your son?"

Both men nodded, watching him.

"What should I call you then?"

Fen's smile turned solemn. "Ruairi, we want you to call us whatever feels right to you. You're free to make your own choices now, and we'll support whatever you decide."

Pesha nodded in agreement.

Air swallowed hard and said, "If I wanted to call you both Father?"

Tears shined in Fen's eyes. Pesha reached for his hand right as he teared up as well.

"We would be…honored." Fen's voice broke. "We would be honored, Air."

"Deeply honored," Pesha said with a tight smile. "We love you."

"I love you both too," Air said, stifling a yawn. "I think I can sleep now."

Both of his fathers leaned in for one last kiss. Together they said, "Sweet dreams, sweet boy."

Air was still smiling when they left, thinking of all the amazing dreams ahead of him as Ruairi Trevanion of Shadowfen Hall.

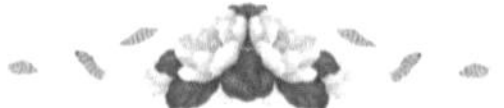

Fen sat in the chair at his vanity, admiring the band Pesha had made him. Carved from the ebony wood of the Darkwood itself, it was smooth and varnished to perfection. The one he'd made for Pesha had also come from the Darkwood, from the amber resin that Lotte sometimes made into syrups for their crepes, thrice cured and as hard as stone.

Pesha emerged from the privy, wiping his eyes. "That hit me harder than I expected."

"Me too," Fen said. He spun the wedding ring on his finger. "I just want him to be happy here."

"He's already part of the Hall. Everyone loves him." Pesha unbuttoned his shirt and pulled it over his head. "Maybe he's been working up to it for a while and just needed us to say it was all right."

Fen bowed his head. "In my heart, I'd already decided who he was to me, but a part of me wondered if that was selfish. What *I* wanted. Not what he wanted."

"I hope his question tonight has disavowed you of such needless worries." Pesha slithered out of his trousers.

"I have to trust what he says is what he wants, so—" Fen looked up. Pesha's naked, chiseled body stood inches away. "I forgot what I was…"

Pesha pulled Fen to his feet, prompting a startled laugh. In seconds he had Fen's clothes off as well, and he'd wrapped him in his arms with a light, rhythmic sway.

"Dance with me," Pesha whispered. He slid one hand down to Fen's and lifted them. The other passed softly around Fen's waist, nestling against his lower back. "Mm. My love."

Fen didn't ask how they were supposed to dance without music. He didn't wonder why they were gliding across their bedchamber floor in the nude. Life with Pesha had been a wonder from the start, and their marriage had begun a new season, one full of equal parts surprise and stability.

"My love," Fen said softly back, resting his cheek against Pesha's collarbone. "Today was beautiful."

"It was." Pesha dipped him and tugged him back. "Our fires are now a blaze."

"One that must be protected at all costs." Fen closed his eyes, remembering the poetry of their vows, and riding the sound of Pesha's heartbeat.

"As long as we are me and thee…" Pesha sighed against his ear.

"Our fire will illuminate the stars in our immortal sky."

"Mr. Trevanion." Pesha dipped down to kiss him. "My sun."

"My stars," Fen said through a gap in their kiss. "Take me to bed."

"As you wish."

The Book of All Things continues with a new story in
The Duke and the Disciple.

The Darkwood Cycle concludes with The Wulf and the Witchling. Farren is finally free of the affliction that imprisoned her for almost a decade, though her heart is still tethered to the brutal past. The more Wulfhelm—her stalwart light in the darkness—tries to get close to her, the more she wants to run. But there's more to her sordid past than even he knows, and once the truth is revealed, the lines between villain and victim will be blurred forevermore.

ALSO BY SARAH M. CRADIT

KINGDOM OF THE WHITE SEA

KINGDOM OF THE WHITE SEA TRILOGY

The Kingless Crown
The Broken Realm
The Hidden Kingdom

THE BOOK OF ALL THINGS

Blackwood Cycle
The Raven and the Rush
The Poison and the Paladin

Southerlands Cycle
The Sylvan and the Sand
The Flame and the Forsaken

Guardians Cycle
The Altruist and the Assassin
The Belle and the Blackbird
The Virtue and the Vixen

Darkwood Cycle
The Melody and the Master
The Hand and the Heart
The Wolf and the Witchling

Sceptre Cycle
The Claw and the Crowned
The Duke and the Disciple
The Tempest and the Tides

THE SAGA OF CRIMSON & CLOVER

THE HOUSE OF CRIMSON AND CLOVER SERIES

The Storm and the Darkness
Shattered
The Illusions of Eventide
Bound
Midnight Dynasty
Asunder
Empire of Shadows
Myths of Midwinter
The Hinterland Veil
The Secrets Amongst the Cypress
Within the Garden of Twilight
House of Dusk, House of Dawn

MIDNIGHT DYNASTY SERIES

A Tempest of Discovery
A Storm of Revelations
A Torrent of Deceit
A Squall of Sedition
A Chaos of Awakening

THE SEVEN SERIES

Nineteen Seventy
Nineteen Seventy-Two
Nineteen Seventy-Three
Nineteen Seventy-Four
Nineteen Seventy-Five
Nineteen Seventy-Six
Nineteen Eighty

VAMPIRES OF THE MEROVINGI SERIES

The Island

and more

THE DUSK TRILOGY

St. Charles at Dusk: The Story of Oz and Adrienne

Flourish: The Story of Anne Fontaine

Banshee: The Story of Giselle Deschanel

CRIMSON & CLOVER STORIES

Available as a single collection, The Shorts

Surrender: The Story of Oz and Ana

Shame: The Story of Jonathan St. Andrews

Fire & Ice: The Story of Remy & Fleur

Dark Blessing: The Landry Triplets

Pandora's Box: The Story of Jasper & Pandora

The Menagerie: Oriana's Den of Iniquities

A Band of Heather: The Story of Colleen and Noah

The Ephemeral: The Story of Autumn & Gabriel

Bayou's Edge: The Landry Triplets

AS RIVER CHASTAIN
(CO-WRITE WITH ELIZABETH BURGESS)

THE COMPLICATED ROMANTIC LIFE OF ROMY DELACROIX

Silvan

Bastian

Dane

For more information, and exciting bonus material, visit www.sarahmcradit.com

ABOUT SARAH

Sarah is the *USA Today* and International Bestselling Author of over forty contemporary and epic fantasy stories, and the creator of the Kingdom of the White Sea and Saga of Crimson & Clover universes.

Born a geek, Sarah spends her time crafting rich and multilayered worlds, obsessing over history, playing her retribution paladin (and sometimes destruction warlock), and settling provocative Tolkien debates, such as why the Great Eagles are not Gandalf's personal taxi service. Passionate about travel, she's been to over twenty countries collecting sparks of inspiration, and is always planning her next adventure.

Sarah and her husband live in a beautiful corner of SE Pennsylvania with their three tiny benevolent pug dictators.

www.sarahmcradit.com

www.ingramcontent.com/pod-product-compliance
Lightning Source LLC
Chambersburg PA
CBHW020246030826
48979CB00030B/2638/J

9781958744406